A Perfect America

By Peter Meredith

I0598722

"If destruction be our lot, we must ourselves be its author and finisher. As a nation of freemen, we must live through all time, or die by suicide." Abraham Lincoln

"Man will ultimately be governed by god or by tyrants." Ben Franklin

"Our Constitution was made only for a moral and religious people. It is wholly inadequate to the government of any other." John Adams

"It depends on what your definition of is, is." Bill Clinton

Chapter 1

The Gay

People scurried out of his way and that was good. Their eyes would flick up as the clack of his expensive Chinese made shoes on the white tile announced his presence. Just as quickly they would look away. When he passed, there came sighs of relief.

Inwardly Phil Tarsus smiled—outwardly he was cool, his eyes were nearly emotionless, save for the glimmer of cruelty that wet them. People—normal people—had trouble looking him in the eye. The innocent ones would glance there once and never go back for seconds. Not true for the guilty.

The guilty would come back for more, searching uselessly for the least compassion in the ice blue of his eyes.

At the entrance to the lower levels Phil waived his badge at a young guard—even he blanched in the slightest at the proximity of an Inquisitor—and the door buzzed open.

"Is the elevator in the green?" Phil asked.

A clicking sound accompanied the guard's reflexive swallow. "No sir. A repair crew is supposed to…"

In the middle of the man's sentence Phil walked away heading for the stairs. A simple no would have been sufficient. Another guard about to head down stopped and held the door open for him. No one liked to have an Inquisitor strolling along behind them; it made them walk funny.

Below him on the stair he could hear a whispered conversation—most conversations these days were of this sort, unless of course the subject was concerning the perfection of *The State* then the volume would be annoyingly increased.

"Uhg! How tough is it to keep an elevator working?"

"It's down for the third time this week," a second voice answered. "At least you only have that broom. I've got to lug this bucket and mop up and down seventeen stories…" The two, a pair of dark workers, slouched along taking up most of the stairwell. They went taut and silent in fear at Phil's approach.

"Step aside," Phil growled. He wasn't about to risk having the perfection of his black uniform marred by coming into contact with a worker. Without a word at his rudeness the two hurried to obey and Phil swept by without giving them another thought.

They were only workers after all; the sludge that made up society.

The lowest level of the Justice building was a far cry from the gleaming steel and white marble of the upper floors. Down here the halls resembled the sad, urine-stinking warrens of the state-run hospitals; the comparison was complete right down to the howling screams.

The dim and dingy rooms, the chill air, the smell: chemicals layered over something unpleasant, all added up to an affront to the senses—purposely so. This was where the Inquisitors did a good deal of their *work*. This was where a version of truth that the State demanded emerged.

In the spartan room he called an office, Phil found a member of the Department of Entertainment sitting huddled around his heater. Had it been anyone but Haley Baker he would've ripped into him for wasting his electricity ration. However, she was long in the leg and her smile made it difficult for him to be angry with her.

"I've a better way to keep warm," he said.

"I'm sure you do," Haley replied with that smile —perfect teeth; full red lips; something secretive and sexy in her eyes. Phil noted that behind the smile there was an unfamiliar touch of unease.

"So what brings you here so early?" he asked. Since she sat in his chair, he took a seat on the edge of his desk, fully aware that he loomed over her. Almost imperceptibly she leaned back. Almost. "The trial isn't for another hour or so," he added.

"I want to look at the case file," she answered, as she bent to her faux-alligator skin purse. When she straightened and checked her platinum curls in a small mirror, she made it into an excuse for her to lean further from him. However he countered this by sliding even closer and now there was nowhere for her to go.

How strange her mannerisms. Phil had known her for three years, since the day he became a full Inquisitor, and she had never been the least nervous around him, despite his overt sexual aggressiveness.

"This guy a friend of yours?" he asked searchingly.

"A gay? Please, don't insult me," she answered tartly. "What would I need with a gay?"

"Then why the sudden interest?" Phil flicked on his computer screen and typed in his password, all the while watching Haley closely. Averting her eyes from the screen, she gave a shrug. He continued with more probing questions, "You've never asked to see a case file before. You don't trust me now?" This was almost a joke. There was no way she trusted him. He had his quotas to fill like everyone else.

"Of course I do," she lied through the ruby red of her lips. "It's just that after what happened to Ellen on Channel One...I want to be extra sure of what I'm reporting. I can't afford to go on air and not have my facts straight."

Now Phil understood. Only the day before, Ellen Mathews, maybe the biggest name in headline news, had been taken before the Secretary of the Inquisitors, Russ Steiner—a man who made even a hard veteran like Phil Tarsus shudder. Her crime: false reporting. She stood charged on seventy-eight counts, a fact that had Phil steaming in anger. He had been next in rotation and the bust should've been his, however,

Russ had pulled rank and had casually switched cases. Seventy-eight counts equaled nearly a fifth of Phil's quotas for the year.

"And you want to be extra careful," Phil said as if thinking it over. In truth he didn't care one whit whether she saw the file, he was just trying to see how he could benefit from this sudden anxiety of hers.

She nodded. "Yeah. Ellen never did any of her own footwork. She probably just made up all those stats like they said. Let me tell you, that's not going to be me."

Phil came off the desk and knelt in front of her, trying to make it seem as if he was in the midst of a terrible dilemma. There was no downside in showing the files. Only upside, and he hoped that the black cloud of having to bother with a stupid fag might have the tiniest silver lining of giving him a shot at Haley.

"Look," he said with a long sigh. "I'm not supposed to show evidence before a trial. After all, he's innocent until proven guilty…"

"Are you saying he's not a gay?" Haley asked sharply, looking for an angle—looking for a juicier story beyond simple treason. She was always looking for something fresh to report.

Phil put his hands on her thighs, midway. "No, he's a gay. But letting you look at the evidence before the trial could get me in some trouble. Maybe we could come to some sort of agreement…" he left off ambiguously.

She glanced down at his large hands on her slim legs. "Do I look like a comfort girl to you?"

He pretended to be outraged at the very thought. "Of course not! I'm asking for dinner is all."

A look passed across her features, one that held a touch of revulsion. He understood. Very few found an Inquisitor to be the most desirable dinner companion.

"Ok, but it'll have to be a hole-in-the-wall. Nothing against you Phil, but I have prospects. With Ellen out of the way there'll be some changes and I'm looking to move up."

"Aren't we all," he replied. With a press of a button, the printer began spitting out a copy of the file on the gay.

Chapter 2

The Trial of Stephen Crown

In the confessional, where the gloom was perpetual, Phil sat across the table from his prisoner. He leaned his big frame back in the steel folding chair, enjoying the long creak of metal; it was an ominous sound.

Stephen Crown twitched.

Phil said nothing. He would wait; comfortably warm in his sharply creased and perfect black uniform. Stephen Crown wore little besides his prison rags and, despite a harsh light beating down on him, he shivered in fear and cold.

Phil's wait wasn't long. The average was eight minutes before a guilty man spoke.

"This isn't right," Stephen whispered from his end of the table. The room was a ten by ten box. It held nothing besides a table, the chairs, two men, and the truth. Not the truth of reality, but the truth of perception, which counted for so much more.

Once a dam burst, it didn't take much to keep it going. "What's not right?" Phil replied in an easy voice—though he had an under-inquisitor, a man named Henderson, Phil never used him for anything of importance; instead, he was his own good cop/bad cop.

"Jailing someone for…this sort of thing," Stephen stuttered. "It's not right. We started this party! We were the ones who began it. We were the intellectual force behind it."

"We? When you say we, what exactly do you mean?"

Stephen dropped his gazed back to the table.

"Well?" Phil asked gently. "Who is this 'we' you're talking about?" After a long wait, Phil gave a theatrical sigh, "Stephen, can we dispense with the bull? Everything you've heard about the seventh level is true. *All of it*," he paused to let that sink in. "But it doesn't have to be that way. We can hold a nice little conversation and get this over with or…"

Both men knew there was so much to that word *or*. The seventh level had a dreadful and well-deserved reputation. *Or* meant a great deal of horrible pain.

Stephen's breath picked up in tempo. "The gays," he spat out. "That's who. We saw the future for what it should be. Harvey Milk and Halperin and Harris and Van Zandt! We started the party."

"So, you are gay then?" Phil asked.

Now Stephen appeared to gag; struck with the inertia of consequence. Being gay was very illegal. Finally, he whispered, "You know I am. Why else would I be here?"

"Oh, there are many reasons," Phil answered darkly. Aggressively he stood, knocking back his chair. He came around the table and saw the fear growing in the little queer's eyes. "You talk of right and wrong, yet you spew this revisionist crap! It was the gays who undermined us from the very beginning. Just like the Jews, you were all one-percenters, hiding your money behind a phony cry of civil rights. But what happened when we finally won? Who had all the money and the power? Who became the new slave masters?" Phil slammed his thick fist down on the table and thundered, "If you read your damned history you'd know the gays and the Jews were the very rich we were fighting against; all the while crying and whining about how bad they had it. In my view you're worse than the Neocons, you are all blood traitors."

The Inquisitor stalked away in a wrath; a fake wrath. Phil practiced his angry denunciations at home at least once a week. He went to the two-way mirror and ran a hand through his short blonde hair, appearing to calm himself. There was no need; he was very calm and perfectly happy. Even though Stephen had barely said anything, he was already good for at least three convictions: Subversion, inciting insurrection, and flaunting the Population Integrity law.

"Where do you work, Stephen?" Phil asked, back in his gentle voice. He knew very well where the little weasel worked.

"Stadler Allegiance Academy," Stephen answered shakily.

"What grade do you teach? How many kids?" The inquisitor came back to his seat and lit a cigarette. Phil didn't smoke—it was a sign of weakness and it ran against the Party's teachings of frugality, but Stephen did. The gay couldn't take his eyes off the cigarette.

A moment later the ramifications of the Inquisitor's question struck Stephen. "Look...I've never said anything to them. Never. You have to believe me."

"I don't believe you."

Stephen made a noise of desperation. "They're innocent kids."

"No one's innocent," Phil shot back, stating the unofficial mantra of the Inquisitors. It was the only thing the Christians ever got right—everyone sinned, no one was innocent. "What did you tell those children about Harvey Milk?"

The prisoner's head swung back and forth in rapid jerks. "Really, I didn't say anything. I didn't. Do you think I could trust a bunch of fourth graders?"

"Who do you think informed on you?"

In astonishment, Stephen's mouth came open. "No...they couldn't have. They never knew. I was very careful not to let on that..."

Moving slowly, like a stalking lion, Phil came around behind Stephen with the cigarette dangling from his lower lip and said, "Here's how this is going to play out: you're going to give up your partners—all of them, right this second. I want names and addresses."

"I can't," Stephen said. "I don't know…"

Phil took a healthy drag on the cigarette watching the orange of it flare bright; he then put it out on the back of Stephen's neck. The man screamed. It was so much like a girl's shriek that Phil looked at him in disgust. When the scream turned into a pitiful blubbering, the Inquisitor moved in again this time fast and aggressive.

"Give me the names!" Phil barked. He then bent closer lowering his voice to a deadly whisper. "Or I'll bring in every one of your students for questioning," Phil said. "I'll have them right where you are now. Is that what you want?"

"You are evil!" Stephen hissed. Phil appreciated this little spark of defiance and smiled, though his victim was not at all comforted by it. There was nothing pleasant to it.

From his breast pocket, Phil took a pad of paper and a pencil. "Names and addresses," he said, slapping them down. "And I know how you immoral bastards rut like goats, so if I don't see enough names I'll be calling for the children…and your students from last year too."

These were idle threats. Only very well connected children went to schools like Stadler Allegiance Academy. Phil went back to his side of the table and watched the gay sacrifice his lovers for the sake of his students. When Stephen paused, appearing to be done, Phil took another cigarette out and lit it slowly, letting the flame linger.

"And you call me immoral," Stephen said, half-under his breath.

Phil shot out smoke from both nostrils, smiling in his cruel way. "You are. I thought as a teacher you'd know this. There is no good and evil and there's certainly no such thing as objective right or wrong. The State dictates what is right and wrong; what is moral or immoral. If the State decrees that being queer is immoral—then it's immoral."

"You have your conscience," Stephen replied. "You can make certain decisions on your own. It doesn't have to be this way."

"The state is always right; it's laws pure and benign. Ignoring them would be chaos." Phil laughed, relaxing. The sight of the six names on the little piece of paper would go a long way to catching him up on his quotas and he was feeling magnanimous. "What would happen if everyone just picked and chose what laws they'd obey? It would be anarchy."

"It would be freedom."

"You're an idiot," Phil sneered. "It would be freedom, alright—but only for the strong. Laws protect the weak."

Stephen slouched looking to ooze lower in his chair. "I'm weak. Who's protecting me?"

Phil glared for a moment and then took a long drag on the cigarette making sure that Stephen got a good look at the red-orange ember before going around behind the man again. His scrawny back shivered.

"You're certainly weak, queer-boy, but you're also guilty. We don't protect the guilty, we punish them. We make an example of their pain as a reminder to all. We hurt them for the benefit of society." Phil paused, basking in the surety of his words. He then said, loudly, "Turn off the video."

It used to be that all the rooms were voice controlled: sound, camera, air conditioning, etc, but a bug or a virus or some such nonsense had infected the computers years ago and now they were useless. Henderson, in the next room ran the controls by hand —he tapped on the glass to let Phil know the video was down.

The Inquisitor strolled again behind his prisoner and taking a good grip of Stephen's hair, he hauled the man's head back. "One more question, fag and we should be done," Phil said, breathing a plume of smoke over the man. "All this crap you're spouting about Harris and Harvey Milk and the gays, I need your source." The smoke might have been warm but the words were like ice. "You didn't just make that crap up, you had to have heard it from someone, who…and before you answer let me warn you, I'm not going to play any games. You'll write down the source or this cig goes in your eye."

Weeping, Stephen wrote and Phil read along, grinning a wolf's smile. "Camera on," he called out a second later after he had pocketed the paper. "Now for the easy part: your confession."

Chapter 3

A Cold Reality

The confession went easy enough; Stephen had known since the moment of his arrest that he was doomed, and with hardly any prodding, barely two dozen punches, and only a few screams of faux-anger on Phil's part, Stephen admitted to three counts of treason against the State. Phil would add at least one more charge: Proliferation of Subversive Materials, when he found the book.

Supposedly, Stephen's 'knowledge' of Harvey Milk and the gays was in a leather bound book hidden between the mattresses of the bed in his dom-box. Phil had rolled his eyes at the childishness of the hiding place, but all the same a piece of propaganda like that would be quite a feather in Phil's cap and he was eager to get a hold of it.

Haley Baker, who had been in the other room with Henderson during the confession, misread the look in his eyes. "Are you going to bring in his students for questioning? It got all quiet in there when you brought up his class."

Before he answered, Phil took the videotape from Henderson who had just exited the taping room. Before he would release the tape to Haley for her broadcast Phil would transcribe it by hand, and then edit it selectively so that he came across in the best light—a defender of the State. He turned back to Haley. "No, that's a headache I'm not prepared to deal with, but…" he paused as he directed her out of the room. In the hall, he whispered, "I have something else—a banned book."

She squinched her face into a look of disgust. "A book? Big whoop."

"It is a big whoop," he said directing her to his office. There he turned the heater on high and it began to bang and rattle. Beneath the racket, he whispered. "Some of these books are worth thousands of dollars in reward money."

Her eyebrows went up at that. Like everyone else, Phil Tarsus made fourteen dollars a day. With his benefits—stealing from the criminals he put on death row—he was lucky to clear a hundred a week. Turning in that book would not only get him a reward of some kind, he would also likely get some extra airtime on TV, and perhaps a Medal of Commendation. Phil just had to get to the book before the Party Reclamation and Redistribution adjuster came out to Stephen's place and stole everything for himself.

Haley watched him shrewdly. "I like the other angle better."

"There is no other angle," Phil said. "Bringing in the children of State officials is the equivalent of suicide. And I'm not just talking about my career; they'd make it look like a real suicide."

"What career? I'm sorry, but you aren't connected. You're lucky to have come this far."

She wasn't lying; it had taken a series of quirky circumstances for him to be promoted to Inquisitor and now he was barely making his quotas. One missed year and he'd be replaced—probably sent back into the military where there was a constant need for cannon fodder.

"Maybe. I got lucky once; I can get lucky again," he said.

"You already got lucky right now," Haley insisted. "Bring Stephen back. Make him denounce those kids. You know he must have warped them in some manner."

Phil was within his rights to bring Stephen back for more questioning, in fact, he was obligated by law to do so, but he wouldn't. "You said it yourself: I'm not connected, which means I'm not protected either."

Haley grabbed his big, callused hands in hers. "This is how you get connected! You take chances— you roll the dice. Bring the kids in. Make them talk. Most kids don't even know their parents, but these ones do. Think of the dirt they'll spill."

A hardy laugh escaped him. "Now I get it. You want a news story. You want a big headline. You want glory...only you want me to take all the risks!"

"Hell yeah I want glory," Haley shot back with a hard look. "But you're wrong about me not putting myself out there. If you go down then I go down. That's why we have to work together. You get me information and I protect you by getting it out where everyone can see. No one would dare go after you..."

With a flick, Phil turned off the heater and Haley snapped her mouth closed in an instant. She glared meaningfully and then pointed at the now silent heater—he shook his head. Finally, she stood, letting out a long sigh. "You're a nobody and you're going to stay that way."

She began to walk away but he snatched her hand. "You owe me a dinner."

"Are you kidding me? You think I'll waste my time with a nobody like..." Still holding her hand, Phil stood. Even with her three-inch heels, he towered over her. "What are you doing?" she demanded, nervously. She had reason to be nervous; unconnected or not he was still an Inquisitor—a dreadful instrument of State justice.

"You promised me dinner."

Haley swallowed loudly under his glare just as Steven Crown had. She wasn't a prisoner, however and she rallied her spirits. "You think a dinner will lead to something else? You think you'll be able to sweep me off my feet? You'll think I'll stoop so low as to..."

"Don't give me that," he interrupted. "I've seen your file. You're as unconnected as I am. You're from the double R block for goodness sakes—and by the way it comes out in your accent. Once I heard you say 'what-er' on TV. It's pronounced *wa-ter*."

Her anger seemed to dissipate. "What-er…water…water," she said quietly, almost under her breath. "You got a hold of my file? You can do that?"

"Piece of cake. You got no patrons. No letters of commendation, at least not from anyone who counts. You're no better than I am, so get off your high horse."

"No better?" she asked. "That's where you're wrong. Take a good look." Still holding his hand, she gave a slow twirl and he did indeed take a good look at the curve of her calves, the slimness of her waist, the way her platinum hair rippled along her shoulders like a golden river. She smiled and he felt something powerful within him stir.

"You see?" she said. "You're a handsome man, Phil. But without connections the best you'll do is some painted-up broad from the steno-pool—while I have my pick of men. I'll get my connections, because I have what every guy wants. What do you have?" His bitter shrug brought her smile out all the more. "Yes, you may be better off than most of those poor shlubs out there, but you're still a shlub, and one who's hit his peak."

Hit teeth ground together, but she scoffed at his impotent fury. "Don't get angry at me. You can change your destiny right now, or you can stay a shlub." She strolled out of his now freezing office, but turned in the doorway. "Call me *if* you change your mind, Shlub."

"Son of a bitch," Phil cursed in a quiet whisper—there were always ears listening. He was mostly angry because Haley had been right about everything. His prospects weren't good. Yes, he was an Inquisitor, but there was no way he would go any higher.

Unless…

Phil sat back at his desk with the hard copy of the Stephen Crown file sitting closed in front of him. He laid a cold hand upon it and leafed back the cover. Right away, he saw the initial, anonymous tip: an eyewitness account of Stephen's 'gayness'. Since no reward had been collected, Phil thought it likely to have been written by a spurned or jealous lover. The next few pages contained the working file on Stephen: his date of birth, his voting record, his State educational attendance record, his address, the names of his neighbors dating back twenty years, his relatives to the fourth cousin, and so on.

The names of his students were on the last page.

Phil had very purposely not looked at the last page. That page was nothing but trouble. What would happen if he brought back Stephen for more questioning? Trouble. What would happen if he brought in the students? Even more trouble. Stadler Academy was ranked as the fourth best school in the capital, which meant that the children who attended wouldn't be children of the highest government officials or the highest ranking military officers—they would be the second highest or third or maybe even the fourth—but it didn't matter. They had power and Phil didn't.

There would be a clamoring for his head; if he was lucky he'd be fired and sent to the Texas front to fight the stinking beaners again. If he wasn't lucky, there'd be some trumped up charge against him and then he'd be right where Stephen was. The thought turned him cold, inside and out.

He glanced at the ugly little heater sitting quiet and cold next to his desk. The dial on the side, showing how much of his heat ration he had left, indicated three and half-hours. It wouldn't be reset for four days, not until February first. It was supposed to get colder.

What would happen if Phil continued to ignore that last page?

Exactly this, he'd stay cold for the rest of his life.

Chapter 4

The Last Conservative

Phil spent the remainder of the morning and most of the afternoon transcribing the videotape of Stephen's confession. It was a job for his assistant, but Henderson was a backstabbing, piece of crap and couldn't be trusted—not for a moment. As usual, he was off running meaningless errands for Phil and would be for the rest of the day.

Once the work of transcribing was complete, Phil typed up the State's case against the prisoner, not forgetting to add, in the most vociferous manner, his personal recommendation that Stephen should be condemned to death for his crimes. Such a recommendation carried absolutely no weight with the jury, it was a strictly CYA maneuver.

He then took the complete case file up to the ground floor where the Deputy-Commissioners of Justice had their offices, and found his boss kicked back in his chair with his feet up on his desk.

"Just the man I wanted to see," Darryl Conner said. The room was warm and Darryl had his uniform coat slung on the back of a leather couch. "Is that the case file against the queer?"

"Yes," Phil answered and handed it over. For the next few minutes, Conner studied the file in a way that wasn't normal. "Is there something wrong?"

Conner held up a finger until he finished and then said, "Your work has been sloppy as of late. But this seems...adequate. Before you go, give the file to Ms. Adleman."

Phil's eyes narrowed. "Ms. Adleman? The Commissioner's secretary? But the case isn't complete; I still have some loose ends…"

The look on Conner's face silenced Phil. "It says here that you got a confession."

"Of course I did. In fact, I got three. Inciting insur…"

"Then you're done," Conner cut in. "Besides, I have a plum for you...one you probably don't deserve. There's a cracked-one up at Polk. Says he's had a vision from God and has been preaching to the other inmates."

"A vision from God?" Phil repeated slowly, while his mind began numbering the possible convictions a case such as this would garner. At a minimum there'd be a charge of subversion for every person the nut case had tried to preach to—the number could be into the hundreds. "I'll get right on it," Phil said and hurried to snatch the file from Conner's hand before his boss could realize that he wasn't first in the rotation. The truth was that he wasn't in the rotation at all—not until the gay's confession had been officially filed.

"Just make sure you drop that report off before you leave. Your travel documents are already at the garage." Conner said and then turned back to his computer screen.

"Before I leave?" Phil asked. "What do you mean? This guy's still up at the prison? You want me to drive all the way out there? Can't I just send Henderson to pick him up?"

"No. The prisoner stays put. You're going to interrogate him there." When Phil opened his mouth to ask why, Conner made a face. "It's the Commish. He tore me a new one this morning over the budget for the seventh level. I'm not about to drag this guy all the way over here just to feed and house him. We'll let the Board of Corrections foot that bill."

Phil kept his face neutral—the way the prisoners were fed, Conner was saving a few pennies at most. Since there was no use arguing, he gave his boss a fake look of understanding and left. The climb to the tenth floor where the Commissioner had his office had Phil warm for the first time that day, though the icy stare of Ms. Adleman was nearly enough to send him shivering again.

As always, the old hag looked as though she had just crept from some cretaceous bog, trailing a run of slime. Her eyes were coal-black and contained all the humanity of a pit viper as she glared at Phil. She was always this way. She lived a life of semi-privilege and that was due only to the acts of her benefactor, Commissioner of Justice Ari Loman. By her look it was clear that she wouldn't just kill for him, she'd burn down an orphanage if that was what he wished.

"Crown file?" she asked without greeting.

"Yes ma'am." He handed it to her and though he meant just to bob his head as way of saying goodbye, he practically bowed.

On the way down to the garage, he growled under his breath, "What a bitch." At the fifth floor, he stepped over one of the dark-skinned workers he had seen earlier. The man lay wailing in a puddle of blood while his mop sat broken and in pieces scattered around him. A bone, like a sharp white stick, stuck out of his wrist at an obscene angle. He had fallen down the stairs apparently.

Slipping past, Phil made sure not to get his shoes dirty.

At the garage level, he signed out a car: a 2104 model Electro. Flicking it on, he groaned and hand cranked the window down. "Hey, moron!" he called to the attendant. "There's only a seventy percent charge on this thing. I've got to get out to Polk and back."

The attendant quailed under Phil's withering look. "Th-that's the b-best car you're rated for, sir. It's been charging since yesterday."

There were other cars in the lot—most even worse than the crappy eighteen-year-old electro, which was at least a four-seater. "Any of those Watts have a good enough charge to get out to Polk?" The Watt was a dreadful box of a car, sporting a top speed of forty miles an hour, and came with no amenities beyond windshield wipers and headlights; they didn't even have heaters.

"I don't think so, but I'm pretty sure that electro will make it back, if you charge it while you're there," the attendant replied.

It would, but it would also be a close call to attempt to go by Stephen's dom-box afterward, which Phil planned to do. His place was a good seven or eight miles out of the way and an Electro with a seventy percent charge could only go maybe sixty miles total. It would be very close. Phil cranked the window back up so as not to lose what little heat was still in the car and nearly ran the attendant over as he pulled out of the lot.

To conserve the battery he turned off the heat and kept his speed down below forty. It made for a painfully long ride, but at least there wasn't traffic to worry about. Besides the usual hang ups at the security checkpoints—one on the outskirts of the city and another roving one ten miles beyond it—the broad sweep of I66 outside of the Capital lay practically barren and he buzzed along with the road to himself.

Just under an hour later, he came upon the castle-like exterior of Polk Federal Penitentiary. Its walls were like battlements; its towers soaring, each topped with the ubiquitous new American flag; the single star in the blue field like a glaring eye.

Unlike the grand exterior, the inside of the prison was a rat-filled dungeon of pain and misery.

As a full Inquisitor he technically outranked every person there, save for the warden, and he showed it by barking out orders to a few loafing guards the second he pulled through the triple-gates and was let into the garage. "You, charge my car. You, get me the prisoner Roland Gentry and take him to the first floor laundry room. You, run ahead and let the warden know that an Inquisitor is going to question one of his prisoners."

They scurried to obey.

Phil had been to Polk on a number of occasions as an Under-Inquisitor and chose the laundry room for two reasons: the ambient noise meant listening devices would be useless and frankly, because it was warm. During the long ride, the cold had seeped into his bones making him feel far older than his thirty-four years and the chill of the prison didn't help.

"Out of the way," he growled time and again as he strode through the maze of halls to the laundry room. Interestingly the prisoners were less intimidated of him than the guards were. The prisoners were emaciated and tubercular, and most no longer feared an Inquisitor as the angel of death—they seemed no longer to fear death at all. They would move, but slowly as if time no longer had meaning to them and more than once Phil shoved men out of his way.

Phil had no fear of them; he was a big man in the prime of his life. He enjoyed violence, since it always came easy to him, and besides, he carried a service pistol beneath his coat.

One man failed to move even after he was shoved. He wasn't a prisoner, but an insolent tech-worker who spun quickly and looked to be within an ace of punching Phil. The man had a sallow, jaundiced cast to his skin that Phil had seen too often —it was this alone that kept Phil from breaking his face.

"Torreon?" Phil asked. Six years before, the fighting had been stiff around Torreon and the Mexicans had unleashed what the GIs called the *Yellow Burn,* as a last resort. Those who faced the brunt of it died slowly and in horrendous agony. Those who caught just the slightest whiff died even slower; over time, their livers crumbled away—the tech-worker with his jaundiced face was under his own death sentence.

"Yeah, Torreon," the worker whispered, before heading down a branching corridor. Phil watched him go, thankful he had been pulled from the line when he had.

A minute later, with the tech-worker already forgotten, he entered the warm confines of the laundry room. Despite the fact that it had been years since he had last been to Polk it seemed that the same press machines were still waiting on parts for repairs. Commandeering two stools from a couple of inmates, Phil prepared a table of sorts at the machine furthest from where any actual work was taking place and waited, allowing the steam to bake in.

Seeing Roland Gentry for the first time made Phil take another look at his file—there it was: date of birth October 25, 2035—the man was eighty-six-years old! Roland was tall and still proud in his bearing. He had a mane of white hair and unlike the other prisoners, he seemed tough and stringy rather than thin and sickly. From across the room his blue eyes were sharp; they took in everything. He didn't seem crazy.

Waving away the guards who had accompanied him, Phil gestured for Roland to take a seat. "My thanks," the old man said, before half-settling himself down on the stool. It was only half because it was clear that after a life time in prison the man was no longer capable of relaxing fully.

"So, Roland Gentry, you say you believe in god?"

The old man nodded and for a second his long hair covered his face. "I do."

"And this god has revealed himself to you?"

Roland took a moment to answer; casually swiveling his eyes around, taking in the room once again. It was a survival mechanism. Phil had never heard of anyone reaching such an age in prison before. To him it seemed impossible.

"God has revealed himself to me, just as he has revealed himself to you…I'm sorry, what's your name?"

"Phil Tarsus. And you are wrong. I've never seen this so called god of yours."

A smile cragged the old man's face even greater than it had been before. "There are none so blind as those who will not see. The scales have not yet fallen from your eyes and thus you see not the miracles that are all about you."

Phil gave a little shrug. "You're right about that," he agreed, genially. There was no use arguing with religious freaks. "But I'm not here to talk about me. Let's talk about you. God comes to you…here in this pit of despair? I bet that must've been something."

"It was indeed."

The Inquisitor waited for Roland to elaborate— crazy religious freaks always elaborated—only Roland just sat there placidly waiting on the next question. Phil blinked a few times, he then said, "And…"

"And we're not here to talk about God. It's clear you have no interest in saving your soul," Roland replied, folding his gnarled and thick-knuckled fingers together. "We're here to discuss my murder."

Chapter 5

A Devil's Bargain

Unruffled, Phil leaned back. "You're going to be murdered? Did your god tell you this or is there some sort of religious war going on here at Polk?" Phil hoped for the latter—the convictions would come rolling in by the barrel full.

"Neither," Roland replied. "The State is going to murder me and everyone in this prison."

"That's not possible. Legally speaking it is beyond the State to murder anyone," Phil explained. "Murder is the *unlawful* taking of a human life. The State makes the laws and so by extension it can do no wrong."

"So right and wrong is arbitrary? What is right one day can be wrong the next?"

Phil loosened his tie; the heat of the room was finally starting to make him sweat. "Exactly."

"And you're ok with this?" Roland asked. The question was tinged with righteous indignation and his blue eyes sparked. However, a second later his lips turned up slightly. "Of course you are. As an Inquisitor you have to be."

"As an Inquisitor I have to put the protection of the State above my own feelings of..."

"Shut up," the old man demanded, unexpectedly. Phil glared, not at all used to being spoken to in such a manner by anyone, let alone a prisoner. Roland hunched forward, his elbows on the flat of the press. "Since your life's work is state-contrived murder, I don't really expect you to care what's going to happen here, but I'll tell you anyway so you know why I'm doing what I'm doing. There's going to be a fire here at Polk—a big one. And no one will survive."

The old man was right, Phil didn't particularly care. "And you know this, how?" he asked blandly.

Roland began to unbutton his shirt. "Seventeen years ago there was a fire up at the federal pen in Marshall. Out of four thousand prisoners only fourteen of us escaped when part of a wall collapsed." He pulled back his shirt to expose the scars of a healed over burn. "Seven years ago there was a riot in Dillings—three thousand dead, by luck I was on a work crew outside the walls when it started."

"This is your proof?" Phil asked taking out a cigarette.

"Both times it started the same: they began by doubling the number of prisoners. There were sudden transfers from other federal pens; mostly career criminals whose transgressions never got to the level of treason. It got so crowded that we were hot bunking it and still had men sleeping on the floors. Then came the tech crews—State operatives disguised as structural engineers tasked with setting the combustibles…"

Phil, in the process of lighting the cigarette, interrupted, "You just said there was a riot, not a fire in Dillings."

"It started as a fire, but the prisoners were able to put it out. When their plan fizzled, the 'technicians' just decided to shoot everyone. It sounded like a battle was raging, only the prisoners were all unarmed. After a while, the gunfire died down and then we could hear the shots come one or two at a time as the last of the prisoners were hunted and executed one after another. The crew I was on sat outside the walls for hours waiting for our turn."

"And why didn't they kill you too? It would've been easy."

"Easy for someone like you, maybe," Roland said, looking past the cig and the smoke and staring with accusatory eyes into Phil's face. "They probably would have killed us as well, but news crews arrived and they had to get their story straight."

Phil looked away, feeling oddly guilty, a sensation that he hadn't felt in years. He noticed that the laundry workers were doing their damnedest to listen in on the conversation. The Inquisitor kept his voice low, "Still, you're only guessing what happened in there. You can't know for sure."

"I can, actually. There were survivors. Those of us who had been outside the walls were forced to move the bodies. There was a man—a friend really— he was shot four times but hadn't yet expired. He told me what happened. He saw it with his own eyes…and

I saw things, too. Many of the prisoners were shot in the back. They were running for their lives."

The cigarette clearly wasn't affecting Roland and it was leaving a bad taste in Phil's mouth. He stubbed it out on the steel of the press. With a shrug, Phil said, "I sort of remember there was a riot once. But so what? A bunch of criminals died, am I supposed to care?"

"You should. Simply out of self-preservation. Remember there is no right or wrong. Today you're an Inquisitor, tomorrow you could be right here with me."

"Not likely," Phil shot back. "I have value. I provide a service that the State desires. What do you do but take up space?"

Unexpectedly, Roland grinned at this. "Spoken like a true, unadulterated capitalist."

"How dare you speak to me like that?" Phil was halfway across the press before he even knew what he was doing—however Roland had anticipated the move and sat back just out of reach.

"What better term is there?" Roland asked, his grin becoming a full-blown smile. "You sell a service that your employer's desire and you have both reached a mutually beneficial arrangement in regard to pay. You act as if this is new to you. If you were a true communist, you'd insist on the same pay and benefits as the lowest worker. Do you?"

In answer, Phil's jaw clenched. Though he was technically paid the same as everyone else, the cafeterias he dined in were nicer and gave out larger portions, his clothes were of a far better quality, his heat ration could stretch to cover a full month and his shoes...Phil looked away from Roland and stared down at his Chinese made shoes; they were beautiful.

"I didn't think so," Roland smiled even larger, showing a full set of graying teeth.

Phil steamed in the heat of the laundry, feeling his shirt next to his skin start to stick. Why was he trading words with this old man? He had a job to do. He had quotas to fill. "What about you, Roland? Are you a capitalist? You turning a profit?"

"Do I look like I have anything to sell?" Roland asked, touching his prison rags—yet he did so with a cryptic look to his eyes, as if he did indeed have something held back. "Now, a long time ago, back in the day, I was a capitalist. I was jailed in '62 for profiteering. I've been in the pen for sixty years for following the natural human inclination to get maximum value."

"To steal, you mean," Phil sneered.

"I never stole from a customer. Profit is not stealing." Roland shook his head in wonder. "It's almost like you've been taught everything ass-backwards. Capitalism only works when each side— buyer and seller is satisfied. As an example: the plumber needs to be paid enough to justify coming out at four in the morning to unclog a toilet, while the homeowner has to balance a hefty expenditure against the inconvenience of pissing in the yard. In this case, who is stealing from whom? Certainly not the plumber; if he charges too much the homeowner will just call someone else. It's communism that's all about stealing."

Phil checked his watch—it was just after four. With the electro needing to charge he had a lot of time to kill and Roland was on the verge of talking himself into his first treason charge. Affecting a bored expression he said, "This should be interesting. How in the world can communism be stealing? It's the ultimate in fairness."

"Communism steals three things from every individual: hope, initiative, and labor," Roland answered, ticking off his fingers. The response surprised Phil who thought he was going to mention taxes or fees or some such nonsense.

Perhaps the old man was correct about initiative. The fact that Phil wouldn't go after Stephen Crown's students was some evidence of that. And maybe he was right about hope; people were generally not all that hopeful, though Phil would never call it a *theft* of hope. But labor? That was just silly.

"The only labor the State 'steals' is from prisoners like you," Phil replied, waving his hand to indicate dull-eyed inmates working the machines. "And you gave up all rights when you committed your crimes."

"I'm not talking about prisoners," Roland replied. "Let me give you another example—let's say you have two lumberjacks, a big guy and a small guy. The large one can cut down three trees for every two that the small guy cuts—at the end of the day who gets paid more?"

"They get paid the same," Phil answered. "Which is only fair since it's not the little guy's fault he's small."

"It's only 'fair' to the little guy," Roland shot back. "The big guy loses out. He's in essence losing a third of his pay, which is reward for work. Can't you see that for a third of the day he is in essence a slave?"

"Wrong," Phil said. "He's losing theoretical pay only. The Equality in Wages law makes sure that each individual is paid at the same daily rate as everyone else."

"Exactly," Roland said, wearing a smirky grin. "And that leads directly into the theft of initiative. In order to fell those three trees the big guy has to bust his ass—how quickly will he realize that by taking it easy and only cutting down two trees he'll get the same pay? Not long, I'm sure. Communism takes the incentive out of working your hardest, trying your best—while capitalism gives you a reason to go above and beyond."

"So in your way the little guy loses out?" Phil replied heatedly. "And you don't care I'd bet? The truth is capitalism is intrinsically unfair."

"Yes," Roland stated baldly. "The smart do better than the stupid; the hard worker does better than the lazy worker. Capitalism *is* unfair, yet communism is worse. And this brings us to the theft of hope."

Phil groaned. This really wasn't going anywhere. Nothing the old man had said so far would amount to treason. "Let's call in Homeland Security!" Phil cried sarcastically. "Someone is stealing hope."

"Scoff if you will, but a lack of hope is killing this country. Hope for a better future drives people to make more of themselves; to become better. Where's your hope, Inquisitor? Is it hope that motivates you, or fear?"

There was no way he was going to give Roland the satisfaction of answering that question. The truth: fear was his primary motivation, but it was something he barely admitted to himself.

"How did we get so far off topic?" Phil asked in a tired voice, as if their debate had exhausted him. "I didn't come all the way out here to argue a dead economic philosophy. I'm here to investigate your crimes against the state."

"Capitalism isn't dead," Roland said. "We're about to prove it, you and I. The hallmark of Communism, from the Soviets to the Cubans to the North Koreans was to get the most out of their people through fear and if that didn't work, then they resorted to savagery. This is how you operate, right Comrade? You'll try to intimidate me and when you see how pointless that is you'll go right to torture."

It was clear Roland had been around the block a few times; there was no sense lying. "Yes, that's it exactly," Phil replied.

"Let me show you something," Roland said standing. He had never fully buttoned his shirt and now he stripped it off exposing the leather of his old man's skin. For a long time Phil sat in silence, appraising what stood before him. Despite his age, Roland seemed hardened, like a tough root from a dead tree. Inured by sixty years of backbreaking labor, his body was a map work of scars with a history of long pain.

"And what am I looking at?" Phil asked as if he didn't know. The torture of Roland would be long and grim, and the convictions few. He wouldn't be easy to crack, not at all. And how would it look on TV for Phil to be brutalizing an old man? Whatever hope Phil had been feeling at this plum assignment was quickly fading

"I'm no fool," Roland remarked. "I'm certain your methods of torture will wring a confession or two out of me. We can go that direction and I'll fight you every step of the way, or…" Here he paused significantly and smiled—unknowingly Phil leaned forward. "Or we can strike a capitalistic bargain, one in which we both gain."

"What sort of bargain?" Phil couldn't see how the old man would gain much of anything. He would die in the end no matter what.

"I know you have quotas to fill," Roland said, buttoning his shirt. "How many convictions do you need?"

An Inquisitor's quotas were based on some obscure formula handed down years ago by a Harvard professor. It was all very scientific and Phil couldn't care in the least. "Let's see…I just got my seventieth, so three-hundred and eighty more."

Roland was just in the process of sitting, but froze in an awkward squat. "Four-hundred-and-fifty convictions? A year? My God! How many Inquisitors are there?"

Phil shrugged. "Nationwide, about six-hundred. But it's not as bad as it sounds. Usually we get about three convictions per person."

Roland finished his sit and looked old, really old for the first time. "Not that bad?" he said in quiet amazement. "That's ninety-thousand people! I don't believe it. The State kills ninety-thousand people a year, all in the name of paranoia."

The Inquisitor folded his arms across his chest. "First, it's ninety-thousand *criminals* a year that are killed. And second, they die to protect the State. America is perfect now and the only way for her to remain perfect is to weed out the bad apples."

"America is perfect…" Roland said quietly and then gave a little humorless laugh. "I never thought I'd live to hear a liberal say that."

"The bargain?" Phil prompted.

"Oh right," Roland came back to himself. "I will get you your three-hundred and eighty convictions. I'll confess to anything you want, but in return, I want out of here."

Chapter 6

The Empty Room

"What do you mean you have to get out of here?" Phil asked, slightly confused. "You want out of Polk?" The idea had trouble catching hold in his mind —prisoners belonged in prison.

"Yes, exactly," Roland agreed. He then leaned forward and spoke in a hushed tone, "And soon. They'll light this place up anytime."

Though he wanted to roll his eyes at Roland's conspiracy theory, Phil was careful to keep his face neutral—there was no sense alienating his meal ticket. "I'll see what I can do," he lied. "But first you have to give me something. You've been preaching your God crap to the other inmates. I want ten names and a full confession concerning each." From an interior pocket, he pulled out a small cassette recorder and held it out to Roland to speak into.

The old man leaned back and crossed his arms again. He remained mute until Phil hit the stop button on the recorder. "You've got a lot to learn about capitalism," Roland said. "You expect me to give you something for nothing? That's not how it works. Show me my transfer papers to the Justice building and I'll give you ten confessions on the spot. Put me in the car, I'll give you another ten—and so on. You see? And one more stipulation, there'll be no torture. If you need to smack me around for your bosses then ok. Anything more and I shut up. Do we have a deal?"

Roland held out his hand. Phil gave it a glance and then surreptitiously looked around. From the corner of their eyes, every inmate was staring at them. "You want me to shake your hand? Why?"

"It's the capitalist way to seal a deal. Contracts are mere formalities designed by lawyers to promulgate lawyerdum, but when two men reach an agreement, they shake hands. It's how you begin to build trust."

The bargain didn't make much sense to Phil. Even if the old man feared death at Polk, he had to know that death would be waiting for him in the dungeons of the Justice building. So there had to be something else…perhaps Roland had a plan to escape? Did he have friends on the outside looking to waylay the electro on the way back to the capital?

It didn't seem likely. Roland had been locked up for sixty years—if he had any friends, they'd be long dead.

"Well?" Roland said, still with his hand out. "What's wrong?"

"I don't trust you," Phil answered.

A great rolling laugh escaped Roland. It was strangely infectious, so much so that Phil smiled. "You don't trust me?" Roland asked with tears in his eyes. "The angel of death doesn't trust me?"

"I don't," Phil insisted. "I'm getting too much out of this deal. It makes me suspect."

Roland wiped his eyes, chuckling weakly. "I know what your problem is; you've been a communist way to long. You have no idea what true fairness is all about. To a communist a deal is when the strong dictate terms to the weak and back it up with force."

The Inquisitor grunted, "Huh," in recognition of the truth. It had only been that morning when Phil had done just that, forcing Stephen to give up the names of his partners in exchange for saving his students.

"Maybe you should look at it this way," Roland continued. "Though you're getting a lot, I'm not giving up much. Just words. And the same is true on your end. What are you really giving up? Nothing. You're simply moving me from one prison to another. Both of us think that we are coming out ahead…and the beauty of it is, we both are."

Again, he stuck out his hand.

Phil was suddenly struck by a wave of indecisiveness—what if Roland refused to speak when he got to the capital…what if he did indeed have friends, religious nuts like him, waiting somewhere along the route back…what if this was a set up? A trap laid out for him by an under-Inquisitor to make Phil look bad? It wouldn't be the first time.

A voice inside him, one that sounded like Haley Baker asked, *What if you stay a shlub your whole life?*

Phil took Roland's hand and shook it.

The only real question was what would happen if Phil couldn't get Roland moved back to the capital? He had been told explicitly to leave the prisoner right where he was. The Haley Baker voice answered, *You beat a confession out of him, and you keep beating confessions out of him until you fill your quotas or he dies.*

That wouldn't be a first time either.

Roland stood, looking relieved. "Let's go. I'm all packed," he said pointing at his thin prison garments.

"Not so fast." Phil shook his head. "There's a load of paperwork that goes into prison transfers. While I take care of that, you go back to your cell and start coming up with names. I want the confessions to go smooth. If I think you're stalling, our little deal is over and I'll peel the skin off you like a banana."

"Poetic," Roland said darkly. "And if you take too long with that transfer, I won't have any skin left to peel."

"I'll hurry," Phil lied. Not for a second did he believe there was going to be an actual fire. Conspiracies of that magnitude would be impossible to contain. People talked—they always talked. They couldn't seem to help it, even with the consequences of talking so blatantly obvious.

Phil snapped his fingers at the guard who had accompanied Roland into the laundry room. "Take him back to his cell," he ordered and left with the laundry workers looking disappointed and buzzing in whispered conversations. It was clear they had been expecting more entertainment from an Inquisitor than just a bunch of talk.

Heading up to the admin offices Phil ran into a string of prisoners standing idle against a wall and one stood further out from the rest looking down the line. He was a big dark fellow. "Out of my way," Phil barked. That the black still had some muscle to him meant he was new and he was quick to scamper in fear out of the Inquisitor's path.

Phil almost smiled at the little hop the black made. That was the reaction he had been looking for. That was the proper attitude. Ever since stepping foot in the prison, he hadn't felt like himself. His aura of power seemed to have faded to almost nothing in the dead world of the prison. He wasn't used to being treated with such little respect—and the worst of the lot was the old man.

Being in Roland's presence had been odd. Unsettling. As if Roland was some sort of parental figure; one filled with disappointment and vast knowledge. It didn't sit well with Phil and now he felt a dark rage. "I'll skin him anyway," Phil said to himself, passing a guard and taking the stairs up. He'd get his confessions and then he'd skin the bastard.

"Let me speak to the warden," Phil demanded of the front desk secretary. She was a pretty little Asian with bones as fine as a sparrow's. Her narrow eyes went as wide as they could when she took in the symbol of the Inquisitors on Phil's lapel—a simple gold key; the teeth of which were long and sharp; and the head: a glaring skull.

"He just left," she answered, the words coming out sticky.

The idea of skinning Roland had brightened his day somewhat, but that feeling left him in a hurry. "It's not even five yet," Phil groused. "Does he always leave this early?"

The girl blanched at the question. "Sometimes...if he has meetings," she replied, hedging her answer. Leaving work early was punishable as theft under the productivity laws—not a one of which had ever done a thing to increase productivity.

"What about the under-warden? Is he here?"

"Yes, of course," she said, eager to please. "I'll show you to his office."

She was up and half-running down the hall in a flash. Phil began to relax again as he followed along, ogling her tight body. Perhaps it was better that the warden was out, he mused. An under-warden would be that much easier to browbeat into releasing Roland without the proper paperwork.

The under-warden's office, dull, grey concrete walls and wearing furniture was warmer than Phil had expected. A heater, blaring away at full power, sat next to the desk. From it, an extension cord ran the length of the room and under a side door. Phil eyed it, letting a sneering, knowing look creep over his features.

The under-warden, a plump man with a sweating upper lip didn't fail to catch the look. "The outlets in here don't work...it's on a meter, honest." Though the two men were technically the same rank—O5, the equivalent of lieutenant Colonel in the army—Phil, as an Inquisitor, had power far greater than his rank would indicate and the under-warden shook as Phil's eyes went to squints.

"Maybe we'll talk about your heat ration later," Phil said, letting the threat sit on the warm air for a moment before adding, "But first we need to talk about Roland Gentry." The under-warden's eyes went from fear to puzzlement as he tried to recall which of the five-thousand prisoners at Polk that was. "The old guy," Phil prompted.

"Oh right—the fossil," the under-warden said with a grin, hoping his little joke would thaw Phil's attitude.

"I need him," Phil said without humor. "He has information concerning a plot against the State. Have him at the gate in fifteen minutes."

"Sure. Of course. That's no problem. I just need a copy of the transfer papers."

"We won't need them. Technically we're not transferring him just yet." The idea came to Phil even as he spoke. "I need to interrogate him properly and you don't have adequate tools here. Do you understand? I'm just going to borrow the old man. You can have what's left of him when I'm done."

The under-warden began to shake his head, letting his jowls swing. "I...I can't do that. Section 3, paragraph 48 of the Prisoner's Right's Act states..." Phil stood quickly, threateningly. The under-warden stopped speaking, though his lips continued to move for a few moments longer.

Phil stood over him and whispered in his most menacing voice, "Aiding and abetting crimes against the State is treason. You understand that's exactly what you're doing."

"I'm not! I swear," the man wailed.

"Maybe not yet, but there is a time element here. What you're doing is delaying a proper interrogation and if the plot goes down...I'll have you in the seventh level like this." Phil snapped his fingers in the under-warden's face.

The man seemed pulled in two directions at once. "We...we have tools here. In the maintenance room...saws and hammers, or electricity. I'll make sure you have whatever you..."

"Shut your fat face," Phil growled. "Have you seen Roland? His scars? The man's experienced more pain than anyone I've ever seen. It's going to take more than electricity to get him to talk."

"Maybe you can go get your, uh tools and come back," the under-warden offered.

"And maybe you can shut up!" Phil raged. "Get me that prisoner or you'll be coming with me instead of him."

The man had his hands to his chest as if to protect himself from a sudden blow. "I can't. It's illegal."

Phil did indeed want to punch the man, but it wouldn't do him any good. "You're playing a deadly game," Phil said. The prison bureaucrat said nothing. He only sat there wilting his suit with sweat. Phil tried again in a calmer tone, "Why would you risk yourself like this? I'd be gone with Roland for a few hours at most. What is it? Is there someone after your job?"

The under-warden nodded. This was always the way of it; the easiest path to success was to tear down the man ahead of you.

"Give me a name," Phil said in whisper. "Give me a name and I'll fix that issue. I'll take them both back to the seventh level and you'll be free and clear."

"He's connected," the under-warden answered in his own whisper, one so quiet that Phil barely heard. "Everyone around here is connected. It's a wonder I've got this far...but everyday they're out for me."

"Stop your whining," Phil said shaking his head. The under-warden was a dead end. More threats would be a waste of time. "I need a phone."

"All the lines are down," the under-warden said, adding to Phil's anger.

He felt it building in his neck and arcing into his shoulders. "What? The phones are down?" Phil clenched his hands into fists—more to control the urge to strike out. "The weather's been clear since… it's been ten days since we had any weather worth mentioning."

"They went down this morning," the under-warden explained. "A tree probably pitched over and clipped a line."

The Inquisitor ground his teeth, "I'll be back in the morning. Have the prisoner ready to go."

Chapter 7

Where There's Smoke

The slow ride back to the capital in the electro, with its half-charged battery, and the bitter cold seeping through the poorly insulated frame only added to Phil's frustration. Even buttoned up, his teeth chattered, while his large-knuckled hands grew stiff on the wheel. Every few minutes he had to swipe away the fug of his breath from the windshield.

As he drove he dwelt upon deceit. Not the morality of it certainly, lying was a morally grey area after all, rather how best to use it to accomplish his goals. Truth wouldn't get him the hundreds of convictions that he'd been dreaming of; unfortunately, lies weren't likely to work either. Phil's boss was a veritable mule when he had an idea stuck in his head. If he thought it would please the commissioner to save a few dollars he'd never sign the paperwork allowing a transfer. At least not without a very good reason and perhaps due to the cold Phil couldn't come up with a single one that sounded at all plausible.

By the time he reached the beltway skirting the capital and passed through the security checkpoint, the only ideas that had come to him regarded Roland. Though he seemed crafty in many respects, the old man probably wouldn't know a faked transfer form from a real one. That would get Phil ten confessions, and if he could get permission from the warden to take Roland down to the garage that would be another ten.

"Maybe I could beat five or six more out of him," Phil mused unhappily. Twenty-six was a good number, but was such a far cry from what he had envisioned that he couldn't help but feel down. He sulked in the light traffic until a warning light on the dash began to blink—the electro's charge had dropped below fifteen percent.

"Crap!" Now he had a decision to make: would it be better to go straight home and swing by Stephen Crown's dom-box in the morning or take the chance of running out of juice? A quick calculation: three miles to Stephen's and then another four back. It would be close. The meters on the electros were notoriously bad...if he were to run out of juice there would be trouble. But if he waited he could miss his chance at the book.

The redistribution adjusters were like vultures. Technically, they couldn't reclaim any property for the State until a jury actually signed off on the death warrant. However, since that was strictly a formality, adjusters had been known to swoop in early and pick a place clean.

Phil likely had a day or two but wasn't going to take the chance and he made the turn away from his home. Ten minutes later, with the meter down to eight percent Phil parked the electro at the top of a steep slope. He was nearly half a mile from Stephen's place but the hill made it worth the walk even with the bitter cold. Starting an electric car on a hill such as this would save him at least half a percent on his battery.

Stuffing his service pistol into the front pocket of his coat, Phil set out into the night sticking to the empty streets as opposed to the sidewalk. He walked quickly, keeping his head on a swivel, taking in the darker shadows and deeper alleys. Every year, to great fanfare, violent crime was reported to be down from the year before and every year hundreds of bodies, bloated and sickening, floated lazily down the Potomac.

The night was especially dangerous, particularly for unwary justice officials. Phil was hardly unwary. He had survived three years on the Mexican front, where a sharp eye meant the difference between life and death. He made it to Stephen's building unmolested.

Strangely, he found the front doors locked. He gave them as ferocious a tug as he could but they were of reinforced steel and didn't so much as budge. Stepping back he looked up at the ugly grey rectangle of a building and checked again the number—the only thing that distinguished it from the thousands of other buildings within the city—QQ443.

It was Stephen's building alright, but why was it locked? There were very few reasons that it would be, quarantine against an infectious outbreak being the most likely. Yet where were the warning signs and the orange tape? Another possibility was a mass arrest, only where were all the Homeland Security vehicles? Without them, the locked door made no sense. Only a member of the Board of Housing could lock these doors—not even the tenants could lock them.

Phil was still staring at the doors when he heard the first scream. His right hand cleared his coat pocket faster than the eye could follow—and a millisecond later a light *snick* came from the black pistol as he thumbed off the safety.

Another scream came from above. Again, Phil stepped back and now saw that the night was darker than it should've been. Roiling black smoke shot from the top of the ten-story building. It curled up into the sky seeming to disappear into the eternity of space. More screams and cries of help came to the Inquisitor as windows began to open all along the side of the building. Desperate faces appeared in the canted glass as the occupants struggled for air.

Phil's mind was slow to catch on. There was a fire? How had this happened so fast? One minute he was checking the door and the next the whole building was going up. He touched the door—it was noticeably warmer than it had been only seconds before. The fire was spreading quickly. Again, he strained at the doorknob, and when that didn't work, he slammed his shoulder into door. He even tried kicking it, but the idea of marring the shine on his shoes made it a feeble attempt at best.

"You! Hey you. Up here!" cried a shrill, panicked voice—one of many. "There's fire in the halls...the

building's on fire. Please, you have to save my baby."
In shock, Phil looked to see a woman, two stories up,
dangling a baby through the small opening of her
window. The windows weren't made to be opened
fully; they would crank back only about six inches,
but somehow this woman had managed to get her
child through the opening. Phil stared, aghast.

"Please, catch my baby! Please, save her!" the
woman demanded and then, since Phil wasn't directly
beneath her, she started to swing the child, who was
making a bleating noise like some sort of barn animal
—a sheep or goat perhaps. Phil blinked in
amazement: the woman was going to fling her child
at him!

The concept was so preposterous that he turned
away, ignoring the pleading and the begging with a
look of disgust. What would he do with a baby? He
was there for a book, not to be burdened with
someone else's problem. However getting the book
didn't seem like a possibility now, at least not from
this direction. Hoping that the rear entrance wasn't
locked as well, Phil left the screaming woman and ran
around the building only to be disappointed.

Not only was the door locked, the air around it
shimmered with the heat coming from within. He
backed away feeling suddenly light-headed. A
noxious chemical smell made him gag. He backed
away even further from the building, noticing that the
screams and cries were growing less. Thinking that
they should've been gaining in volume instead, he
again looked up. Lifeless arms stuck out of a few of

the windows, but the for the most part they were empty—no more scared faces, no more people.

"What the hell?" he whispered under the hungry cracking sound of the still unseen fire.

Poison, his mind whispered right back in answer. That was the only explanation. Someone had deliberately set fire to Stephen's building and to make sure no one survived, they had added some sort of fast acting poison to the fuel.

Phil continued to back away, staring up at the building. Other than the smoke, nothing moved. After a minute flames began to appear in the windows of the lower floors and a fleeting vision of the woman dangling her baby came to him. This annoyed him on some previously unknown level and he turned and strode purposefully back to his car. What happened to that woman wasn't his fault. And saving that baby wouldn't have done it a whole lot of good. The state run orphanages were practically slave work camps—if anything, he had done that mom a favor.

In this day of hunger and disease and torture, a quick death was a good death.

Sulking over the loss of the book, but feeling justified with regards to the woman, Phil trudged up the hill to the electro and only when he went to open the door did he notice that he had never tucked his gun away. Before he did, he gave another closer look around him, realizing only then that the fire had been set deliberately. It had been set professionally, but for what purpose?

Stephen Crown's rather feminine face sprang to mind. "No, he's just a fag," Phil said, tucking his gun into its holster. He then leaned into the car, released the break, set it in neutral, and began to push. When gravity took over, Phil leapt in and turned the motor on but didn't engage the electric engine till he hit the bottom of the hill.

"He's just a fag," Phil repeated, turning for home. "No one would a torch a building full of people over a fag. Not even if they knew about the book." Still the thought haunted Phil the rest of the night—as did the image of the baby dangling by her skinny little arm.

Chapter 8

The Thin Ice

The idea that Stephen Crown had something to do with the fire was such an insatiable itch to his subconscious that Phil was up the following morning earlier than usual and headed back to the Justice building before his watch—an ancient Timex given to him as a failed bribe the year before—had a chance to hit seven.

A distinct feeling of unease accompanied the subconscious itch and as he strode through the building, the usual heady, bloated sense of self-importance that he normally carried about with him had disappeared. If people scurried out of his way, it went unnoticed. If they seemed afraid to look in his eyes, he couldn't tell as his own had a touch anxiety to them and he kept them, for the most part, on his Chinese-made shoes.

The fire had been the work of a professional and this meant that someone with a lot of pull was behind it. And someone with that much pull could squish a shlub such as Phil Tarsus like a bug.

"The elevator's in the green, Inquisitor," the same guard from the day before said in a hopeful tone.

Normally, Phil would have heard the butt-kissing notes in the man's voice, however that morning he looked at the cramped elevator with trepidation bordering on paranoia and missed it completely. "I'll take the stairs."

You're being stupid, he groused at himself. He was. There were far easier methods to kill a man besides rigging an elevator. The thought didn't do much for his anxiety. Neither did running into his boss.

"Thank goodness you're here," Darrel Conner announced with a slap on Phil's back. "The Commish is in a mood! He wants the Crown case wrapped up ASAP and I was starting to worry that I'd have to run the show myself. Not that it would be a big deal...I mean I've done thousands of these in my time. It's just been a few years. You know what I mean?"

Phil didn't. His mind was lagging again. What did Conner mean about wrapping up the case? "The Commissioner wants Crown executed? Today?"

"This morning actually," Conner said. "I've got half a jury rounded up and—fingers crossed—the rest will be here within the hour. Though I bet we'll be waiting half the morning for the news gal to get her fanny down here." The deputy-commissioner paused, scratching his cheek and eyed Phil shrewdly. "So, do you know what's up? Why the Commish is all over this? I mean this Crown guy's just a fag, right?"

It took all of his will power to keep his face neutral at the question. "As far as I know," Phil replied.

It was official in Phil's mind now. There was more to Stephen Crown than he had realized. Loose ends were being trimmed...and it wasn't out of the realm of possibility in the paranoid America of 2122 that a full Inquisitor could be gotten rid of as easily as someone convicted of treason.

"I didn't really get that in-depth with him," Phil went on, practically gushing out the words. "He confessed to being gay right away...I mean it was quick...nothing surprising. The transcripts cover everything."

"Then you probably missed something," Conner said. "Phil, we have tools for a reason. Tools and training. It's no wonder you're constantly behind in your quotas."

For just that moment he was glad he was behind. Whatever secret Stephen had held back was one Phil didn't want any part of. "It won't happen again," Phil replied. A thought struck him and he went with it. "I promise...in fact I have a tough nut in that prisoner down at Polk. I'd love to bring him back here and really put him through his paces."

"What? The guy at the prison? Isn't he like eighty years-old?" Conner asked dubiously, raising a mocking eyebrow. "You're telling me you can't break a senior citizen? Are you kidding?"

"I can break him," Phil said defensively. "Don't worry about that. I just wanted to use the skinner on him...and they don't have any mirrors in the prison big enough." Phil never had a prisoner not break after seeing their full-length body without skin; not only was it visually horrifying, mentally it destroyed them.

"No. The geezer stays at Polk. Like I said the Commissioner is being crazy over the budget."

Phil smiled and nodded, though inwardly he felt his chest tighten. This sudden stinginess over the budget was out of character for the Commissioner. Was Roland right about the possibility of arson at the prison? Was Phil's strange investigation there just a set up? A reason for him to be at the prison when it just happened to go up in flames? It was possible; a man as powerful as the Commissioner of State Justice could arrange all sorts of "accidents."

"That's no problem," Phil said. "I'll bring some of my tools with me the next time I go out." At this Conner canted his head and looked at Phil quizzically.

"The next time?" he asked.

It would be almost a dereliction of duty for Phil not to go back to the prison immediately after the execution of Stephen Crown. "Later today, I meant," he added.

"Good. Also, remember to make it legal. Just because you're having your 'talk' outside the Justice building doesn't mean you can skirt the law. Make sure you bring the news with you."

"Of course," Phil answered, talking to Conner's back. The man had turned away, heading back to the warmth of his office, leaving Phil standing there feeling chill and brittle inside.

Was it all a set up?

"Don't be stupid," he chided himself in a whisper. Just like with the elevator—there were far easier ways to kill a man than to burn down an entire prison.

Someone burned down Crown's building, a voice within him reminded. Attempting to ignore that voice, Phil went back to his office, where, in a fit of despondency, he turned his heater up high and sat considering his paranoia and wasting his precious heating ration.

"There's ten dom-boxes per side...ten stories high...about three people per..." Phil lapsed into silence as he realized the death toll of the fire from the night before. "Six hundred innocent people killed. For what reason?"

No one is innocent. His words to Stephen Crown from just the day before came back to him.

To the State, the dividing line between innocence and guilt was so thin as to be almost invisible, and as an Inquisitor, Phil ignored it altogether...and now he realized he was being a perfect fool by even questioning whether someone powerful enough to torch an apartment building would hesitate even for a second to burn down an entire facility crammed with convicts.

Phil began to pace, hoping to find a hole in his own logic—it was glaring, yet in his growing fear it was a minute before the obvious struck him: incinerating a prison just to kill one Inquisitor was outrageous, especially when there were so many easier and less costly methods to silence a man: an assassin's bullet; a hemlock infused cocktail; an "accidental" fall from the top of his building. No, if he would be killed it wouldn't be in a prison fire.

He didn't know whether to be happy at this or not. Feeling shaky, he sank back into his chair. "That damn fag," he whispered harshly. Crown had done something...or knew something...or...Phil didn't know what. He only knew that if it wasn't for Stephen Crown, he wouldn't be sitting there in a fearful sweat.

Like a magnet, the computer on Phil's desk drew his eyes to it. The Crown file was just there, a few clicks away. He didn't want to know. Whatever mystery was there, he truly didn't want to know. He just wanted to go back to his normal life of sending people through the meat-grinder of justice and forget Crown. Still, his hand went to the mouse and gave it a shake—though he didn't *want* to know, he *had* to know.

Nothing happened. A renewed spike of fear had him rattling the mouse back and forth in a blur. The computer should've been whirring into life; however, it just sat there cold and lifeless. Phil jabbed the power button—and breathed a sigh of relief when the machine kicked on. Maybe there had been another power outage or maybe one of the cleaning crews had shut it off while attempting to clean around it.

The old computer, a 2101 People's Desk Top, took its usual sweet time coming to life, running through its start-up functions and all the while Phil sat drumming his fingers on his desk. Finally, he highlighted the working-file and read...down...the...list...

The Crown file was missing.

Phil ran down the list a second time, going one-by-one, reading the names of the men he had recently condemned to death. No Crown file.

Desperate, he checked the deleted files and was reading through them with growing desperation when Haley Baker came barging in, making him jump in his chair. "What's the deal?" she demanded, her brows showing thunder—this did nothing to detract from her beauty. "What's so damn important about this fag that you had to get me out of bed so early? Is this your way of getting back at me because I won't go out with you?"

Phil's hand slid out from his coat—it had shot to grip of his pistol in a fraction of a second when the door had come open. "Hardly," he replied, relaxing just the slightest. "It's the Commissioner's idea. Don't blame me."

She didn't appear to believe him. "And is it also the Commissioner's idea to drag my ass all the way to Polk?" she asked icily. Phil began to shrug his innocence but Haley cut that off, jabbing him in the chest with a slim finger. "Don't give me that crap! Who does a confession at a damned prison? I mean what kind of lighting will we have? Have you thought about that? Have you thought about our ratings? I'll look like I'm reporting out of a fricking tomb!"

Her petty complaints did nothing to evoke sympathy from Phil. "First off, it's Conner who's making me go down there. Second, if you're so worried about lighting I'll make sure to bring my blowtorch."

She had been about to continue her blustering rant, but the idea of the blowtorch turned her complexion a light green. The smell of burnt flesh made her nauseous and out of deference, he usually used other means to elicit confessions.

"Sorry," he mumbled, unable to stay mad at her even in his current state of mind. "Hey, why don't you look on the bright side? Everyone gets the same shots from the seventh level: the same old confessionals, the same old blood covered slabs. But getting a confession from Polk...that's rather unique."

Haley's eyes went to the floor and she began to pace. "Maybe...maybe," she murmured to herself. Suddenly she stopped and she began to nod. "This could work. A grim, gritty backdrop. A cold darkness...I like it. Tell me, what's the victim like? Is he a hard gangster type? Lots of scars, tattoos anything like that?"

"You just called him a victim," Phil said, sitting back and staring in astonishment.

"What? I...I did? No I didn't, did I?" Haley stammered. She put her hands on Phil, pleading; her panicked fingers grabbing at his wide lapel. "That's not what I meant. I meant the criminal...he's a criminal," she insisted.

Dropping the wrong word like that could destroy a person. A part of Phil wanted to make her sweat— she had busted his balls on too many occasions and had it been any other day he might have used her slip-up to exact either revenge or force a date on her. Yet just then, he still felt unsure of himself, as though he stood upon a frozen pond with white lines zigzagging out from beneath his feet.

He let her off the hook, saying, "The *criminal* is not what you'd expect." Phil pictured Roland: the long white hair, the scars, the confidence. This last was something Phil couldn't understand. How could a man left to rot for so long still have so much mental strength? "He's different, that's for sure. He'll look good on camera. He has a presence."

"Ok. Good. That's good," she said in relief that Phil wasn't going to make anything of her accidental slip. Haley then pulled herself together and forced a smile on her face. "First we have to get this execution out of the way. I hate to say it, but the ratings on the confession were...not so good. It wasn't you. Your denunciation was better than usual. It was the fact that he's just a gay." She made a face. "People are tired of gays. Can you make him cry? It would help if you could."

Phil shrugged, feeling more defeated. His ratings had always been below average—though he was handsome, his cold demeanor turned the women off, and while he was brutal and cruel, he seemed to lack the passion for hurting people that men looked for in good television.

He glanced again at the computer screen. The Crown file was gone, probably erased forever and now it was time to do the same for the man himself. Phil's stomach hurt. Would he be next? Was he to be erased as well? With a flick, he turned off the heater and immediately the cold, which had been held at bay, crept back to coat him.

Chapter 9

A Stone's Throw

Phil stood fidgeting outside the jury room, waiting for Haley to finish her lead in. If they were going to get any sort of ratings, she would have to carry them with her looks and perky outlook on executions. He was in no state of mind.

How close was he to death? Would he be assigned a rigged car? Would there be someone waiting for him in his dom-box? Was the water in his taps even then being poisoned? Would it be a knife in the back; a bullet to the brain from two-hundred yards; a garrote from behind...

Henderson, Phil's under-inquisitor, stuck his head out of the filming room. His eyes went to squints as he saw Phil's right hand slip up under his jacket. "Sorry. Didn't mean to scare you," Henderson said. "You're on in fifteen seconds."

"Good." Phil kept his hand where it was until the puzzled assistant retreated back into the room. Even then, Phil was slow to pull his fingers from the dimpled grip of his service pistol and he had to fight the urge to re-check the load.

Fifteen seconds ticked away, but it was another twenty before Phil could force himself into the jury room.

The jury, a group of twelve people pulled at random, sat in their numbered chairs and despite the bone-chilling temperatures, each sweated in their finest clothing, the sheen on their faces catching the light and glinting. Lips were drawn lines; hands were clasped to keep the shaking from being noticed. They were afraid and had every right to be. A wrong word; a moment of hesitation; a show of patriotism a shade less devout than the person sitting next to them could mean their own death sentence. Jury duty was a horrific event for the condemned but in some ways it was worse for the condemners.

"Good morning," Phil said, walking slowly along the length of the table. Though his mind was a confused jumble of paranoia and his insides were beginning to cramp and hurt, the malevolence of his position washed over the jurors and from an outside perspective, nothing as yet seemed wrong.

Each of the jurists sat up a little straighter becoming more attentive, though they had no real need to be. They weren't there to decide innocence or guilt—no one was innocent after all. The single purpose of the jury was to add the slimmest veneer of legitimacy to the outrageous proceedings.

Usually Phil made a circuit of the table before he went into his canned speech, a rah-rah performance designed to get the jurors' bloodlust pumping. However, just then his mind was a blank; empty of all his words and in the void the image of Crown's apartment building going up in flames came to him.

That was no accident, a voice in his head spoke. *And that file, someone deleted it. And this execution, someone hurried it along. And your trip to Polk...*

Phil squeezed his eyes shut. When he opened them again the image of the fire was gone yet still his speech didn't come to him. It was as if it had been deleted along with the Crown file. His mouth came open and then shut again. The onset of panic set in. His throat began to tighten so much that even if his speech did come back to him he didn't think he would be able to spit it out.

After a near minute of the Inquisitor just standing there, one of the jurors, a girl with dirty-blonde hair that sat lank upon her head, had the audacity to glance up at him. That had never happened before. Normally, the jurors were deathly afraid to attract any attention to themselves and as a rule they kept their eyes straight ahead unless spoken to.

For the moment, this riled Phil enough for him to feel like his old self. How dare she even glance at him? He held her gaze wearing a look that was a combination of fear and fury. The girl paled beneath his stare but was too afraid to look away. As they locked eyes, his usual speech came to him:

...Let me just say, thank you for coming down here this morning. I want you to keep in mind that jury duty isn't about one person's innocence or guilt, it's about protecting the State. It's about protecting

our way of life. It's about keeping America as perfect as she can be...

That was how he normally began, but just then nothing was normal. He felt like his whole world had been turned upside down. And for what? One gay? One useless fag? It made no sense. He was just doing his job...his duty to his country. Angrily he turned from the girl and faced the two-way mirror that made up one of the walls. What was happening to him wasn't fair, but then again, fair and duty didn't always go hand in hand. Whenever that happened duty, as a rule, won out.

"Do I need to tell you your duty?" he asked, harshly, looking at the tall man with the black uniform and the regulation haircut standing just inches from him in the mirror. The jurors glanced at each other, wondering who had been asked the question. When no one answered, Phil demanded, "Well?"

Heads began to shake. "No sir," one man said and then all answered the same way in a running mumble.

The Inquisitor turned from the mirror and his eyes fell on the empty screen opposite him on the far wall. "Stephen Crown has admitted to his crimes," Phil said, just then remembering a little of the ceremony of death. "Watch."

The elevators could sit unrepaired for weeks; the computers could crash twice a day; the electricity was hit and miss, but the machinery that ran State justice never failed. A projection of Crown's tear-stained face lit the screen. The jurors watched as he listed his transgressions against his fellow man and as always they sat there waiting for the "Big Crime" that would justify the death penalty, and as always their faces went purposely blank when the screen did.

"I can read your thoughts," Phil scoffed at them. "You're all thinking: *That's it? He's just gay?*" The blank looks remained and the two jurists who had their backs to him, shivered. "Yeah, just a gay," he continued. "Just a man who doesn't feel he has to obey our laws. Who here would like to ignore our laws whenever they felt like it?"

Not a hand went up. Phil stood in front of twelve sweating statues; even their eyes were frozen in their sockets. Each of them clearly fearing that even the slightest move could be interpreted the wrong way.

"Of course, none of you would even think about it," he said. "That's because you not only respect our laws, you respect and love your country. This gay, on the other hand, seeks to destroy our country as sure as any bomb throwing neocon. He just seeks to do it from within...he's like an insidious rotting cancer."

This sort of talk was more in line with what the jury had been expecting and they nodded along, eager to do their duty and get out of there. Unfortunately, this was all Phil had. As he spoke he'd been eyeing the jurors with the growing suspicion that one among them was an assassin—his assassin—the man charged with killing Phil Tarsus. He tried to convince himself that it was only paranoia fueling the idea, but the notion of an assassin among them drove everything else out of his head and another silence settled uncomfortably on the thirteen of them.

Phil's mouth came open uselessly. He ran a nervous tongue over his lips and then swallowed loud enough to be heard by everyone in the room. Someone tapped on the two-way mirror in an effort to get Phil speaking again. He started to shake his head, thinking he would make an excuse about being sick and then run from the room, but just then another of the jurors took a peek at him.

Was this him? Was this the assassin? Phil's hand headed to his shoulder holster under his coat, but just in time, he brought it to his chin where it shook slightly. Angrily he balled it into a fist. Why on earth was this happening to him? Why had he been singled out? He did his duty. He had always done his duty. He put his country first in all things like a true-blue American patriot, and now...

"Are you a patriot?" Phil asked the man, surprising them both with the question. The juror who had glanced at him was somewhere in his thirties. He had slickly oiled black hair and seemed oddly thick through the shoulders and arms. It was this that caught Phil's eye. So few people these days were this strong and well fed. An assassin certainly would be.

"Yes," the word shot out of the juror's mouth as if he thought he was being timed in his response. He seemed properly nervous...but then again Phil figured assassins were trained to blend in.

"What's your name, Patriot?" Phil stared hard at the man, looking for the tiniest falsehood; ready to act

74

if he found one. His right hand stayed close to his chest. He could have his service pistol out and put a bullet through the juror's eye before the man could blink.

"I-I'm David Key," the juror said, rushing his words together. Phil said nothing to this, but only continued to fix David with his soul-searching gaze, his hand inching closer and closer to his gun. After a moment of quailing beneath the look, David went on, "I'm thirty-four and I'm a cook over at the Transportation Ministry and..." David's shaking hands went to his chest as he slowly leaned back away from the ferocious look on Phil's face. "And...I'm a patriot."

Phil's hand came out from beneath his coat. He had been surrounded by lies for so long that the truth usually stuck out like a sore thumb. The juror wasn't lying. He really was a cook, which explained the extra weight.

"Good," Phil smiled at him, showing his feral white teeth, trying, and failing, to appear friendly. David blanched at the sight, which only made the deadly smile grow larger.

One down, eleven to go. Phil then turned to look at the next juror, "And what's your name?"

The juror, a stick of a girl with wide, unblinking eyes answered, "Abby." Her voice was a tiny thing, barely a squeak. She looked as though she thought Phil was going to eat her. "I'm just a secretary," she added as though she thought that being 'just a secretary' would make her less edible. She began shivering in a manner that couldn't be faked. Phil looked to the next person and as he did Abby let out a long breath.

"And your name?" Phil asked each in turn, going around the table. They answered, growing more nervous rather than less. So far this was unlike any pre-execution council that any of them had ever seen on TV. Normally there was a cold anonymity to the proceedings; the jurors saying nothing except to pronounce their verdict at the end. And normally the Inquisitor stuck to his script and kept the ritual moving along in its time honored sequential manner.

When the last had spoken, Phil leaned up against the table feeling his stress ease slightly. The assassin, if there even was one, wasn't among them; these were just people. This realization caused a short barking laugh to escape him, which only had the jurors looking even more uncomfortable. He didn't care, however he still had an execution to conduct, and for the life of him he was too frazzled to get back on track. Though what did it really matter anyway? What was one botched proceeding? With nearly fifteen hundred executions a week who would even remember this one?

Your boss will, you idiot!

And if Phil was marked for death did he care what Conner thought? Not at all. "Well," Phil said with an odd twisted smile. "I guess this is my lucky day. I have a room full of patriots who know their duty. Let's see if that's true."

The stunned jurors watched as their Inquisitor walked out of the council room and into the execution room.

"Is it time already?" the squeaky voice of Abby asked.

Phil went to the long table in the execution room and picked up a stone from the top of the pile. The stones at the top were small, about the size of a golf ball. They were for pain, for punishment. The ones further down were larger, the killing stones.

"Yes, it's time," Phil said, looking at the bound figure of Stephen Crown and bouncing the stone in his palm.

Chapter 10

Fear Unleashed

"What is this?" Stephen asked in a carrying whisper from across the room. His eyes were wide and though he spoke to the Inquisitor, he couldn't stop staring at the piles of rocks in their bins. Some of the rocks were new—and grey, but many were old and wore a coating of dull maroon.

"You know what this is."

"No. No...no y-you c-can't be serious," Stephen babbled. "You can't stone me."

"There are worse ways to go."

Seeing his slow death laid out before him, Stephen wasn't at all consoled. "Please don't do this to me," he said, his face pale and dripping with tears; his Adam's apple worked up and down as though he were choking on the very air he breathed.

Every once in a blue moon Phil would feel the slightest bit sorry for a person he condemned— usually this would occur with a women if she were young and pretty enough, but for Stephen Crown, Phil felt nothing but a vicious hate.

"I'm not going to do anything to you," Phil replied. "Everyone knows it's illegal for a government official to take part in an execution. But if I could...

He held the rock up to Stephen's face and gripped it so that his knuckles went white, wishing he could hurl it at the queer who was ruining his life.

Maybe he's not ruining your life, a voice inside himself spoke up hopefully. *Maybe there's no assassin. Maybe the missing file and the fire and the odd behavior of the Commissioner is all just a coincidence.*

He didn't believe this for a second. It wasn't how his world worked. His world was very black and white. A thing, good or bad, was always purposeful. A file didn't go missing by accident. Executions weren't hurried along on a whim. Buildings weren't torched for the pretty colors. Everything was done for very specific reasons. But why Polk, he wondered. Why go to so much trouble for one...

Crown interrupted his thoughts, "I'm begging you...please don't do this. I was wrong. I admit that, but I can change. Please, I should have been more..."

Like a switch had been thrown, Phil's hate turned to fear in an instant. There was still a chance, a one in a million chance that his lack of thoroughness would save him; that his very ignorance and incompetence would make it not worth the effort to kill him. But if Crown were to gush out his secret right there, they'd all be dead. The jurors, Henderson, Haley, even her cameraman—all dead.

"Shut your mouth!" Phil screamed, his voice sounding strangely high and girlish in his own ears. "It's too late for your excuses or your lies. It's too late for...everything."

Crown, who stood almost naked and with his arms flung out and trussed to the wooden beams in the normal fashion of execution, dropped his head and for a moment the image reminded Phil of something he had seen while fighting in Mexico. It had been a statue carved from ivory of the old American God, Jesus Christ. There had been many of these in Mexico and none were ever suffered to remain intact.

Hurriedly, Phil turned away from the man. He had no time for reminiscing. At any moment Crown could blurt out the poisonous secret he had squirreled away in his brain.

The milling jurors stood in a glump behind the table; nudging close to one another as if proximity equated to security. They were sheep in Phil's eyes. Sheep about to be transformed into wolves.

"Spread out!" he barked. "Form one line. Make sure you have enough rocks in front of..."

"Do you believe in God?" Crown whispered from behind.

At Crown's first syllable, Phil's shoulders hunched and went taught as a steel cable. The question didn't bother him; he had heard it asked many times before in the execution room. What bothered him was Crown's voice; he could breathe death at any moment simply by uttering the wrong combination of words.

Yet the question couldn't remain unanswered; people would wonder why. "No," Phil scoffed. "I don't believe in a sky fairy that grants wishes."

"I never knew if I really did either," Stephen said. "I've always wondered, but now...now I know. He's real."

Phil was about to scoff some more since it was the only sensible thing to do, but there was a strangeness to Stephen's eyes that stopped him momentarily. Where just a moment before they had been filled with terror, they were now alive and bright, more so than any set of eyes that Phil had ever seen. Normal people had eyes that were not windows to the soul, but lead vaults containing little besides fear and mistrust.

After a second, Phil had to glance away. "Do you not see those rocks?" he asked incredulously. The jurors all froze, many with their arms full of the stones. "That's your death. It's going to be slow and horribly painful. Look at them and tell me how you can possibly believe there's a God."

Crown did as he was told. He stared without blinking, until a slow smile started to creep up the edges of his mouth. Infuriated, Phil pointed at the jurors and then whispered so low that the cameras wouldn't pick it up. "Look at those people. They're going to kill one of their own. Why? Because I told them to. You've done nothing to them or to anyone that would justify this. Is that right? Is that just or good? No. It's evil. I'm evil. Everyone in this room...hell, everyone in this building is evil. Maybe everyone in this city is evil. People are evil. They give up their babies. They turn informer on their neighbors. They cheat and steal all day, every day and you're going to stand there and tell me there's a God? A god of love and happiness and damned cupcakes?"

Amazingly, Crown nodded. Phil was never so close to purposely killing a prisoner than at that moment. His fury was volcanic—a blaze within himself that truly didn't make much sense. Who cared if the fag believed in fairies and leprechauns? He'd be dead in twenty minutes one way or the other. And at least he was spouting this nonsense instead of his secret.

Phil managed to warp a sympathetic smile onto his face and said, "You're afraid. I get it, but don't feel bad. A lot of people find God at the end. I personally don't understand it. What is there about this room that elicits such a strange reaction?"

Stephen surprised him by answering. Though he spoke to Phil, his eyes never left the rocks. "It's just what you said; it's the evil of this place that tells me the truth. God has been removed from this room more thoroughly than in any place I've ever been. He's not in you and he's not in them." Crown lifted his chin to the jurors who were picking through the rocks in front of them, looking for the ones with the least blood on them, the way they always did, as if they could keep their own hands clean in some way.

As usual, Phil sneered openly at how the jurors picked over the rocks and then wiped their hands on their clothes in a useless gesture, not realizing that those hands would be forever stained with guilt. The jurors were as complicit in these executions as Phil was; hell as complicit as all of America was. This was why he sneered. The way they sweated and shook, they acted as though they were sheep being lead to a slaughter, when in truth they were sheep being lead to murder.

This was the true, undeclared purpose to the perpetual executions: to unite the country in fear and blood. What most people failed to realize was that along with the 90,000 executions, the country generated over a million state sponsored murders every year in the form of jurors. And it was these new murders who were the most ardent supporters of the practice.

Undoubtedly skinny little Abby would leave and tell everyone later that: "It wasn't that bad" or "It was the right thing to do" and definitely she would add: "I did what every American patriot would've done." Thus adding another layer to the State's veneer of legitimacy and making it that much easier for the next batch of jurors to come through and kill—everyone does it, after all.

Phil turned his sneer back to Stephen. "God isn't in them because God doesn't exist."

Stephen smiled cryptically, "Where there's love there's God. My mother said that to me on the day she died. It was the one and only time she'd ever spoken about God and it's haunted me ever since. Maybe because it's true. Those jurors are certainly proving it. They're filled with fear. It oozes from their pores and is infecting everything around them, including you."

"Me?" Phil said, his eyes flaring again in anger, but also uncertainty. Was his fear really so obvious?

"Yes, you Inquisitor. You're more afraid than the rest of them. I don't know what it is; maybe you're afraid I'll die too quick and that you're bosses will be mad at you because I didn't suffer enough. Or that I'll take too long to die and you'll lose your TV audience to a better death. Or is it you're afraid one of them will balk and not join in? What would happen then?"

They'd all die is what would happen. It occurred every few years; a juror would take a stand against the whole ghastly affair or one would just be overcome by the thought of the criminal's suffering, or some such nonsense and if the Inquisitor couldn't get the proceeding back on track...they'd all be put on trial. And the trials always ended up one way.

Phil didn't want to give Stephen the satisfaction, but the urge to look back at his jury was too compelling. His eyes went immediately to the weakest of the lot: Abby. She had made a pile of the very smallest rocks and had both her hands over it. Phil thought at first she was attempting to shield the rocks from the other jurors; perhaps to keep them from poaching "hers" but then he noticed that Abby refused to look down at them.

"Damn," Phil said under his breath. She was using her hands to block the sight of the rocks. That was a terrible sign. If she couldn't look at the instruments of death, there was a very good chance that she wouldn't be able to use them either. Would she freeze up during the execution? At the thought Phil's chest constricted around his heart so that he could feel every beat vibrate through him.

"But most of all I think you're afraid of what I know," Stephen said.

The words spun Phil around. "Huh?" He felt caught between two fires: Stephen on one side threatening to spill what he knew and Abby on the other threatening to come apart at the seams.

"You're afraid—deep down—that I know something you don't. That I know the truth about..." The time between words stretched out and it became the slow motion hell of a nightmare. Phil reached for Stephen to shut him up, but too late the queer finished his sentence "...the truth about God."

"What?" Phil asked, his mind a moment behind. "The truth about God?" Phil actually laughed with relief. "You mean the truth that God is all a lie made up by the neocons to enslave the masses?"

"No. The truth that there really is a God. A loving God that will be calling me home soon. Maybe...maybe this whole stupid trial has been a blessing in disguise. I've wasted my life, living in fear, feeling like a rat slithering among all the other rats. When have I ever been *good*? You know what I mean? When have I ever been a good person, really? I haven't been evil, not like you, but I've never been actually good. The fear always stopped me. The fear of pain and death. How stupid! But now ha-ha! I'm not afraid at all."

He certainly didn't look afraid, though he did have a manic air to him. His eyes were fever bright and his grin bizarre.

"I'd be afraid if I was you," Phil told him. The Inquisitor had seen his share of death and stoning ranked as one of the most painful—if it was done right; slowly.

"Oh, I'm sure it'll hurt, but perhaps the pain is a necessary atonement for my sins. I feel them now, my sins. They're a weight on my soul. The lies I've told. The times I've stolen from others. It's too late for forgiveness but maybe there's still a chance for heaven."

"I've heard enough," Phil said, turning his back on the condemned man, wondering why he had listened to even a syllable of what Stephen had to say. Heaven! What nonsense. At least he had kept his real secret to himself; Phil thanked his lucky stars for that.

The jurors had formed their line and picked out their rocks. Each looked uncertain, but none more so than Abby, who had backed away from the table and was trying as furtively as possible to keep David, the greasy-haired cook, between her and Phil.

Phil groaned inwardly, wondering how this day could get any worse. Would Abby throw the rocks as she was supposed to? Or would she just go through the motions and hope nobody would notice? Because if so, she was a fool. The cameras would pick it up and people all over America would see, and they would think to themselves: if Abby doesn't have to kill her neighbors why should I have to? That was the greatest fear of the State: that somebody would stand up to them even in the smallest way. They would never allow it to happen. The video would never air and none of them would see the light of day again.

"Crap!" Phil muttered. How on earth was he going to fix this? A speech maybe? A real one this time; one that would focus on the importance of duty? Or would patriotism work better? Or a speech on the evils of homosexuality? Probably no speech would work. Abby had undoubtedly heard every speech he could give a dozen times already. Americans were raised on a steady diet of them from the moment they could walk.

If not a speech, then what? He could hope. He could just start the execution and hope that she would take part.

Phil didn't have a better idea, so he moved to the front of the table, only to see Abby slide even further behind the cook. He had to stifle another groan at the sight; the girl was definitely going to be a problem.

"David...could you, uh," Phil began and then paused. He was about to ask the cook to move to his right so Abby would be seen, but then he had a better idea. "Could you step forward?" The cook did, moving right to the edge of the table, his hands gripping two rocks as if they would fly away if he didn't.

"David, you've seen the evidence against the accused, how do you find?" Phil asked.

The cook blanched, going wide-eyed. Jury members were always asked what their verdict was as a group; never as individuals.

"Guilty," David choked out.

Phil's idea was to put Abby on the spot. She looked like she would hide if she could, but he wasn't going to allow that to happen. But he couldn't exactly single her out either, so that meant all the jurors would have to give their verdicts as individuals.

"Well?" Phil asked, expectantly.

David's mouth came open. He looked down at the rocks in his hands as a deep silence swept the room. The cook was alone in bringing "justice" and Phil thought he saw the conflict set in: kill or be killed. There was no middle ground in this.

Grimly, David set his jaw, his face becoming a hard mask. "Traitor!" he denounced and then hurled the rock in his right hand. From that distance, a bare fifteen feet, he could hardly miss and the rock thudded solidly into Stephen's chest.

Traitor? It was rare for a juror to add anything beyond the word guilty. "Sarah Johnson," Phil called out over the grunt of pain from Stephen. "How do you find the accused?"

A woman, a nurse at a state hospital stepped forward. "The bastard's guilty," she spat out and then zinged her rock, clipping it off the top of Stephen's head.

A second juror adding something? This was going much better than he hoped. But there was still, "Abby Jacobs," Phil said. He made sure to look at her calmly, in the most reassuring manner he possessed. "How do you find the accused?"

The girl stared around the room as if she was the one on trial. When two seconds passed, a long time in the situation they found themselves, one of the other jurors gave her a tiny nod, which seemed to help. "Gg-guilty," she stammered. Another second leapt by and she just stood there until Phil inclined his head toward Stephen. "Oh right. Traitor!" she screeched and threw her rock.

"Good aim," Phil said. The girl's rock had hit Stephen square in the mouth. Abby beamed and when Phil had finished going down the list of the twelve jurors, and Stephen sagged against his ropes weeping lightly, she asked, "Can we go again?"

"Of course you can."

Chapter 11

Half Past Fear

Haley pushed through the exiting jurors with barely a glance at the sagging, blood dripping hunk of meat that used to be Stephen Crown. "That was...that was genius," she gushed. "We're going to re-runs for sure with that one. I thought you were losing it the way you started, but it was all a plan, wasn't it? The way you acted as if you didn't care. Oh my gosh, I was like, what the hell's happening? For a moment, I didn't think there was even going to be an execution, but then I started to see what you were up to. You put it all on them and somehow it brought the passion out. I've never seen a jury so excited to kill."

Kill or be killed, the thought ran through Phil's head. At first he thought that the jury had reacted instinctively to his odd behavior, protecting itself by going to the extremes, each juror trying to out-do the last. "Yeah it was all part of the plan." It had been all luck—but was it good luck? It didn't feel like it. As the execution progressed Phil realized Abby hadn't been worried about the killing at all; she had been worried about her accuracy. At one point he had to remark a second time about her aim, it was so good.

"I've been practicing," she had said. "I was so scared that I wouldn't be able to hit him and be the only one not a part of it."

Haley pulled out her compact and checked her look, saying, "If we do go to re-runs, and I'm almost certain we will, I'll take you up on that offer of dinner. And we should go somewhere nice. You know, to be seen."

"That'd be great," Phil replied, forcing an excited attitude where it should have come naturally. The execution was bothering him. For one, Crown hadn't stopped staring at him, as if he was trying to impart something in his looks alone. Secondly, the jurors had actually enjoyed the killing. That wasn't at all normal. And it wasn't right. The jurors were supposed to be afraid. They were supposed to kill out of fear of what would happen to them if they didn't. But they had liked it.

Haley, adding more red to her lips, said between coats, "Just a hint with the editing, the only thing I'd change is to drop a second or two off your pauses, but no more. That was part of the fun—the way you looked as though you were just going to walk away from them."

Phil gave her a half-smirk over the top of a half-shrug. "I might just leave it completely alone. Not change it a bit." He was worried that a second viewing would only confirm the bloodlust, the real bloodlust, the unfabricated desire to kill that he had seen in the eyes of the jury. Had it been a fluke? Or had he inadvertently uncovered an ugly change in the population, one in which they cheered death rather than feared it?

And what would the Commissioner and the other people in power think about that? They certainly wouldn't be happy. Though they spoke of patriotism at every turn, all they really had to sway the masses with was fear. And if they no longer had that, what would happen then?

He didn't want to think about it. Whatever happened there'd be blame, and in this day and age, it was perfectly acceptable to kill the messenger.

Feeling the day's anxiety creep over him, coating him in doubt thicker than before, Phil left the execution room. He made his way back to his office and was deep in the process of using up the last of the month's heat ration when his boss, Darryl Conner came in.

"I don't want you to change a thing on that video tape," Conner ordered. He then held out his hand. "In fact, I'll take it as is."

"I haven't transcribed it yet."

"What the hell have you been doing? You're due back at Polk in two hours."

For the last couple of hours Phil had been drifting into a state of apathy but now he sat back in his chair, his eyes hooded and dangerous. His right hand coming to rest on his tie, comfortably close to his pistol, but not overtly so. "Why two hours? The old man going somewhere?" The suspicion in his voice was obvious and his boss picked up on it quick.

"Of course not. What's wrong with you?" Conner replied with anger. "You're supposed to be there in two hours because I had a talk with the warden up at Polk this morning. He told me that you tried to browbeat some moron into releasing Gentry to you, *despite* the fact that I told you the old man stays put! What do you say about that?"

"Uh...I was going to borrow him only," Phil answered. "The facilities up there aren't at all conducive to..."

"I don't give a rats-ass about the facilities at Polk," Conner said in low venomous tone. "You get up there and get the confessions. I don't care how you do it or how long it takes. You had just better get them or I'll have your insolent ass back fighting the Mexicans where it belongs."

"Yes sir," Phil replied, dropping his gaze sheepishly.

Conner stood there for a moment, seething, and then added, "You have one hour to get me those transcripts."

When he left, Phil took a moment to drop his head on the keyboard. "Maybe I'm wrong about this whole Crown business," he said, and was too frazzled to argue with himself about it. Instead he bent to the work of typing, something he had never been particularly good at. As he watched the tape, stopping every ten seconds or so, he saw himself the way Haley had. It was strange. He had seen himself on tape many times before but this was something else. The fear that he'd been feeling had come across as anger and when he had sneered at the jurors it sure appeared as though he was about to wash his hands of them and leave them to their fate.

All in all, it was a good execution. Even the parts where he and Stephen had whispered to each other.

Enough of it had come across to make Stephen look like a religious zealot and Phil a logical defender of the State's position.

"I told you it was good," Haley said from the doorway. "The best I've seen in years. Those jurors...they started off meek as kittens but then they really got into it."

"Yeah that was great," Phil said, finishing up his report.

"You sure are acting strange," Haley remarked.

Before Phil could give an answer, Conner came in, pushing past Haley. "That's because I chewed him out for not following orders. I'll take that, thank you," he said grabbing both the report and the video. He then turned back to the reporter. "You have access to a news van, right? Be a doll and let Phil and Henderson ride out to Polk with you. Thanks. Oh, and here are your travel docs." He dropped the paperwork into her hands and was gone before she had a chance to protest.

"I guess I'm giving you a ride."

"He's being crazy over the budget," Phil said, apologizing for his boss. "Please, tell me you have heat."

Haley's van was a wonder to Phil. It was only six months old and everything still worked on it, including a fabulous heater. He was instantly jealous.

"How do you rate such a fancy ride?" he asked, settling into the faux-leather seat.

"We have to keep up appearances, don't we," she said, nudging her cameraman, a lanky fellow named

George. Though George hung around the Justice building six days a week he was terrified of inquisitors and because of the proximity of two them, he had the steering wheel in a death grip. He didn't smile as Haley was. She rolled her eyes. "Relax, George. They won't hurt you."

"That remains to be seen," Henderson said in his practiced tough guy voice. It was Phil's turn to roll his eyes. His under-inquisitor never turned it off.

"I'd be nice to him if I was you," Haley said. "George is an expert with the camera. He can make you look really good or really bad. Think about it. Image is everything. That's one of the mottos of the Board of Entertainment."

Phil raised an eyebrow. "One of them? How many mottos does one Board need? We don't have any in the Board of Justice." *No one is innocent* was strictly an unofficial motto.

"The other is: perception is reality."

Henderson, who had seen Phil rolling his eyes at him and was clearly in a pissy mood, said, "Reality is reality. When you say perception is reality you might as well say lies are fact."

"You couldn't be more right," Haley said, turning back from the front seat and patting his leg. "But that's exactly what we do, and that's why the Board of Entertainment is the most powerful board. We shape reality."

"No you don't. All you do is make lies more palatable," Henderson shot back. "And it's Justice that's the most powerful board. I could have the lot of you arrested like that." He snapped his fingers, eliciting a second eye roll from Phil.

"Henderson, you sound like a second grader—*My teacher can beat up your teacher*," Phil said faking a child's voice. "Why don't you shut up before your tongue does a number on you?" Though Henderson was an ass, in this instance Phil had to agree; Justice was easily the more powerful board. "I still can't get over how nice this ride is," he added to smooth over the conversation.

Haley ran a gloating hand on the smooth plastic of the dash. "It certainly is. And there's a reason people at Entertainment get these, but your under-inquisitor isn't going to like the answer. It's because image *is* everything. We're the face of the State so it's important that the public sees only the best—the prettiest people, the nicest cars, the finest clothes."

Henderson breathed loudly out of his nose, clearly wanting to say something. Haley couldn't help but hear. "In some ways it's the same for you over at Justice. Who cares what your black cars are like on the inside? When they go by people shudder. Right? Or what about the Justice building itself. Outside it's beautiful—insides it's a hideous dungeon. Justice is a facade."

Her words were borderline treasonous and she knew it as soon as they slipped out. "I meant the building only. Not...not the board or the uh...the concept."

The ride went silent. Eyes flicked about; each wondering if Haley had gone too far, knowing that people had been arrested for far less. The concept of justice was a corner stone of the new America, though for the life of him Phil hadn't a clue why. It was never practiced as it had been taught in grade school.

Henderson had a smug look about him, but held his tongue and Phil was glad for the silence and not just because he didn't want Haley in trouble. They had already spoken more than was normal for members of such a mistrustful society and the hidden burden of anxiety over just such a slip always gave him headache.

He rubbed his temples, staring out the window until the dark, stonewalls of Polk Federal Penitentiary appeared. It was strange to him that such powerful walls had been erected around such a foul and dilapidated prison. What he also marked as strange, something he had never noticed before was that the walls seemed to have been constructed by a confused architect. They appeared designed both to keep things in as well as out.

Phil smiled at a sudden thought: maybe the architect had been an Inquisitor.

No one is innocent; conversely that meant everyone was guilty. How do you build a wall with that knowledge? Which side was the good side? The safe side? He decided there couldn't be one and after just coming from a room where twelve strangers had almost gleefully stoned a man to death over the breaking of an outdated law, Phil would have felt a might bit *safer* entering a prison where most of the inmates were incarcerated for the theft of food, had it not been for Roland Gentry and his paranoia.

That paranoia had infected Phil the day before and its fever had only gotten worse. Instead of barking orders when they pulled through the main gate he stared around, looking for anything that seemed out of place. Nothing did. It seemed the same numbers of guards manned the walls and towers as they had, and none looked at them in a manner that suggested they were party to a secret.

The one difference that afternoon was the presence of the warden. He was a bull of a man who was clearly helping himself to the rations of his inmates. Phil couldn't care less about that; it was the self-important look to the man's face that he cared about. It worried him. No one but someone very well connected would dare to look so smug in the presence of an Inquisitor and even then they were usually cordial about it. The warden looked anything but.

Chapter 12

An Imperfect Deal

"It's about time," the warden growled.

"It's about time for what?" Phil replied as evenly as he could. Though the man was clearly connected, he wasn't *that* connected. He was just a warden after all. However, the manner in which he was acting made it seem otherwise. "About time for you to take off early again?"

The warden shook his head as if to say: nice try. "Conner told me you were a putz. Listen, my hours are my own to keep. There's never been an allegation against me regarding shorting the minimum. What I'm talking about is you taking your sweet time getting down here. And now I'm late to a meeting with the Commissioner of State Infrastructure."

"Infrastructure?" Phil was quick to ask. "What are you meeting with them for?"

"As if that's any of your damned business," the warden said, pushing past Phil. He paused halfway to his car and turned. "While I'm gone, Brewer's in charge. I've had a good long talk with him so don't try any of your Inquisitor crap on him again. As a favor to Conner, I'm letting you interrogate Gentry in the machine shop. You'll have the place to yourself, so you're responsible for any mess. Here..." the warden tossed a set of keys. "One's to get down to the lower levels, the other's to the machine shop."

Phil caught them and forced a sycophantic smile onto his face. "Sir, if you don't mind, I need five minutes with Gentry up here. I can't tell you why, but..."

"Dietl," the warden interrupted Phil, calling out to one of the guards. "If the Inquisitor attempts to bring any prisoner up here, shoot them both."

"Yes sir."

"Good bye," the warden said and then climbed into his car, the latest version of the Electro.

Phil's pathetic smile drooped, turning into a grimace: there went ten easy confessions.

"Why would you want to interrogate someone here?" Haley asked, skeptically looking around at the uneven and crumbling asphalt.

Phil sighed before answering. "The old man's a head case. He thinks that someone is going to burn down the prison and the only way he agreed to talk to me is if he thought we were going back to the Justice building."

"Does he think he'll be safer there?" She laughed for a moment and then sobered, turning angry. "The guy's an old man? How old? People don't like to see the elderly tortured you know. It makes terrible TV."

"He's very old, but also very tough." Phil sighed a second time. "Look, it is what it is. I have to interrogate him and you've got to film it. Let's make the best of it. I want you to set up a camera in the laundry room on the first floor, and if the old man asks, make it out that it's only temporary and that we're leaving soon."

"Why are you going to so much trouble?" Henderson asked, taking a hold of Phil's sleeve as he made to enter the prison. "It's an old man. Just beat the confessions out of him and let's get out of here."

Phil stared at his assistant in an unsettling silence until Henderson looked down. He then rasped, "You think you can talk to me that way because the warden was an ass to me? He's connected; you're not. Listen close: if I get any more lip out of you, I'll find myself a new under-inquisitor."

The threat had sharp teeth to it. An unconnected man got only one shot in his field. "Yes sir," Henderson replied with the proper respect, lowering his gaze.

"That's better. George, you and Henderson set up another camera in the third sub-basement. There's a machine shop down there," he paused long enough to press the keys into his assistant's hand. "It's where we'll do the majority of the interrogation. I want a good background. If you have to move stuff around to get it, that's fine by me. I plan on leaving a mess that'll give the warden fits."

Ten minutes later Roland entered the warmth of the laundry room, his blue eyes taking in Phil, the camera, and the single legal document laid out on the flat of the broken press, all in the space of one second. He then looked at Haley and couldn't seem to look at anything else. He wasn't the only one; the other prisoners stole peeks every other second.

"Goodness gracious. I'm Roland Gentry. Pleased to make your acquaintance," he said to her, offering his hand. She was very reluctant to take it, making his face droop slightly. "Is it something I said?"

"You're a criminal, Roland," Phil put in, laughing quietly. "It's not proper for a lady to associate with criminals, even a lady in her profession."

Roland managed to pull his eyes away from Haley just long enough to ask two questions. "Her profession? What profession is that?" His eyes shot back. "Are you an Inquisitor, too?"

"No, she's a reporter," Phil answered for her. "It's been the law for years; all interrogations and trials are televised, after some editing of course. Now, this is the transfer paperwork I promised you."

Roland took the paperwork, glanced at it briefly and then stared again at Haley. "Your skin is perfect. Your lips...it's been sixty years since I've seen a woman and I don't think I've ever seen one as beautiful as you."

It was clear the man wasn't lying about this and Haley dipped her head in acknowledgement. "Thank you," she said giving him a white smile.

"You're welcome," Roland replied, spellbound.

"Roland?" Phil prompted.

"Of course. I'm sorry. It's been...it's just...I...I'm sorry. I've been anxious to leave all day but now I could stay here forever. Really..." Roland spluttered some more before he managed to pull himself together. "I'm sorry. Back to the business at hand. Our deal is for ten names." He recited the names with ease. "These are men I preached to. They've all been baptized."

"And did you ever suggest that they preach to the other inmates as well?"

Roland glanced again Haley's way and then nodded to Phil. "I did suggest that." Phil smiled inwardly—Roland had just given up twenty confessions, two for each of the names. Section twenty-three of the Establishment of Religion Law made it illegal to practice any portion of a religious ceremony. While section forty-one forbade the promoting or promulgation of any religion. Now Phil would go for conspiracy.

"And were these meetings designed with the..."

"Hold on," Roland interrupted, lifting up a hand. "We'll stick to our bargain, if you don't mind. I've given you ten names as I said I would. Now you hold up your end."

"Yeah, about that," Phil said sitting back with his hands clasped behind his head, relaxing, making it clear he wasn't worried in the least about the place burning down—and he wasn't. Nothing at all seemed out of the ordinary. By the minute, his fears laid themselves gently down to slumber. "I think I'm going to need ten more names before we go."

This centered Roland's attention. It was as if Haley had disappeared from the room. The old man's blue eyes seared into Phil. "Ten more names? That's a strange request, especially when I've already given over ten freely with the promise of so much more."

"Let's just say, I don't trust you," Phil said. "What do you want most in the world? To get out of here fast. But what then? I have no idea you'll come through for me when I get you down in my confessional."

"Your confessional?" Roland asked amazed. "You call your torture chamber a confessional? That's blasphemous."

"Ten names," Phil insisted. When Roland just continued to stare, he added, "Hey, isn't it the capitalist way; to take every advantage; to screw people over for the least penny? You're the one in a hurry. You're the one with his back against the wall."

"It's not just me. *We* don't have time for this."

"Ten more names."

"You are so clueless when it comes to capitalism," Roland sneered. "You'll only get one more name out of me if we do it like this, but I can guarantee you won't like it."

This caused Phil to take pause. What name could a prisoner possibly drop that would worry an Inquisitor? Maybe the old man was bluffing. Then again Phil had little choice but to continue his own gambit. "Ten names," he demanded, glaring.

"You just screwed yourself," Roland stated. "You know what your problem is? You've mistaken the tenants of communism for those of capitalism. It's the communist way to steal from those who have, and give it to the have-nots. While the capitalists believe the have-nots must work to get what they want. You see how you acted true to your upbringing? I have names—many, many names and you tried to steal them without giving what I asked for in return. And now you're screwed."

This was all a bunch of bull to Phil. Everyone knew that a capitalist would sell his executioner the rope that would eventually hang him. The rest was all talk. "I don't see why you're making such a big deal about this. You're going to give me those names one way or the other."

"I'm making a big deal out of it because now I don't trust you," Roland answered. "I offered you a cush deal and you throw it in my face. There's a reason. What is it?"

"I've told you, it's you who can't be trusted. I guess we're not going to the garage after all," Phil said as if he were truly disappointed.

Roland nodded, smiling grimly as he did. "I get it now. You couldn't get me out and so you thought you could trick me. That's too bad."

"Wrong. We can leave any time. I want ten names now and ten more when we get to the car. That's the new deal."

"No. You'll get one name from me. Would you like to hear it?"

Phil took a second to answer, feeling suddenly wary of what this strange old man would say. "I guess we can start with one."

"Sure," Roland said calmly. "A man came to me recently. He was afraid for his future. Afraid that powerful people were out to get him. Though he didn't come right out and say it, I knew he was afraid of what would happen to him when he died. Afraid for his very soul."

"His name?" Phil insisted.

"The man's name is Phil Tarsus."

Chapter 13

The Zealot

Phil drew in a long breath—confused—bewildered really. His own name was the last he had expected to come from Roland's lips.

Roland filled the silence. "He came to me, this Phil Tarsus, afraid, looking for guidance. It seems there was a man that wished to kill him. And it wasn't just any man; it was his boss, Darryl Conner."

The Inquisitor rocked back in his chair as if struck. His eyes were wide, refusing to blink. They felt to grow in his head until it was as if they took up half his face. "How...how do you know that name? Tell me now!"

"You gave it to me, remember?" Roland answered as if innocent as a child.

"I didn't," Phil gasped, trying desperately to remember their conversations. He was sure the name of his boss had never come up. They had talked of nothing but politics and religion. "Stop the tape!" he ordered belatedly in a hiss that sounded as mechanical as the machines operating at the other end of the room. With his paranoia swelling within him Phil jumped up. Going to the camera, he first checked to see if Haley had actually stopped it, but then he thought better and popped out the tape and stuck it in his pocket. Haley kept her face as neutral as she could, but it was obvious that she was nearly as confused as Phil was.

Phil swung back to the prisoner. "You're going to tell me how you know that name or else."

"I will if you can get me out of this prison."

"No, now!" Phil raged. Suddenly, his fear from earlier came back in full force. "Who do you work for? Is it the Commissioner? Is that who's after me. He set all this up didn't he?"

"I work for myself," Roland answered simply.

"Then who's paying you to kill me?" Phil bleated. Roland only stared at him in an odd way. Phil looked down at himself to see that he had pulled his service pistol, though strangely he was cradling it to his chest as if afraid someone would take it from him.

"You couldn't get me out, could you?" Roland asked. Phil shook his head and the old man sagged. "Relax, Phil. The name Darryl Conner was on the transfer paperwork. I figured he was your boss."

"Then that story...what was that? Your idea of a joke?"

"I was teaching you a lesson. There are ramifications to screwing over a business partner."

Phil ran a shaky hand over his forehead, wiping away the sweat that hung there in drops. "We're not in business together and I'm not your partner. And you can stop with the lessons in capitalism. You're wasting your..." Phil paused in mid-sentence as a distant, repetitive, metallic sound came to them. "What's that?"

Roland went grey, but stayed silent. The sound grew nearer until Phil recognized it as someone rapping on cowbell.

A guard came down the corridor striking the bell and calling out, "All prisoners to their cells. All prisoners to their cells."

Just like that the hall filled with the rag covered stick figures who used to be men. Haley and Phil shared a nervous look before the Inquisitor asked of Roland, "What's happening?"

The old man refused to speak. His eyes went to the floor. "Damn it," Phil muttered. He then tried to fight his way through the prisoners, but the guard turned down another corridor before he could get close.

"You! What's going on?" Phil demanded of one of the men, pinning him to the wall like a squirming bug.

"A drill? Or a lock down? I don't know. Please let go. They beat you if you're one of the last."

A drill? Was this a coincidence? Or was there more going on? Phil shoved the bleating man away and looked around, trying to make some sense of the world—and that was when things went from strange to really strange. The hall had been a carefully precise chaos, like the inner workings of a hive where the comings and goings of busy bees seemed always on the edge of slipping out of control. But then Haley stepped from the laundry room and a tumult exploded like Phil had never seen. Men walked into walls. Some tripped over each other or went in circles. Fights broke out among them, while others stopped with their mouths hanging open and their feet paused in the middle of steps as if they were frozen in time.

"You better come back in," Roland said, gently pulling her back. He then looked at the hand that had touched her in wonder.

"What's going on?" she asked of the old man.

Roland considered his answer, but before he could say anything Phil pushed his way back into the laundry room and said, "It's just a drill...I hope. They have lock downs all the time. It's probably nothing to worry about."

"Don't lie to her," Roland said. "There's going to be a fire, Ms. Baker. They're going to burn this place down."

Haley's eyes went wide. "What? When? Now? Oh my gosh! We have to get out of here."

She began to rush back into the emptying hallway, but Roland caught her arm. "Not that way."

"But that's the way out!" she screeched.

The old man shook his head sadly. "You're not getting out. They won't let you go," he said. He then turned to Phil. "Do you want to tell her or should I?"

"Tell her what?" Phil demanded. The fear that had been his constant companion all day came out as anger. "They aren't going to burn down this prison just to kill a crazy old man and an Inquisitor. Please! It's unbelievable for you to think that we're the focus of some elaborate plot. Now stop scaring her."

"What plot?" Haley demanded. "What did you do?" This she asked of Phil.

"I didn't do anything," Phil answered defensively. "Don't listen to him. There's not going to be a fire. It's only a drill and it's only coincidence that we're here when it's going on. Now come on. They'll let us out or I'll see heads roll."

The three pushed through the last of the scurrying prisoners, many of whom were too preoccupied with the thought of a beating to even notice a woman there. They made their way to the main gate but were too late.

"Open this right now!" Phil demanded of a group of six guards, who were slacking against the bars nervously, as if they wished they were on the other side of them—the safe side. When they didn't jump at his words Phil's gun leaped into his hand as if by magic. The gun and the wild-eyed Inquisitor riveted the guards. They looked to one of their own, a sergeant who hurried from a nearby guardroom springing sweat at every pore.

"I'm sorry, I can't open the gate," he whimpered. "I don't even have the keys. It's the under-warden who has them but even he can't open it. We're in a lock-down and the laws states no one but the warden can open the prison back up."

Haley, spoke before Phil could, "Why is there a lock-down? What's wrong? Is there a fire?"

Phil watched the guard closely as he answered. "No, ma'am. We're running a drill only. There's nothing to be afraid of."

Both Haley and Phil breathed a sigh of relief—Haley because she was gullible and believed anything if someone in uniform said it and Phil because it was obvious the guard wasn't lying.

He holstered his gun and then tried to get his wits back. Despite what he had said to Roland, a very large part of himself had been sure that someone was going to burn the place down. "How long will this drill last?" he asked, calmly, acting as though not two seconds before the trigger on his pistol hadn't been halfway back as he demanded answers from the sergeant.

"Only a couple of hours at the most."

"Oh man," Haley moaned.

"I wouldn't be worried if I was you," the sergeant told her. He glanced at his watch. "The prisoners will be locked up tight as a drum any minute now. And you can hang out here if you wish...we have tea in the guardroom and a halfway decent couch. I know it's probably not like you usually have but it'll do in a pinch. You're Haley Baker, right? You're my favorite news-woman."

"Why how sweet of you. Some tea would be nice, thank you," she said, switching to celebrity mode in a flash, giving her fan a radiant smile.

Phil began relax, but Roland, who had kept quiet and in a subservient mode around the guards, whispered in his ear, "The tech crews that have been all over this place, they all left."

More than anything Phil wanted to ignore the man's words, but he hadn't relaxed that much and the creeping fear within him wouldn't allow it. "Those tech guys I saw yesterday; what were they up to?"

The sergeant could barely tear his eyes off of Haley. "The tech guys? Those lazy bastards were supposed to be re-wiring this whole place with a new P.A. system, but they left with the job unfinished. That's why we had to use the stupid cow-bells as usual."

Roland gave Phil a meaningful look.

"It doesn't mean anything," Phil insisted. He turned from the room without wasting a moment on being polite. "Haley, stop your flirting and let's go. I still have an interrogation to conduct."

Haley had been smiling at her fans but now she looked alarmed as she hurried to catch up with Phil's long strides. "But...but the drill?" she said and then whispered, "And the fire."

Phil tramped on, shaking his head. "There's not going to be a fire. He just made it up to try to get out of here." The Inquisitor reached the door to the lower levels. It was a great slab of iron on hinges that took him quite a bit of grunting to heave back. "My guess is that he probably had some plan to escape."

"Really?" he heard her ask the prisoner as they began descending the stairs to the lower floors. With each step, the light grew less and the air closed in on them. He felt he was moving further and further from any sort of safety but swallowed that fear just like he had swallowed all of his growing fears that day. What other choice did he have?

"Actually no," Roland answered. "Other than escaping the total destruction of this place I didn't have a plan. And yes, there's going to be a fire. The Inquisitor wants to ignore the signs but I can't."

"W-what signs?"

In mid-stride Phil turned with a hard look. "Don't listen to him, Haley. He's a zealot. Just ask him. I'd bet you twenty dollars that he thought God had sent us here to save him."

"You're a zealot?" she asked, her disgust wrinkling her face.

Roland nodded. "Very much so. Proudly so. People always misuse the word zealot. How can one love God with all his heart and not be a zealot? It's impossible. And by the way, I wouldn't take him up on that bet. I prayed to be rescued from this place. But as the old saying goes: God works in mysterious ways. It turns out I'll be the one doing the saving."

This made Phil shake his head as if overcome with weariness.

"You need me," Roland mentioned as he passed the Inquisitor on the stair.

"I don't."

"I agree it's strange. I thought I needed you, but it's the other way around. God has answered my prayers and yours too I'm betting. You see this place is going to burn down any minute and I'm the only one who can get you out of here."

Chapter 14

The Lesson

The third sub-floor held little besides a number of dimly lit storage rooms and the machine shop. The shop was a handyman's dream; it seemed every tool known to man was represented there. They hung from the walls and dangled from the low ceiling. They lay about in rusty piles or gleaned in neat stacks in shiny bins. Phil's first thought was to consider which of the tools he would steal.

"How'd it go?" Henderson asked. He ran a professional, but disapproving eye over Roland's unmarked face. "I take it he gave it up easy."

Phil glared. Since when did he answer to his assistant? Never. "I don't like the lighting; it's too bright. And what the hell were you thinking using those tools as a backdrop? You've got practically a dungeon feel here, but the tools look brand new. Get some of those old rusting ones up on the wall, damn it."

The set up for the interrogation that Henderson had concocted hadn't been bad, but Phil was in a mood.

Roland had stopped, statue-like, his left hand out to the wall and his head cocked as if trying to catch the tiniest of far away sounds. After a moment he blinked as his mind caught up to what Phil had been saying. "You're still going to go through with this?" Roland asked. "Did it occur to you that I might not want to save you if you mistreat me?"

"What occurred to me was that you are a prisoner, and that if you could escape you would've done it a long time ago. Now, if you don't mind let's get you tied up."

"You're forgetting our deal. You try any of this barbaric crap on me and I'll clam up...except for one name, right? That name I'll sing over and over."

Phil shrugged. "I thought our deal was over. Are you telling me you have a new one? And if so why on earth would you trust me...and really, why would I trust you. I admit I screwed you over. I lied right to your face. Clearly, you can't trust me and because of that I don't think it would be all that smart for me to trust you. You see what I'm getting at? Your capitalistic theories are worthless, which means all I'm left with are my communistic ones."

"Fear and intimidation?"

"It's what I'm good at," Phil answered.

"You're not as good as you think," Roland retorted. "Your heart's just not into it. I can tell. And yes, I have another deal. You see the basis of capitalism is the understanding of human nature and using that understanding to further one's ends. While the basis of communism is the warping of human nature to further one's own ends. Let me give you an example. Take competition. The mother of..."

"Stop," Phil said. "I don't care about this crap. I truly don't. If you really have a deal let's hear it."

Roland beamed. "Yes, my capitalistic friend, I really do have a deal. I will give you twenty-five names right now and in one hour, if I'm not hurt in any way, I'll give you another twenty-five."

"And after that?" Phil asked.

"If there's a fire, then we escape. If not then we'll see where our bargaining gets us."

"Let's make it thirty-five names now and only a half-hour wait," Phil haggled.

A laugh escaped the old man. "Very good. Thirty-five names it is. You see? Understanding human nature is always so much more effective. Another Inquisitor might have tried to change my nature and gone right on with the interrogation and what would they've got out of that?"

"Probably just their own name repeated back at them over and over," Phil answered.

Roland nodded. "Exactly. But in this way you get something: thirty-five names. And I get to stay pain free while we wait on the fire. It shouldn't be long."

"Then you better get cracking on those names," Phil said. "Take that chair and try not to look so smug. An interrogation isn't only about names and crimes committed. Haley, are we in the green with that camera?"

"Yes...but is there really going to be a fire? They said it was a drill." Superficially, Haley was unchanged, but the undercurrent of fear that her situation had generated was doing a number on her just below the surface. The skin of her face, which was generally the perfect combination of tight and smooth, had sagged away from the bone almost, but not quite, imperceptibly.

Phil caught it, only he couldn't find the words within him to soothe her. The truth was that as much as he wanted to deny the possibility of a fire, he couldn't. Too much had happened to him that was out of the ordinary.

Roland did what he could. "There will be my dear, but I should be able to get you out."

Haley seemed comforted by the words, while Phil thought they were pie in the sky. "Let's get to those names."

Without a pause for a break, Roland rattled off thirty-five names. When he was done, he said, "As I was saying about the warping effect of communism. Take competition..."

Phil let out an exasperated groan. "We're not done. A name doesn't mean much if there isn't a crime associated with it. Did you preach to these men?"

"Yes."

"Was this in conjunction with a Christian ceremony?"

"Not exactly."

Phil smiled, but his teeth were gritted behind it. If the old man would just say yes to his every question, this would go a lot smoother. "Did you preach the gospel?"

"Yes."

"Then it was a Christian ceremony. Was that so hard to say?" Roland only shrugged and after a pause, Phil continued. "And did you suggest that these men go out and preach as well?"

Roland nodded emphatically. "A true Christian is always an evangelical. Especially in these times."

"Evangelical?" Phil only had a vague notion of the term. People always used it to suggest that a religious person was extra-crazy, that maybe they worshipped snakes or conducted blood-orgies, but the way Roland had said it made it seem otherwise.

"Evangelical comes from the Greek meaning 'good news'. An evangelical Christian feels it's his duty to proclaim the good news, that is, the word of the Lord." Phil just looked at him, wondering what word that was precisely. Roland saw the look and added, "When I say the word of the Lord I'm talking about the gospel."

"Right," Phil said. "The gospel. And when you were, uh, spreading the word did you hear confessions?"

"Not like your confessions," Roland joked. When no one cracked a smile, he shrugged. "I'm not a priest. In my opinion a man's sins are between him and God. So that's a no. But I did perform baptisms. It's a common misconception that baptisms have to be done by a priest."

"Yeah I get mixed up on that all the time," Phil said dryly. "Now tell me about the future. Did you ever plan to meet on the outside to continue to spread your filth?" This was Phil's attempt to add a charge of conspiracy to each of the names.

Roland's lip curled at the word filth, but he let it pass. "No. So few live to see the sun again that making plans was considered a waste."

Damn it, Phil cursed inwardly. "Ok...what about the government? Everyone knows that Christians hate communism. Did you ever plot or maybe suggested an overthrow with any of these men?"

"No," Roland said in the open way of his. The clear lack of falsehood in his demeanor again disappointed the Inquisitor. Undaunted, Phil tried again from another tact but Roland cut him off, saying, "Look. The rule of man has been charged to man. Remember: Render unto Caesar the things which are Caesar's, and unto God the things that are God's."

"And that means?"

"In this case it means that the form of government a nation takes is up to the people of that nation and not God. So, no I didn't preach an overthrow. I felt my mission was the saving of souls."

Haley shook her head, making a sign to Phil for him to stop. "You know what?" she said. "This isn't working. It's really, really dull. You're going to have to spice it up or our ratings will tank."

Phil understood. Religious crimes tended to be uneventful, especially compared to the state's constant characterization of zealots: barbarians worshipping trees and burning children alive to appease their mad God.

"I'm sorry Ms. Baker," Roland said. "But it's not my fault that my crimes aren't really crimes."

"Deluding impressionable people into giving over their lives to a lie is crime enough for me," Phil chastised. "It may not be as exciting as, say murder, but religion is like that. It's slow and devious. It's like having a colony of termites eating at your house. You see one tiny bug and it seems harmless enough, however if you don't stamp it out fast the next thing you know your entire house has crumbled away to nothing."

Haley gave him a wan smile and then pointed at the camera. Phil interpreted this to mean: *That's a little better. Keep going.* He had no other choice. "What about you, personally. Have you ever considered the overthrow of our government?"

"Of course," Roland answered easily. "Even when I was young. It was instinctive to me. I knew before my father did that the system couldn't be allowed to persist. I tell you, my father was a brilliant man; smarter than any man I've ever met. He could buzz through the Times crossword puzzle in half an hour. He could put you in checkmate in two minutes. I could ask him anything on any subject and he always had an answer. The man was always right, except one time."

Roland paused and held up one finger. He had such a presence about him that everyone leaned in. "He was wrong one time. This was about...seventy-five years ago. America had been transforming from a free-market to a socialist society for decades and then communism became all the rage among the 'learned' class. They agitated endlessly about it, telling everyone who'd listen about how wonderful and perfect America would be when the worker's paradise finally came into being.

"I was in the fifth grade at the time. Every day the teachers had us making banners or signs or marching in parades. It all sounded so good. Equality, justice, fairness for all. And on the other side was only evil or so it seemed. Anyone who stood up to the communists was vilified or shamed into being quiet, or if that didn't work there were always union goons who would beat them into silence.

"One day we were marching, as always...at the time I thought it was so cool. I mean what kid wouldn't want to be outside on a fine day instead of cooped up in school. Anyway, we were marching and there was this old couple holding flags and singing something about freedom. They seemed pleasant enough but the song really bothered everyone. Soon they were being mocked and spit on by the marchers and then our teacher started yelling at them to shut up and before I knew it she was beating the old man with her sign.

"I was so shocked I just watched—everyone did, at first. But then the fellow's wife tried to help and suddenly it turned into a frenzy. Our teacher screamed for help, and as I stood there shocked to my core, my fellow classmates rushed at the lady like a pack of jackals.

"They killed her. They beat her with their signs and when that wasn't enough they kicked and stomped her until blood came from her ears and she lay there limp. The man seemed mostly dead. No one did a thing for him. We just kept on marching. It wasn't right. When I got home, it still bothered me and I told my father about what had happened.

"He grew sad and said, *They're doing it wrong, again. How many times are they going to screw this up?*

"*What do you mean?"* I asked.

"He answered: *In principal Communism is a beautiful thing. In practice it's the most brutal, repressive form of government man can inflict on each other. It's a hideous blight upon this earth.*"

The room went deathly quiet. No more blasphemous thing could possibly have been uttered. Phil glanced to George and his camera, making sure that the light still showed green. It was.

"Now which part did you think your father was wrong about?" Phil asked. "You don't think communism is repressive? Or is it you thought that the gold induced slave-society of the old America was far more brutal?"

"Neither," Roland replied. "My father was wrong when he said that the principals of communism were a beautiful thing. It isn't. Not at all. *From each according to his ability, to each according to his needs*, is the very essence of warping human nature. And this warping isn't even for the betterment of either.

"The needy man only grows more so when he lives off of handouts. He grows dependent. He learns that work is for suckers and eventually he becomes a human parasite. He becomes addicted to the handouts, and the only time he shows the slightest motivation is when he gets off his lazy butt to demand more. And as an addict he always wants more.

"It wasn't enough to get free money. They demanded free food, free housing and free medical care. Eventually they wanted everything without working for anything; free medications, free abortions, free phones, free TVs, free sex change operations. It was never ending, because what did the dependent man care? He felt entitled to it all. That's what they used to call the dole: entitlements. How crazy is that? The poor man was entitled to free stuff on the basis of need alone. In other words we rewarded being poor and punished being rich.

"And what was the pathetic justification behind taking seventy-five percent of a rich man's earnings to give to someone who refused to work a day in his life? Simply: the rich man could afford to give it to him. The rich man had more than he needed and by golly he would share even if we had to make him share at gunpoint.

"And of course the rich man was warped by all of this as well. The rich person learned not to work as hard, not to try his best, or take risks, or persevere when times got tough. Why should he bother? Was he ever thanked? Was he ever praised? Never. What did he receive for his toil and sweat? Constant guilt, constant blame, and demands for more, more, more! There was a song from the hippie generation that summed up what the communists think of the rich beautifully. It went:

Tax the rich
Feed the poor
Till there ain't no rich no more.

"That was always the aim of the left; not the eradication of poverty, but the destruction of the rich. Isn't that a bizarre mindset? The conservative's mindset was to make it possible for everyone to have a *chance* at being rich. While the left wanted to make it straight up impossible for anyone.

"They took away the incentive for the average man to strive for more, but perhaps worse, they stifled the world of ideas in the process. Tell me, where have all the great men gone? Where is the new America's version of Bill Gates or Steve Jobs? Of Edison, Einstein, or Ford? Of the Wright brothers or Lindberg? Where is your equivalent to Washington, Lincoln, or King? How many great men have come along in the last century only to have their ambitions beaten out of them? Their dreams crushed? And their ideas deemed a danger to society?

"And of course without great men you have lost the ability to come up with new ideas. In my father's time there was always something new. A new vaccine to combat disease—a new pill to fight hair loss—a new computer that was always smaller but better—a new cell phone that held more computing power than the old space shuttle. Now what is there? I'm really asking, because I haven't heard of any advances in decades."

Roland waited for an answer to his question, but none of them could say a word. The truth was that in general people acted as though there wasn't anything left to invent; nor anything left to discover or no new worlds to explore. They acted as though the pinnacle of human thought had been reached and now beyond it was nothing but empty space.

"That's what I thought," Roland continued in smug anger. "And look where you are now. Instead of embracing the most ambitious and brightest among us, and holding them up as paragons the left did everything they could to hurt them."

Roland paused for a breath and Phil, who decided it would be good to stop this long diatribe, said quickly, "The rich got exactly what they deserved. After all they only got their money in the first place through theft and slavery. It was right to return it to the people." This was the standard line of reasoning and Phil would've been well out of bounds not to insert it.

"You couldn't be more wrong about slavery," Roland answered easily. "The slave masters of the old south had their lands burned and their livelihoods ruined during the Civil War. It took over a hundred and twenty years for that area to prosper again, and when it did, it wasn't due to slavery. And to further destroy your insipid argument, the richest parts of our country never knew slavery. As for theft? Who did the rich steal from?"

"The natives for one," Phil answered. "And the immigrants."

"Again wrong. Neither the natives nor the immigrants had anything to steal. Really the idea is silly on its face. How does one get rich stealing from people with nothing? And in case you don't recall, most immigrants came here as poor as church mice— they came here looking to make their fortunes. Now I suppose you could make the argument that we stole the land from the natives, but it would be a weak argument. By their own standards the land belonged to whichever tribe was strong enough to hold it.

"Think about it. Had there ever been set lines marking the permanent boundaries of lands between the Sioux or the Cree or the Seminole? No. Just like everyone else they practiced social Darwinism. The strong tribes flourished and pushed around the weak ones. When the white man came they were the stronger and so claimed what they would. That's the way history has worked since the dawn of man but somehow only the whites were criticized for it." Roland looked to be enjoying himself and added: "What else have you got?"

A sneer turned Phil's features. "Everyone knows that in America the rich stole from the workers. That's not even in question."

Roland chuckled. "Oh, you mean the same workers who had the greatest standard of living in the world? The same workers that averaged over two cars per family? The same workers that had a minimum of two weeks of paid vacation? Are these the destitute workers you're referring to?"

Phil looked down at his hands. Just then, the justifications that he'd been taught in school seemed somewhat childish. What was worse, with his eye trained to spot lies from a mile away Phil had failed to catch the old man in a single one. Was what Roland said all true? And if so what was he supposed to do or say about it? Clearly, the standard party talking points were pathetic in the face of Roland's logic, and this ruled out saying anything.

And that left only doing. The smart thing to do was to edit Roland's remarks to make him seem pathetic and out of touch. A dropped word here or an added sentence could make anyone look stupid. A few more sound bites—ones that he could rearrange to suit himself—would do the trick.

"Tell me more about..."

"What's that noise?" Haley interrupted. Her eyes were wide and staring up at the low ceiling. From that direction a dim rumbling could be heard.

Roland took a deep breath. "That's either our fiery death or our salvation, depending on whether or not you put your trust in God."

Chapter 15

A Mysterious Way

Phil's first response—after feeling his insides explode with butterflies— was to take a look at the camera; the green light still glowed. Though he could erase whatever he wished it was best not to take chances.

"Will God be sending Santa Claus to whisk us up the chimney or will the Easter bunny tunnel down here and save us with chocolaty goodness?" Phil quipped. Affecting an air of smugness at his quick retort, he turned to Henderson in a leisurely manner. "Find out what that sound is."

"Shouldn't we be getting out of here?" Haley asked. "If there's a fire, we'd better..."

"Turn off the camera," Phil ordered, thankful that Haley had given him an excuse. When George straightened up, Phil's relaxed manner evaporated. "Maybe it's nothing...it's probably nothing. But if it isn't; if there really is a fire, especially one professionally set, there'll be no escape. We'll all die down here."

Roland, who had been looking around them in a speculative and calm manner, said, "We'll escape. I've prayed on the matter of my deliverance and not for a moment have I doubted."

"How? How can we get out?" Haley asked. She got up and went to the door to look out. "This place is locked down. Even the guards can't escape. Wait! Have you been tunneling through the walls? Is that how we're getting out?"

"No. That would be an impossibility. The walls are three feet thick and latticed with rebar. You can't get through it. I know because it's been tried fifty times."

"Then how?" Haley asked in a high voice—the fear in it was undeniable. All eyes, including Phil's, went to Roland.

"Through prayer," Roland answered simply.

Phil groaned, while Haley's face screwed up into a tight, angry mask. "Prayer?" she demanded. "How on earth will that help?"

"I believe it will help a great deal. We shall follow the dictates of Matthew seven: Ask, and it shall be given you; seek, and ye shall find; knock, and it shall be opened unto you."

"He's crazy," Haley stated. She turned from him as if he no longer existed."Phil, what are we going to do? How the hell are we getting out of here?"

Phil only had time to shrug his shoulders before Henderson burst in saying, "There is a fire! There are alarms going off all over the place up stairs and I smelled smoke the second I opened the door. Grab the cameras we gotta get out before...what? Didn't you hear me, there's a fire!"

No one had budged except for George, who did little besides look to Haley for instruction. "We can't get out," Haley said. "There's...there's a drill. They won't let us out. They w-won't. We asked but they wouldn't...couldn't open the gates. They d-don't have a k-k-key!" She began to cry, great splashy tears. Phil wanted to go to her and hold her, but the advent of his death had left him too weak to even stand.

"We're trapped?" Henderson asked. "No. No, they'll let us out. We're Inquisitors. They have to let us out. We'll make them!" With this, he pulled his gun and went for the door.

"Do not go up there," Roland ordered.

"*You* don't tell me what to do," Henderson seethed. Phil had never seen the man so worked up. Normally Henderson was an emotionless automaton of State justice. His role as under-inquisitor never required him to denounce, cajole, or even threaten. He was supposed to be apathetic to the proceedings to the point of inhumanity—so clearly uncaring that Phil would seem the only real human in the eyes of the damned.

Henderson made to leave and Phil said in a dusty voice. "They don't have the keys. The guards...they don't have them. The under-warden does, and knowing him he'd rather be shot or burn to death rather than break any of the Warden's rules."

"We're really trapped?" Henderson asked in a carrying whisper. "But there's a fire."

The air felt to be growing heavy, thicker; it made Phil's chest work to expand. "They won't let us out," he said. He was sure of it. He had walked into a trap and it had closed around him.

"We can't just stay here," Henderson said. "There has to be a way out."

At this, all eyes went to Roland and he nodded. "We put our trust in the power of the Lord. These walls, built by man, will crumble at his least word."

"He's crazy!" Haley practically screamed. "He said himself that the walls were three feet thick."

Again, Roland nodded. "Yes, and with steel bars running through them."

"You're crazy," Haley repeated, before swiping the arm of her jacket across her wet eyes.

"I say we let his God save us," Phil said. His mind had split into two pieces. On one side, he knew the power of the State—the absolute power of the State to kill. When it wished you dead, you died. On the other side was the natural desire to live. That side would do anything, even grasping at straws.

"They're both crazy," Henderson said. "I'm taking my chances upstairs. I'll put my faith in my gun, not some stupid sky fairy. And you'd be smart to come with me." This last he said to Haley, but despite having called Roland crazy she shrank back into him. The fear of fire was too great in her.

He left and Haley said, "We're going to die."

"It'll be ok," Roland said in an attempt to calm her.

"What do we do?" Phil asked nervously. "How do we get this God helping us?" As every child in school had, Phil had been inundated with horrific and graphic drawings and representations of Christian rituals—the drinking of blood, the eating of human flesh, the human sacrifices. But he was desperate.

"Just open your hearts, and your mind and body will follow. George, come here. Stand next to the Inquisitor. Everyone hold hands and bow your head." Roland took a deep breath and then said in a loud voice, "Lord, as you freed your children from Pharaoh, we ask for your help, your guidance and your blessing as we flee the chains and bars that keeps us from the journey that you have for each of us. Please bless us. Grant us strength and courage, and guide us in the darkness that is to come. In Jesus' name we pray. Amen...say amen."

"Amen," the three repeated. They then stood, waiting to see what would happen. Nothing did.

Roland went to the wall and tugged down a sledgehammer. "We'll need another one, and that wedge. Hopefully, the rust hasn't made it worthless. George, grab that acetylene..."

Phil's brows came down in sudden anger. "What are you doing? What about your God? Didn't you say he could melt walls or whatever?"

"Yeah!" Haley put in, looking cheated.

"The Lord helps those who help themselves," Roland answered easily. He then handed over the sledgehammer to Phil. "God has put the power of his love in each of us. We just have to use it. Forget the camera, Ms. Baker. If you can carry the hack saws, please."

Bewildered, she took them. "The power of love? The walls are three feet thick...you said so."

"And now, thanks to God's plan, we have sledgehammers and a gas-powered reciprocating saw. It should be enough."

Just then, Henderson came back in breathing hard and coughing up black phlegm. "The smoke! It's moving down. I couldn't get through."

"Then we better hurry," Roland said. "Please, take this saw, Mr. Henderson. George, that acetylene torch, if you don't mind. Inquisitor, lead the way."

"What? What's going on?" Henderson asked.

"Roland's God is getting us out...somehow," Phil answered. Without looking back, he left the room, toting an eight-pound sledgehammer in each of his large hands. The stairs were already awash in a thick grey fog that had the same chemical smell that had emanated from Stephen Crown's building. Taking a deep breath and holding it, Phil started up, only to be called back by Roland.

"You're going the wrong way. We're going down."

"There's no way out down there," Henderson said. "There's nothing down there but the boilers and the pump room; and if you think water will save us, think again. If the smoke doesn't get us, we'll be baked alive, and soon after that the whole prison's going to come down on our heads. There's only one way out and that's through the main gate."

Roland stopped and looked at them all in amazement. "Even if you can cut your way to freedom before the fire gets you, what do you think will be waiting for you when you get out?"

"I don't know? Fire trucks?" Henderson replied, sarcastically.

"Really you are very gullible," Roland said. "Why is it only the Inquisitor seems to know your plight?"

"What plight is that?" Henderson asked. His brown eyes were steeped in suspicion. "What did you do, Tarsus?"

Phil glared right back. "I didn't do anything. It was Stephen Crown. He knew something—I don't know what so don't ask. But someone is looking to take out everyone who was close to him."

Henderson started to say something but Roland beat him to it. "We're fast running out of time. Make a decision." The old man then went down the stairs two at a time. Phil went with him; behind he could here Haley and George hurrying to keep up.

Henderson stood for a moment on the landing until the gathering smoke choked the indecision out of him and then he too followed. "I can't believe you were all that close to that fag," he said.

"Don't be an idiot!" Phil shouted over his shoulder. "I did his interrogation. Obviously they thought Crown might have talked about more than being just a fag."

"But what does Crown have to do with Roland?" Haley asked. She had the hacksaws clutched in one hand and lugged one of the two cameras in the other. "Was Crown a Christian? Did they know each other?"

"I don't think so," Phil replied. "He started in with the God crap at the end like most of them, but before that I don't think he was a Christian. And he'd never been in prison."

"Hurry!" Roland cried from the bottom of the stairs. He stood in front of a second massive steel door, identical to the one at the top. This one led to the water pumping room. When Phil got to the bottom, he looked at Roland as if he were crazy.

"It'll take all day for a sledgehammer to even put a dent in that," he cried. "What were you thinking?"

"I was thinking that I would use this iron wedge, Inquisitor. We should be able to force a gap large enough to get the reciprocating saw in there. It's designed to work in tight spaces like that. We cut the dead bolt and the door opens right up."

Roland shoved the thinner tip of the wedge in the seam of the door just above the lock and said, "Don't miss."

Now that he understood what the plan was, Phil went right into action. He hefted the sledgehammer and swung hard. He didn't miss, not once. Sparks flew as the heavy hammer drove the wedge deeper into the seam. Six hits were all it took.

"Mr. Henderson! The saw, quick!" Roland yelled. "All you have to do is fit the tip right in the gap and cut downward. The bolt is maybe an inch thick at the most."

With the smoke of the fire drifting down the stairs at them, Henderson pulled the cord and the saw's motor buzzed loudly into life. Though the blade was barely three inches long it took both hands to hold the machine. The blade became a blur as it racked back and forth, doing in ten seconds what would have taken a man with a normal saw an hour to do.

"Yes!" Roland cried triumphantly. "Everyone in. Get in!" No one hesitated for even a second.

"Now what?" Phil asked, though he thought he knew. The pump room was a maze of pipes and machinery that had only two purposes; one was to send fresh water throughout the prison for drinking and bathing, and the other was to send the waste out to the sewage treatment plant for recycling.

Haley caught on in second. "You can't be serious! You're kidding, right?"

Roland shrugged. "What did I say? God works in mysterious ways."

Chapter 16

Escape

"I don't think I can do this," Haley said. She had dropped the hacksaws and stood clutching her belly. "We're going out through the sewers...where all the poop and the oh man! I'm going to be sick just thinking about it." She began breathing heavily, puffing out her cheeks.

Roland ignored her. He even ignored a rolling thunderous crash from above them that vibrated the walls and made the pipes hum. Instead, he went to the larger of the two pipes that fed into the south wall.

"Black water waste. This is it." He didn't look altogether happy at their option either. Climbing up on the pipe, he went to an access port. "George, I'll need those wrenches I gave you, and Inquisitors, I'll need your muscles."

The pipe was cool to the touch and had a putrid smell about it, though this last might have been Phil's imagination. He couldn't stop picturing what they would find in the three-foot tall pipe when they opened it up—a river of the foulest sludge no doubt. A shiver escaped him.

"Seriously, I don't think I can do this," Haley said once more.

"And seriously, I don't care," Henderson shot back. He wrapped his wrench around one of the four massive bolts and began straining. He then spoke in short bursts as he put his all behind the work, "If you don't...like it...find your own...way out."

Phil had his own worries about being able to stomach the escape and kept quiet. He managed to struggle the bolt he'd been working on half way off when Haley spoke again. "What's grey water?"

"What? Grey water?" Roland asked in puzzlement. He slid off the pipe and went to the second, smaller one and examined it.

"Just ignore her," Henderson said. His bolt had loosened as well and he was working the wrench in circles as it threaded upward. "If she wants to be an idiot and die down here, that's her deal. That's the problem with women. They don't have what it takes without a man to..."

"Stop what you're doing!" Roland ordered, his voice filled with excitement. "This is a grey water pipe. I don't believe it. Get over here and get this panel off."

Since anything would be better than swimming in a river crap, Phil was quick to come off the black water pipe. "Why?" he asked. "What's the difference"?

"Grey water is from showers and sinks and the laundry," Roland explained. "It's ridiculously inefficient to have a separate system like this, but who cares. As long as..."

A longer, louder rumble shook the room and then the lights went out. Then a crash, that wasn't at all far away, sent splinters of wood and rock over them. Haley screamed. Someone large—probably Henderson fell into Phil sending them both to the ground in a jumble of curses.

The dark last only for seconds and then the emergency lights flickered on. Roland was quick to restore order. "Don't lose the tools. We'll need them. Ms. Baker, you left the hacksaws back there. Please get them, now. Quick, the access panel. Mr. Henderson was right. This place is coming apart faster than I thought possible. How can it burn like this?"

"They're using Crete-melt. You can tell by the terrible smell," George said. "It's some sort of phosphorous compound. It burns hot enough to use rock as fuel. Well maybe not rock, but anything porous, like concrete. They shelled Mazatlan with it two years ago when I was in the army."

Everyone looked up at the ceiling for a space of two seconds and then rushed back to their assigned jobs. Phil and Henderson attacked the bolts holding down the access panel; Haley scurried after the saws she had dropped and George used the light on his camera to point the way when the emergency lights also failed.

"Forget her!" Henderson rasped. "We need the light over here if you want to get out."

"Ignore him, George. We can work a wrench by feel alone," Phil said testily. "We'll need those hack saws if we run into chains or more bars, which we probably will."

A minute later, the rust holding the last bolt in place gave way with a squeal of metal and Phil worked the wrench in quick circles. "It's off," he said, tossing aside the cover. "George, let's have that light. I want to check this out."

"What's there to check out?" Henderson said and then started working his big frame into the hole. With the cover off it looked positively tiny to Phil and to see Henderson squirm to get in gave him the chills. Haley 'helped' by shoving Henderson down like she was stuffing clothes into an overloaded washer.

"George should go next," Roland said. "And then Ms. Baker. I'll go last."

George, tall and thin, folded his body as if he were hinged at odd points and was through in half the time it took Henderson. Haley, as slim as she was, simply stepped into the pipe, bent her knees and disappeared. Phil made to go next, but his inbred distrust flared. In his mind's eye, he pictured Roland calmly reattaching the access cover after Phil had climbed in, blotting out the last of the light.

"I'll go last. You are a criminal after all," he said to the old man.

Roland had been looking up at the ceiling, listening to the hungry fire eating away at the concrete. "If you say so, but you have nothing to fear from me," he said and then went through the hole, stiff and grimacing, showing his age.

Now Phil stood in the gloom alone with the sound above, seeming to grow in the dark. He hurried to the opening and bent and squeezed and squished himself, but without passing through.

"Turn yourself." Roland's muffled voice came to him. "Go in at a diagonal. First one arm and shoulder and then the other."

Phil did so but only managed to wedge himself tight. He could feel hands on him below, yanking and pulling but still he could go neither in nor out. Then Roland said something about finding the problem and took Phil's pistol from his holster. This gave him an extra inch and just barely he slid the rest of the way into the confines of the pipe.

In the dark, Roland squatted, holding the pistol, looking at it in a strange manner. "What is to stop me from shooting you?" he asked in an odd whisper. "I can kill you if I wish. I have the power."

The pipe was too low for Phil to squat. He had to remain on his hands and knees—it was a horribly vulnerable position. "But...but you just said you wouldn't hurt me."

Roland considered this for a moment and then smiled. "Up there I was a prisoner. Yessuh boss. Nosuh boss. Please don't hurt me none boss. Now it's different, isn't it? I'm different. Do you know what I am now?"

Way down the tunnel Henderson and the others were crawling away as fast as they could through ten inches of flowing, ash smelling water. This left Phil alone with a self-ascribed Christian zealot and one who was likely a neocon to boot. In his world, there was no more dangerous creature than that.

"You're an escaped prisoner," Phil said.

"Wrong. If we had more time I'd make you keep guessing until you came up with the right answer. But since we don't I'll tell you what I am. I'm a free man. I'm a slave no more. I'm free to sin or free to live in God's light. I'm free to laugh and love or free to hate. I'm free to pull this trigger and never was a man more deserving of death than you. It would be an injustice to the hundreds of people you've tortured to let you live. What have you to say for yourself?"

The only light in the tunnel was cast by George's camera and this was far away and dim and so Phil's shrug went unnoticed. It wasn't a proper answer anyway and he knew that Roland wouldn't accept it, so he strove to come up with a better one...and failed. What could he say? The world was the way it was. A man either swung the whip or felt the lash. There was no other choice and was he supposed to apologize for doing what anyone else would have? Of course not, but again this wasn't an answer Roland would accept either.

Since there was no right answer, he decided to stall for time. "You should put down the gun, Roland," he said in tone that was at once soothing as well as authoritative. "You still need me. If you think you've escaped then you're way off."

"Stop. You're just embarrassing yourself," Roland said, wearily. He let his shoulders sag and pointed the gun away. "I've never needed you. Not for one second. You have always needed me and you still do. But since you are still blind and see not God's plan for you, I think you should take back your gun. It is who and what you are, after all. At least for now."

Phil took the gun but was slow to holster it. God's plan? Roland's zealotry was all nonsense and to be perfectly honest it made a very logical man look like a buffoon. Perhaps it would be best to just shoot the man right then. Put him out of his misery. With his God talk, Roland was doomed no matter what. Perhaps they all were, but Roland was for sure.

The more Phil thought about it, the more he thought that it would probably be a mercy to shoot Roland.

Mercy? The word struck an alarming chord within Phil. Since when did he think in terms of mercy? Mercy was for the weak. Mercy was for those gutless cowards who got sick at the sight of blood or felt all bad inside when someone started mewling in pain. Mercy ranked up there with guilt and empathy and worst of all, sympathy as those parts of the human mind that were utterly useless.

He shook off the feeling, letting his old self take control again. Roland was right about one thing. Phil was a gun. He was cold, hard, and deadly. That's who he was, not some panty-waste. Yet he still had to force a swagger of confidence into his voice, "Let's get going. We still have a long, hard road ahead of us."

Chapter 17

The Dark Road

The hard man that Phil saw himself to be was tested beneath the earth, and as the pipe gave no sign of ever coming to an end his confidence ebbed quickly. Still he went on ceaselessly and despite the slime coating the bottom of the pipe and the warm water, his hands became raw and his knees ached, and still the pipe went further, beyond what his imagination could inspire.

It could be worse, Phil rationalized internally. What disgusting atrocities would they have suffered had they chosen the black water pipe? A shiver went up his spine and his lunch threatened to come up at the first image that came to him. He decided that it was best not to dwell on the subject of the black water pipe.

Instead, he thought about Roland creaking along at a snail's pace just in front of him. How had the man made it in prison for so long? Especially as crazy with God fever as he was. It didn't seem possible...unless he was connected in some bizarre fashion. Could he really be connected in prison? Did he have a relative —a nephew or niece that nobody knew about?

Phil was just about to ask him when George dropped his hand-held camera in the water and the light went out. Urgently Haley tried to get it working again, only her efforts proved fruitless.

Now their world was absolutely without the least light and the darkness became solid. It felt tangible as if the air had mixed with it, and it pressed on their bodies, warm and damp, so that time and again Phil would ineffectually swipe at his face. The black air was also harder to breathe. It was hot and had a used taste, and though he worked his chest like bellows, he only seemed to be able to take in so much.

"What do we do?" Haley asked in a tone that was part shriek.

"What do you think?" Henderson replied, and even as the words left his mouth he could be heard moving on. The little train of crawling humans pressed forward with him—all but Phil. The dark had a hold on him. It was an affront to his senses and sensibility. Nothing seemed right; nothing seemed the way it should and it was only when the others drew away and their sounds grew faint that a gnawing fear forced him into motion.

The sensation of complete dark was difficult to render into a mental substance that Phil could comprehend. Sometimes it felt as though they crawled uphill, but that was impossible because the water slithering past moved along just as it had. And sometimes the walls of the pipe seemed to open up infinitely and it was a surprise to Phil when he put his hand out and it would be just there. More frequently however, the pipe seemed to be growing smaller in diameter and he would pause every once in a while to attempt to measure it against the length of his arm from his elbow to the tips of his fingers plus a part of his other arm. The measurements were always off because he could never tell when he was measuring the exact center of the pipe.

His ability to perceive the others in the pipe also changed. After a while in the dark they ceased to have faces that he could recall. They became only the noises they generated. Roland was the occasional groan of a man on his deathbed. Haley was the fearful breathing of someone from a horror movie. George was the frequent thunk of skull upon metal—his spacial capacity seemed to have diminished more than the others. And Henderson was the constant cursing mutter of an eternally outraged gnome.

Who knew what Phil Tarsus was? What were his sounds and what did they mean to the others? There was no way to know.

In the endless dark, he knew little, though he did know fear and confusion in equal parts, yet he didn't know which was worse and sometimes didn't know which was which. Sometimes his fear was confusing because it didn't make sense—the shrinking pipe as one example. And sometimes his confusion struck him cold with fear.

Who knew what Phil Tarsus was?

That was a confusing question that in the dark had no answer. How long ago had it been, with the least light upon him, that he'd been the tough guy who was cold, hard, and deadly? Ten minutes ago? A half hour? Two hours? There was no way to know. All the same that tough guy came and went. When he was gone, in his place was an anxious stranger that Phil knew only distantly.

The stranger had strange feelings. He worried when Roland would groan. He felt protective of Haley and wanted to hold her. He felt sympathy when George would knock his head because he did it too. And he could empathize with Henderson. With the tunnel expanding and shrinking, and moving up and down, and generally going on forever he felt like cursing as well.

The stranger and his feelings scared Phil, mainly because they kept reoccurring. He had never been devoid of feelings, but always before he could ignore them or defy them. Like when the lady from Crown's apartment building dangled her baby and made to heave it at him. The frantic look in her eyes had sent a spear of grief into his heart. He knew her desperation, her fantastic need to save her child, but still he had been able to turn away. What benefit could he possibly derive from a baby? Zero benefits. Babies were all downside, and dealing with one then would've been dreadfully inconvenient. He had made the calculation in a heartbeat, ignored his feelings, and turned away.

That was the real Phil Tarsus. This namby-pamby in the dark version was not. Though it was surprisingly persistent, and worse, powerful. He couldn't seem to force the feelings away, or if he did they'd be back at the next groan of Roland's, or Haley's next whimper. *It'll be alright*, he wanted to say to them. *The tunnel can't last forever*.

Perhaps this is what he hoped someone else would say to him? Someone like Roland, who was clearly fearless and held within him an otherworldly level of wisdom and knowledge.

Would it be all right? he asked himself as he touched his face once again. He touched himself frequently because along with the confusing personality changes, had come a fear that his face had changed as well. His features felt different, larger than they were and irregular. He tried to tell himself that his face was no different than it had been and that it was just his fingers had pruned up to a degree that was alarming. The tips of them seemed huge, craggy, and alien.

The idea they were growing out of proportion was the next thing to lay siege to his sanity and he was just in the process of trying to gauge them against what he hoped was an object with a fixed measurement—his nose—when Haley screamed.

"We have to go back!" Her voice had a hollow quality. It ran down the pipe, kicking up a flat echo that came back to Phil's ears in a mumble. *Go back*, it said. "Please! The pipe is shrinking. Everyone turn around before it's too late."

"Let me assure you, my dear," Roland said in a calm rumble. "The pipe is the same width. It's our perception that is different."

"No it's not," Haley bleated. "I measured it. It's smaller. It's getting smaller and soon we'll be squirming on our bellies and what then? We won't be able to turn around and the water will be higher and we'll all drown."

"Please try to relax. Inquisitor, can you give us a little light?"

"Light?" Phil asked.

"Yes. You lit a cigarette yesterday," Roland said. "I assume you still have the lighter on you."

"He does! He does!" Haley cried frantically as if Phil was trying to hold back on them.

"I do," Phil said amazed at himself. How had he forgotten that? Quickly he sloshed onto his side and fumbled out the lighter.

The little flame was like a miracle. It dispelled his primal fears and made everything normal again, including the pipe, which went back to the size it had been. He felt giddy; so much so that he smiled at the flame. The others smiled too.

"You see, everything's going to be alright," Roland said, in that gentle grandfatherly rumble. Haley practically melted at his words, however Phil felt a sharp uptick of fear. There had been an element of untruth in Roland's demeanor and Phil picked it out in an instant. The man was nervous, more nervous than when the dark had held sway over their lives.

What was it? He looked at the others and apart from their faces being covered in grey slime, they seemed ok. The pipe was fine. The water was...the water level had risen! When they had first entered the pipe it had been maybe six inches deep. Now it was easily double that, making the pipe about a third full.

Roland turned back to Phil and gave him a meaningful look. "We shouldn't waste the light."

"Right." Phil read the look to mean it wouldn't do any good to mention the water. He snapped the lighter closed and felt an odd moment of afterglow—a ghostly image of the others squatting or kneeling in the water. "We should get going. Henderson, start..."

"Wait!" George cried. "Turn the light back on! The water level has risen."

"There's no need for light," Roland said. "Yes, the water has risen a bit, but it's nothing yet to worry about..."

"It's more than just a bit!" George shouted gripped by a sudden panic. "It's a lot and we could drown. We could all drown."

George wanted to say more, but there was a commotion in the dark—a great deal of splashing and a strangled yelp. Then Henderson spoke in dangerous tones. "Yes. If we sit here whining we just might all drown. If you want to keep it up then move aside and let those who want to live pass by."

Phil thumbed the lighter back into life to see Henderson crushing George's head against the wall of the pipe. "Let him go," Phil ordered. When Henderson did, Phil nodded downstream and said, "Lead the way."

Just then, a pulse flowed through the water and as they watched, a tiny wave, two inches high, rippled along it. A second wave followed the first.

"We'd better hurry," Roland said. Now there was new meaning in his eyes as he measured the fact that the water had risen six inches in the last minute.

Chapter 18

Rebirth

Where before the dark had ballooned to take over
Phil's mind, and warp his senses, now the water took
its turn. And it was far more urgent and immediate. It
didn't allow for a consuming imagination to make it
more than it was. That was hardly needed.

Within minutes, the water level had risen so
much that crawling wasn't at all required, instead they
were able to doggy-paddle. That only lasted so long
and then as the current picked up they were swept
along like so much debris and it became a struggle to
keep their heads above the surface.

What was going on back at the prison to cause
such a torrent? There were only two options in Phil's
mind: the inmates and the guards were fighting the
fire with anything they could and down in the pipe
they were getting the run off, or everyone was dead
and a major water pipe had burst and was flooding
part of the facility.

"It's getting deeper!" Haley cried, unnecessarily.

For each, panic was readily setting in. The
universal dread of drowning had been multiplied a
hundred fold by the infinite dark and the terrifying
constriction of the pipe. They tumbled along

spluttering and coughing and sometimes screaming. What would happen when they ran out of pipe? What would there be at the end? What happened if there was a low point and the pipe filled completely?

Phil was close to losing it when Henderson yelled from far ahead, "There's another pipe. It's dry."

"The light!" Haley screamed. "Do you still have the lighter?"

Phil would rather have given up his gun than lose the lighter. It sat in his clenched fist as if it was the only thing that could keep him alive. He waited until he was swept into a tangle of bodies before attempting to light it.

"Hold on, damn it!" It felt as though a hundred hands were pawing at him attempting to get at the lighter. He flicked it on. The five of them gasped in unison. The water was only four or five inches from the top of the pipe. In the dark, it was hard to tell exactly how bad their situation was.

"Where's this go?" Henderson demanded of Roland. Even with the light, it was hard to see. The five were all crammed in one spot, making a bottleneck that had the water frothing white foam into their faces.

"Who knows?" Roland answered.

"Maybe we should go further down," Henderson said. "Maybe there's another pipe."

Now it would seem obvious for them to take the dry pipe that went off at a forty-five degree angle upwards, only it was small. Phil, as the largest of the men didn't think he would even fit.

"Is there another pipe?" he asked Roland.

Roland shook his head. "I...I don't know what's down there. All I know is that the pipe runs to a water treatment plant. What's between here and there, I have no clue."

"What?" Henderson demanded. He then spluttered out a mouthful of water. "This was your idea. How could you not know what was down here?"

"It was our only choice," Roland replied. "Now we have two choices. Which way to go? I say up the smaller pipe. It's likely a run off pipe from a storm drain. If so it'll be tight but it also won't be that long a crawl."

Haley, as the smallest of them, was ready to brave it. "Look out. I want to take it. You guys can do what you want."

"Hold on Ms. Baker," Roland said. "You can't go first. If there's a manhole cover, you'll never get it off and we'll all have to come back down here to switch positions. Someone else should go first. Mr. Henderson, it should be you, if you plan on taking this way."

Henderson swallowed heavily at the sight of the pipe. It seemed a bare eighteen inches in diameter and he was nearly as thick as Phil. "I'll do it," he said after what felt like a very long pause. "Just give me room. Don't try to crowd me...and I'll need the lighter."

Phil flicked it off at the request—it was getting too warm to hold, and he felt like hiding it. "We'll pass it up as soon as we're all in the pipe," he said.

The idea of waiting there in the dark as the pipe filled all the way was too much.

"No, I want it now. I don't think I'll be able to reach back once I'm in. My arm will get stuck."

There was that. "Fine," Phil said handing it over. Giving up the lighter was like giving up a part of himself. It hurt, physically. And then watching Henderson squirming up into the pipe made Phil want to vomit.

"You'll fit, Inquisitor," Roland said. "Take off your jacket and your holster. Shove that stuff in front of you as you go. But I want George to go next and then Ms. Baker. Forget the cameras. They're useless, but do take the hacksaws."

They each crawled up one after another, leaving Phil and Roland, both of whom now could only breath by craning their head to the side and practically kissing the top of the pipe.

"Still don't trust me?" Roland asked. "Or would you like to go first?"

"You go," Phil said and then wondered why. He did trust the old man, especially since it didn't seem like there was any mischief that Roland could get into. So why had he given up a better spot in line? It didn't make sense.

He had only seconds to wonder at this before he was forced to hold his breath and wait while Roland wiggled up the tunnel like an inchworm. Finally, the pipe was clear and Phil began the process of getting stuck in the smaller tube.

Even compared to the last, this pipe was a nightmare. Time and again, panic would grip the big man as his wet clothes seemed to adhere to the sides of the pipe. His great chest would then begin to work uncontrollably as he hyperventilated in fear and at the feel of his ribs pressing rhythmically against the steel, he would feel an overwhelming terror.

This would send him into spasms of jerking muscles and kicking feet...none of which did a damned thing to help him.

"Inquisitor...may I call you Phil, instead?" Roland said from above him in the pipe as he went through the third of these terrors.

It took him a moment to find his voice. "I...I don't care. I...I'm stuck. I can't move. I can't move. I can't breathe. I'm going to be trapped down here forever!" Panic had him near hysterics and he felt like a child.

"You aren't going to be trapped," Roland said easily. "The pipe here is the same diameter as it was when you first got in. Logically, if you didn't get stuck then you aren't really stuck now. Does that make sense?"

"Yeah...yeah I guess so, but I can't move. My clothes are like glue. They're glued to the walls."

"Try twisting one way and then back the other. It'll loosen the hold."

It worked. Phil was able to go a few more feet before the walls gripped him even fiercer. Roland must have heard this new onset of panic because he began to talk again.

"How did you become an Inquisitor?" he asked. "I have trouble believing it was a childhood dream."

"I'm stuck again. I'm stuck!" Phil could think of nothing else.

"Remember twist and if that doesn't work try going back an inch or two before making another try. Now you were going to tell me how you became an Inquisitor."

"It was..." Phil grunted as he twisted the smallest amount. It seemed to loosen the hold just enough and he was able to breathe easier again. He took a moment to collect himself as his heart raced. "It was an accident. I was fighting on the Texas front near Torreon when an Inquisitor came through filling his quotas."

"They arrest soldiers too?" Roland asked, surprised.

"Oh yeah...an inquisitor...doesn't have to...worry about quotas...down south," Phil said pausing to catch his breath. He had scooted maybe eight inches on that try. "He just has to worry about getting shot."

"You wouldn't think the Mexicans would shoot at a man in your uniform. Seeing as you probably do more damage to your own cause."

Phil had to laugh. "You're right. An Inquisitor has to worry more about getting shot by one of our soldiers."

"Right."

"You...bet your...ass...right," Phil said, struggling another foot upwards. "Anyway, someone did take a shot at the Inquisitor but hit the under-inquisitor instead. I was right there when it happened. The Inquisitor just looked around and his eyes fell on me. *Pick up that gear. You're my new Under-Inquisitor*, he said. Later he told me he picked me because he thought I could carry more of his stuff."

"That's it? There wasn't a test or anything?"

Phil squirmed another few feet before answering this time. "There's a test. You have to pass it within six months. That's how it is with most under appointments in every field. The reason is that connected people bounce around a lot and for them it's never about the test but about who they know."

Roland paused his climbing. "And how did you become a full Inquisitor? I'm guessing that you aren't connected to someone important."

"No I'm not. I got lucky. My Inquisitor's benefactor died and so I informed on him and it left a hole that I got to step into."

Roland paused above him and Phil accidentally pushed himself into the soles of his shoes. "You informed on your own Inquisitor? The guy who gave you your start? Isn't that sort of underhanded?"

"That's how the game is played," Phil answered. "It's the same for me. Henderson has been looking to knock me off since I hired him. And I only hired him because I thought he was dimwitted, which he faked admirably."

"Communists," Roland said. Phil squinted up and could barely see the old man shaking his head. "How they get anything done is beyond me." He sighed a long weary sigh, but then he cried, "I see light! Phil, I see real light!"

Roland left him then. In his excitement, he wiggled and squirmed like mad and within minutes, Phil was alone in the tube. He got stuck twice more and both times his heart raced and his breathing went into overdrive, but the light above helped and eventually he pulled himself through a gaping manhole cover.

They found themselves on the side of a road. It was a two-lane road that Phil was sure he had never been on before in his life.

"Praise the Lord in heaven!" Roland cried...literally cried. Tears of joy ran down his old man's face. He knelt in the brown January grass next to the road with his hands in the air, looking to the sky. "I have been swallowed by the whale and have emerged whole. I have tasted the bitter dregs of Satan's hate and they have washed over me and because of the Lord above my soul is clean and whole. The Lord of..."

The sound of a hammer being drawn back on a pistol can be mistaken for nothing else. Roland's words choked off in an instant. He looked back to see Henderson standing tall over him with his service piece drawn and pointing square into his face.

"It's about time you got out of that pipe, Phil," Henderson said. "I know it's rude to shoot another man's prisoner without his permission, but I nearly did it. He's been going on about God for at least a minute! But now that you're here, you want to take care of him or should I?"

Roland's eyes darted to Phil. "What's he talking about? He wants to shoot me? Why? I got him out of there. Without me he'd be dead."

Henderson chuckled. "It's not just me."

Roland again looked to Phil, questioningly.

"Sorry. It's the law. An escaped prisoner is to be shot on sight. No questions asked," Phil told him with a shrug.

Chapter 19

The Survivor

"Have I been cast as a modern day Moses?" Roland asked the cool air above him. A sharp breeze and his wet clothes reminded Phil that it was still winter. He hugged himself, glancing to see Haley snugged up tight against George, whose face was pinched and nervous.

"What are you talking about?" Phil asked.

"Moses led his people from Egypt but was denied the Promised Land," Roland answered. "But I am no Moses. I am just a man. And you still need me."

"Wrong, zealot," Henderson shot back. "Since you've said your prayers already I guess there's nothing left to do but..."

"Stop!" Phil ordered. His pistol shown in his hand, slipping from beneath his coat. He was a deadly shot. Henderson knew it too and lowered his gun somewhat, wearing a nasty look. Phil kept the gun pointed where it was; he had an inexplicable desire to protect Roland. "Let's hear him out, first. Tell me, old man, how could we possibly need you? We're looking at our own death sentence if we *don't* kill you."

This caused Roland to laugh. "The lot of you are already under a death sentence. You escaped from that prison as much as I did."

"Don't be stupid," Henderson barked. "There's a big diff..."

"Remember that fellow Crown you were talking about earlier?" Roland interrupted smugly. "Have you forgotten about him? You weren't in the prison today to question me, you were there to die. Really! I can't believe I have to make this point. All four of you escaped your death sentences when you got out of that prison and when they find out, they'll come after you with everything they've got."

"Who is *they*?" Haley asked.

Roland shrugged and looked to Phil. "I don't know," the lead Inquisitor said. "Maybe the Commissioner of Justice? He acted very strange in regard to Crown and he forced me to come out here. But how did he know there was going to be a fire? Unless he ordered it set."

Haley rounded on Roland, her eyes glinting. "What about you? How did you know about the fire before hand?"

"Because I know people. Because I can read them well. And besides, prison fires have happened before and I saw the signs. They aren't too subtle when you know what to look for. I just can't understand why they do it. Rebuilding after a fire is expensive."

"Hey, there's something wrong with George," Haley said, suddenly. The man's lips were a blue-purple and he couldn't stop shivering.

Roland gave him a close look and said, "You'll have to decide my fate later. We have to get a fire going to dry off before we all die of hypothermia. It'll be best to start it in a little grove in the land so that we're hidden from sight. Do any of you know where we are?"

Phil stared around at the wooded hills surrounding them. Nothing looked familiar. "I've only come out here a few times and have never got off the highway except for the Polk exit."

"Same here," Henderson added, holstering his gun. "It all looked to be forest on the way in. There weren't any towns that I could see."

"Either way we can't stay here. It's too open," Roland said. "Follow me."

They moved off, Roland taking the lead and directing the others as if he were in charge. He was a natural leader and all but Henderson hurried to obey. When they found a spot sheltered by some moss covered rocks and had built a fire from the plentiful dead wood in the area, Henderson was the first to speak.

"I still don't see why we need the old man. Let's say someone is out to get us, running around with an escaped convict who's also a zealot and likely a neocon is only going to make things worse. Besides, he stands out. Look at that hair. People will stare."

Men with hair only wore it one way: regulation —short and kept neatly trimmed on the sides and back. Phil couldn't remember the last time he'd seen a man with a different style; Roland, with his white locks hanging to his shoulders would indeed draw attention.

Roland seemed to understand this and he nodded gently, but then he said, "Sure, I might stand out, but have you seen yourselves?" They each glanced around and even with the fading light of the coming evening they saw the truth; they were a sorry lot: bedraggled and dirty, huddling as close to the fire as they could without getting burned.

"So what?" Henderson said. "We can say we got in a car accident. Or fell in a river. This still doesn't answer the question of why we shouldn't kill you. What good are you?"

"He got us out of the prison," Phil put in.

"That was great, don't get me wrong," Henderson said, honestly. "But I don't think his escape artist skills will be all that needed in the immediate future. So I ask again what will he do besides slow us down? If someone like the Commissioner is really after us, it means we're in huge trouble. It can only be worse with a zealot around."

Phil had no idea what to say to that. How long had it been since he'd been contemplating mercy killing the old man—and how long had it been since he had been planning on torturing him? He checked the Timex on his wrist, which was, amazingly enough, still running, and saw that the prison fire had been set only an hour before. It felt much longer.

Roland waited patiently for someone to come to his defense. When no one did, he frowned. "The least you could do is let me go my own way. I'd be far safer that way since no one on earth will be looking for me. There are very few people alive who even know I exist and even fewer who care...apparently."

Henderson shrugged as if contemplating Roland's words, but Phil knew better. When there was the least doubt, his under-inquisitor went by the book. Perhaps Roland sensed this as well, because he added, "But I don't really want to go my own way. I've been watching you four and a word springs to mind: institutionalized."

"What?" Henderson scoffed. "Us?"

"What's institutionalized?" Haley asked. "It doesn't sound good."

In Phil's mind, it didn't sound good for Roland to be grasping at straws like this. "It's when someone has been in prison for so long that they become dependent on the routine of the place. Every day is the same there and they don't know how to break out of the daily mold."

Haley's forehead wrinkled in triple lines. "That's absurd. We were in there for like two hours."

"There are other ways to become institutionalized," Roland said. "And the phenomenon is not just a matter of routine. In your case, it's a matter of thought. Inquisitor, where do you eat lunch? Or dinner?"

Phil took a second to run his tongue over his teeth before answering, "At work or my dom-box cafeteria, same as breakfast, why?"

"And where is the closest grocery store to you?"

"There are no grocery stores," Phil answered. "The very idea is archaic; part of a greedy past where food wasn't a right. You should know. I bet back in the day you stood in lines all the time only to be gouged by money-hungry merchants. The last one closed before I was born. And by the way we don't have horse and buggies either."

Roland took the jibe in stride. "And I take it you need to show your ID when you go to these cafeterias." Phil nodded slowly, suddenly nervous, and Roland went on, "And if you are wanted by the authorities would that ID be accepted?"

Phil hesitated before answering. Not because he didn't know the answer, but because of the ramifications of the answer. "No it won't."

The old man didn't seem surprised at the response. "And so how would you eat?"

"Wait. How are we going to eat?" Haley asked. "If we're marked as outlaws our ration cards will be useless. Oh man! We don't even have to be outlaws. If they think we're dead, we'll be cut off." The four looked back and forth at each other as the truth of that sunk home. Eventually they all looked to Roland who took that moment to ease himself down onto a log.

"And who is the one institutionalized?" he asked. "The system has been set up to control you. The government tells you where to eat, what to eat, and how much to eat. You can't pop into a grocery store and grab the fixings for a four-course meal. Why? Because there are no stores."

He groaned a bit as he stretched his toes to the fire. "I remember back before I was sent to prison. The year they outlawed profit was the same year the liberals came up with the idea that universal access to food should be a human right. So of course you know what happened next." Here he paused, but it was only for effect. He was in story telling mode. "The law of supply and demand kicked in. Prices skyrocketed. There was a shortage of everything and then came the long lines for the least item."

"That's what I said," Phil murmured.

Roland ignored him and went on, "And so what's a liberal's answer to everything, especially a problem of their own making? More government intervention; more laws; more misery. They tried to take over the retail food industry and ended up destroying it. The lines went out the door, around the block, and halfway to kingdom come, all for a loaf of bread and a stick of butter. People grew angry so the government blamed the problem on the wholesale food industry and so they had CEOs and managers arrested, and then they took over that sector of the economy also.

"Well, without people experienced in running businesses of that size, the expected mismanagement set in and the lines for food only grew longer. People became angrier and so more arrests were made and more blame was spread. It's the greedy farmers we were told—so the government nationalized farms, but since bureaucrats make terrible farmers, food supplies dwindled even more. Next it was the meat packers, and then the canners, and then the truckers, and so on.

"Finally the government discovered the real problem. It was the people who were at fault. Those damned citizens were the greedy ones. They always wanted more food. That was bad, but what really galled them was the people also wanted different types of food. How dare they demand bananas *and* oranges! How outrageous that those greedy slobs would want wheat bread and white...tell me, have any of you ever heard of pumpernickel bread?"

None had. Phil answered for them, "No. It sounds weird."

"It's not. It's wonderful," Roland said. "Oh the smell. I love bread...or I should say I loved bread. When I was a kid the stores stocked all kinds: pumpernickel, rye, Jewish rye, Russian rye, potato bread, French bread, French rolls, baguettes..." he paused to smile, his eyes looking dreamy.

"What does this have to do with anything?" Henderson demanded.

"The bread? Nothing. But the rest has to do with the fact that you four were born and raised in a system that controls your lives totally. You are the ones who are institutionalized. You have almost no free will left to you. For example, who decides what you wear?"

Eyes darted about, but no one wanted to admit that the Board of Apparel made the decision on what each profession would wear and how many sets of clothes a person was allotted.

It didn't matter, Roland seemed to know. "The government tells you. And who decides what you watch on TV?"

The government ran the three TV channels that were available. Many of the programs were mandatory. Again, the four of them remained silent. Now they each stared into the fire.

"And who decides what you read? And who decides what job you have, and who decides where you live? These are all decisions that a free people make, but you aren't free. You are slaves. You have a slave mentality. You do what master says. You go where master tells you to go. You think what master wants you to think. You four are the ones who are institutionalized. You have lived your entire lives in one giant prison.

"That's why you need me. I may have lived in Polk for sixty years but in some ways, I was freer than you were. I could think what I wanted. That may not seem like much, but my mind is my own. None of you can say that. You've been subject to a constant brainwashing from the moment you were born. The government raised you. The government schooled you. The government dictates what you see and what you hear, and thus the government controls your mind.

"And it shows. They have corrupted you. You are humans with only the thinnest shreds of humanity left to you. Do you even know what hope is? Do you know what love is? So many of your emotions have been warped or deleted from your collective subconscious that it's scary. I can barely understand your thought processes. All of you.

"Take Mr. Henderson. You can't even manage gratitude properly. I saved your life, but you can't think past the law to show it, let alone feel it. And you, Ms. Baker. You are a disgrace to your gender. Did you attend *Damsel in Distress Academy*? All you are is a pretty face with nothing behind those perfect eyes. And you, George, you're practically a robot. You cower to anyone in the least authority—including me and I'm an escaped convict. I could see you were freezing before, but you were so afraid to say anything that you let me go on and on."

"Like now," Phil growled. He could see that Roland was about to turn his acid tongue on him and he wasn't happy about it.

The old man simply ignored the words, but not the speaker. "And you, Inquisitor. You came out to Polk knowing you were going to die. Your boss said: go to your fiery death and you couldn't think of a single thing to do besides go. You should've seen yourself. You jumped at every sound. Your hand went to your gun at the least movement. You were worse than a sheep led to slaughter. Unlike the sheep, you have awareness. You knew you were supposed to be killed. You saw the trap and you came anyway because you haven't learned to think."

Roland waited after he said this. It wasn't a theatrical pause. He waited to see who would respond. None did. What could Phil say to such obvious truth? At their silence, Roland nodded his shaggy head. "And that is why you need me. I'm a survivor."

Chapter 20

The Farm's Edge

"You don't know how it is for women," Haley said a few minutes later, her voice brittle with anger. Phil was surprised her silence lasted as long as it had. When Roland made his 'Damsel' remark, the storm clouds had gathered on her brow instantly and he knew that it was only a matter of time before they broke.

Roland seemed unperturbed by her seething emotions. "If you're going to tell me that it's oh so hard living in a man's world, don't bother. I think I've heard it before."

"Hearing it and living it are two separate things," Haley shot back. "No one looks at a man and sees only his exterior; only his hair or his face or his...his rear."

Roland seemed to find her sudden embarrassment endearing and he smiled, however there wasn't a smile in his words, "Your beauty must be quite a cross to bear." Haley showed her teeth like an animal, but her fury prevented her from speaking so Roland went on, which he seemed to do at any silence. "Is George a part of this 'Man's world'?"

"What do you mean?" she asked, her animal look replaced by wariness. She suspected that she was being set up.

"Is George part of the 'Man's World' as you see it? I ask because I get the idea he doesn't think so. Not that he isn't a man, but rather he doesn't see living in a 'Man's World' as some great privilege. Do you, George?" The gangly cameraman gave a half-hearted shrug. Roland took that for a yes. "See? And I bet people...women I should say, judge him on his exterior all the time. Do they?"

George had a beak for a nose that to Phil seemed comically large whenever he put his camera up to his face. He also had a sad, mopey look to his eyes. He wasn't handsome in the least. "I don't know," he said, however this was accompanied with another shrug and a bit of a head bob.

"What's your point, besides being mean?" Haley asked.

"I don't wish to upset anyone I was just pointing out that to be a survivor you have to stop making excuses. You, me, George, everyone, has to overcome not only their own personal weaknesses but also the weaknesses of the society in which we live. Being a man isn't magical. You aren't handed over the keys to a corporate jet when you turn eighteen just because of the thing between your legs. You work for what you want and you use the talents that God has given you."

"Still, it's not fair," Haley said.

Roland smiled sadly. "Nothing ever is. However, in your case this unfairness works to your advantage.

174

Your beauty has propelled you far. Just think where you'd be if your nose was a little bigger, or your skin not so perfect. Where would you be if you had bad teeth or a hairy mole on your cheek?"

The fire crackled as each stared into it. Phil watched the tiny glowing motes leap upward from the flames to safety and as he did, he considered that had it not been for his size, he would be dead. His unit had died to a man a week after he'd gone off with his Inquisitor.

"My make-up gal, she's almost pretty," Haley said in a far away voice, her eyes on the flames. "When I do live shows I get my own gal and while she's fussing about, I have nothing to do. I can look either at her or at myself in the mirror. Sometimes I do both. She's almost pretty. So close. Her hair is blonde, but it's thin and hangs blah. And her eyes are too close, but only by millimeters. Still it's enough. She's plain."

"I like her," George said.

"Really?" Haley asked smiling up at her cameraman. That smile in the gathering night with the light of the fire on her face gave Phil a twinge beneath his breastbone. He knew all about unfairness. Love was rarely fair.

"*Georgey has a girlfriend*," Henderson teased in falsetto. The high, childish voice bothered Haley, who gave him a stern look. She then turned back to George, who was in the process of running a shade close to tomato.

"Are you going to ask her out?" she asked. How quickly it seemed that Haley had forgotten their plight. George seemed to as well.

"I don't know. Maybe. Maybe you could uh..." the man paused. Too embarrassed to look Haley in the face he had turned away from her and the fire when he answered. Now he stuck out a long thin arm. "What is that? There's a light."

Nervous alarm caught up the air in Phil's throat as he turned his head this way and that to catch sight of the light. Had they been found out so quickly? Was that possible? Would there be dogs? Everyone moved from the fire to see, and there it was far off between the swaying trees, light.

"Maybe it's a town," Haley said. "Should we go?" Her words were directed at Roland. They all looked to Roland, even Henderson, though he did so with an intentionally loud sigh. At some point— probably when he was pointing out the truth about how their thinking had been corrupted by the government—Roland had become more in their eyes.

There was no denying he had a presence that blanketed the group, affecting each of them. For Phil he was a man of exotic wisdom; a font of knowledge that, although the Inquisitor attempted to fool himself into thinking was only a mixture of zealotry and neocon boloney, he craved nonetheless. He sensed that the knowledge the old man carried was key to answering a question he had heard on many occasions as an Inquisitor: *Isn't there more to life?*

When people got right down to the wire, when they saw the stones arrayed and the jurors frightened but excited, that question would come to them. Sometimes they spoke it aloud and sometimes Phil read it in their eyes.

No one ever had an answer. The question was deadly enough; to utter the words: *Isn't there more to life?* was a death sentence in itself. Phil had never seen someone ask that question and live. And this was true outside the Justice building as well.

Once on the Texas front, a soldier in his company had said those words, and more besides. The man had so many questions. He had sat there with a slack jaw and a mind made numb from days and days of battle and had asked: Isn't there more to life? Why are we here? Is there any meaning to life whatsoever? Phil had scampered away from him. He was more dangerous than the Mexicans. The next day the Inquisitors came and he was gone.

Phil had forced the soldier and his question, *isn't there more to life?* from his conscious mind. They were such dangerous words. To the State, a citizen lived only for the State, and any question as to whether there was anything *more* was equated to suggesting that the State was *less.* The State could never be less. It had to be the totality of existence for man. It had to be the be all and end all to man. From birth to death, from sunrise to sunset, the State was everything and controlled everything. And this was why the existence of God could not be allowed. The

State was its own god and the State was a very, very jealous god.

Phil knew this on a subconscious level. Consciously, however the State owned his mind or nearly all of it, yet there was still that little part that would sometimes secretively ask: *isn't there more to life?* And that little part, since the moment he had met Roland the day before, had become like a tiny, incessant itch in middle of his back that he couldn't reach, nor put out of his mind.

Phil stared at the old man and wondered: what did he know that made him so sure of himself?

He acted as if he knew the answer to the secret question. He acted as if he knew there was more. If asked, Phil was certain that Roland would say it was God. That God was the answer, maybe the answer to everything.

But no one else thought that. Not a person in America. God had been obliterated. God had become the punch line to a joke. God did not exist. Yes, there were a few, who at the edge of their lives, entrusted themselves in a blind hope, but they were acting on desperation only. Yet Roland was different; he knew God existed just as he knew that fire was hot. He knew it so fully that it bothered Phil, yet all the same he looked to Roland, as did the rest.

Just then the old man had his back to the fire and was squinting down his nose at the lights. "None of you know this area at all?" Heads shook all around.

"No, but it doesn't matter, we should go down there," Haley said.

Roland thought on it for a moment before saying, "I don't know. It's a risk to go..."

"But it's a risk to stay," Haley shot back. "We could freeze." Despite the fire, she shivered constantly.

"There are risks to life whatever path we choose," Roland said to her. "If we go we could be arrested and let me assure you that the cold of prison is far worse than this."

"Well my stomach tells me we should go," Henderson put in. "There's nothing to eat out here. What good would it do to starve to death?"

Though Phil was hungry as well, he said, "At least for the time being we're going to have think with our heads and not our stomachs. But I think we should go. Let's say the Commissioner is after us, he has to assume we died in the fire. It's probably still burning. We should be safe."

A sigh escaped Roland. He turned from the lights and put his hands out to their little campfire. "I know the problem. I've diagnosed the problem, yet I have trouble with your institutionalized thought processes. You fear cold and hunger, but we have a fire and there's food in the forest; perhaps not a lot and certainly unprocessed, but food nonetheless. Do not be afraid of freedom. Do not be afraid to rely on yourselves. I say we don't put our heads back through the noose. I say we don't go."

Henderson scoffed, "And live like animals, scrounging around for a few nuts and berries? What kind of life is that? If that's freedom you can keep it. I say we vote on it. Raise your hand if you want to go?"

Roland folded his hands in his lap.

"I think we should go," Haley said. "You guys are Inquisitors. No one messes with Inquisitors. We'll be safe. I think we'll be safe." George nodded his agreement with her.

With the numbers against him, Roland stood and began kicking dirt on the fire, smothering it. "Lord, please be with us."

"It'll be ok," Haley said, though whether she was trying to reassure Roland or herself it was hard to tell.

"I'm sure it will," Roland agreed. "I keep faith that the Lord watches over us."

Bringing up the Lord seemed to unsettle Haley even more. "Why is everything politics and religion with you?"

With the fire out the dark seemed more intense and it was some minutes before their night eyes could catch up. Roland took Haley's hand, not for her sake but for his. "Because little in life is as important," he answered. "One governs the order of our lives on earth while the other governs our souls. Both must be actively considered and acted upon, for if one doesn't, he leaves such things to others. America is a prime example of what happens when you don't make politics and religion a priority."

They walked in a single line with Henderson pressing ahead. "Do you ever stop talking?" he asked Roland.

"I do. Especially when I should be listening. However, the Lady asked me a question and it would've been rude not to answer. But if everyone wishes for me to be quiet I'll be quiet."

And he was quiet right up until Phil said, "You're wrong about America not making politics a priority. Sometimes it feels as though that's the only topic of conversation. We have classes on communism, plays on communism, film festivals on communism."

"That's not you making politics a priority, that's the State continuing its brainwashing..."

Henderson interrupted, "Why did you get his mouth started again?"

Phil wasn't going to answer but Roland gave him a look that reinforced the question. "I don't know," Phil said. "Maybe because he has a different point of view. Maybe because I'm curious. I don't know."

"It's your funeral," Henderson replied. "It's best not to listen to another word."

"I'll decide what's best," Phil said. "Besides I was just telling Roland he was wrong. It's a strangely satisfying experience."

This had Roland chuckling. "What I meant was where we are now as a nation is a result of people in the past not paying attention to politics. Most people never considered politics except for a few days every four years. They'd complain about how bad the choices were; they'd pick one, and then go back to their lives thinking they had done their civic duty."

"That's why our way is better," Henderson said. "Everyone is an active part of the government."

"Much like a slave is an active part in a whipping," Roland rejoined. When Henderson didn't respond but just kept walking Roland shrugged and said, "Either way with no one minding the politicians they did what politicians do: they abused their power. They made laws to benefit their friends. They corrupted the system so that it was almost impossible to get them out of office, and they twisted the will of the people to fit their agendas."

"Sounds great," Henderson put in. "And you neocons want to go right back to that? Wait. Don't answer that. In fact everyone hush. You see that?" They had crested a hill and could see the lights better. They were strung out and spaced along a curving line that disappeared in the rolling hills. "Is that a fence?"

"Yeah," Phil answered. "And those are guard towers. What the hell is that about? And what is that smell?"

Roland took a deep breath, seeming to enjoy it. "That's a farm."

Chapter 21

The Truth Shall Set You Free

"You can smell the fields and the fertilizer," Roland said. "It's a farm alright, but why do they need towers? That doesn't make any sense. I can understand a fence, but towers on a farm? Is it because of theft? Is it that rampant?"

"Probably because of the neocons," Haley said. Her voice was pitched far lower than Roland's. At this he chuckled as though she had made a joke. "It's true," she insisted. The others nodded sagely in agreement. This only made him laugh harder; in seconds he dropped to his knees, overcome.

Henderson moved close and lowered his mouth to Roland's ear as he chortled, pink faced and happy. "You need to hush. If there are Homeland Security fellows in that tower we could be in trouble; they tend to be trigger happy." This sobered Roland up until Henderson added, "Besides the neocons really are saboteurs."

Roland couldn't help himself. The laughter gushed out from between his fingers, which he had clamped to his mouth. He was forced to walk away, though stagger was a better word. The others followed, none sharing in his mirth. Eventually he calmed, breathing in great gasps. "Oh my...oh my...saboteurs. That's funny."

Henderson huffed, "Fine don't believe me, but the neocons are for real. Everyone knows that. And what they do is real; sabotage is sabotage. It's not funny."

In a second Roland rolled to his back and clutched his stomach, making snorting noises as he tried to hold in the laughter. Haley dropped down low and whispered, "Roland, pull it together, please. They'll hear."

"Ok...it's just you guys are being so ridiculous. Sabotage! Let me guess: they've gone after heavy industry? Automobiles, farm equipment that sort of thing?"

"Yes," Phil answered for them. "It's been going on for years."

"Of course," Roland agreed. "And what about power generation?" Phil nodded. "And textiles? And computer systems? And coal output? Tell me, do these nasty saboteurs go after the trains too? Keep them from running on time? I bet they somehow have gotten into Jonny's second grade classroom and knocked down his test scores."

"What are you saying?" Phil asked. "Are you saying there aren't any neocons? I know..." he lowered his voice so that the night three feet away couldn't have heard. The act was ingrained; pure self-preservation. "...I know the government will finesse some numbers here and there, but the sabotage really is wide spread."

Roland shook his head in the gloom. "Don't you know when you're being played?" Though he spoke in his normal voice it seemed very loud. They hadn't moved that far away from the tower, and in alarm Haley touched his lips with her small fingers to quiet him. "Fine," he said in a lower voice. "How many neocons have you captured? As inquisitors? With them being so prevalent you must have had your share. And I'm talking about real neocons, not people who've stolen a sandwich and you've tortured into confessing to a lie."

Phil sent a look Henderson's way before he shrugged and said, "Twenty or so. They're usually not in the capital, and when they are they're very well trained and hard to catch," he added defensively.

"Twenty?" Roland asked, his voice rising in anger. "You've interrogated and tortured how many people? Four hundred?" It was closer to five hundred, but Phil only gave a half-hearted shrug as a way of saying yes. This only made Roland angrier. "Out of four hundred people you only captured twenty neocons? Really?"

"Really."

"Really?" Roland demanded again, his eyes boring into Phil's with such intensity that the younger man had to look away.

"I don't know the real number," Phil admitted after a moment. "People say things when they're being questioned. If they admit to being a neocon what am I supposed to do? Call them a liar?"

"You're an idiot," Roland hissed, getting to his feet. There was no sign of his laughing fit left to him. "No...no you're the liar. That's what you are. And it may be ok that you lie to save your hide, I don't know, but you also lie to yourself. You're self-delusional. You're...never mind. Forget I said anything to you. Anything at all. Ever."

Phil stood amazed as Roland stalked away, blending in with the night in seconds. What was more amazing was that he found himself hurrying after. "Roland, wait. You shouldn't be so mad. This is how the game is played."

"It's not a game," Roland replied. "These are people's lives."

"What about my life?" Phil asked. "I know it's been sixty years for you, but these days you either swing the whip or feel the whip. There's no in between."

"Then you feel the whip," Roland said without a pause as if there could be no other option. He began to walk away, but stopped with his head bowed. He took a few deep breaths before saying, "Look, I can't stay unless you can start admitting the truth to yourself at least."

They were far away enough from the others for Phil to be himself, yet he really didn't know who that was anymore. "What truth should I admit to? That capitalism is perfect and that it actually works? You want me to admit that truth even though it's been proven to be a failure every time it's been tried? Or do you want me to admit that there is a sky fairy beaming down rays of joy on us? No. I can't do that. Your prayer in the prison did nothing. You got us out, not God."

"No, that's not it." Roland came close so that Phil had a good look at the man's pale features. They seemed ghost-like in the night. "That will come in time. What I want you to admit is something that seems patently obvious to me, but you can't seem to grasp: your government lies to you."

Such a thing, true or not wasn't so easily spoken aloud. It wasn't even easy to contemplate. All too frequently, thoughts became words and words became death.

So it was with difficulty that Phil asked himself: Did the government lie?

An answer came to him quick and slick as oil: No, the government didn't lie; people lied! Some bad people within the government lied. Like the newscaster, Ellen Mathews that Haley was hoping to replace. She had been falsely reporting on the state of the economy for years. The government hadn't lied, she had.

Just then, a voice spoke up inside him: *But where had she got her numbers from? She couldn't have just made them up.*

Was that true? Phil turned from Roland and stared up at the stars, thinking something wasn't right. He felt a step behind, as though his ability to reason was just waking up from a long sleep. What was he missing? Had she made up the numbers? If so, why hadn't the Board of Production said something long ago? Why did they wait until now to blow the whistle on her?

Stop being an idiot, the voice said. *Stop lying to yourself.* Where was the truth? What made sense?

Who gained from Ellen's lie?

Ellen didn't, not really. Yes, it was always nice to report good news, but the downside to lying—arrest, torture, and death—far outweighed that. This meant that the Board lied. The Board gained from the lies; the lies made them look competent; and now that the truth was so obvious, they gained by turning on Ellen, making her the focus of the problem instead of them.

The truth clicked in. Just like an odd shaped piece into a puzzle; suddenly all the edges lined up. Ellen Matthews would die simply because the Board of Production could no longer hide the fact that the cost of living standard had fallen another five percent. You could blame a drop in automobile manufacturing on saboteurs, because who would know and in truth, since no one owned cars anymore, who would really care, but when a person received water instead of milk with dinner, and had to make by with two pairs of socks a year instead of three, there was no hiding that.

Ellen was a scapegoat for the government's lies, plain and simple. In fact, it was very plain and very simple, so much so that it should've been embarrassingly obvious all along. How had he missed it? How had he heard Ellen spout those rosy statistics everyday and not have looked around at reality and known that she'd been lying...

Phil groaned and reminded himself that Ellen hadn't been lying. "I guess the government lies," Phil said. "But what do you care that I can admit that? What can you possibly gain?"

"Because you need to be free. Your shackles hold you back," Roland said. When Phil gave him a puzzled look, Roland explained. "The truth shall set you free—it's an old saying, but it has never been more appropriate. You are shackled by your belief in this government. They have enslaved not only your body but your mind as well. To be free you have to question everything that you've been taught."

"Even all the other stuff you've been yapping on about?" Phil asked.

"Yes. Do so. Set my truth against their lies and see which rings true in your heart and in your mind."

The Inquisitor gave a non-committal shrug. "I still don't get it. Why do you find it so important what I think? Are you looking for validation? Are you looking for someone to nod along as you go on and on?"

"No," Roland answered simply. "It's important that you know the truth and can see the truth and not be fooled by the lies that surround you."

"Again, why?"

Roland's face lit up with a big grin. "Because God sent you to me. I prayed for deliverance to continue my work and God sent me you."

"This is about God?" Phil asked, grimacing, as if the subject pained him, which it did. He felt the slightest bit sick. "You have definitely got the wrong guy. You know I don't believe in that fairytale nonsense. Maybe you should try Haley or George. Has it ever occurred to you that maybe God sent them and I just tagged along."

"The word of the Lord is open to all."

Phil glanced to where the others stood apart, each not happy about the delay. Henderson especially. "What about him? What about Henderson? I see that you haven't tried all that hard to have him come around to your way of thinking." Picturing the attempt struck Phil as funny and he let out a short laugh. "He'll tear your head off if you try. He's not nearly as understanding as I am."

"The word is open even to Henderson," Roland replied. "As I said, it's open to all, however there are those who close off their hearts and minds and would rather live in lies than die for the truth. I hope I'm wrong about Henderson; he seems to be one of these. What's strange is that you are not. As you say, you're more understanding. It's a rather odd quality in an Inquisitor."

For a moment Phil stared. Had the old man just implied that he was soft? That he was an easy touch? Or maybe just gullible? He turned from Roland and walked back to the others, saying over his shoulder, "My understanding only goes so far and I think you've reached the limit."

Chapter 22

Into the Farm

"What the hell did you go after him for?" Henderson demanded, as Phil rejoined the others. Roland trailed after, walking with a slight gimp. Henderson pointed and said, "He's going to be trouble. Mark my words. He's going to bring a world of trouble down on our heads and it'll be your fault."

Phil stopped. First Roland thinking he was soft and now Henderson speaking that way with such impunity? A fire seemed to roar up within him. In a flash Phil struck his under-inquisitor to the ground; the blow, vicious and unseen in the dark. He stood over the top of Henderson.

"Say another word!" he dared. The dark made him seem even larger and fiercer. Henderson didn't rise to the challenge. In silence he touched the side of his head where the punch had landed. Phil nodded and said, "That's right. You listen to me; it's not the other way around. You do what I say, and right now I'm telling you keep your damned mouth shut."

"Violence begets violence, Inquisitor. It should be avoided if at all possible," Roland said. He began to kneel down to check on Henderson, but Phil hauled him back up. With his fury adding strength to his arm, Roland seemed to weigh little more than a kite would.

"And you," Phil growled. "I'll have no more of your yapping. I mean it. If you can't hold your tongue, I'll remove it."

Unbelievably, Roland stood unflinching. He smiled easily and said, "Your tempter-tantrum aside, what are we going to do? Are we going to this farm?"

Phil felt his last nerve fray and he was about to deck Roland as well, when Haley said, "We have to do something besides fight. I'm turning blue it's so cold. Here, feel." She moved close and put her icy hand on Phil's cheek.

"Yeah." Phil breathed out the word. Just like that his anger fled and it wasn't the temperature of her hand but rather her proximity and the way she gently touched him that cooled his anger. "Your hands are freezing. Let's go. I'm betting that's the main gate over there." He pointed to where two of the guard towers sat closer together than the rest.

Without a glance back at Henderson, Phil took them on a looping path through the trees in order to keep well away from the closer towers.

"What are we going to say?" Haley asked as they walked. "Our travel docs don't give up permission to be out this way."

"I would refrain from lying," Roland advised. The night and the cold air had brought out a wheeze in his voice. He attempted to cough it away. "There is...power...in the truth."

Henderson mumbled something unintelligible and angry. Phil had to agree. Ignoring the old man's advice he said, "We'll just tell them that there was an engine fire with the van. That's believable enough. And that we saw lights in the distance and followed them here. If they try to give us lip, I'll just brow beat them. It should be as simple as that."

At first it did seem that simple.

As they came within shouting distance of the main gate, they began haling the nearest tower, hoping not to be shot out of hand. Seconds later a spotlight stripped the night of any calm and in its glare they walked the last few yards; keeping their hands across their brows against the raking light.

At the gate a group of soldiers accosted them. "Who are you and what are you doing outside the gate after sundown? It's illegal."

Though the soldier's tone had been annoyingly arrogant, Phil kept calm. He had played the pissing contest game before. It was nothing new to him. "We had an accident back on the highway; engine fire. I'll need to talk to whoever's in charge."

"Then you need to talk to me," the soldier replied, his tone growing haughtier at Phil's confession of weakness. Had they been a group of electrical workers or line technicians their situations might have been embarrassingly bad, but they were not. Phil had his collar up to help keep out the cold. He stepped away from the others and right up to the fence so that the spotlight was less harsh.

He brought his shielding hand down and adjusted his collar so that the death's head key with its four sharp fangs, the symbol of the Inquisitors, shown clear.

"Perhaps the first thing we'll talk about is your lack of manners," Phil said quietly, dangerously, turning the tables on the soldier.

There was a moment of stunned silence and then: "I-I'm sorry, sir. I didn't know. I couldn't tell. Please forgive me," the man said in a breathless panic. Though it was difficult, Phil kept his smile from showing.

"Forgive insolence? Forgive rudeness? I don't do that," Phil said growing steadily quieter. "What I do...what's your name?"

"Sergeant Taylor," the soldier squeaked.

"What I do, Sergeant Taylor is when I find a soldier who is as rude as you have been I like to bring them back to the Capital with me. I like to bring them down to the seventh level. I like to strap them to my favorite table and I like to use my very favorite knife on them. Do you know why?"

Taylor shook his head and now Phil did smile; it was a smile that suggested he was hungry to inflict pain. Taylor's features were difficult to make out in the night and the sharp slanting light, yet his eyes were obvious. They were huge and round.

Phil stared into them and said, "When a soldier is this rude, he's usually hiding something..."

Taylor interrupted, "I'm not! You have to believe me."

"Sometimes it's treason they're hiding..."

"I'm not. I didn't do anything," the sergeant said, gripping the chain-link fence.

"And sometimes it's that they have a really small penis and they're just over-compensating, but by then it's too late for them."

"I have a small penis!" the sergeant cried, seeing his chance.

"That's what I thought," Phil growled, knowing instinctively when to switch to anger. "Now if you don't want me to burn that tiny thing right off you then you had better get that damned light off of me and get this gate open in ten seconds!"

It took six seconds.

"I'm sorry, I'm sorry," the sergeant repeated over and over again.

"Who's really in charge?" demanded Phil. "And what is this place? A farm?"

"Yes sir. It's a farm sir. People's Farm 332. When I said I was in charge I only meant that I was in charge of the gate for the night. Colonel Heinrich is in charge of the entire facility and Mr. McCew is in charge of the actual production aspect. The workers just laid rows of asparagus. They'll be putting in the peas in the..."

"I don't care," Phil said.

He was about to ask whether Colonel Heinrich was army or Homeland Security when Roland asked, "What's with these fences?" It was only then that Phil noticed that there were indeed two fences with a run of about ten yards between them tracing the huge perimeter of the farm. Not only that the towers were built with two searchlights; one for the interior and the other for exterior use.

That Roland would say anything was bad enough, but the question seemed especially stupid and it sent a stab of anxiety spiking in Phil's chest. Obviously one fence was designed to keep the workers in, while the other was designed to keep thieves out.

Just then a moment of confusion slipped through his anxiety. The walls at Polk had been similar and he remembered wondering: which side was the safe side? The same question could be asked of People's Farm 332.

Before Phil had a chance to glare, Roland followed up with, "Is this a penal farm?"

The sergeant, who was leading them past a number of dim outbuildings, replied, "No. I don't think so."

Behind the soldier's back Phil glared in earnest, putting a finger to his lips. Rolland nodded and mimed locking his lips and throwing away a key. This only grated on Phil.

"Right though here," Taylor said. They had come to what looked like a pre-civil war plantation. It was a two-story manor with white painted brick and tall columns like sentries standing guard in the front. They entered through a massive wooden door and Taylor stopped them just beyond it and showed them to a sitting room.

"I'll get the officer on duty," he said.

Phil checked his watch, 6:48 pm. "No. I don't care what protocol is. I'm sure Colonel Heinrich is still awake; I want to see him."

"Yes sir," Taylor bleated and made a beeline down a hallway of polished wood.

"I wouldn't have done that," Henderson whispered. "Some low ranking nobody would've been easier to deal with."

"Wrong. It doesn't matter what peon they have on duty, once our travel docs were seen you know they would've ran right to Heinrich. This way we deal with one man. The fewer people who see us the better."

"I love this woodwork," Haley said, touching the banister of a large staircase that swept down from above. It had been hand carved with intricate vines twisting and turning along its curve. "How come they don't make banisters like this anymore? Or any woodwork for that matter? You almost never see anything so nice."

"Do not answer that," Phil ordered Roland. The old man had just drawn in a long breath. "In fact do not say anything while we're in this house."

"Isn't he grumpy," Haley remarked. Henderson and George refused to agree, so she sidled up to Roland and whispered, "I want to know why. This place is like two-hundred years old, but it's nicer than the dom-boxes we have today. Why is that? It shouldn't be that way. Right? We're more advanced but our stuff isn't as nice. I mean look at those lace curtains. They're so lovely."

"You have begun with a faulty premise, my dear," Roland said. "And don't glare so much, Inquisitor. You knew I was going to answer her."

"You will get us all killed," Phil whispered.

Roland ignored him. "We aren't more advanced. Yes, in some things we are, but that's only because of the technologies gifted to us by our fathers and grandfathers. However in many ways we have regressed and are at a very similar level of advancement to the 1860s. They had their technologies, yet they still relied on the human animal for so many things. Farming for instance. Humans sowed the earth, weeded it, fertilized it, and finally picked the fruits of their labor. Now, did any of you notice the implements that hung from the outbuildings we passed?"

They all shook their heads, save for Henderson, who rolled his eyes and moved away as if he didn't want to be associated with them.

Roland didn't seem to care. "There were hundreds of hoes for turning up the ground. Dozens of buckets and ladles for manure. And I couldn't count the numbers of trowels and flat carts for the actual planting of the crowns. But what I didn't see was more important. I didn't see a single tractor or plow. Nor any tillers or cultivators. There wasn't a single piece of machinery in sight. Who knows how many thousands of acres are out there and it's all worked by hand." Roland shook his head as if he couldn't believe what he was saying.

"You're right," Haley said. "That doesn't sound advanced at all, and it's not like what I see on TV. There are programs about farm life. They make it seem very nice. Really wholesome. You know, bright skies and rainbows; rivers full of trout. That sort of thing."

"Did these television programs ever show fences topped with barbed wire and guard towers with machine guns?" Roland asked rhetorically.

"Never," Haley admitted. She looked down at the wood of the banister again. "So what happened to all the technology? People just don't forget that sort of thing."

"They did during the dark ages," Phil said. "That's what they taught us in school. They said the Catholics made it so no one could read..." Phil stopped in mid-sentence at Roland's look.

"Hardly," the old man said. "The priests and monks kept the written word alive until Gutenberg invented his press. To answer your question, Haley, the technology of an advanced people relies on a synergism that is not compatible with communism. Not on a grand scale. Take the Chinese. Yes they can turn out computers and phones yet the majority of them live in abject poverty. You might be amazed to know that over forty million of them live in caves and who knows how many millions more live in huts with thatched roofs."

"Sounds dismal," she said.

"It is," Roland agreed. "And the soviets before them. They could fire a nuclear tipped missile halfway around the world yet they couldn't feed their own people. Communism can only focus on a few things at a time, while capitalism with its incentives can unleash the great potential in everyone and by doing so can do so many, many things better."

The heavy tread of footsteps thumping on hardwood came to them. Phil hurriedly grabbed Roland's arm. "You need to zip it. You're in prison rags for goodness sake. You speak out of line and it'll be expected that I beat you."

"You should beat him anyway," Henderson suggested. "I would."

Chapter 23

A Lack of Papers

"Colonel Heinrich, it's nice to meet you," Phil said, his words and manner cool. Since the colonel outranked him, Phil wasn't going to have an opportunity to force his will on the man. And to act in any way friendly would only create suspicion. So instead Phil decided to act just as if he had really gotten in a car accident: he would show barely hidden anger and embarrassment.

As his footsteps had sounded, the colonel was a large beefy man. He had huge hands and a round, red face that seemed more so above the grey Homeland Security uniform that he wore. "And you are...Inquisitor...?"

A lie would be found out in a matter of seconds so Phil answered, "Tarsus."

"Well Tarsus, is there some reason that you failed to hand over your travel documents? Let's have them."

Phil had to obey and gave the colonel the wilted remains of his travel docs, explaining that their van had blown a tire and had taken a spill in a river.

Despite the water damage the documents were still somewhat legible and it didn't take long for

Heinrich to lift his face from the papers. "There are four names on here, but I see five of you."

Phil jerked a thumb at Roland. "He's a prisoner not a person."

"I don't care if he's a border collie," Heinrich seethed. "I need paperwork on him. Everyone has paperwork."

"He doesn't, which, if you really want to press the matter, is Brewer's problem up at Polk. Not mine."

Heinrich stared, astonished. "Not your problem? Do you think you are above the law? Paperwork is the only..." The colonel paused in midsentence, staring at Phil in a shrewd, calculating way; clearly considering the eternal question: is the man I'm about to ream, connected? And if so, how connected? He glanced back to the paperwork as if the answer would come from there.

His head came up quick as he realized something. "Brewer? The under-warden?" Heinrich asked, his eyes going to squints. "He let a prisoner out without a proper transfer form? That's not the Brewer I know. The Brewer I know won't tie his shoes unless the law gives him permission. He's as by the book as they come. So that means you have something on him, or this is illegal somehow."

The two men stared eye to eye, neither blinking. "Why don't you give him a call," Phil said, nonchalantly, as if it wouldn't bother him in the least if Heinrich did. And in truth, it wouldn't bother him. Even if the phone lines had been repaired in the last day, the fire most assuredly had melted every phone in the prison.

"Can't, the phones are down. They've been down for days."

"Then I don't know what to say," Phil said. "Look, I can give you the number of the Secretary of the Inquisitors. When your phones are working again you can give him a..."

"How bout I radio Brewer instead?" Heinrich asked, cutting in. "I have a short wave upstairs."

"That would be fine too." Phil's right hand went to his tie and gently fingered the polyester, while his mind ran down how the evening would play out: Heinrich would not be able to raise Polk on the radio. His suspicions would grow. He'd send someone out to Polk. By electric car, the prison was probably not more than fifteen minutes away, which meant that Phil had thirty minutes to escape...or he could draw his pistol right there.

How would that play out? He had just begun working down that unpleasant scenario when Roland disobeyed orders—his one order—and spoke: "Why is it always a pissing contest with you, Inquisitor? Show him the paperwork and be done with it."

"What?" Heinrich asked. "What's he talking about?" Before Roland could speak again, Henderson backhanded him across the face. The old man went to the floor spitting blood. Now Heinrich's face went redder than ever and thunderclouds grew behind his brow. "The carpet, damn it! If you get blood on the carpet you won't make it back to the Justice building to be killed. I'll stone you right out in the yard. I swear I will."

"Damn it, Henderson," Phil snarled. "Pull him over to the wood."

The under-inquisitor did as he was told and when Heinrich was convinced that his carpet hadn't suffered, he rounded on Phil. "What game is this? You have paperwork but you're withholding it? That's illegal. That is very illegal. I could have you jailed right here."

"Then we'd be in quite the dilemma," Phil answered back in a sinister tone. "You'd be keeping me from executing my assigned duties and you know as well as anyone that it's illegal to interfere with an Inquisitor when he's in pursuit of justice. It's treasonous." That was a weighty threat and it was also Phil's ace in the hole, justice being such a malleable word.

Heinrich stared; his eyes wild in his red face. "Who sent you? Whoever it was made a big mistake! I'm connected. I'm connected and I'm sure I'm more connected than you."

"No one sent me...or rather my boss did, Darryl Conner." The name clicked in his mind and now he knew what Roland was talking about. He had paperwork of sorts, the fake transfer documents that he had shown to Roland, only he had left them in the laundry room back at Polk and they were either burnt to ash or buried under piles of rubble. "I had the forms, but they were destroyed in the accident."

"Then why didn't you just say that?" Heinrich asked, calming slightly. He ran a damp hand across his forehead. "Instead you start in with treason! You had me going, I tell you. I was thinking that...never mind what I was thinking. Sometimes you fellows act as though you are too big for your britches." He sighed as if he'd just had a close call.

"Yeah, sorry about that," Phil said, trying to hit the perfect note: a blend of apologetic machismo. "I guess I'm a bit worn out. I get cranky when I'm tired. Do you think you might be able to spare a few beds?"

Heinrich bobbed his head. "I think we can do something for you, but first I have to radio Polk. Rules are rules."

Phil had been working a semi-fake, tired smile onto his face. It froze unnaturally in place. Heinrich saw this. Tension mounted and there was a moment as the two stared into each other's eyes. Then came another moment—a much faster one as the two men drew their weapons; Heinrich from a holster at his hip, Phil from beneath his jacket.

Phil was hot and ready. His gun cleared the black of his jacket like a striking steel snake. Now came a third moment as the two sized each other up. Heinrich had his gun half out of his holster. They both knew he wouldn't be fast enough to get a shot off.

"If you shoot you'll be a dead man," the colonel warned.

"Clearly you don't understand the situation," Phil said. "If I don't shoot I'll be a dead man. I can't leave you to make your calls. Someone very high up is after me."

"We can make a deal. I'm connected..."

"You're not that connected."

Slowly, Heinrich took his hand off the butt of his gun and lifted it up, palm out. "I think you're wrong. My second cousin is the Commissioner of Homeland Security. You don't get much more connected than that."

Phil shot Henderson a look and then lifted his chin toward the colonel. Henderson went behind the man and took the pistol from his holster. He then frisked him, slowly and expertly.

"Clean."

Lowering his gun, Phil said with a touch of sadness, "That's not connected enough."

Heinrich's eyes flared in surprise. "Who's after you?"

"The Commissioner of Justice."

"Oh man!"

There was always a question as to who in government had the most power, but whenever the question came up, the Commissioner of State Justice always ranked in the top three.

The colonel went to one of the plush chairs and sank himself down. Shaking his head he asked, "What did you do? Wait don't answer that. I don't want to know."

"What are you going to do with him?" Roland asked. He and the others had done their best to stay back and unobtrusive. Now they came up and stared at the colonel as if they had never seen one before.

Henderson shrugged. "Kill him. What else can we do with him?"

"There are two other options, both of which are far smarter," Roland answered. "The first: we take him hostage. At the least, it will get us off the farm and maybe this cousin of his might be able to help in some manner. Are you close to him?"

Heinrich made a face, which Phil interpreted, "No. They're not close. I'm guessing the colonel kisses his ass: sends him birthday gifts and the like, but I doubt you get much from him other than the ability to name drop. Am I right?" Heinrich shrugged, which Phil took to mean: yes.

Roland's face drooped slightly. "Rats. That leaves option two. It's a little more complicated and requires some trust."

"I don't like it already," Henderson said.

Phil ignored him. "Let's hear it."

"It's simply this: we tell him your secret. What I mean is we tell him why you're being hunted. In detail. You see?"

Phil didn't, and he could tell by their looks that no one else understood either. "No I don't see. How could that possibly help anyone?"

"It's like this, by letting him in, he becomes a part of the group." Roland had an expectant look on his face but when no one said a word he went on determinedly, "Phil, you say that someone is out to get you and is willing to kill anyone close to you. If you were to tell Colonel Heinrich everything, then you would share a common enemy. You could pool your resources, giving you both a much better chance at coming out of this alive."

"Oh..." the colonel said, clearly not enthused."I have to say that it doesn't sound like such a great idea. I think I'd rather take my chances as your hostage than be on the bad side of the Commissioner of Justice."

"I agree," Phil said. He went to the chair next to the colonel and plopped down, holstering his gun. "Besides I'm not sure who's after me for certain and I definitely don't know why."

"Perhaps you should tell us the whole story and we can help you figure out the particulars," Roland suggested. Everyone agreed, but the colonel.

"Would you be so kind as to tie me up over in the corner before you start?"

Chapter 24

A Slave's Wage

"That was his crime? Being gay?" Roland asked when Phil had finished going over what he could remember of his conversations with Stephen Crown. His memory of their two encounters was spotty at best.

"Yeah, that was his crime," Phil answered vaguely, fingering the fanciest pen he had ever seen in his life. It was long and elegant with a brass back and nub. They were currently in Heinrich's bedroom suite. It was posh in every regard: silken sheets lay upon a massive four-poster bed, the furniture was of dark wood and it all matched, right down to the roll top desk, where Phil sat touching the smoothness of the pen.

The flippant response made Roland's face torque into a maze of wrinkles. "That doesn't make any sense. Why kill someone for being gay?"

Phil shrugged. "Population decline or something. It's not important." He groaned and rubbed his head. "I know I'm forgetting parts of our talk, but I don't know what and I don't know if what I'm missing was all that important."

Haley nudged him. "You talked about God right before the execution. Did he mention any names?"

"God's name. I don't know."

Looking into a hand mirror that she had found beside the bed and running her fingers through her blonde hair like a comb, she said, "You're not being much help. What about those names of his lovers that he wrote down?"

Phil pointed to the pad of paper that he carried around. It sat deformed and still wet on a side table. He had tried his best to pull back the pages, but they were made of cheap paper and had become yellow mush.

"I meant can you remember any of the names."

"All I know is that one guy was named Benny. Don't look at me like that. I didn't think I'd have to memorize the names. And it doesn't really matter since I would have noticed if someone was named Commissioner of Justice Ari Loman."

"My guess is that the answer was in the computer file. And there's no way you could've deleted the file by accident?" Roland asked.

Shaking his head, Phil said, "No. I would've had to have accidentally deleted it twice. Once in the active file folder and a second time in the deleted files folder. I know I didn't do either one. Someone had to have done it on purpose, and now it's gone forever."

Haley waved her hand for Phil to come closer. "Have you forgotten? You made me a copy," Haley said in a whisper so low everyone dipped down close in order to hear.

Excited, Phil asked, "Did you read the names of Crown's students?"

He had been a touch too loud. They had not seen anyone besides the colonel in the house, but people could be heard walking around. She hushed him before saying, "Of course I read the names. I want to be someone, remember? Unlike you, I don't want to be a shlub all my life. But...but there were no Lomans or Gilchrists or Mendels or any of them. None of the big names were on the list. But I wouldn't really expect them to be. Stadler is a slightly lower ranked school."

"And is the file in a safe place?" Roland asked in a whisper.

"As long as no one burns down the offices of Entertainment it'll be safe. I put it where no one would think to look."

They all paused waiting to hear where that is. "Well?" asked Phil.

Haley sat back on the bed. She pursed her lips, thinking for over a minute. "I'm not telling," she said finally. "You two have your guns and your Inquisitor status. Roland has his brains and his magic God. All I have is this secret and George. Don't worry George. You're on my team."

"No, no, no," Henderson said. "What do we do if something happens to you?"

Phil answered, "We won't let anything happen to her. We'll protect her."

Henderson rubbed his eyes. He looked a mess. His black uniform sat crumpled on his thick frame and his hair spiked in a hundred directions. When he looked at Phil, it was obvious he appeared the same way. "I just don't get you. She's just a piece of tail. Don't get me wrong, Baker, you're a hot piece of tail, but in the end that's all you are."

"What the hell is your point?" Phil asked in a gravely, dangerous whisper.

"My point is, what do you care about protecting her? First, you keep grandpa around even though he won't shut up and is nothing but trouble. You know where we'd be if we had shot him like I wanted? Probably downstairs having a warm meal, while our clothes were being cleaned. You know I'm right. Our travel docs would have held up and old Heinrich wouldn't have to die."

"He still doesn't have to die," Roland pointed out.

"You see? He's crazy," Henderson said. "It's absolutely no use talking to him and I think it's rubbing off on you, Phil. We protect her? You've never said anything so stupid. Let me tell you, Ms. Baker, here's the deal: if something happens to Phil, I'll keep you around as long as you have a use for me. It's a dog eat dog world; sorry but that's the way it is."

"Then all the more I'm glad I didn't spill," Haley snarled right back.

Henderson gave a tired laugh and said, "That's the other thing. Who cares about the file, or the names, or any of the gays? You guys act as though there's some great mystery. Commissioner Loman is after us...really he's after Phil and we're just collateral damage. But other than Loman, who else could it be? Who's got this much power?"

The short answer was no one.

"Could this commissioner stage a prison fire?" Roland asked.

Phil and Henderson shook their heads. "I wouldn't think so," Phil said. "The Board of Corrections is separate from Justice. Loman can't just burn down prisons and he wouldn't do it just to kill you and me."

"But he'd burn down an apartment building?" Haley asked. "That's the Board of Housing. I forget who runs that, but I bet he isn't too happy right now."

"Maybe he is, maybe he isn't. We don't know," Phil replied. "Unlike prisons, there are thousands of apartment buildings. He may not care too much about a single one. And maybe he's getting a kickback of sorts—you know, a future favor, or perhaps the disappearance of an over achieving subordinate."

Roland looked confused. "Why on earth would you want an over-achieving subordinate to disappear? Wouldn't you rather have your under-achieving subordinates disappear?"

"Why do you ask stupid questions?" Henderson said. The old man shrugged.

"They're gotten rid of because they pose a threat," Phil said, putting his head back and letting out a sigh. "I don't know. I don't know what we're going to do. I don't even know what to do about him." He pointed to Colonel Heinrich. He sat in the far corner of the room with a curtain sash tied about the wrists. His ears were stuffed with cloth and he had a makeshift blindfold on.

"What do you mean you don't know what to do about him?" Henderson asked. "You've gone so soft, it's like I don't even know you. He's a hostage. We get everything we can out of him and then shoot him in the head when we don't need him anymore. What's there about the concept that's so confusing?"

Phil refused to look in Roland's direction as he answered, "I guess there's nothing confusing about it. Let's get him untied, I want some food."

"And I want a change of clothing," Haley added, pulling at her blouse. "I've been chaffing in these damp rags since we climbed out of the pipe. Excuse me, Colonel? Can we get our garments cleaned and pressed by morning? Do you have facilities like that around here?"

Heinrich blinked up at her. "Don't I know you? Aren't you on the news?"

For hours, Haley had worn a pinched look on her pert features, but now she unfurled the smile that millions saw everyday as she cheerily reported on the next execution. "Why yes I am," she said, holding out her hand. "I'm Haley Baker, channel 2 news."

Heinrich took the hand and shook it. He seemed slightly dazed. "That's right. You are Haley Baker. Wow. I'm a big fan. I thought I recognized you, but with everything going on..."

She laughed. "Don't worry about it. Really, I don't see how you even knew it was me under all this grime. I'm such a mess. Speaking of which." She pointed to her blouse and skirt, both of which were filthy. "Is there anyone here who can help me out?"

The colonel gushed, "Of course. For you, anything."

"Hopefully that pertains to us as well," Phil said. "We'll all need our clothes cleaned and pressed by morning, in fact before the break of dawn. I want to be out of here before the sun rises. And I'll need clothes for him." The inquisitor pointed at Roland.

"A uniform?" Heinrich said with a twisted lip. "At his age he can't pass as Homeland or really much of anything."

"Find him a tech uni. Henderson, let me have the colonel's gun." Phil cleared the chamber and took out the clip. It was now useless; he tossed it back to its owner and then rummaged through the colonel's wardrobe. The two men were nearly the same size, with Heinrich larger through the belly and Phil broader across the shoulders. Fortunately, Phil found a pair of crisp battle fatigues that fit him.

After he changed, he gathered everyone's clothing—Haley wore a sheet and somehow made that sexy—while the others wore Heinrich's extra uniforms. All save Roland, who would have looked ridiculous.

"Congratulations on your promotion," Heinrich said dryly as Phil clipped the eagle to the collar of his camouflaged jacket. The insignia bumped him up a full rank.

After glancing at himself in a full-length mirror he said, "I like the Inquisitor's uniform better. I may not have the rank, but it carries more weight. People respect it. Even colonels."

"I suppose we do."

"There is something people respect even more," Phil said, pulling his service pistol. "Colonel, you need to know that I will kill you if you step out of line in any way. One false word, one false move and I will kill you. Do you understand?"

"I'd do the same if our situations were reversed."

"Then we have an understanding." Phil tucked the gun into his front right pocket and then glanced over to Roland. "Pick up the clothes. You're coming with us and not in any advisory role so keep your mouth shut. I don't need or want any more of your life lessons. Do *we* have an understanding?"

"I doubt it," Roland said pleasantly. "You understand little besides the boot, the bat, and the bastinado."

"Then we do have an understanding."

"Yes we do. You're threatening me again. I get it." Roland made a bundle of the clothes and hefted it easily in his long stringy arms.

Colonel Heinrich led the two out into the night, chatting easily as he went. "I've got this lady who does a great job at getting out stains. And her ironing is probably better than what you big city boys get. She'll be a little put out with me showing up so late but whatever."

"How many people live here? There are so many buildings." Roland asked, once again disobeying his one order. They had already passed five rows of low barracks style buildings and there seemed to be many more all laid out in grid.

216

"Somewhere upwards of a thousand. It takes a lot of workers running a farm of this size. With the two annexes we till ten-thousand acres. Lots of peas; lots of carrots. Here we go: Woman's B-3. Man on deck!" he hollered and then strode into the building.

There was a great flurry of activity. Women of all ages and in various stages of dress flew in every direction, many squawking in fright. Heinrich stared openly and in some cases lecherously, while Roland gawked in amazement for a full three seconds and then hid his face.

"Sorry...sorry. I'm sorry," he mumbled mainly to himself. His cheeks burning a fiery red.

Phil reacted completely different. He found himself ill at ease and not because of the women's sexuality, but rather because of their lack of sexuality. There wasn't a one among them that stirred him in the least. They were peasant women; farm hands. Unlike Haley, who was willowy and graceful, these women were skin and bones, yet tough. From their work and the constant sun they were old before their time. Each wore an array of wrinkles on their leathery skin and their hands were forever stained by the dirt in which they toiled.

Like the soldier he once was, the women lived in bunk beds, each getting a stand up closet measuring two feet wide and two deep in which to store all of their worldly possessions. Most had room to spare. The only thing of any actual value in the room was the giant television that mumbled away in the center of the room. Not to have one in every residence, be it a single dom-box or a thirty person barracks was illegal.

"Where's Marge Fishman?" Heinrich bellowed. Hands pointed to a middle-aged woman with coarse black hair that ran specked with grey. "Marge, excellent. Take these clothes to the washroom. We need them by five tomorrow morning. And use the good soap. These are my guests. Oh, also get me a uni that'll fit this old fellow."

"Yes sir." Marge had almost no voice. She reminded Phil of the juror Abby who had been so afraid, but this was different. This woman's fear was deeper and far more ingrained, as if she were perpetually afraid.

"Should we tip her?" Roland asked.

"What do you mean? Tip her over?" Phil asked, wondering why he would want to hurt the woman.

"No. I mean pay her. We should give her a little money."

This seemed illogical to both Phil and to Heinrich. "What's he on about?" the colonel asked.

"I'm not sure," Phil answered. "Roland, the State pays people. We don't."

"Then what do you use your money for?"

"Is he mad?" Heinrich whispered to Phil.

"Sometimes I think so. Listen Roland, people get paid by the State to do their jobs. I'm not going to pay this lady when she's already getting paid, and I'm sorry if her job calls for her to work late. It happens to all of us. And what I spend my money on is my business."

Roland held up his hands, palms out. "I'm sorry. I just wanted to make sure we are doing right by the lady. Sorry ma'am," he said to her. She wanted nothing to do with the conversation and just stood in silence. Roland bobbed his head as a way of saying good-bye and was just about to turn away when he looked into her closet. What he saw there caused him to stare.

"What is it?" Heinrich asked with growing suspicion. "Contraband?" The colonel pushed Marge aside and rummage through her meager belongings: two pairs of grey work trousers, two long sleeve shirts, a single flop hat, and a pair of black boots that didn't seem like they would fit a woman of Marge's small stature.

"There's nothing here," Heinrich said with some disappointment.

"Exactly," replied Roland. The word held a stinging rebuke, but it was lost on the camp commander; Heinrich only looked at him blankly. "Don't you see? There isn't *anything* in her closet. Marge, what do you spend your money on?"

"What money?" she asked in confusion.

Chapter 25

Values

With his hand growing warm on the hidden pistol, Phil hustled Heinrich and Roland back into the night.

"Where's her money?" Roland demanded. "You're stealing from her. Hell, you're stealing from all of them!"

"You better leash your dog, Inquisitor!"

Phil pushed the old man back with a gentle wave of his thick arm. With his other hand he flourished the pistol so Heinrich couldn't miss it. "In case you forgot," Phil said to his hostage.

"How could I forget?" the colonel fumed. "But I don't need to be lectured to by this old piece of crap. Does he know my costs? Does he know what my allowances are? Does he know what I have to trade away just to get enough heating oil in the winter? Son of a bitch! A damned prisoner in rags has the gall to lecture me. My people get their fourteen a day! It may not get them much, but they stay warm in the winter. They're clothed well enough; and we have a doctor! A real doctor not some nurse wanna-be. How many people's farms can say that?"

"Every one of them should be able to," Roland said.

"Well they can't," Heinrich spat back. "Maybe one in five. But still that's better than the mines. You ever see the mining camps? They work those black boys to death. So pardon me if I get a little angry if some nobody questions how I do things in my own damned camp!"

"You seem to be doing alright," Roland said. "Unlike those ladies, it doesn't look like you've missed a meal."

Heinrich began to charge at the old man, but Phil's pistol came between them. "You're going to have to shoot me, Inquisitor because I'm going to kill him." Phil brought the hammer back, which had the effect of letting the air out of the colonel. With his bluff called, he sagged back like a week-old party balloon.

"This is not our fight, Roland," the Inquisitor said. Gently, he thumbed the hammer back down and put the gun back where it couldn't be seen. "I just need to know one thing, where is her money?"

The colonel shrugged. "After we deduct for food, medical, housing, and her heat ration there's nothing left of her fourteen dollars. It's just how the numbers go."

Roland bowed his head in disbelief. "Come on," Phil said, tugging his arm and walking back toward the colonel's place. "I tell you, Haley was right about something, this place is nothing like the commercials."

"How could it be otherwise?" Roland said, his energy fading as well. "Who would come out here to work if they knew it was so bad?" Heinrich said nothing to this. Roland hadn't expected an answer and added, "I tell you, seeing this whittles my heart down to the bitter nub. What I can't understand is why you don't use real farm equipment. Where are the tractors or what are those big things called...combines?"

"The last one we had broke down about nine years ago and we could never get parts for it..." Heinrich paused to look out at the darkened fields.

"Five bucks says he blames the neocons," Roland whispered to Phil.

"...The neocons kept sabotaging the plant where they were being...what?" Heinrich asked as Roland snorted with mocking laughter.

"Don't worry about him, he's being an ass," Phil said quickly, trying to keep the peace. "Tell me; is the double fence about the neocons as well? Do you have some in the area?"

"Maybe. That's the official theory, but I don't think so and neither does anyone else around here. The outer fence is for the scroungers. Every year we lose people. They go under the fence you know. But once on the outside they don't know what to do with themselves. How would you live out there, right? So they sort of hang around trying to sneak food off the farm."

"Speaking of food," Phil said. "I'm starving."

As they walked back on the deserted roads Roland said, "So when am I going to get that five dollars? I won the bet."

"You really are a money grubbing conservative," Phil said testily. His hunger had come on like a freight train and had put him in a mood.

"Phil, you are both right and wrong," Roland said. "If you were to give me five dollars I'd run it right over to Marge and hand it over to her as payment for her work. I wouldn't consider that money grubbing. However, I do love aspects of money. I won't deny that. Money has always had a bad rap, which really makes no sense since it's only a symbol. Money stands for something."

"Money stands for something? What the hell is that supposed to mean?" Heinrich asked. Phil began rubbing his temples. He didn't think he had the energy for another lecture.

"Food first, please."

Roland agreed about the need for food and he kept his mouth shut. The three walked back to the plantation house in silence, which was broken the second they walked through the front door. There upon Heinrich began yelling for the officer on duty to fetch the cook.

Before dinner, Phil had time to shower and he felt refreshed when he came down to the largest feast that he could remember.

"You never know what tomorrow will bring," Heinrich said. "So I decided to splurge." The table was spread with two whole chickens, plates of beets, mounds of broccoli, and a basket of biscuits.

"I think he's trying to bribe us with this meal to let him live," Henderson joked as he helped himself.

"I think it's working," Phil said, and in truth, he felt much more in the way of gentleness for the man when his stomach had been filled.

"All right," Heinrich said, halfway through a bite of chicken. "I can't take it anymore. What does money stand for?"

"What?" Henderson asked.

"He says that money stands for something," Heinrich said of Roland. "I want to know what."

The under-inquisitor stood and stretched. "You are all wasting your time with the old man. He's as cracked as they come. But before you get started, we need to work out shifts to keep watch on the colonel. I think we should do two-hour shifts. Haley goes first, if we can trust her with a gun. Then George, then myself and then Phil."

"You can trust me," Haley said defensively. She still wore only the sheet, though she had somehow fashioned it to resemble a dress. "I'm not going to shoot my foot off."

Henderson shook his head. "I don't care about your foot. My worry is that you won't be able to shoot the colonel if it came to it."

"I trust her," Phil said. "Just keep him away from you, Haley and don't let him talk. If he acts in anyway suspicious just holler and if he tries to come at you, aim and pull the trigger and keep pulling the trigger until I get there or you run out of bullets."

Heinrich looked a little green at the discussion and put the leg of chicken back on his plate, unfinished.

"Then that's settled," Roland said in the awkward silence that followed. "Now who would like to hear what money really means?" Henderson snorted and walked away, while George raised his hand meekly. "Good for you George. It's really quite simple: as a wage, money is a universal description of a person's value to society."

Haley had been toying with her food and casting glances at Heinrich, the man she would possibly have to kill. At Roland's words, she came more awake. "And what do you mean by that? Is a millionaire worth more as a human than a peasant?"

"I said as a wage. Money as an accumulation of wealth stands for something else, namely purchasing power and job creation, but that is a discussion for another time. As a wage, money equals relative worth, but only in a free market. Here in America we are a communistic society and thus money has almost no meaning what so ever."

"Of course it does," Heinrich put in. "Everyone gets their fourteen dollars, and with it they buy clothes and food. You know, necessities."

Roland shook his head. "That fourteen dollars has no meaning. Look at where you live, Colonel on your fourteen dollars and compare that to the squalor right down the road. Look at your closets full of clothes. Some of those shirts are silk. What do they wear? Coarse wool and denim. And look at what you eat. So, is there any relationship between wages and standard of living?"

The question had been directed at Phil and he was quick to answer, "No. Not that I can tell."

"Correct. What matters is rank, which begs the question: why use money at all?" Roland took a minute to butter a biscuit and eat it. In that time no one spoke. Savoring the remains, he said, "There are two reasons. I'll give you one, but you'll have to guess the second. The main reason a currency is used is to make it easier for the State to trade with other countries. It's simpler to rate one currency against another in order to buy and sell than to attempt to barter. You know, how many gallons of oil is equal to how many bushels of apples? That's a pain to do."

Roland then ate another biscuit. "I told you I love bread."

"What's the other reason?" Heinrich asked when his patience had dwindled.

Haley blew out in noisy exasperation. "He said we have to guess. Is it because of fairness? To make it fair that we're all paid the same."

Roland got excited. "You are so close! That's the stated reason we're given but what's the truth?"

When Roland said the word truth, he emphasized it and the answer kicked in to Phil's mind. "We're paid the same because the State wants to create the illusion of fairness, when they're not fair at all."

"Ding! Ding! Ding! We have a winner," Roland cried out beaming. Phil smiled at the man's excitement, while the others sat in varying degrees of unease. When Roland noticed this he said, "Oh I forgot, you three still believe in your government."

Heinrich leaned away from Roland. "What do you mean by that?"

Phil decided on a biscuit as well; they were perfect. "He's just saying that the government is always lying to us."

"How can you say that?" Heinrich asked, aghast. "Aren't you an inquisitor?"

"Today I don't know what I am. Maybe a dead man walking...or eating, I should say. Pass the butter, please. So Roland, money is equal to a man's value to society? How much am I worth?"

"You are worthless," Roland answered. "An Inquisitor contributes nothing to society. They are a drain only."

The table grew even more quiet. Phil heard only static in his ears for quite some time, as if his mind had just disconnected itself from his reality. Eventually he spoke, "You don't lie, do you?"

"Never."

"Then what about me?" Haley asked with a touch of desperation. "What's my worth?"

"You are worthless as well. I'm sorry," he added, when Haley's mouth came open.

"No," she said.

"Yes. If anything, your job is worse than his. You glamorize torture. You give murder a sexy smile. You export the worst of America. You help to create and maintain this culture of death we find ourselves in."

George's eyes went wide but he didn't dare ask about himself and Roland didn't offer. Colonel Heinrich turned in his chair and with a red-faced glare asked, "Well?"

"You have value," Roland stated.

This seemed to surprise the colonel. He nodded judiciously. "We feed the people here."

Roland blinked like a basilisk. "You are a slave master and nothing more. The value you possess is the ability to wring blood from stone. Congratulations."

Chapter 26

And the Lion Shall Lay Down with the Lamb

"And what of you?" Haley asked sharply. "Where's your value, Prisoner Gentry? What's your worth? You're a penniless nothing, whose only talent is running his mouth."

"And betraying his friends," Phil added. The static that had numbed him had drained away and in its place was a sour taste. He dropped the biscuit that had been halfway to his mouth. "How many names were you going to give me? How many men were you going to condemn to save yourself?"

"None."

"Then you *do* lie," Phil snarled, feeling a sudden justification in finding out that Roland wasn't as good as he had made himself out to be. That he was as bad as the rest of them. Perhaps it was true as well that all the crap he had spewn was equally as fraudulent.

Roland shook his head, his long white hair swinging in his face. "I do not lie. You asked for the names of the people that I preached to and I gave them to you and was prepared to give you many more. However, these were names of men who are long dead. Most died before they had a chance to be released from prison. The few who did get out were picked up very quickly and stoned to death by men like you."

"You tricked me," Phil said. "You tricked me and that's like a lie."

"No. You asked me a question and I answered it honestly. Just like when I told you what you were worth. Next time if you want a different answer ask a different question. As for my worth? It has yet to be revealed. Maybe it will tomorrow; right now I'm going to bed." He stood slowly, his knees popping, and then walked out of the room, but came back quickly to grab the last biscuit.

"He bothers me," Haley said, when he left a second time for good. "I don't like the way he looks at me."

"Maybe it's the fact that you're wearing a sheet," Phil posited, though he knew what she meant. He knew it better than anyone.

After making sure that the sheet was still in place, Haley said, "No, it's not the sheet. It's something else. Like he's always judging me, or he's expecting me to do something."

Phil understood. "I get the feeling that he expects me to change all of a sudden. To stop being who I've been for so long and just...and just change." He didn't tell her that he had the feeling that Roland wanted him to become more, or perhaps better. But Phil didn't really know what being 'better' entailed. His knowledge of God being so jumbled that the very term 'good' was next to meaningless, while 'holy' had a cartoon feel to it.

A yawn escaped Haley and she nearly lost the sheet. Unlike with the farm girls Phil found himself staring as she re-hoisted the makeshift dress. Colonel Heinrich stared as well and said as if speaking to Haley's barely concealed breasts, "That's because he's a zealot. They always hope they can change a person, but they can't. A leopard can't change his spots. A turtle can't learn to fly."

"Up here," Phil said, snapping his fingers in Heinrich's face to get him to stop staring. "The old man is right about something; it's bedtime. Haley, are you sure you can handle him? We can put him the master bedroom closet and bar the door with a chair. What do you think?"

"Yeah, sure." She didn't seem sure. She seemed turned around and tired and a little afraid.

"I'll come with you and make sure it's ok. Oh, and good night George." The cameraman had sat so still and quiet after dinner that Phil had forgot that he was even in the room until his chair scraped as he stood. George bobbed his head in reply, but there was something in his eye as if he had something to say.

"Yes?" Phil asked. Always shy, George turned pink in the ears and dropped his chin. "Is there something about Roland that you wanted to say?" It was just a guess.

"He wants me to be happy."

"Oh." Phil had no clue what to say and so he gave a crooked smile that conveyed exactly that.

Happy was a convoluted concept, much like good. It meant different things to different people. Yet to the State, happiness had gradually come to be frowned on. It was like a second cousin to greed.

So few people were happy that there was a growing suspicion of those that were. It was generally assumed that the happy person was in possession of something that was not only secret but very likely illegal. The thinking went: why would the washerwoman from down the block be happy? Her life is crap just like yours and mine. There must be a reason. What does she have that I do not? Extra food? Had she found money? Or was it that she had swiped a pair of mittens...

People tended to keep their happiness to themselves.

"Ok. Well good night again, George." Phil turned away.

"I think he wants you to be happy as well," George said and then ducked through the door same door that Roland had used. They were sharing a room on the first floor.

"What does he mean by that?" Heinrich asked with a sidelong look at Phil.

"Who knows?" Phil answered tiredly. He then lifted his hand to indicate that the colonel should lead the way to the master bedroom. Despite the meal and all their talk, Phil had not once relaxed his guard, while Heinrich had looked for a chance to make a run for it at every opportunity.

There would be no opportunity; the Inquisitor was too alert. With Haley covering the colonel, holding Phil's pistol with a surprisingly steady hand, Phil emptied the closet so that it was bare wood, and after the colonel went in with nothing but a throw pillow, Phil locked him inside.

"You'll be fine. He can't get out and the two hours will go in a snap." Phil walked to the door, though his eyes stayed fixated on Haley. She sat on the bed; her sheet no longer looking like a dress. It looked very much like a bed sheet with a naked woman under it. One of her long slim legs stuck out.

"Stay," Haley whispered.

"I could stay," he answered. His room down the hall was fancy enough, but there was nothing in it that was more enticing than Haley Baker. The sheet had drooped in front exposing her left shoulder. How different she was from the farmwomen. Her skin porcelain and perfect. Her muscles smooth and soft. The delicate bones below her neck much like a bird's; he felt the need to touch the skin with his lips.

He came to sit next to her, his hand on the exposed thigh. Her flesh was softer than he imagined, and hot. She was alive. The muscles jumped and without meaning to, his hand gripped them.

He had not hurt her but she hesitated. "Not like this...he's right there."

"And you're afraid."

She was afraid. He knew fear a thousand times more intimately than love. Like some jungle predator, he could sense it. Normally it invoked anger, or hunger, or the passion to cause pain, perhaps to justify the fear. However, now there was something else, a strange need to sooth.

The feeling was bizarre and unnatural, but not at all unpleasant. Taking his hand from the warmth of her thigh, he raised her chin and was smote by the blue of her eyes. He realized then that this wasn't Haley Baker.

Haley Baker was beautiful and sexy, but Haley Baker was also plastic and fake. She presented herself exactly how the State expected her to present herself. She had conformed to such a degree that the real Haley had never been seen except in little glimpses.

The woman in front of Phil wasn't a woman at all. She was a girl. The term woman would suggest a natural maturing, but this girl had skipped many steps along the way. She was a girl. She was afraid and vulnerable and needy. The combination was intoxicating. It made Phil know he was a man in the fullest meaning of the word.

Though there was a sexual component, the feeling was greater than that. It was a feeling of being complete all at once. For his entire life, he had been a jumble of puzzle pieces but never the finished product.

He had known need, but only rarely. He had felt love, but it was so long ago that his mother was only a blur in his mind. He had felt compassion, but he suppressed it as weak. He knew a sense of duty and though he claimed it was a duty to the State, he really only knew a sense of duty to himself. He felt and understood all of this, but also he felt something different. A desire to cherish. A desire to cherish an actual person. To protect her and to love her. But more, there was the desire to be loved and to be needed.

Who really needed Phil Tarsus? No one at all. If he were to die, another Inquisitor would take his place and the world would not even blink.

Except that here was a girl who did need him. Only she was desperate and would take the old, jumbled Phil; the incomplete Phil. He saw this in her eyes and he saw too that she really needed him to be so much more.

Phil bent his face to hers. "No..." she whispered. "Please, no." He ignored her and brushed his lips against hers. So amazingly warm and soft! Just like that, his need grew close to overpowering. It raged in his loins and the old Phil Tarsus would have taken her and then sneered at her in the morning for being easy.

However, this Phil Tarsus was, at least for the moment, complete. He laid down next to her and pulled her close. "It'll be ok," he assured her when she resisted. Gently he pulled her to his chest and set her cheek in the pocket of his shoulder. "This is all I want," he said, running his hand through her hair and breathing her in.

Chapter 27

George's Trial

A soft knock woke Phil seven hours later. He was the type of person who woke instantly; his mind and body fusing back with reality before his eyes would even open.

"What?" he groused, hoping to sound like the colonel might when woken so early.

"You asked me to wake you up at five, Sir. It's five. The clothes that you wished cleaned are ready. I've put them in the hall. Is there anything else, Sir?"

"Breakfast," Phil said, lowering the pistol he had snatched from the bedside table.

"Yes Sir."

Phil waited until the sound of the man's footsteps retreated before falling back onto the pillow.

"Did we really sleep straight through?" Haley asked. She sat up, blinking and rubbing the sleep from her eyes. Suddenly she looked alarmed. "What about the colonel? Is he still in there? Colonel?" she called. "Are you still in there?"

"Where else would I be, damn it. Now open this door. I gotta take a leak."

"Me first," Haley said, taking her sheet and rushing into the bathroom. Phil stood and stretched before he opened the door, making sure to keep well back, with the pistol in his hand.

"Generally I frown on it when my hostages give me orders," Phil said. Heinrich shrugged with one shoulder. He looked a mess; his hair jacked up and going in three directions, and his uniform wrinkled like a dog soldier's. "This morning will go nice and easy if you don't make trouble," Phil told him. "We have breakfast. We pack some food for the road and you get us a vehicle that'll fit all of us, and one with plenty of juice."

"And what happens to me when you get up into those hills?" Heinrich pointed through the window. The coming dawn had just given them the first inkling of an outline. "You going to kill me?" Now it was Phil's turn to give a half shrug. "Because I don't think I want to go to all the fuss of driving up there if you're just going to kill me anyway."

"You don't have an option."

Heinrich went to his closet and began eyeing his uniforms; Phil kept close, his gun at the ready. "I have options," the colonel said, flicking through the wardrobe. "Only in every one of them I end up dead or very likely dead."

"Trust me you'll be dead."

"That's the problem." Heinrich took a crisp dress uniform out and laid it gently on the bed, making sure not let a single one of its sharp creases bend. "I die in every scenario, so why do I help you? Why don't I accept my death right here in camp, knowing full well that you'll never leave it alive?"

Phil didn't have an answer, or at least a good one. "Because you never know what the future holds. Something could happen. Perhaps you could escape."

"Please!" Heinrich groused. "I didn't sleep at all last night. I spent the hours running down every option I had, and 'just hoping that things would work out' was the first one I jettisoned because it was so moronic."

"Then it seems like hours wasted," Phil sneered, not happy with the suggestion that he was a moron. "I spent my time in the arms of a beautiful woman."

The colonel's red face went redder still. He seemed about to explode at Phil's impudence, but then he blew out loudly and the red faded. "I didn't waste my time. I've come up with a plan, or rather I've decide to accept the old man's second option. You tell me everything and then we'll be in it together. I could help you; a full bird colonel carries a lot of weight."

"I don't know. I'll only have your word that you won't try to screw me over. And we both know promises are empty."

"I know," Heinrich said. "That's why I'd put it in writing. I write out a full confession. I say I know everything and agree with it all, whatever it is. Then we mail it before we leave. I can't take it back at that point now can I? We'd be in it together. We might die or we might not, but in this way we have a fighting chance."

Phil rubbed his chin, feeling the sandpaper texture of his face as he considered the colonel's words. "It sounds like a good plan, but I'll need to talk to the others."

Heinrich eyed him strangely. "Why? You're in charge, Inquisitor. You're the leader. They'll do what you say and we don't have time to dicker around. Do we have a deal?"

There was that word again: deal. It was a word he had never trusted before he met Roland. Deal...both sides giving something in order to gain. The colonel gained by having a shot at staying alive, but what did Phil gain? Another ally? If so it was a dubious ally.

What would the others think? Henderson would be upset, because he had no trust, while Roland would be happy because he had too much. Haley would agree with whatever Phil decided and George would agree with her. Which left it to Phil. The old Phil would never trust the colonel.

"Yes, we have a deal."

The colonel beamed.

While Haley showered, Phil told Heinrich everything that had happened to them in the last few days. "They burned down Polk?" Heinrich asked. "I guess it had to happen. That place was ugly."

"I guess it was," Phil replied uneasily, seeing his old self in the colonel's response. That thousands of people burned to death hadn't fazed the man. Phil went on describing everything he knew and everything he guessed about the Commissioner of Justice. With so much supposition, it was difficult for the colonel to write much.

"How about I just denounce him? It'll have the same effect; there'll be a bounty on my head."

Phil agreed to this, if only to save time. He planned to tell the others about his decision concerning the colonel at breakfast, but there always seemed to be soldiers or service personnel running around. Besides, the group of fugitives was in a hurry; he wanted to be out of the gate before the camp really got going.

Heinrich filled out new travel docs for them, ordered up a van, and had extra food packed. When it was found out that the colonel was going to leave as well this caused a touch of surprise among the soldiers, but with Heinrich's power absolute within the camp no one said even a single word. He also made sure to demand that his letter was mailed out as soon as possible, tipping Phil a wink when he did.

Breakfast consisted of porridge and would've been dull, but there was real butter in it and it helped. What helped more was that Haley would look for any reason for her hand to touch Phil's, though she warned him early with a well-crafted look that she wanted their night together a secret.

Roland ate in a nervous silence and then after breakfast, as they waited for the van, he tried to engage Phil in conversation concerning the fate of the colonel.

There were too many soldiers near. Phil gripped his shoulder, digging his nails into the leather skin of the old man. "You need to shut up about that. Now is not the time." He relaxed the grip and put on a fake smile. "I like your new over-alls. They're quite a step up from those rags you were wearing."

Roland looked a hundred times better. He was clean-shaven and pink from a recent bath. His clothes, though not new were newish and smelled pleasant. The old man didn't seem to care. "I prayed to the Lord for you. That you would show mercy on the..."

"The van!" Phil exclaimed, loudly, trying to drown at the man's words. "Thank the...the goodness."

"Thank the what?" Henderson needled. "I swear you almost said lord. Did you get too much sleep? Or not enough? If you know what I mean." He nudged Phil and pointed toward where Haley stood with George. She looked a hundred times better as well; golden haired and fresh.

"Just get in," Phil said, eyeing the old van. He wanted to be angry at Henderson's teasing, but the appearance of the van allowed only trepidation. It seemed composed mostly of rust. "What year is this thing?"

"I think it's an '84," Heinrich said. At Phil's shock, the vehicle was thirty-six years old, and looked it, he added, "It should get us to the Capital just fine. Look at the battery gauge. Ninety-six percent is as good as we have. I asked for this van specifically."

Heinrich supervised the loading of the food, with Phil hovering nearby, and since it would've seemed odd if he didn't, the colonel drove, with Haley sitting in the front passenger seat. Phil still didn't trust the colonel completely and sat just behind him, trying not to let his newly laundered uniform touch anything.

When they had left the farm a few miles behind and the rolling hills had started to bore him, Henderson asked, "So how did everyone sleep?" He didn't wait for a response. "I was a bit lonely, seeing as I was the only one of us who slept by themselves."

"I was alone," said Heinrich.

Henderson ignored him. "Yep, pretty chilly being all alone. How'd you fare, Phil?"

"As if it's your business."

"My you are testy," Henderson teased, holding up his hands in mock fear. "I guess your *sleep* wasn't as good as one would've thought."

From the third row, which he shared with George, Roland said, "You are acting like an immature boy, Mr. Henderson. It's unbecoming."

Henderson ignored him as well. "What about you George? How was snuggling with Grandpa? Did he drool when he took out his teeth?"

"I didn't sleep with him," George was quick to protest.

Like a cat with an injured mouse, Henderson was quick to pounce. "You shared a room. There's only one bed," he said, stating the facts as though the cameraman was on trial.

"Nothing happened," George answered, his sad brown eyes large with a sudden fear. George knew only too well what an accusation of being gay meant. He should have left it at that, but he added, "I swear it. He slept on the floor and we only talked."

242

"Slept on the floor?" Henderson was skeptical and even Phil thought it a strange enough response to look back. This didn't help George who looked back and forth from Inquisitor to under-inquisitor in growing terror.

"I swear!" he bleated a second time.

"It's true," Roland said without a trace of fear. "He seemed very uncomfortable with the idea of sharing a bed, so I slept on the floor. I'm used to it; they didn't have beds up at Polk."

"That's what happened," George agreed, eagerly. "We just talked."

"About money no doubt," Henderson said. "He seems fixated on it like every other neocon. Greedy bastard."

Henderson had only spouted the party line, something that should've been readily agreed to, but the words hung in the air oddly and there was a silence in the van save for the whirr of the engine and the thumping of the tires on the pothole riddled road.

Finally, George swallowed loud enough for everyone to hear and said, "I don't think he's greedy. He doesn't care about money. He cares about fairness and what's right."

That George had the courage to actually stand up for Roland was shock enough for Phil to look back again. The abrupt change in a man so shy had him wondering: what had they talked about?

Henderson had the same question. He stared at George through narrowed eyes. In true Inquisitor fashion he asked, "What did you talk about? Nothing illegal I hope." George's mouth came open, but no sound emanated. This was enough to answer Henderson's question. The under-inquisitor turned on a smile that Phil had worn on his own face hundreds of times. It was an evil smile. It conveyed the message that there was pain in the offing and that he was only too happy to inflict it.

George blanched at it. Henderson dialed it back, expertly. "Maybe we shouldn't go into specifics," he said, turning on the faux charm, going with the slow play. "You know the laws, but old Roland may not be up to date. Which ones did he break? The propaganda laws?" As he spoke, he nodded gently like an old friend in an effort to get George to agree.

Of course, by agreeing, George would be admitting to one count of treason. Receiving subversive propaganda was as illegal as spreading it and both carried the ultimate punishment.

Phil watched this play out and saw that Henderson had learned much as his assistant. Like a chess master, he drove in relentlessly for the mate. If George happened to wiggle out of this question there would be only more coming. It would feel endless and eventually he would break or make a mistake and then would come the pain, and of course, more questions.

The car went quiet as each waited to hear what George would say. So ingrained was it among Americans to not get involved—to avoid even the whiff of treason, that it was indicative that no one else but Roland came to George's defense.

"Aren't we beyond this sort of thing now?" Roland asked. "We are all fugitives. I thought that would be enough to open your eyes, Mr. Henderson."

His blood was up and shark-like, Henderson switched to a new victim without pause. "Beyond what? Please tell me."

Roland only smiled at him sadly and said nothing.

"Beyond what?" Henderson demanded. Where before he'd been calm with an undercurrent of deadly menace, he was now angry. "Beyond what? Beyond the rule of law? Is that where *we* supposedly are now. Because I'm not. I'm not beyond it. This is still America. The perfect America. What is beyond that? The chaos and poverty of your neocon capitalism? Is that what you're after? Or is it the mind control of the religious right, where you either..."

"Stop!" Phil thundered. He'd had enough of hearing exactly how he had always sounded. "This isn't a trial, Henderson. There aren't any cameras, so you can save your canned speech for another time."

"Canned?" the under-inquisitor asked in a deadly voice. "What I said wasn't canned. I believe it with all my heart. America *is* the greatest country on earth. It's perfect. Militarily we are unstoppable. Our standard of living is the highest in the world. We're the only country in the world without hunger, or poverty, or even unemployment. Who else can say that? What other country?"

Hearing this grade school lesson, Phil felt his blood rising and his face grow hot. He was close to replying to Henderson with a punch to his smug face when Roland spoke: "You should answer his question, Inquisitor. You should answer it honestly. What other country?"

Honestly? What did Roland mean by that? What was he trying to say? "No other country could make those claims," Phil answered, honestly. Roland raised his eyebrows in an unspoken: Annnd? Confused by the look Phil repeated, "Really, no could make those claims unless they were lying."

This was what Roland wanted to hear and he smiled, cat-like. Just like that, Phil understood and he matched the smile with one of his own. "Henderson, no other country could make those claims. We're the only one with the balls to lie that big."

Chapter 28

A Question of Innocence

A bark of outraged, surprised laughter erupted out of Henderson. He turned to the window and the passing scenery and shook his head at it. "Wait until we get back. You're done. You are through...and that's ok with me. That's just fine with me, because that's the way it's done, isn't it? That's the way it's always been done. You racked your Inquisitor and now it's my turn. I'll have you up on that rack until my ears bleed from your screams."

The van went deathly quiet, and still. No one dared to budge. The two men sat side-by-side—two scorpions in a bottle—and neither made the slightest move. Henderson was lucky that he didn't. Though Phil was a big man, his years fighting on the Texas front had made him quick and deadly.

Seconds passed and then Roland coughed, just a little clearing of his throat.

Phil's gun seemed to leap into sight on its own and before Henderson could twitch it was pressed against his temple. After a moment of shock, the under-inquisitor affected a bored expression and went back to looking out the window.

"Is that supposed to scare me?" Henderson asked, contemptuously.

"It should," Phil growled. "You've made it clear what your intentions are. I think I would be justified in pulling this trigger."

"What my intentions are?" Henderson said in astonishment. "You act like this is something new to you. We both know I've been intending to denounce you from the day you hired me. That's the way the world works. You did it to your Inquisitor; he did it to his, and so on. Why do you act like this is such a shock?"

Phil held the gun in place for a moment and then it suddenly felt very heavy. It came down. It came to sit in Phil's lap and he could only stare at it. Henderson was right. This was how the world worked. And he knew it. He wasn't connected. He wasn't protected. He was at the mercy of fate, and fate was cruel. Life was cruel. Life was pain. Life was torture.

Isn't there more to life than this?

The question came as it usually did: unexpected and unwanted, and as always unanswered.

After a while Haley spoke, "Is that what we're doing? Are we going back? Is that the plan?"

Even though the question had been directed at him, Phil only looked at his gun, while the others glanced one to the other. Finally, it was Colonel Heinrich who answered. "Yes. We're going to kill the Commissioner of Justice."

"We? We?" Henderson asked, outraged. "What's this *we* you're referring to?"

"I've decided to take Roland's advice," Phil said, still with his head down. "I told the colonel everything. He's with us now."

Roland clapped Phil on the back. "Good for you! I prayed for exactly this. Well maybe not the part where we kill anyone but..."

"Stop! Stop the van," Henderson ordered. "Stop it right now."

There was no use arguing with Henderson's anger. The colonel sighed and brought the van to a stop in the middle of the road. They had wanted to avoid the highway with all of its security patrols and so they were high up in the hills on a two-lane blacktop. There was no traffic and likely none for weeks to come.

As soon as the vehicle slowed Henderson swung open his door and stomped away. Everyone got out and stared around them. The morning was crisp and perfect and smelled of nature. It wasn't something that Phil had much experience with. Mexico had smelled of blood and bullet-casings and dust, while the Capital smelled of chemicals and pollution and rotting garbage.

This was so much better. It was primal and earthen and calming. The smell woke a desire in him for a simpler life; a peaceful life.

It did not have the same effect on Henderson who came stomping right back still in a rage. "Are you an idiot, Tarsus? This man can't come with us. And do you know why? He can't come with us because he's a dead man. The plan was to kill him."

"We're all dead men," Phil replied. He had never holstered his gun, but he did so then. It seemed silly to have it out, seeing as he didn't think he could kill Henderson with it. "If we don't stick together what chance do we really have? Be honest with yourself."

"You be honest with yourself!" Henderson screamed. "We can't trust him. Whatever crap he spewed to get you to keep him around was all a lie."

Phil shook his head. "No. He wrote a letter denouncing Loman. I read it and you saw him order it mailed out."

Henderson gripped his hair in anger and then walked away to the side of the road. Far below them, the sprawling remains of a large town took up a length of valley. It was dead and the early morning light only made it seem more so. The town had been put to the torch. What was left of the buildings was black and crumbling. Nothing had ever appeared so ugly.

The under-inquisitor grunted in its direction as if it had spoken to him and he was answering. "You deserve the death that's coming to you, Tarsus. The weak only deserve death. It's just like what they taught us in school: survival of the fittest. Remember all that? You are a prime example of evolution at work. The weak perish and the strong survive."

"You have mistaken compassion for weakness," Roland said. The others kept well back, while Heinrich stood apart.

"Wrong," Henderson stated bluntly. "Phil, it's a sign of weakness to listen to anything a zealot says. What do they have to offer? Nothing? All you ever get from a zealot are a bunch of promises about some sort of future reward that you only get when you die...*be my slave on earth and I'll pay you good when you get to heaven.* What a complete joke. Religion is the biggest con job in history and you, Phil are buying into it."

"I'm not," Phil replied defensively.

"Then why do you let him go on and on? The only other reason that I can figure is that you're going soft. Turning weak. You couldn't even make it with Haley. You got a girl, naked and in bed and what did you do?" Phil dropped his eyes and Henderson smirked. "You cuddled. Was it sweet? Was it tender?"

"I think you need to shut up," Phil said, his hand itching to go for his gun.

"Not until I've had my say," Henderson replied. "And don't bother pulling out your gun and waving it around. We both know you won't shoot me and we both know why. Because like I said, you are weak. And here is the finest example: Colonel Heinrich. He'll say anything to live. Anything! He wrote a letter? We both know how pathetic the post office is. It could be a month before that letter travels the fifty miles to the Capital. You don't think he'd shoot us in our sleep and go back to intercept it?"

"I wouldn't," the colonel said, quickly. "We're in this together now."

"I wish I could trust you," Henderson replied, though whether he honestly meant it was hard to tell. His bloodlust seemed to have awakened and he looked excited to kill. "Just like I wish I could trust Phil. I'm not going to lie, I need you, Phil. But I only need the Phil Tarsus that walked the halls of the Justice building like a bad ass. I need the Phil Tarsus who was such a terror to the Mexicans. I need the Phil Tarsus who could kill a man without blinking. If we're going to live through this I need that Phil Tarsus. I don't need this wimpy version."

Roland came to Phil and put a hand on his shoulder. "Don't listen to him, Phil. It takes strength and courage to trust. Take a look at us. According to the society in which you were raised which of us, if any, should you trust? Certainly not me. I'm a man who believes in God. And not the colonel; he's your hostage. You can't trust Mr. Henderson; he'll kill for your job. He'll stab you in the back at the first chance. What about Ms. Baker? I'm sorry to say, but ratings mean more to her than life and love. And that only leaves George, the gangly, soft-spoken cameraman who cringes every time you look his way. Do you trust him?"

Phil had never given the cameraman much thought before. He gave a glance his way and of course, George was staring at his feet. "Yeah I guess," Phil said.

Henderson scoffed, "You guessed wrong. If there's anything I learned from you, Phil is that you don't trust anyone. Let's just think about the facts. By a quirk of fate and through no fault of his own George is suddenly an outlaw. When he's caught, the Commissioner is going to have him tortured. They're going to rip him apart and make him feel pain like no one ever has. And he'll talk; he'll spill about everything you ever said and did."

George had begun to quiver in fright and Haley sent a look Phil's way, pleading with her eyes for him to come to George's defense.

"I wouldn't blame him," Phil answered. "Spilling under torture isn't a reason not to trust him."

"Again so wrong. You say you can trust him and maybe you can in the bright light of day." Here Henderson lifted his arms and looked up at the sky. "But what about later? What about when we get close? He knows our chances are lousy; he knows the pain that is waiting for him. Will you trust him then? Because I won't. The question goes through my head: what would George do to avoid his fate?"

"Nothing," George said. His sad eyes were no longer sad. They were wide and unblinking, and he never took them off of Henderson.

"Would he turn you in at the first opportunity, if it meant saving himself from that pain?"

"No...I wouldn't. Please I wouldn't."

"Would he kill us while we slept and toss our bodies in a ditch? Maybe thinking he could try to sneak back alone and rejoin his life."

"I wouldn't. I couldn't."

"Would he run away at the first sign of trouble and leave us right when we really needed him?"

"No! I wouldn't," George wailed. "I swear wouldn't do any of that. Please, you have to believe me. Please, don't hurt me."

"We won't hurt you," Phil assured him for Haley's sake alone. The Inquisitor wore a smile to calm the man, but it sat crooked on his face. Henderson was probably correct about George; the man was pitifully weak; perhaps even dangerously so.

"You know I'm speaking the truth," Henderson said. "I can see it your eyes. And if you can't really trust George, how can you possibly trust Heinrich. He has every motive to kill us and get that letter back."

Roland put himself between Phil and Heinrich. "You can't listen to him. Henderson is exactly what I've been telling you about. He's institutionalized to the point where he can't think beyond his paranoia. The colonel is on our side. Too many people saw us come and go; he won't be able to hide it, which means getting the letter back would be useless to him."

"You can listen to whoever you wish to, Phil, but I'm going to shoot him." Very casually Henderson pulled his gun as he said this. "The colonel runs that camp with an iron fist. He can get that letter back just as easily as he can execute every person who laid eyes on us."

"I wouldn't do that," the colonel said. "Those are my people."

Henderson thumbed off the safety and said, "They're your slaves. Isn't that right, Roland? Didn't you call him a slave master? That's correct, Mr.

Paranoid heard your whole conversation last night and I had to agree with that part."

"I was talking about value," Roland answered. "And speaking of which, he still has value."

"A colonel of Homeland Security only has so much authority and when we get to the Capital, Phil and I will have all we need." Henderson took his eye off the colonel and asked Phil, "So, do I pull the trigger? Or do you want to do it? The reason why I ask is that I'm thinking you need to get back up on that horse."

Phil's head swam. He felt slow and unsure of himself; unsure of who he was anymore and Henderson's mention of a horse only added to his confusion. "What are you talking about? What horse?"

"It's an old expression," Henderson said, easily. Unlike Phil, he seemed completely in his element. He could kill without a twitch to what little conscience he had left. Just then Phil envied that. Henderson didn't worry about right or wrong, good or bad. He was operating as a self-sustained unit, accepting anything he processed as a benefit and destroying anything he viewed as a negative.

"Back in the old days," Henderson went on, "When people would ride horses sometimes one would buck them off. It would make a person nervous of riding, so the cure was always to get them back up on the horse. Now I'm thinking you've been around this crackpot for too long. He's melted your brain with all his talk. He's made you weak. And I believe the way to cure you is for you to get back to doing what you do best." He indicated the colonel.

"We had a deal!" Heinrich cried angrily.

"You can't kill him," Roland added.

Phil turned from them. He turned from them and looked to Haley. She had her back to the men and was gazing down into the valley. "What is that town down there?" she asked. George pretended to look at the town as well, but Phil could see his eyes shifting all around; he seemed close to bolting.

Phil had no clue what the town was. Nor did he have a clue what he would do about his deal with Heinrich, and he had no clue as to whom he could trust, or what he would do about Henderson or Roland. He felt pulled between them, like he was the rope in their game of tug of war. One, his future; the other, his past.

No! Phil rebelled against the very thought. Roland couldn't be his future. Magic gods, fairy spells, voo-doo magic? It was all nonsense. That couldn't be the way he was heading. But all the same, Phil could see Henderson clearly now for the first time. He could see it all—the ease of giving pain, the ability to kill and smile about it. The closed mind when it came to his reality.

"Kill him," urged Henderson. "Your gun is out. Use it." A glance down proved that Henderson was correct. His service pistol was in his right hand, yet he did not remember drawing it.

"You cannot kill an innocent man," Roland warned, sternly.

256

This made Phil almost laugh aloud. Heinrich wasn't innocent. Not by a long shot. He was the commander of what could only be described as a slave camp. His people were more like prisoners of war than citizens. *No one is innocent.* The familiar refrain came to him and only added to his turmoil. Was that right? Was it true that no one is innocent? The Christians thought so and so did the communists.

No one is innocent, his mind sung out a second time with gaining strength. *Yes,* he wanted to shout. *No one is innocent, but so what?* Maybe Heinrich wasn't innocent, but did that mean he deserved death? What about George? He wasn't innocent either, did he deserve death? And what about Phil Tarsus? If anyone deserved death, it was Phil Tarsus.

The thought sobered him and the shroud of chaos that had muddled his mind lifted. "I don't think we should kill him," Phil said. "Put away your gun."

Henderson didn't. Instead, he sighted down the barrel at Heinrich. "No. One of us is going to kill him. For your own sake, I think you should be the one. But if you don't do it, I will for all our sakes."

"Damn it, Henderson! Put the gun away," Phil ordered.

This only elicited a derisive laugh. "Look at you, Phil. What an embarrassment. Who are you trying to fool? Your gun is at your side. If you cared about this clown...if you really cared, it would be pointed at me. Think about it. Where would your gun be pointed if I had a bead on Haley?"

The image of sighting down his service piece, aiming at the sweet spot, the 'lights out' spot just behind Henderson's ear came unbidden and fast. "What's your point?" Phil said.

"My point is you haven't had some great epiphany. The king of the sky fairies hasn't come down and put a spell on you. No, you've just gone soft. You are weak. For some reason you are suddenly afraid of death. You don't want me to kill this bastard, but you won't stop me either."

"You can," Roland said to Phil. "The Lord commands: *defend the weak and the fatherless; to uphold the cause of the poor and the oppressed*: psalm eighty-three. Killing in such a manner is justified, as it is also in the case of self-defense. The Lord gave us life and the instinct to preserve it."

"You see that, Phil? You can do it. You can shoot me," Henderson chided. "So why is your gun still at your side? Is it because you know I'm right about Heinrich, but you've just become too soft to do it yourself?"

"I don't want either of you to die," Phil explained. "We need each other. We have to..."

Henderson made a face, rolling his eyes, and then returned to his aim, thumbing back the hammer as he did. "I'm going to count to three and either I'm going to shoot him or you're going to shoot me. One...two..."

"Wait!" Phil shouted. His hand came up, but it was the wrong hand. It was his left and it was empty.

"Three," Henderson said and fired.

Heinrich crumpled to the blacktop, bleeding from two wounds: one small in the center of his forehead; the other large, a gaping, yawning hole in the back.

Chapter 29

More Than Life

Roland rushed to the body of Heinrich and knelt there with his mouth open and his eyes wide, while his hands acted in a manner disconnected from his brain; they began a half-hearted version of CPR. This accomplished nothing besides pushing more blood out of the back of Heinrich's head, adding to the pool that haloed around him. After a few pathetic compressions, Roland stopped and leaned over the body in misery.

Without looking up he said, "I'll pray for you, Mr. Henderson. I'll pray that God has mercy on your soul."

"Then you better get praying quick," Henderson advised as he swiveled the hot barrel of the gun in Roland's direction. "You're as much of a danger to us as Heinrich was."

"If you keep killing people, there'll be no *us*," Phil said. His body jittered as if the sound of the gunshot had set off thousands of mini-avalanches within him. Yet his right hand was steady as he held his pistol straight out before him. "Now put your gun down, very slowly."

This brought a smile to Henderson's face. "That's a little more like it," he said. "A little more like the old Phil. That's all you had to do; point that gun like you finally mean business. Maybe you're not lost yet." Jauntily, Henderson stuck the pistol back in its holster beneath his black jacket. He then turned his back on Phil and went to the body of the colonel and began rummaging his pockets. Across the body from him, Roland stiffened but whether he did so in fear or anger Phil didn't know, though he guessed anger.

"May the Lord in his love and mercy guide the soul of Colonel Heinrich..." began the old man in prayer.

It seemed more than a prayer. It was as if Roland was using the words to taunt Henderson. If so it worked. The under-inquisitor's face screwed up in disgust and he raised his hand to crack Roland, but Phil cleared his throat. His gun still sat in his hands, but unbeknownst to anyone it no longer felt like a gun to him. It didn't feel to be made of steel and springs anymore. Instead, it seemed to Phil that he held a hunk of stone and he was sure that the trigger had seized and that no hand of man had the strength to pull it.

Just then the gun was useless to Phil, save as a tool to bluster with.

Henderson didn't know Phil's state of mind. He saw only a gun pointed his way, though he didn't seem all that worried. He snorted and, ignoring Roland, went back to his scavenging; pocketing items he found valuable and casually tossing aside those that he didn't. One of the latter, an old pen with a chewed on blue top struck Roland. Unperturbed, the old man ignored the affront and never ceased in his praying.

Standing away from them, Haley had her chin down and from the corner of her eyes, she watched the men. She didn't look at the body. Her eyes flicked away and then back again, indecisively. When she caught Phil looking at her she asked hurriedly, "What do you think that town is? It's freaky looking."

Phil glanced first at the useless gun in his hand and then at the town. "Who knows?"

"I wish I had my camera still," George said, quickly. The body bothered him as well for some reason. "I'd love to capture it; you know the feel of it. It's haunting; you know? But I guess it doesn't matter. They'd never let me show it."

George was right about that. Apart from the endless executions that were televised the only other programs aired never depicted America in any way depressing. And the sight below them, the charred and skeletal remains of what once must have been a pretty place in a pretty valley was nothing but depressing.

"What do you think it is, Roland?" Phil asked; his gun hung at the end of his arm in his slack hand. He was tired of the weight of the thing. For years, he had carried it around and had done nothing with it besides wave it about. Just then, he wanted very much to throw it in the bushes that grew near the road, but he couldn't. He might still need it.

The thought was depressing, the town was depressing, and what Roland was doing was depressing. Praying over a dead man? It bothered Phil and holstering his gun, he asked again in a louder voice, "The town? Do you know what it is?"

Roland ignored the town and the questions; he kept his head bent over the body and went on praying.

Henderson made a sound of weariness and came to the brink of the road and looked down the steep slope at the distant town. "It's a burned up bunch of buildings. You guys act as if there's some mystery behind it." He glanced at Roland and then back to Phil. "Look if you don't want me to shoot your pet monkey, fine. But I'm not going to sit here all day while he prays to the mumbo-jumbo gods. What's he hoping will happen? Does he actually think Heinrich will go to the Christian heaven? You saw his people, they were like wraiths. He was starving them."

Phil didn't exactly know what Roland was hoping to accomplish and he didn't want to. Seeing the old man praying so fervently made him suddenly anxious and he wanted to leave right then and not talk about death anymore.

Or think about it.

That proved impossible. Somewhere in the last few days, he had become suddenly introspective. Before he had met Roland, life had happened to him, and he only floated along reacting as required. Now however, there were questions where there had been none, and emotions where there had been only apathy.

Phil knew that there was something going on within him. It felt like an awakening, or a release. It felt as if something inside him had suddenly been unchained, but what it was he didn't know. He was on the cusp of revelation; there were ideas that seemed just within reach and at the same time far beyond his grasping fingers. The ideas confused him and scared him. He wanted both to know and not to know; there was danger either way.

Standing high above the dead town the secret question came again to him: *Isn't there more to life?*

He felt he had the answer to that now. The night spent in Haley's arms had solidified it. There was more to life; something much greater than what America in all its current "perfection" afforded. Yet exactly what it was he didn't really know; he only knew there was more.

Phil now had an answer to his question, and the answer was no great surprise. The truth was he had always known there was more to life, and the real, secret truth was that the answer frightened him. If there was more to life then it stood to reason that there was more to death, and if that was the case...

"We should get going," Phil said, purposely trying not to follow his own train of thought. Henderson nodded but didn't move. He stared down at the town with flinty eyes.

Just then that old familiar voice in his mind spoke up, however the question had changed: *Isn't there more to death?*

The new question—the new unwanted question had Phil groaning. No, there wasn't more to death! How could there be? Death was death. It was a state of non-being. How could you live after you died? That there was more was so impossible that even magic fairies and gods couldn't make it happen. And what's more, he didn't want it to happen. He had heard of the Christian death—heaven for the good, hell for the bad.

That couldn't be the way it went, Phil hoped. Because what would happen if it was true? What would happen to Phil?

"If we're going to go, we should go," Haley said with another furtive look at the body. George agreed.

"Yeah, you're right," Phil said. He tried to appear blasé but his feet betrayed him and he hurried for the van, wanting to leave death behind him. "I hope there's a map. I'm a little turned around in these hills."

Roland spoke up, "Wait. We have to take care of him."

"Take care of who?" Phil asked. "Heinrich?"

With knees popping, the old man got to his feet. "Yes. We can't just leave him out here. We have to bury him."

Agitated, Haley began to breath heavily and spluttered out, "No...no. That's just...no. Someone else will take care of that. We should go." George agreed, nodding and wearing a queasy smile.

"Who do you think will take care of this?" Roland asked. He spread his arms and indicated the valley and hills and empty forest. "There's no one here but us. That makes it our responsibility."

"Somebody will," Haley stated as though it were fact. "He's dead, ok? He won't care...I don't see why you do."

"Because I follow Jesus' greatest commandment, that's why," Roland said.

Phil was just about to climb into the van to search for a map and now he stopped. *His greatest commandment?* Jesus' greatest commandment had to do with death? Phil blinked once and then ducked in and began to furiously dig through stacks of papers. Whatever this commandment was, he didn't want to know.

"There's a *great* one?" Henderson drawled. To him it was a joke, as it should have been for Phil. He had been taught from a young age not to believe in any of that after-life crap. You lived, you died. That was it. End of story....except Phil heard once again the question in his mind: *Isn't there more to death?*

No! He didn't want that to be the case. No way. He wanted the lights out version; the end of story version. He wanted it all to be gone in a blink. He had seen and been a part of torture for so long that the idea of a land like the Christian Hell, where it was an eternity of pain, haunted his subconscious. However, now it was subconscious no longer.

His anxiety had him by the throat and he said in a high voice, "Let's not worry about any stupid commandments."

Roland's eyes narrowed at Phil's choice of words. "It's hardly stupid. When asked which of God's commandments was the greatest, Jesus replied: Love the Lord your God with all your heart and with all your soul and with all your mind. This is the first and greatest commandment."

That was it? Phil let out a pent up breath in a long sigh. Love God? But...but what did that have to do with death?

Henderson was just as perplexed as Phil. "That sounds not only fruity but also pathetic. And really what does that have to do with burying someone?"

"I'm not done," Roland answered. "Now this commandment seemed so obvious to Jesus, so intuitive that he added a second: Love your neighbor as yourself. Most people interpret it as the golden rule: Do unto others as you would have them do unto you."

Now Phil felt the anxiety creep back in. Would this rule work in reverse? Would all the bad things that he'd done to others...would that happen to him? Was that how it worked in hell?

Isn't there more to death?

Images of a horrific nature flashed through his mind: quivering flesh being pulled off the muscle in long wet strips; tears and blood running together—neither mixing, each separate and distinct; hands without fingers; feet with toes crushed beyond recognition; teeth cracking; teeth splintering; mouths without tongues but filled nonetheless—filled with...

"No!" Phil yelled, strident and hoarse. The images clung to his vision; he had done all that, and much, much more. He put out a pointing, accusing hand to Roland. "No. You're changing it around. It's either one or the other."

"What are you so worked up about?" Henderson asked. "Who cares?"

Phil gave a nervous chuckle. "I don't care. It just seems stupid. You can't go changing things around whenever you feel like it."

"Changing what around?" Roland asked. "It's very straight forward. Let me put it this way..."

"No, we've heard enough," Phil interrupted in palpable anger. There was no way he wanted to hear Roland's explanation. The old man knew too much and was far too convincing.

Concerned, Roland walked over to the van and asked in a low voice, "What's wrong?"

I'm going to Christian hell! Phil wanted to scream.

If there was such a place, no one deserved it more than Phil Tarsus.

Chapter 30

A Change of Heart

Phil's insides, just below his breastbone began to jitter. He shook his head at Roland unable to speak just at the moment.

There is no hell, he thought to himself. There is no God. Death is death. You're here one second and gone the next. Anything else is only fantasy and wishful thinking.

So why was he so scared to hear what Roland had to say? What was it about the old man that bothered him?

He's always right, a voice within him spoke up. It was the same voice that always asked those unwarranted questions. *He's always right, and he always has facts and logic on his side. What do you have?*

Phil had the rote answers he had learned in school. He had his training and his position as an Inquisitor...and he had his faith in the government, which up until two days before had been rock solid. And he wasn't alone. There were over two-hundred million people who believed everything he did. They had to be collectively smarter than this one man was. That had to be true, he told himself.

"What's wrong is that I spent even one minute of my life listening to you spill your crap," Phil growled at Roland. The words felt false on his tongue but he spat them out anyway. "We're leaving. Everyone get in the van."

Roland shook his head. "I'm staying to bury Colonel Heinrich. I'll follow along after."

Leaning on the hood of the van, Henderson suggested, "We should kill him." Roland gave him a sad look then walked away, unafraid. "What an idiot. I'm not kidding you know. We should really do the old crackpot. I could shoot him from here, easy."

Phil looked at Roland pulling up a stone half the size of his head. Was the old man right? Was there a Christian God? Was there a Christian hell? Again, he hoped not, and he didn't want to know, and that meant he had to get away.

"No. Don't waste a bullet on him," he said, shutting the door and buckling his seat belt. "If he wants to stay and die out here alone, then...I guess that's the way it is. Which is fine by me...what the hell?"

When he had turned the key, the dashboard lit for a brief second and then went blank. He tried it again and this time there was nothing. Cursing furiously he popped the hood and stared at the electric engine, though what he was looking for he didn't know. Mechanics fixed cars, not Inquisitors.

Next to him, Henderson looked equally lost; he grimaced at what appeared to be a serviceable engine and then shouted to George, "Do you know anything about engines?"

"No."

"Do you think it's the battery?" Henderson asked. He touched a few of the cables and gave each a wiggle.

Phil shoved his hand away. "Stop that! For all we know you're making the matter worse. The battery was in the green. When we started it was over ninety percent and we've only gone about ten miles...I think. It has to be something else, but I don't have a clue what."

"He might," Henderson said, pointing with a quick finger at Roland. The old man was slowly covering Heinrich's body with the largest stones he could find. With the forest so close, it was hard to find many.

Phil didn't want Roland's help—it would come with a price. There'd be a lecture and then maybe a damning of his soul for all eternity. But what choice did he have. Phil slumped over and laid his head on the cool metal of the van and then gave a sideways nod.

His under-inquisitor called, "Hey Zealot! Get over here."

"When I'm done," Roland answered, hauling another rock.

"Son of a bitch!" Henderson cursed. "I said get your butt over here right this second, you damned..."

"Shut up," Phil said. "He's as stubborn as a mule. You know that. There's only one thing that will hurry him and that's to get the job done with. Go help him. George go help too. There are some stones over here. Haley you can help as well. Go around and point out some of the larger rocks."

"And what about you?" Henderson asked. "What the hell are you going to do?"

Phil screwed up his face in an imitation of anger. "I'm going to try, with all my heart, not to shoot you for your damn insubordination. I'm this close to doing it. Now get moving."

Since all Phil could actually feel was a gut wrenching anxiety, his charade was a bluff, but one that Henderson wasn't quite ready to call and so he stumped off to collect his rocks. He did so with attitude and didn't so much as place the rocks on Heinrich's body as hurl them down on it. The sound was unpleasant and Haley walked further and further away to find rocks for them.

Henderson sneered at her. "What's your problem, Haley? Since when do you get weird over a body? You must see three a day."

"Yeah, but I never like them," she answered, safely behind a stand of prickly bushes where she couldn't see the body. "It's the way they smell; it's gross. And it's how they look fake. You ever notice that? When they're dead they look like broken puppets. But really, I hate their eyes. They look at you. It's like, wherever I go they watch me. They follow me with their eyes. I hate it."

Phil turned to see what she was talking about and there was Heinrich looking at him. His eyes were open, staring and accusing. *It wasn't me!* Phil wanted to yell. *It was Henderson. I'm innocent.*

The eyes kept on staring, probably because they knew that no one was innocent.

Just then Phil felt as though he was going crazy. In the last few days he had gone from one emotional extreme to the other. He had gone from the verge of understanding life to the lowest depths that fear could generate. He had gone from the hell of fire to the warmth of a woman's arms. He felt broken; or torn inside and his retreat to what he knew: being a cold-blooded Inquisitor, was only a mask, and a thin one at that.

And now with the lurking specter that hung just beyond death invading his subconscious it was getting too much. He wanted to run away into the forest and leave it all behind and that was when Haley said simply, "Here's a rock."

She pointed with a fine finger, but instead of looking to the rock he followed that hand to where it met her slim wrist and then he gazed along her arm until he saw her. It seemed that it didn't matter where she wound up, she was beautiful no matter what. Under the trees, with the soft light all about her and her golden hair flowing she resembled an elf or some sort of magical forest creature that he couldn't possibly name.

She took his breath away.

Phil picked up the rock with shaking hands and she smiled. For her the smile was a shabby thing; nervous and thin, but for him it was exactly what he needed. Just like that, with almost no effort, she calmed him.

"Good enough," Henderson said after nearly an hour. The day was warming and he had a fine sheen of sweat around him. They all had worked up a sweat and now that the body was safely hidden away, each seemed more relaxed.

"Just five more minutes," Roland said. "I need to make a cross."

"Phil? Are you going to kill him or am I?" Henderson asked, trying to gel their relationship back to the way it had been. He seemed to have realized, possibly with the killing of Heinrich, that he had gone too far. "I've never met a bigger pain in the ass in my life."

"Give him his time," Phil replied. "If he can get the van working you'll probably be changing your tune. It's a long walk back to the Capital."

It turned out that the van was beyond Roland's ability to fix. "Ok. This is probably the issue," he said. "See that right there. The duct tape. It shows the engine had been jury rigged."

"Heinrich rigged the van to breakdown?" Henderson asked in wonder. "How stupid can you get? Was he suicidal? What did he think would happen to him?"

Roland tried not to appear too superior when he said, "No. The van was rigged to stay operable. This holds the fuse cover in place, but this is fresh tape. I bet it was put on this morning." Roland peeled it away and inspected the fuses. "Here's the problem.

This fuse is blown and judging by all the scraping in the housing I'd guess that it blows frequently. Check the glove box or the trunk for more."

There weren't any in the glove box, but in the trunk there was an emergency kit with a pouch on the outside marked, 'fuses'; it was also empty.

"That really doesn't make any sense," Phil said. "To take a van that needs fuses and not bring any. He even asked for this van in particular..." Phil broke off, feeling a sudden need to draw his gun and just start shooting.

"What?" Henderson asked.

"It's quite simple." Roland pointed in the trunk at the extra food. "If you remember Heinrich helped to load the food. He probably took the fuses then with the intent being to sabotage his own vehicle. It would have been nothing to drop them on the ground as we were all getting in."

"I even saw him move that kit, but I was only worried about a stashed gun," Phil said. "So he takes the fuses from the kit? Why?"

Roland laughed without any humor. "To screw us over in the event that we killed him before we got to the Capital. Which is exactly what happened. That fuse connects the starter to the motor and probably other aspects of the engine. He must have known that the fuse would blow after each use—after each time the vehicle was started."

"Is there any way to fix it or bypass it?" Henderson asked, in a tone that was far less abrasive than his usual. He sounded almost pleading.

"No. At least not with the tools we have here," Roland replied. "There is, however, a ghost of a chance that we could find a fuse down there." He pointed to the burned out town.

Chapter 31

Deductions in Primitive Logic

The distance from where they stood, to the edge of town was five miles in a straight line. The actual distance they traveled was closer to eight miles. Between them and the town lay a maze of hidden, partially frozen marshes, which Phil refused to set one foot in. He had his Chinese made shoes to consider.

He wasn't alone in wishing to steer clear of the marshes. Haley was afraid of them on the basis of snakes and crocodiles, neither of which were in evidence. Henderson wanted to walk on firm ground due to the fact that Phil had forced him to carry the lion's share of the load seeing as he had killed Heinrich in the first place. George needed all the solid footing he could get. He was unaccustomed to walking on anything but concrete and like a drunken stork, fell constantly, tripping over the least stick. Eventually he sprained his ankle and limped along grimacing in pain.

Roland enjoyed his walk and probably would have even if they had slogged through the marsh. He sang to himself or hummed happily and went out of his way to touch different plants and especially delighted in the feel of bark or cold moss. He would skip stones, walk across fallen logs with his arms flung out for balance and generally acted as the world's most wizened teenage boy.

Phil felt a little like a teenage boy himself. He used Haley's fear of imaginary reptiles to keep her as close as possible and he found any excuse to touch her. Every log in their path seemed to require him to take her hand to help guide her over it. And when she put her palms out to touch the furry ends of the tall grass, he would as well and their fingertips would brush.

For him it was magic.

In fact, to him *she* was magic, a very strange magic. She was both a revelation and a curse. Because of her, he'd had his first secret question answered: Isn't there more to life? Which led directly to the second: Isn't there more to death? Revelation/curse. Yet what was really magical about her was that she was also a protection against the curse.

When she was near and he could feel her eyes on him; when he could see her white smile, or even just nudge her shoulder as they walked, his fear of death drew away and became hazy and easily dismissed.

The walk made him happy—an exotic and taboo sensation for him—and because of this he made sure to draw it out. The group strolled rather than hiked. They lingered over lunch and it was near one in the afternoon when they finally made it to the town, only to stand on the edge and contemplate the wisdom of entering.

"How old do you think those are?" Henderson asked. All along a thin strip in front of them were thousands of bleached bones that hadn't been at all visible from the hills. They had been deliberately placed on the ground, though not in any semblance of a formed skeleton. Ribs and vertebrae, tarsals and metatarsals, long bones and flat bones were sprinkled here and there and acted as a border to the town the width of a sidewalk.

Roland fearlessly went to the remains and picked up a broken husk of femur. He studied the head of it, even going so far as to sniff it. "This has been here at least four months...this is January? Yes I'd make it four months, but I'm no expert in forensics."

"Then how do you know?" Phil asked. He too went to the bones and toed them with his shoe. With his time in the war and his position as an Inquisitor, he had seen his share of dead bodies, and had seen literally tens of thousands of bones, but had never once taken the time to consider the factors involved in their deterioration.

"I know that bones found outdoors, in this sort of climate, likely won't last more than two years. This femur is worn, especially the head which is spongy and porous relative to the rest. Four months is only a guess, but I'm not likely off by much."

"There are so many," Haley said in a whisper. With the forest encroaching so close on the town, Phil could only see about a hundred yards to the west of them and counted eight skulls along the border. With the thousands of bones visible, he figured there'd be more.

"It might just seem that way," Roland said. "There are two-hundred and six bones in the human body and some of these are broken. You could spread them over quite a distance. And look. This..." he went to an odd shaped bone and picked it up. "Isn't even human. It's part of a cow or deer skull."

Haley shrank back behind Phil and said, "It's still too many. And those are heads over there. Who lives out here?"

"Heinrich mentioned scavengers," Phil said. At the sight of the bones the magic feeling Haley gave him had been replaced by worry. Not the worry over the fate of his soul, which was eating away at his subconscious, but the fate of his living body, which was more immediate.

"Scavengers?" Haley said, in a manner that made it obvious she equated scavengers to cannibals. "Could they really do all this?"

His gut told him that scavengers hadn't done it, but if they hadn't, who had? The government? In his mind, only the State had the power to kill in such numbers and only the State would be so uncaring of the remains of people. But this begged the question: why would the government do this?

Roland and Phil shared a look. It lasted but a second yet in that time, it reignited the strange bond between them. Roland seemed to read his mind. "People living as scavengers would be too few to kill on this scale. It could be the government doing this.

Maybe the bones are here to scare off the stray scavenger."

Henderson made a face. "I don't think so. First off, why would they, when they could just kill the scavengers? If you ask me, this is primitive, you know? Like zealot behavior."

"The State would never allow zealots to exist in the numbers this would take," Phil answered back. "And you saw what Roland did to Heinrich. That's normal for you people, right?" Roland nodded and Phil went on, "They bury their dead, while the State cremates theirs. What does that leave?"

Roland gazed up at the blue sky, but he didn't appear to be thinking, only enjoying the view. When he sensed Phil growing agitated, he said to him, "You know the answer to this."

If the others weren't all staring at him Phil likely would've been angry. Instead, put on the spot, he stalled. He went to the nearest skull and picked it up. It was incomplete: the jawbone was missing, there were a few gaps in the teeth, and a hole in the back of the cranium. He turned it over and looked inside. Besides a brown stain around the hole there wasn't much to it.

Finally, he said, peevishly, "I don't know the answer. It's why I asked you."

Roland went to Phil and took the skull. He gave it a glance and then handed it back. "You know death. Probably better than anyone alive. The answer is in this skull. What does it say to you?"

The skull held the answers? Phil shrugged. He'd never heard of such a thing before.

"How did the person die?" Roland asked as he bent and examined more of the bones. "Was he stoned to death?"

The answer came quick. "No. There'd be more damage. He was struck on the back of the head."

"Would the State kill in such a fashion?"

Again, Phil answered without hesitation, "No. They could of course, but they don't like to. It's over too fast this way. I don't remember the last time...or anytime I've seen someone killed with a blow to the back of the head."

"And was this person from the Capital?"

Now Phil was slow to answer. How on earth would he know that from a skull? He looked at it closer, felt the graininess of the bone, and even gave a front tooth a wiggle. "Wait," he said. "The teeth. There aren't any fillings in them, not a one. And this tooth is cracked. This person has never seen a dentist before. He's not from the Capital."

"He could be from one of the farms," Henderson put in. "Heinrich bragged about his having a doctor, but not a dentist."

Roland came back with a handful of bones, most of them ribs, but also another skull. "In a camp like that a doctor or a nurse would double as a dentist, at least when it came to crude fillings like these." He held up the skull in his hand and in one of the few remaining teeth was a filling of grey.

Something clicked in Phil's mind. "There were people from two different camps here, which means they aren't really scavengers as Heinrich used the term. Maybe they've formed their own outcast society? Banded together, if you know what I mean. If so, it would likely be primitive. And thus the bones."

"And thus the bones, what?" Haley asked. She stood nudged in near to George and hadn't come any closer to the ring of bones than she had to.

"I'm just saying it speaks to a primitive side of man. Maybe they think it's religious in nature," Phil theorized.

Roland gave him a sharp look. "Wrong. Try again."

Phil gave a little laugh at Roland and was just about to tease when the voice in the back of his head reminded him that he was in no position to make jokes. *Isn't there more to death?*

He hoped not, at least for himself. Yet for these people there might have been. "The bones were put here for a reason. If it's not religious then...it has to be a warning. But to who? Not to the government, that's for sure. If they knew people were out here, they'd come after them quick."

"And that leaves?" Roland prompted.

"Other primitives!" Phil cried. "There must be other bands of...of scavengers, or nomads, or whatever they might be. If I was an outside group of them coming up on this town. I'd be scared of all these bones. There's no way I'd go in."

Roland smiled in acknowledgement of Phil's answer. He then sobered slightly. "You're only missing one thing. In case you don't realize it, you are part of an outside group."

"Yeah, but we're not scavengers," Phil answered back. "And we're not primitives. Hell, we're from the government."

"And that's so much worse."

It wasn't Roland who said this.

Chapter 32

Trials

Before the last word had left the man's mouth, Phil had his pistol drawn and had a bead on a very odd form of a person. He was brown-eyed with a great unkempt mop of thick brown hair that grew wild on his head. He was small, and skinny to the point of undernourishment. His clothes were a shredded mish-mash of uniforms, with the shredding purposeful. He had turned his outfit into a gilly-suit that allowed him to blend in to his surroundings. To add further to his camouflage his face was painted in lines of green and brown.

In his hand, he carried a spear of all things, but despite that he seemed unperturbed by the sight of Phil's gun. He was not alone. Men much like him in appearance materialized around them. All were armed; most with weapons just as primitive: bows, cudgels, axes. A few, however, carried actual guns. At first, they carried them at the ready but not aimed, yet when Phil displayed the quickness of his hand they remedied that and brought their weapons to bear.

"Drop your weapon," the man ordered in an odd accent: 'drop' came out as if had an E on the end, and 'your' sounded like yer.

"No," Phil stated plainly. "Have your men back out of range. So we can talk in peace. If not I will kill you."

"The government man said peace!" the primitive chortled. His fellows did the same, laughing quietly. "There is no peace with the government. There is only war. And as for your threat: no commie can intimidate me, because I do not fear death. What about you? Can you say the same?"

Phil's hands came down. "No."

"What is this?" the primitive asked. "An honest killer?"

"He's getting there," Roland said, striding forward. He held his hands out rather than up. "My name is Roland Gentry. This is Phil Tarsus. Ms. Haley Baker. Nick Henderson. And this is...George. Sorry I don't know your last name."

George didn't offer a second name; he only shook his head and stared around him as if he was about to get sick.

"I am Joseph. Governor of the Dwellers." As Joseph introduced himself, he all but ignored Roland and stared openly at Haley. "Drop what weapons you have, slowly."

Phil let fall his pistol and it thumped to the ground. Next, he drew out Heinrich's piece and tossed it as Henderson did the same with his. Immediately the other primitives rushed forward and bound their hands. Up close, Phil noted that they were exclusively Caucasian and that the tallest barely reached his chin. They smelled of earth.

"What do you plan to do with us?" he asked Joseph.

Strangely, the question quieted the Dwellers, who had been whispering among each other sounding much like the passing of a breeze.

Joseph took a moment to eye them each in turn and then in a formal manner he cleared his throat. "The two men in black I sentence to die in one day. The other two men will be judged by the merits, which they have to offer pending their own death sentence in two days. The woman will be given the option of joining us or choosing release. All contingent upon review by the assembled quorum."

More whispering came from this proclamation. George moaned as if in agony, and asked, "What does that mean? Merits? What's that mean?"

Roland answered so quick that it was obvious that he wanted George to stop talking. "When he says merits he means what we have to offer the people of the Dwellers. As an example they wouldn't kill a doctor or someone skilled in metallurgy." George started to shake his head and Roland smiled in a tight way. "Don't worry for me, George. I may not be as strong and able a fighter as *you*, but they may take me anyway."

While George appeared bewildered, Haley caught on. "Yes, George you don't have a thing to worry about. You're big and strong and...and you can fight. Right George?"

"If they really wanted fighters they would've chosen us, instead of him," Henderson said to Phil in a carrying whisper.

Phil shot him a glare before softening his features. "George, you'll be fine." It was all he could manage to say, because in his mind the dreadful new secret question began to replay itself: *Isn't there more? Isn't there more?*

Joseph had been watching with an appraising eye. He grunted, "Mr. Gentry understands much, but not everything. The Dwellers need warriors, yes. But we also need people who are loyal and who inspire loyalty. Now. Enough talk out here in the open. Bind their eyes."

"May I beg one favor?" Roland asked with an uncharacteristic quaver to his voice. "I have been imprisoned for the last sixty years. I haven't seen the sun and the sky and the trees in so long. May I not be blindfolded? Please? You have nothing to fear. From what you say I will either be dead tomorrow or a part of your group."

Joseph ran a hand over the paint of his face as he contemplated. Finally, he said to the group of primitives, "Who thinks the old man should walk without a blindfold?"

There were thirty or so men gathered around them. It seemed each raised his hand. Henderson saw this and asked, "What about me?"

"What about him?" Joseph asked.

Not a hand went up. Except for Roland, they were all blindfolded seconds later, and then led along a path that went up and down. Sometimes Phil could feel the crunch of old leaves beneath his feet, or the whisper of long grass against his pants, and at other times there was the sound of water flowing. Rarely could he hear their captors; they moved in dead silence. Unfortunately, he heard George the most. The gangly man tripped frequently which must have undermined the little bit of confidence he had and before long Phil heard him weeping.

By then Phil almost didn't care. As they progressed, apathy stole over him. He was going to die. He was part of the government—the worst part of the government and that meant he was the Dwellers' enemy. They would never give him a chance. They would kill him and spread his bones out in the sun to dry.

Isn't there more to death?

Phil was afraid there was. He was going to join countless others in a running, open-air grave. Eventually his bones would be ground under foot. They'd snap like twigs and then over time they'd turn to dust and be swallowed by the earth.

And that was only if he was lucky. If he wasn't then he'd be bound for the Christian hell.

The thought ate at him, turning him weak and then he too began to stumble. Small hands came from either side and held him up and propelled him along. He slouched into the men who helped him until he finally tripped and went sprawling. The ground was dusty and tasted of ash.

He refused to get up. "Why are you bothering dragging me all over the place? Just shoot me now."

One of the Dwellers hissed, "I'm not going to waste a bullet on you."

Hadn't he just said the same thing only a few hours before? Déjà vu struck Phil like a slap. "What do you mean?" he asked. "What?"

"You know what."

He was pulled to his feet and pushed along in a black world of misery. Finally he felt the air change and the group went underground. Here the path evened and there was no reason to fall, yet he still did, because there was also no reason to keep going.

"What a headache!" someone complained. "Take off the blindfolds. They're so deep only the Devil can help them now."

The blindfolds were removed and they found themselves in a natural cave from which a road of sorts had been carved. They followed it, taking turns which seemed random to Phil, but which got them to their destination: a large subterranean amphitheater.

Though it looked as though it could hold hundreds, only a few people loitered about. These people seemed far more civilized. They were unpainted and their clothes were worn but still recognizable as government issue. They were small, and, like the others, had masses of hair. They came over to stare and whisper.

Roland tried to engage them in conversation but they moved away. He also tried the guards who sat nearby making lists of the food and belongings that had been taken from the prisoners. They told him to shut up. He didn't bother trying to talk to Phil and the others, who sat listlessly on the stone floor.

Hours went by. They were given water, but nothing to eat. They grew cold and huddled close for warmth. Haley leaned on Phil and he tried to forget everything but the feel of her, the smell of her. She was the answer to his question: Is there more to life? And every time she was near, the answer was a resounding: Yes! Even there beneath the earth, she was the answer and it gave him a touch of strength.

He felt sorry for the others that they didn't have this same feeling. George cried and couldn't be consoled. Roland meditated a few feet away and appeared lonely. Henderson simmered in anger. Time dragged.

At first, the amphitheater was lit by a few dull bulbs, but after a long while people started to filter in and more lights were added. This seemed to be an excuse for their whispering to become actual talking and the place began to buzz. Eventually the place was filled to capacity and the buzz grew. It made Phil nauseous. His insides rattled and hummed as if connected to a motor. He wasn't the only one. The others sweated and looked green, all save Roland.

Somehow, he kept his composure. He sat silently; sometimes with his eyes closed, sometimes watching the people as intently as they watched him.

"All rise!" a voice called out.

Like a switch, silence reigned where moments before the air had been alive with words running past each other. Joseph strode into the room. Gone was the gilly-suit and paint, only the boots that he wore remained of his old outfit. He wore an old-fashioned vested suit and his hair had been cleaned and was now parted. Still Phil knew him.

He went to what could only be considered a throne in the middle of the room and sat down in it, stiff and formal. At this, everyone sat except the prisoners.

Two newcomers came into the room then; one went to Joseph to stand next to him, the other stood just next to Phil. He refused to smile or make eye contact.

The man standing next to Joseph said, "One by one step forward and state your name and occupation. And here let it be known that lying before the court will be grounds for termination."

"Termination?" Roland asked. "Do you mean the death penalty? If so your threat is quite silly. Two of are to be killed no matter what. Logically it behooves them to lie at every turn."

"Either way, that is the law," the man stated. "And your name and occupation?"

"I am Roland Gentry. I don't have a formal occupation, seeing as I was in prison as of yesterday, but I do work. I'm an evangelist for the Lord. I spread the message of Christ's love to all who have the wit to listen, though currently I'm on a bit of a hiatus."

"Hiatus?" the man seemed unsure of the word and he gave a glance to Joseph who only raised his eyebrows.

"Yes, hiatus," Roland agreed pleasantly. "I'm taking a break. I'm on a spiritual journey you might say."

"So you are a priest?" This caused a stir, but good or bad, Phil couldn't tell.

"I'm sorry. I didn't catch your name," Roland asked.

"My name is Bertrum. I'm the annual prosecuting attorney. And next to you is Edward. He is the annual defense attorney."

"Nice to meet you," Roland said genially. "In answer to your question. I'm not an officially sanctioned priest of any religion, mainly because all religions have been banned. However, I am a Christian and I have a duty to the Lord."

More whispering commenced at this. Joseph asked something of Bertrum, who dutifully sent it along, "You say you were in prison. On what charge?"

"I purposely broke the Anti-Greed laws. I ran a successful business, employing people and servicing my customers satisfactorily, and for that I was jailed for six decades."

"Oh," replied Bertrum. "Next. The girl I think would be good."

"That's it?" Roland asked. "My life hangs in the balance and you only ask me four questions? Is this a sham court? Are your minds made up already and you're just going through the motions? Our attorney has done nothing but stand here for goodness sakes."

Joseph shot a look to Edward who finally spoke, "Our laws and our methods are our own. But to answer your question, yes, most of us have already made up our minds. You are a man of God and clearly learned. There are many with questions concerning the soul. And you're old, no one will vote to kill you. And we always need more women, so the lady is safe. The other three will likely be killed."

"Just like that?" Roland asked in amazement.

"Yes," Edward stated matter-of-factly. "Miss? Your turn."

Haley shook so badly that she couldn't move. Phil went to her and put his lips on her forehead. "You're going to be fine, Haley. They'll probably all fall in love with you, just like I did. If you're not careful they'll make you queen."

Never more in history was the word *love* equal to the word *fool* than in present day America. It was sad but true; those who were stupid enough to display the feeling were always taken advantage of, and along with pity, shame, and remorse, love was universally considered a sign of weakness.

Just then he didn't care what kind of fool he appeared. With his death imminent, it didn't seem to matter.

Haley caught the word and it widened her eyes, but it also softened them. She smiled through her tears and after kissing Phil—just a warm touch of her lips on his, she found the power to step forward and give her name and occupation. They asked her no questions and George went next.

After hearing how the vote would go, he cried and shook and generally made himself out to be pathetic, but it hardly mattered with his death pre-ordained. Henderson refused to say anything and only flipped off the entire room with both hands; moving in a slow circle so that everyone could get a taste of his anger.

Then it was Phil's turn and he was in a sudden hot mood. "My name is Phil Tarsus and as you can tell by my uniform I'm a dirigible pilot. And this person who was flipping you the bird..."

"What the hell is a drig-able pilot?" Bertrum demanded.

Phil shrugged as if the question seemed too obvious. "Someone who pilots a dirigible."

"Answer the question," Edward said under his breath. "He wants to know what a dirigible is."

"It's an airship of course. A zeppelin. A blimp. You ever heard of these?" Phil had seen one only once as a child and thought it wonderful and silly all at the same time. "Well my copilot and I ran afoul of some nasty weather..."

"Enough!" Bertrum cried. "Your uniform is that of an officer of the Board of Justice. Admit it!"

"I bet that carries your version of the death penalty," Phil asked in response. When Bertrum nodded smugly, Phil began again, "So there we were at twenty-thousand feet when a flash tornado took our blimp and spun us like a top..."

"Stop it!" Bertrum strode at Phil and pointed to his collar; at the skull's head and the four sharpened teeth. "That is the symbol of the Board of Justice. Admit it."

Behind Phil, Roland said, "The Lord gave unto Moses ten commandments. Thou shalt not bear false witness was number nine. Do not lie to the man."

A sigh escaped Phil and he let his proud shoulders slump. What good was it to hold anything back? He was as good as dead one way or the other. "This is *not* the symbol of the Board of Justice. It's close. It's the symbol of the Inquisitors."

Bertrum jumped back as if Phil was diseased. Even Edward moved away. All the while a furious hissing came from the crowd. From his throne, Joseph looked on the verge of exploding. His brown eyes were black with anger.

"I ask the quorum that we move up the final action against Phil Tarsus!" he thundered. "Any objections?"

The cavern went quiet and the Dwellers glanced from one to another but not a hand went up. When Roland saw this, he came forward with a hand raised. "I object. You have not even had the vote on whether there should be a final action at all. And now you want to move it up? Is that how your laws are?"

"Actually yes," Edward answered, speaking quickly. "Joseph is the current Governor. He can order things how he wishes and only by a sixty percent vote can the people go against him. Anyone of us can ask for that vote to be taken."

"And has anyone asked for a vote to be taken on our behalf?"

"Not yet," Edward answered. "We haven't had the chance yet."

"Right there!" Roland said loud enough for all to hear. "Every governing body has its rules, otherwise there'd be chaos. Is the Governor allowed to make multiple decrees on a subject, one after another without the opportunity of the people to have their say?"

Heads began to shake among the audience and Roland caught up on it in a flash. "No he cannot! And for good reason. Let's say that sixty percent of you vote *not* to murder Mr. Tarsus. Wouldn't that nullify the second decree of moving up the execution? And wouldn't it be too late at that point?"

Heads began to nod and Roland did too, trying to become one with the people. "That's right. You are governed by the rule of law, not the by rule of the mob, or the rule of emotion, or the rule of a single man."

The crowd began to murmur in agreement. Joseph stood up from his throne in a black rage. "You claim to be a man of God, yet you defend an Inquisitor? They are the blackest of sinners! How can you take up with such filth?"

Roland did not back down. "How can I not? Should a man of God only go about with those who have no sin? If so, I would be a very lonely man. Perhaps you, Governor could show me the men among you who are without sin."

The governor ground his teeth, but could say nothing about sinners. However, he could say something about procedure in his own throne room. "We shall now rule upon the merits of the prisoners. I decree that the woman shall become one of us. Any objections?"

There were none and Haley had her bindings cut. She was taken to the side by a gaggle of women and given something to drink and small hunk of bread, which sat forgotten in her hand. Phil could feel the distance between them.

"On the merits of George Tuney, shall he be one with us? All in favor, raise your hands," the governor said and then surprisingly raised his own hand. Enough of the Dwellers did as well and George, shaking like a leaf at his unexpected release, stumbled to stand next to Haley.

"On the merits of Roland Gentry, shall he..." Joseph began, but was interrupted by Roland.

"I am not destined to be one of you," he said loudly. "I am destined to share the fate of Phil Tarsus. If he is to die by your hand then I will die by your hand."

Chapter 33

The Internal Road

The governor stood for a long time eyeing Roland as the people whispered. Finally, he said, "Then you will die as well."

Roland nodded. "If my death in any way serves the Lord then I will die at peace."

"It's not going to be peaceful," Joseph warned. "From what we know the Lord hates sinners and it will be the fiery pits of hell for you."

"Please do not take offense Mr. Governor," Roland said. "But the Lord loves all his children, even the wayward ones. They just have to be willing to come to him."

Now Joseph smirked. "I will make sure you go to him, that's for certain." He then raised his voice and asked, "By my decree the following people shall be put to death..." He paused and cast another look at Roland. "Shall be put to death tomorrow at midday: Phil Tarsus, Nick Henderson, and Roland Gentry. Is there any dissent?"

Even with Roland added to the mix, no one stooped to voice a defense of a pair of Inquisitors. The room was still and quiet. Joseph let it go on for near a minute and the entire time he looked at Roland, almost begging him with his eyes to reconsider.

Finally, one voice rose in dissent. It was a small voice and trembled with fear. "I dissent," Haley Baker said. People backed away from her. "You said I was part of your group. I'm allowed to do this, right?"

A spasm of disgust splashed across the governor's face before he nodded. "All who oppose my decree raise your hands." Only Haley and George lifted their arms. Joseph went on perfunctorily, "My decree stands. Take them to the cells."

The three doomed men were hustled from the cavern by their guards so quickly that Phil wasn't able to catch another glimpse of Haley. This was a blow to his heart and he marched along the endless tunnels in deepening despair.

Eventually they came to a long, low room that had been rough-cut out from the main tunnel. A single bulb lit it making it very gloomy. Cages lined both walls; they put Phil in the first, Roland in the second, but when they went to put Henderson in the third, he balked.

"Do you mind if I go in the last one?" he asked. "The priest over here is going to talk all night and I just don't want to hear all that mumbo-jumbo."

"If he really is a man of God then you would be smart to stick near him," the lead guard advised. "We get a God type coming through here every once in a while and from what they say, the fires of hell are very hot."

"Scary," Henderson said, flatly. "After this winter I could use the heat." They put him at the end of the line of cages.

Roland wasted no time and asked, "What about you, Phil? Are you up for some mumbo-jumbo?"

Before he answered, Phil glanced around at his little cell. There was a bucket as a toilet and a single bowl of water that reminded him of a dog bowl. There wasn't anything else to the cell. Not even a bed or blanket.

"I don't think so, Roland. Whenever you start in, I just get confused. I don't know who I am or what I'm supposed to be doing. Or even what's right or wrong."

"Yes you do," Roland replied. "Everyone knows right from wrong. The problem is most people lie to themselves about which is which. Just like people lie to themselves about God's reality."

Phil sighed tiredly at Roland's attempt to turn the conversation back to mumbo-jumbo. Without Haley near as his protective totem, the fear of death was hard upon him and he didn't want to hear Roland tell him about Christian hell.

"Do you think Haley will be ok here?" he asked instead. "I just don't like the way Joseph had an eye out for her. I'm surprised he kept George around. That was at least good of him."

"I wouldn't say that was good of him, necessarily," Roland replied. "Don't get me wrong, I'm glad George has found a safe refuge—he'd never make it where we're going—but that doesn't mean Joseph had pure intentions. I think the opposite. He chose George to throw a bone Haley's way. To get her to see that even though he's going to have the three of us killed, he's really not such a bad guy."

Phil hadn't thought of that and he kind of wished Roland hadn't pointed it out. It was one more thing to worry about. "Damn," he said without much emotion. "You're probably right. Say, what did you mean when you said, *he'd never make it where we're going?* Where do you think we're going?"

His subconscious mind answered: Hell.

Roland had a different response. "We're going to the Capital. Isn't that the plan?"

"The Capital? Are you alright?" Phil asked, giving Roland a close look, checking for signs of a break down. There were none. The old man appeared distinctly unruffled. "We're not going to the Capital. We're not going anywhere. We're going to die...tomorrow."

"We won't die tomorrow, at least not here. I have faith in the Lord and you should as well. Did he not release us from prison? Did he not save us from a horrible death?"

"Those were coincidences, not miracles," Phil said. "We got lucky." At this, Roland only smiled in that frustrating way of his. The smile said he knew better. Phil's blood grew hot at the sight of it. "You know, I don't get you. Everything I believe can't be the opposite of what you believe. It's not possible."

The old man's smile grew wider. "It's possible. Even the things we think we agree on, we do so for opposite reasons. In your society you have taken the single greatest authority: God, and you've replaced him with the weakest of creatures: man."

"That's silly. Man is not weak."

"Man is the weakest creature both mentally and emotionally. A squirrel knows what a squirrel knows and you'll never change his mind about it. Nor will he ever cry about what he knows or feel remorse over his decisions."

"I guess so," Phil conceded, not bothering to argue the fact that man was also far more complex compared to a squirrel. He just knew that Roland would only tell him that something more complex did not necessarily make it better. "But who cares if God's been replaced. It shouldn't lead us to be such opposites."

"Of course it should. My beliefs are absolute and unchanging, while yours are based on the whims and shifting consensus of billions of people, each looking to satisfy their own needs and desires. Even your science can't be trusted. Almost everything you think you know is based on research that was either fund driven, politically contrived, or simply a fad. And that was before the communist took over. Now they simply just change facts to suit themselves. That we have opposite views seems logical to me and I don't think it could be any other way."

"I guess," Phil replied dubiously. "I mean I know the government changes things. They do it and we're not supposed to react. We just all play along. Two summers ago there was this big heat wave in the Capital. They said it was global warming due to coal use and they cut back on our electricity ration. This year it's been a bad winter. They called it global cooling and somehow they blamed it again on our over use of coal and again they cut back on our ration. They act like we're morons and are supposed to believe everything they say just because they're the government. Like everybody else, I only smile and act like everything is just normal."

Roland pulled off one of his new boots and inspected a blister. He grimaced at it. "That's exactly my point. There's God's truth and then there's the truth of man."

"I was talking about the government."

"Which is made up of men. Men who pervert the truth for their own ends. God would not do that. He is truth. God is light and in Him is no darkness at all. Wait...I keep forgetting you don't want to hear all this mumbo-jumbo."

"I don't. You're right. It's all nonsense. And besides, I just don't understand how you could believe some of it. I mean, you talk of love, while at the same time everyone around here talks of burning pits of fire."

"This sounds much like curiosity to me."

Phil spluttered, "It's...not. Not really. It...it passes the time." Their cells were silent for some minutes and then Phil demanded, "How can some sky fairy create the universe? Tell me that?"

Roland shook his head, disappointed. "You only embarrass yourself when you use terms like sky fairy or flying spaghetti monster. It's juvenile to call names rather than to have a logical debate. And secondly, I should ask you about your *beliefs*. How can you believe that the universe just popped into being all by itself? Scientifically it's flat out impossible. Thus the universe had to be created by something greater."

"Let me guess...God?" Phil shot back. "I could ask the same about him. Where did God come from?"

"The age old question. I have two answers for you," Roland said with a smile. "One: I don't know where he came from, and maybe I'm not supposed to know. Not yet at least."

Surprisingly, Phil was disappointed by Roland's response. "That's not much of an answer."

"It's as valid as yours," Roland replied. Phil began to splutter again and Roland held up a hand. "I haven't given you my second answer yet. Number two: The concept of God is of a being who is all knowing and all-powerful. He is perfect in every way. By that definition nothing is impossible for such a being, including—one—always existing. *I am the Alpha and the Omega, the First and the Last, the Beginning and the End.* Or two—he willed himself into being."

"What? No, that's impossible."

"It's not impossible for a perfect being. Neither of my answers contradicts my beliefs. You cannot say the same for your beliefs."

"Beliefs?" Phil said. "That's the second time you said that. I have facts; you're the one with the beliefs."

Roland shook his head. "No, we both do. Your belief in the creation of the universe is an act of faith since it's not an act of logic. Science tells us that matter simply cannot create itself out of nothing. You deny that God created the universe; ergo it must have created itself, which your very science states is impossible. In other words you believe that which you don't believe. You see the difference between our faiths is that mine is logically possible, while yours is not."

How was this being turned around on him, Phil wondered. "I'm not a scientist," he replied. "So maybe I can't argue the facts. I just know that no one believes what you do, not in America."

"Do numbers equate to the truth?" Roland asked. "Because if so we'd never have progressed beyond the concept of the flat earth. Numbers don't matter. Faith does. Trust does. Do you trust your instincts when your soul cries out for something more?" Phil drew a sharp breath and Roland cocked a white eyebrow at the sound. "You do, don't you? That's why you're talking to me when you know I'll only spout the mumbo-jumbo. You want the answer to other age old question: Is there anything more to life?"

"Yes." The word was dry as dust. It was one thing to say it to one's self, to admit that there may be something greater than the State, but it was altogether different to say it aloud. It was terrifying. Phil wanted to cringe. He wanted to throw up a shielding arm.

Roland didn't gloat. He didn't cheer or sneer, as Henderson would have. He only nodded sagely as if there could've been no other answer. "You are not alone. Every person who has ever walked the earth has asked the same question."

"And you think the answer is God?" Phil asked.

Roland shook his head. "No. I don't *think* the answer is God. I *know* it. I know it! I know it! I know it with all my heart. Tell me, Inquisitor, what do you know with all your heart?"

Phil had been standing at the bars and now his mouth came open and he started to blink. Nothing came to him. A few worn facts from school, history...and geography...nothing that could compare to Roland's fact; Roland's absolute certainty.

The old man read his expression perfectly. "You don't know anything with such surety, because you can't. Because of how you were raised, you have more anti-knowledge than real knowledge, but you can't deny the heart! That's where that question arises. Right here." He gripped his chest through his shirt, rubbing it as if it was more than thin cotton over tired muscles.

"This in here is true fact," Roland continued. "A fact that can never be altered. God is here. He is right here!" Roland thumped his frail chest. "And I rejoice in that knowledge as much as I weep when I meet an unbeliever."

Roland dropped his boot and suddenly scrambled to his feet. He went to the bars and took Phil's hand. "Phil, ask me where I'm going when I die."

"Why?"

"Just ask me!"

Phil huffed, "Ok. Where are you going when you die? Heaven?"

"Yes! Yes, heaven! Angels, cherubs, clouds, harps, angels, bliss...utter bliss. That's where I'm going. The very idea fills my heart with so much joy. It makes me complete...no that's a poor word. Perfect. I feel as close to perfect as humanly possible." He sighed and let his shoulders drop. "Yes, I feel perfect. What do you feel, Inquisitor?"

Not perfect. He didn't feel even close. But he could tell Roland did, and always had. From the moment Phil had met him, the man had been so eerily calm. Fearless even. Which only made sense if he believed he had the Christian heaven to go to if he ever died.

"What happens if you're wrong, Roland? What happens if you die and it's just nothing? No angels, no harps, no bliss. What if you're just gone?"

"You're not the first to ask me that. What you really want to know is do I think I'll have wasted my life if there's no heaven? Not at all. Having heaven—even the possibility of heaven as a reward has given me peace of mind and hope. I've been in prison for sixty years and I still have hope. Without God there is no hope. It would be the saddest thing to live your life without the hope of heaven. You eat and drink and have sex and sleep. When it starts to wind down you just sort of wait for it to end. I can't imagine a life like that. Can you?"

Phil walked away. If he could have left his cell, he probably would have. Instead, he went to the far corner and leaned there. He was just a shadow in the shadows. In the dark, the terrible images came back to him. They had grown more distinct: the blood redder, the tongues at the end of his forceps a glistening pink, the molars clicking and bouncing on the tiled floor, a lovely ivory.

"Yeah...I can imagine there being nothing at the end," Phil whispered. "It's what I want."

"Why?" Puzzled, Roland laughed out the word.

"Because even if there is a Christian heaven, I wouldn't be allowed in. I'm an Inquisitor. There's nothing worse. There's nothing lower. Nothing. You saw how they all reacted. They hate me...everyone hates me."

"I don't hate you, Phil. But I understand. You deny God out of fear."

More images came to Phil, more screams. He shoved them aside and tried to answer despite that his tongue had gone dry. "Yes, because if there's a heaven then there's a hell. And that's where I'll go and they'll do unto me right? They'll do to me what I did to all of them. They'll tear out my eyes and hammer my toes and I'll scream and scream and..."

"Phil!" Roland reached out through the bars. "Come here," he said.

"There's no point," Phil said in a choking voice. He sniffed back tears and then laughed in misery. He was crying! What a way to start on the road to hell; crying like a baby.

"Let me explain about hell. There are no demons or fiery pits. Hell is the absence of God. Look at this world the State has made. It has removed God and all that is left is misery and hate and suspicion..."

Phil barked out, "And torture. And pain. And tears." He sniffed his own tears back a second time and ran his sleeve across his face. "The last guy I t...t...tortured, he told me God wasn't in me."

"He was wrong," Roland said. "Where there is love, there is God and I know..."

"That's what he said!" Phil interrupted in a shout. "The man I killed, Stephen Crown. He said that about love. Did you know him? Did he talk to you? No, wait...you couldn't have; you were in prison. So how did you know?"

"Truth is universal and no one man may hoard it as his own," Roland answered.

"Universal..." Phil whispered. It was universal, only it wasn't. He was the exception. He was the angel of death. He was merciless, he was pitiless, he was godless. "Crown wasn't wrong about me."

"I believe you. The Phil Tarsus that I first met was devoid of love," Roland accused. Phil nodded, a bare motion of his head to the vertical. Roland caught the movement and said. "That was true then, but is it true now?"

The question, though spoken softly, had great power. It swept away the horrible images of torture that had been playing nonstop in his mind and drew forth a new one: Haley Baker as she looked in the forest hours earlier, pointing out a rock. This wasn't the made-up, sharp angled, perfectly coiffed Haley Baker who smiled her way through executions.

This Haley Baker was real; scared but trusting, beautiful but naturally so, her blue eyes were soft, not the hard diamonds that normally hid her soul. This Haley Baker was so much more.

"I have love," Phil admitted. There could be no denying it to himself now. Not with his heart swelling in his chest at the thought of her.

"Then you have hope," Roland said. "And you have God."

Chapter 34

One of the Many Forms of Death

There was no sleep for either of them that night. Roland talked, and taught, and explained about God until he was hoarse, and Phil soaked it in despite that it all seemed so foreign. He knew that somewhere in all those words was the key to life and death, and maybe salvation. Yet when new guards came to replace the old, bringing with them a breakfast of a few crusts of bread, he was still struggling internally. The chains that bound his soul had not loosened and in some ways had grown tighter.

There were some concepts that he just couldn't grasp. Forgiveness being one—it was antithetical to the State's teachings of Darwinism. Another was the role of Christ—why was he even needed when God was so powerful? And lastly: the idea that God had a plan for each of them.

"You keep mentioning that he has a plan for each person," Phil said. "That doesn't seem right, unless his plan is for most of us to be miserable."

"Hardly," Roland said, and drank heavily from his bowl. The water tasted like iron, however the old man acted like it was fine wine, smacking his lips before answering, "God actually plans for us all to be happy if that's how we wish to live our lives. He has given each of us life as a gift to do with as we please, with the only stipulation being that we must live with the consequences of our actions."

"Consequences," Phil muttered through gritted teeth. For years, his actions had been unrestrained evil. That was the burden of Phil Tarsus. Those were the chains that bound him internally and held him back. During the night, Phil had grudgingly accepted what Roland had to say—there was a God. For most of the criminals that Phil had killed this had been a joyful revelation. It made Phil's intestines run afoul of themselves.

"Yes, I'm sure you are starting to understand consequences more than most," Roland said. "We have free will and that is a wonderful gift, yet it can be a terrible one as well when we misuse it. And sometimes our actions have far reaching consequences that may outlive us by hundreds of years."

Phil couldn't bear the thought of anything in his stomach just then and he handed his bread through the bars to Roland. "Hundreds of years?" he asked, skeptically. "When they kill us, no one will remember me tomorrow. I don't think I affect the future at all, and you've been in prison your whole life."

Roland waved away the crust. "You may want it for later. And yes people's actions affect the future, sometimes subtly, sometimes not so much. Take America as an example. We are still dealing with what our grandfathers laid on us. And if we don't do anything our children will be burdened by our inaction."

"Are we supposed to do something about it?" Phil asked in a low voice. "Is that God's plan for us?"

"I really don't know," Roland answered. "I don't know God's mind. I just know that we aren't destined to die here. I am firmly certain that it's our destiny to go to the Capital; after that our conscience will direct us."

"Go the Capital and do what? Kill Loman?" The idea sent a fresh wave of panic rippling along Phil's nerves. "I don't think I can. After last night...after everything you've said about God and love and the commandments, and the burden of my consequences...If all that's true, I can't kill any more."

From a few cells down, Henderson spoke for the first time since he'd been locked away. "You are such a joke, Tarsus. How many people have you tortured and sent to their deaths? Four hundred? Five hundred? If you have a soul, there's no saving it. I bet it's so black, light can't escape...so why do you suddenly care? Have you ever thought that maybe this is God's plan for you? That he wants you to be a killer? That he wants you to kill Loman?"

"Don't listen to him. He's thinking only of himself. However..." Roland paused in anguish. "I fear there will be more death to come, but you must refrain, unless it's to protect others. As he said, your soul is stained. But...but I don't know what part we play. Maybe it will only be our role to help undo the

314

sins of our fathers. Maybe our role is to show others a better way. Maybe we die and we'll never know."

Phil began to rub his chest where a pain had begun to grow along with the fear. "I wouldn't know how to undo things...I don't even know how America got the way it did; I mean other than greed. That's what they taught us in school. That the neocons were so greedy that the people finally rose up against them."

"It wasn't greed," Roland said. "It was shame that changed America."

"Shame? Because you were all so money-grubbing?" Phil threw this out simply to keep Roland talking; when there was a pause in their conversation, even a second's worth, Phil's dread didn't creep back in to nag at his mind, it roared in like an invasion

"They've really got you brainwashed," Roland replied, annoyed. "We've talked about this: no it wasn't money-grubbing. The liberals discovered the one great weakness of a moral society—shame."

"Is that a sin?" Phil asked before Roland could draw another breath. His mind was now constantly trying to categorize actions into sin/not a sin, afraid of adding to his soul's burden.

"No, it's an emotion. One that's a powerful catalyst for action. Let me give you an example: We'll take the gays for instance. The liberals promoted them at every turn..."

Phil raised a quaking hand, stopping Roland. "That's wrong. If the liberals changed into the communists, then you're all turned around. The communists hate the gays."

"They do now, but they didn't then. Just like every other totalitarian government, America turned on the people who put them in power. With the Soviets, it was the students, the Jews, and the intellectuals. The Nazis killed their own thugs, the SA or the Brown Shirts. The Cubans killed their own revolutionaries. The Chinese..."

Roland paused as a new group of the Dwellers came in. They flung a pair of torn-up pants and rat eaten shirts to each of the prisoners, and one among the men said, "Strip all the way. We don't want to get blood on all your finery. They'll be needed when you're gone."

"From rags to riches to rags again," Roland said, peeling away the work uniform he'd worn for only a day. "That's the story of my life." He laughed as he said this. Phil couldn't laugh. The pain and fear sat like a heavy stone in the middle of his chest.

The men, like all the Dwellers they'd seen, wore a mishmash of government issue clothing that were years out of date. They exclaimed over the black uniforms of the Inquisitors, holding them up to the single light, and each cast greedy glances; especially at Phil's shoes. Roland ignored them and plopped back down in his new rags completely at his ease.

"Where was I?" Roland asked. "Oh yes. The communists hating the gays. You're confused on the subject because you don't understand the sequence of their thought. When they were weak the liberals destroyed the dominate culture by dividing it in any way they could. Black against white, gay against straight, woman against man, theists against atheist, poor against rich. It was a constant agitation—a constant friction. And always they used shame as the principal tool."

Cold without his uniform and starting to shiver, Phil sat in a ball on the rocky floor. "Shame is a weak emotion. Wouldn't anger have worked better?"

"The common response to anger is more anger," Roland answered back. "Anger is primal; shame is evolved and insidious. The common response to someone shaming another is guilt. We were shamed into giving up our laws, our borders, our religions, our constitutional rights, even our culture. The left made us ashamed of being Americans. It seems so impossible now. We were the greatest force for good the world had ever seen. No country was ever so strong militarily, yet we never conquered. We protected the weak. We fed the hungry. No country was ever so generous. Yet we weren't perfect and the liberals made the shame of that the instrument of our downfall."

"So the liberals just used the gays to create shame?"

"To destroy the dominant culture, yes. A culture is made up of a common language, a common history, and common values. They used illegal immigrants to wear away language. They used revisionists to distort history, and they used gays and criminals and the poor to distort values. And always shame was the tool.

"Who could deny a poor immigrant access to services just because of a language barrier? Did they care that this kept immigrants as permanent second-class citizens? No. Who could consider the actions of the founding fathers as brave or noble in any way? They owned slaves and that made them evil. Everything else they had done was moot. Who could deny gays the right to marry? Thousands of years of history didn't matter in the face of love, right? And who could deny criminals their luxuries in prison? TVs, weight rooms, cigarettes, conjugal visits? They were people too, right?

"All of this to wear down society until there was no dominant culture anymore, until people grew ashamed of their flag and their country and their history."

Phil shook his head at all of this. "And how do you think we can fix it? It's too much."

"Maybe it's too much for two people, however if we teach and try to bring God back to a Godless world, maybe it won't be. Maybe we can bring others to our side."

At that moment, another man came in and stared at the three prisoners driving all thoughts of America and gays and the culture right out of Phil's head.

The man was older than most they had seen, with grey running through his brown hair and wrinkles lining his face. Very solemnly, he said, "It's time." The room went quiet—all save Phil's heart, which began to pound so loud he could hear it as a drum in his ears. Without being told, the guards bound the prisoner's hands behind their backs and the group began a slow march back through the dim caverns.

Despite the unhurried pace Phil's pulse ran a sprint within his chest and his breath came ragged from his throat. Henderson was quiet, sulking in anger, while Roland walked along easily and continued to chatter to ease their fears. It didn't work. Ahead Phil could hear what seemed like hissing; it sounded like a thousand angry snakes. He began to stumble.

"Put your faith in the Lord," Roland said. "We will not die just yet. Though you should be prepared, for you do not know the day of your death. Jesus said: It will come like a thief in the night. So you must set your soul to rights."

"I can't. I can't do it. Henderson was right. My soul is black. I've done too much." Phil said this and then let out a moan of fear. The hissing had become the whispering of hundreds of people and he imagined that they were his victims come to pass judgment. How many faces would he recognize? Would they be the crushed-in faces that his victims wore at the time of their deaths or would they be whole?

Henderson groused, "Tarsus, you are so damned weak! So pathetic."

Phil understood Henderson's anger and had it not been for Roland he would have been angry as well. Generally, Inquisitors had no other emotions. They did not have fear, they caused it. They did not have love, they used it. They did not have joy or sadness for those were signs of weakness. Inquisitors had anger.

Without it, they had little left to them. "I am weak," Phil admitted. At the moment he felt tiny and confused, trapped somewhere between Roland's surety of heaven and Henderson's anger over his knowledge that it didn't really exist.

Roland stopped and the entire group came to a standstill. The guards were puzzled and because of his age, they only gently nudged him to get him going again. He ignored them and turned to Phil. "Have I spoken all night in vain? You are only as weak as your faith in God. Trust in him. Trust your soul in him. God forgives those that seek forgiveness."

Before Phil could find his tongue to answer, Roland demonstrated his own trust in the Lord and strode forward into the same rock-hewn chamber they had been in the evening before. It was filled with eager, hating people.

When Phil stepped into cavern, one among the Dwellers shouted "Devil!" This set off a chant of, "Devil! Devil! Devil!" The people pushed forward in a mood for blood and the guards only just held them back.

Without fear, Roland went up to the crowd and protected only by a gentle smile he parted the masses and passed through. Henderson tried to follow closely in his wake but the people closed in. He cursed them and spat; they replied in kind and his fury grew animalistic. He lashed out, kicking and biting anything in reach.

Phil went last. At first, he had two guards moving him along, but they fell back, afraid of the ferocity around them, as the people became a mob. Phil was the embodiment of everything they hated and feared. Blows rained down on him and he hid his face, tucking his chin down. Air became hot with the fire of their rage and he found his chest laboring for breath. In panic, he began to run, bouncing off people, or smashing full into them. They became only a blur of fists and snarling teeth. He had no idea which way he was supposed to go, but somehow found the edge of the crowd and staggered up to Roland.

"I can't do this," he cried upon seeing the old man. "I can't! I'm too afraid."

"Have faith. God forgives," Roland said, as the guards seem to materialize from the mob. They turned the three prisoners around and forced them to their knees.

"How?" Phil asked in desperation. The Dwellers surged at them, only to be held back by the desperate guards. Fights broke out all around them, but Phil didn't care; his soul was on the line. "How does he forgive? You make it sound too easy. Especially...especially for people like me."

Roland nodded in agreement. "You're right, Phil. Forgiveness is not easy. It's never easy and the greater the sin the more difficult it is. It's the same when asking for forgiveness. It can't be casual. It has to come from the heart. Are you sorry from the heart?"

Before Phil could answer, Henderson snorted and yelled over the screaming crowd. "He's not sorry, he's only afraid. He's afraid of all these crazy people. And he's afraid of the Christian hell. He doesn't care about the people he's hurt."

Was this true? Phil couldn't tell. Not then with the crowd shrieking, and surging, demanding his life. He couldn't tell one emotion from another.

Roland saw the confusion and said, "It's alright to feel more than one emotion. You have an overwhelming fear of death; that's natural. But beneath that, do you feel the sorrow, the regret for what you've done?" It was so hard to think beyond the crowd that Phil couldn't say a word. Distressed, Roland put his face in Phil's and said, "Think of the last person you wronged. What if Stephen Crown were here. What would you say to him?"

Phil pictured the man's face as it looked when he had entered the execution room: he was wild eyed and blubbering tears. The pain in Phil's chest grew; he could barely breathe.

Henderson laughed at Phil's reaction and asked, "How bout this? What would you say to Crown if he showed up here with a rock in his fist? That's the question."

An image of Stephen flashed in Phil's mind: the man was small and weak. He was a skinny little thing. He wore the black uniform of the Inquisitors and it swam on his thin frame. In his hand was a stone; an old dirty one and at his feet was a pile of many more. The look he wore on his gentle face was of burning hate.

"I know what you'd do," Henderson laughed. "You'd fall to your knees and whine and cry and beg him not to hurt you. Just like he did."

Phil looked at Henderson's evil face, but saw nothing as his vision passed clear through, remembering how Crown appeared right before his death. He had been calm...maybe more than calm. He had been confident, and when the rocks rained down, strangely silent.

"You're wrong, Henderson," Phil said. "At the end he didn't whine or beg. He...he accepted what was happening and he knew..." What had he known?

He had known God, Phil realized.

At that moment, a thunking sound echoed in the room and the Dwellers went silent and withdrew. Joseph had arrived; he passed through his people carrying a heavy miner's pick; both ends of which were stained the color of rust; though it wasn't rust. It was old blood. Blood that had purposely not been wiped away. Phil kept some of his own tools in exactly the same state; he always thought the terror it elicited to be delicious.

Henderson saw the blood and went green. Phil felt calm. "I know what I'd say to Crown if he were here," he said. The room had gone so quiet that everyone heard, though no one understood.

"Be quiet," Joseph ordered as he came to stand before the prisoners. In his eyes he held the finality of judgment. "Your time of death is on you," he said. "Who shall go first?"

Phil knew perfectly well what he would say to Stephen if he were there standing before him alive and ready to kill.

"For the sins I've committed, I deserve death," Phil said to Joseph. "Kill me and know that I hold you blameless, and if what you do is a sin; for my part I forgive you."

Joseph stared as if Phil had spoken a foreign language, while Roland smiled and said, "You are not an Inquisitor any longer. You are now a child of God."

Chapter 35

Free to Pursue Death

It took a few moments, but then Joseph reacted in self-righteous anger. "You forgive me? How dare you get off thinking you can forgive me. I've done nothing wrong, unlike you, Inquisitor. We are at war!"

"We are not your enemies," Roland answered, because Phil couldn't. Just then he was beyond arguing. He was in such a peaceful state that the crowd and the blooded pick barely registered on his conscious. He could be forgiven. His sins could be washed away. There was hope for his soul.

"Liar," Joseph accused Roland.

"I do not lie. We have a common enemy. The very government you battle has put a death sentence on us."

"They're with the government. He's a liar!" cried someone from the crowd. The people began to chant: "Liar! Liar! Liar!" Joseph hefted his pick and demanded more enthusiasm from the Dwellers, but the chanting didn't last more than a minute.

A commotion and a shouting sprang up from the back of the crowd. A small group of people were pushing a cart of some sort through the mob. Haley and George were with them. Timid of the crowd they kept close to the cart.

"What is this...who is this?" Joseph asked when he saw what was laid upon the cart.

"It's Heinrich!" someone squealed. "The colonel from 332. He's dead!"

The amphitheater erupted in a cacophony of cheers. People danced around the mangled corpse, while others rushed up to spit on it. Joseph didn't take part in the sudden celebration. He went to one of the men who brought the body in and began to question him. The man pointed at Haley and then towards the Inquisitors, but spoke under the noise.

After a moment Joseph stood apart, thinking, letting the people revel in their victory. When the crowd began to cool down, he came back to the center of the room. "Quiet! Quiet! I want answers. You, Priest," he said, pointing at Roland. "How did this happen? Why did you kill one of your own?"

"I told you, we are not your enemies. We are...hold on. If you don't mind...my knees. They're killing me. I need to stand." Joseph waved to one of the guards who helped Roland up. "And my hands, if you don't mind. I assure you I'm harmless."

"No. Leave him tied," Joseph said as the guard had begun to work at Roland's bindings. "This corpse is meaningless. You are still slated to die."

"But we are not your enemies," Roland repeated.

Henderson heaved himself to his feet and said, "I wouldn't call them friends either. Not the way we've been treated."

"Friends? Who said anything about friends?" Joseph asked in a rage. "You are Inquisitors! You don't deserve the consideration of a guest. You deserve only death. Ask him, he said it." Joseph pointed at Phil.

"I do deserve death," Phil said. Neither the body, nor the jubilant crowd had affected his state of calm. It was an unbreachable wall. He had the surety of knowledge that no scientist ever felt. God loved him. Despite being the worst person in the world God loved him and would forgive him. "But I also need to live," he added.

Joseph almost went berserk in fresh outrage. He stomped around gripping the pick with both hands. "You need to live? I had a brother who was tortured to death by Inquisitors. He needed to live. My father was stoned to death after his torture. Didn't he need to live too? Ronald over here had his entire family killed by Inquisitors. Every one of us in this room has had loved ones killed by Inquisitors. Yet you think I'm going to let you walk away because you need to live? Why? Let's hear it. Why do you need to live, Inquisitor?"

"Atonement," Phil answered simply. His tone was easy and quiet, causing the crowd to lean in to hear him. "I've killed hundreds of people...maybe even some of your loved ones. I don't know. I do know that it was wrong. And I do know I need to beg forgiveness from the families of each my victims, but more, I know I need to make things right. Even if they torture me and stone me to death, I need to go back to the Capital and make things right."

"The scales have fallen," Roland said.

"Yes," Phil agreed.

"What are you talking about?" Joseph asked. His voice was far less angry.

"I see now the error of my ways," Phil replied. "And I see atonement is my only recourse."

"No...no," Joseph said, shaking his head. "Take it up with God, if there is one. Because you are not leaving this room! You are a dead man."

The Dwellers gave a halfhearted spasm of cheer. Some clapped, a few booed, but most turned to their neighbor and started whispering. The hissing snake was back, but this time it held no fear for Phil.

Roland spoke over the people. "Phil Tarsus is a dead man. The State has laid a death sentence on him. So if you kill him now, you are only acting as an executioner for the State."

The hissing came back stronger and for once Joseph seemed unsure. "And how did Heinrich figure into all this?" he asked.

"We should discuss this alone," Roland advised.

With the crowd so volatile, Joseph agreed. They were led to a small room off the larger chamber, where their bindings were cut and they were allowed water. Haley and George came in and seemed uncertain where to stand; did they side with Joseph or Roland? Haley came and pressed herself to Phil. She was warm and fresh smelling; her heart was a bird's flutter beneath her skin.

"I thought they were going to kill you," she whispered, though not as quietly as she hoped.

"We still are going to kill him," Joseph said. "First, I want to know what's going on. Horace, tell me again how you found that body."

One of the Dwellers stepped forward; he was lean and angular. His eyes were the color of stone and dark with suspicion as he glanced toward Phil. "The Lady told me this morning about the body. She said Heinrich was their hostage and that one of the Inquisitors killed him, because they didn't need him anymore."

"And you speak of atonement?" Joseph seethed.

"May I explain from the beginning?" Roland asked, and as usual for him he didn't wait for the permission he had just asked for. He spoke for half an hour and recounted everything flawlessly from Phil's first encounter with Stephen Crown all the way up to the killing of Heinrich. "So in my opinion your choice now, Governor seems obvious. You should let us go. Our enemy is your enemy."

"It's not obvious to me," Joseph shot back. "Your Inquisitor has taken the exact wrong time to go soft. You want me to turn you lose on the most powerful branch of the State, yet he's meek as a kitten. Sometimes you God people are more trouble than you're worth."

Roland couldn't ignore the swipe at his faith and replied, "I can assure you, Governor, there is a big difference between finding God and going soft. Not to mention..."

"Not to mention you have me," Henderson said, interrupting. "I haven't found God, nor do I want to. I want to kill Loman. I want to get my life back. Actually I want his." He pointed at Phil. "I want to be a full Inquisitor when this is all over."

A pained look swept Roland's sagging features. "That's not likely going to set his cares to rest, Henderson. From the Governor's point of view, he'll only be trading one Inquisitor for another. Maybe if you told him that you wouldn't come looking for him later..."

A laugh shot out of Joseph. "He can come looking all he wants. He'll only find death like all the rest of them. Do you think he'd be the first agent of the State to come after us? Ha! I have to say, Gentry your condescending attitude is worse than the straightforward evil of this Inquisitor. You think we're primitives, don't you?"

"I don't mean to be rude, but you seem relatively primitive," Roland replied. "There wasn't any evidence of crops when we came, so I have to assume that you are a society of hunter/gatherers. Your clothing, your weapons, your tools all were produced by the State. There isn't any artwork about or a clearly defined culture, there is a general confusion of religion, and your government is the most rudimentary form of a democratic republic. And what's more, you live in caves. You are quite literally cave men. All of this is indicative of a primitive people."

"You call us cave-men?" Joseph asked in growing anger. "You speak of culture? You think art makes a society?"

"I don't actually," Roland answered. "Especially in a society dedicated to war."

Joseph scoffed, "We're not dedicated to war. We're dedicated to survival. The Dwellers have been here for forty-three years. We were one of the first of the freedom fighters to break away...actually, we were simply declared outlaws for not complying with Re-urbanization laws. You saw that town. That was Williamston. The State burned it to the ground because my father and the fathers of almost everyone here took a stand. Which is a lot more than could be said for your fathers."

"I never knew my father," Phil said. He had been taken from his mother and put in a State run academy at the age of three. This was compulsory, not a matter of maternal fitness.

"I knew your dad," Joseph said, he then laughed at the puzzled look on Phil's face. "Your dad was a little wimp who rolled over and took it up the ass because the State told him to. Just like your grandpa before him. Yeah, it was you limp-wristed Capital fellows that got us into this mess in the first place. My how big in the britches you were, calling us rednecks, and toothless bumpkins, and racists. Always with the racism crap. My granddaddy used to tell me he kissed every black ass from here to Chattanooga and still he was called a racist simply because of the twang in his voice. But things sure did change for the blacks when you libs got full power."

Roland sighed. It was a sound that marked his age—dry and tired and almost used up. "That was a sad time."

"It's a sad time now," Joseph growled. "You can call us primitive if you wish, but we are at war. This is how a society appears when it's under siege. We don't have frescos on the ceiling and we don't do poetry readings. We fight every day. We scout. We forage. And sometimes we do a very difficult duty and slay unarmed opponents, because it would be the death of all of us to release them."

"You have to realize that's not what we are. We are not your enemies," Roland said.

"Speak for yourself, Grandpa," Henderson said. "He's my enemy...at least he will be when I take out the commissioner and resume my place in society. I would think nothing of it to come back here and wipe the lot of you off the map."

"He's not my enemy," Phil said. He blinked as if waking up. "My enemy is the State that has ruined not only lives, but also souls. Though I have a question, Joseph. Can you ever win?"

Haley cut across him before he could answer. "Of course he can't. The State is too powerful. The real question is how are you even here? And for forty-three years? How has the State ever allowed that?"

"They don't *allow* it," Joseph answered. "They just can't stop it. In fact, they started it with that Re-urbanization law. They thought it would be easier to control people if everyone was lumped altogether in big cities instead of spread out in lots of little towns. All they ended up doing is moving people with the spirit and mentality of sheep to the city. The rest of us fled up into the hills."

"But...how are you still here?" Haley asked. "Why haven't they crushed you yet?"

"The State is not all-powerful. They want you to think so. They want you to think they are invincible; that they know everything, but they don't. We see them coming from miles away and we just, poof...disappear. Only to reappear hanging on their flanks, picking off stragglers. They don't know anything about mountain fighting. Still...can we win? No. Not by ourselves. I doubt we could even if we banded together."

Phil's eyes narrowed. "Who are you talking about? Who could band together?"

"Groups like us," Joseph said. "Other freedom fighters. The entire stretch of the Appalachians, from Maine to Georgia are riddled with groups like this. Hell, some have their own kings. No joke. And it's not just us. I've heard of groups in the backwoods of Alabama and Mississippi. And, if rumors are true, you got headhunters in the swamps of Louisiana."

"Headhunters?" Roland asked dubiously.

Joseph nodded sagely. "I'm not joking. We get wanders, pilgrims, desperadoes...all sorts creeping up and down the Appalachian Trail looking for a better life. Most want to stay here among the Dwellers. They say we're the most civilized. You may call us primitives, but we have a society of sorts, however some of these others are...nasty."

"But real headhunters?" Haley asked.

"Yes, and they'd love you," Joseph leered good-naturedly. He then turned to Roland. "And they'd hate you. Most of these groups are even less disposed to God types than I am."

"Because God represents a challenge to authority," Roland said.

"I think the reason is that God and war don't mix," Joseph replied. "At least they shouldn't. But what do I know other than battle?"

"You know deep in your heart that we aren't your enemies," Phil said. "Even Henderson isn't. Let's say he gets his wish and kills Loman...and me for that matter; he won't be coming back here. Inquisitors don't fight battles, nor would they ever suggest fighting an unwinnable one. It's very bad for the career."

"He's probably right," Henderson agreed. "So where does that leave us?"

Joseph stared down at the table for well over a minute, before he said, "You can go. The old man is right about being the State's executioner. If you're wanted, they'll get you, but maybe you'll get a few of them first. And that's a win in my book."

Chapter 36

Out of the Fire

"I want to stay here," George stated in a voice that trembled. Though Joseph spoke next all eyes were on Haley, especially Phil's. Which way would she turn? Would she stay or go? With all his heart, Phil wanted her to do both. He couldn't stand the idea of leaving her behind, but at the same time, what lay ahead of them was near certain capture and death.

The governor gave a little shrug. "Of course. You and Ms. Baker can stay. We think you both will be an excellent addition to our community. We have a lot to offer here."

Henderson snorted and Phil jabbed him with his elbow. "I think you'll both be happy here," Phil said. It hurt him somewhere beneath his breastbone to say this.

"I don't want to stay," Haley said and then shot a look of pain at George. "But you should. You made the right choice, George. Going to the Capital is a big gamble and even if it pays out for us, it won't really for you. You'd still just be a cameraman. Do you know what I mean?"

Before George could answer, Phil blurted out, "You have to stay as well." Feeling odd, he stood abruptly and paced a single turn of the room before coming to stand right in front of her. "Please stay here. Going to the Capital really isn't a gamble. It's more of a one way ticket to the seventh level of the Justice Building and it will kill me if you suffer even in the slightest."

She tried to convey something with her eyes but Phil didn't have a clue what. "Can we have a little privacy?" she asked the room in general. Everyone cleared out but the two of them and as soon as the door shut, Phil crushed her to his chest.

"I can't bear the idea of you getting hurt," he said. "You know what they'll do to you down in the seventh level if things don't go our way. You know better than anyone."

Haley pulled away. "I don't even know what our way is. You've changed, Phil. You've changed a lot and real fast. It's...good, I guess, but I'm a little lost about where we are as a group and where we are as...us. I mean, is there an us? There wasn't before, but there is now and I don't really know..." she trailed off with her thought incomplete.

Phil began, "Roland says we..."

Haley put a finger to his lips. "I don't care about Roland. I care about you, and I'm pretty sure you care about me. And I know damn well that Henderson cares about Henderson. He's going to try to kill you. His plan is obvious: he'll use you to get close to Loman and then kill you both."

"Probably," Phil agreed reluctantly. If Henderson did this and disposed of the bodies, all he would have to do is throw a bluff Conner's way. It wouldn't be hard. A simple: *I never even went to the prison. Phil told me to stay here*—was all it would take. Conner wouldn't know the difference since Loman would never include him in his plans.

So what option did that leave Phil? Stay there among the cave men? That was out of the question. He had his atonement to consider and that meant going to the Capital with Roland. It felt to be the right choice, but what would happen once they got there, he didn't know.

"Here's the thing, I know I have to go," Phil said. "But why do you want to? Henderson may be able to fake his way around things, but you can't. You can't really say you didn't go to the prison, because they'll find the news van eventually and then they'll come after you. So why go? Why chance it?"

Haley stared at him before answering, her eyes darting back and forth from each of his as if she couldn't tell which one held his soul. "First off, these Dweller-people aren't going to make it. Maybe it'll be this year or the next, but the State is going to find them eventually and when they do, they'll kill everyone one of them. The second reason is more urgent: you need me more than you realize. I'm the one with a copy of the Crown file, and I'll watch your back better than that old man can."

These were good reasons if Phil actually thought something positive would come of their journey. The truth was that he pictured them being picked up by the first security patrol they happened upon and brought to the seventh level for questioning. He wasn't nervous in the least for himself, but the idea of something happening to Haley terrified him.

He started to argue again and she added, "And there is a third reason." She kissed him then, long and slow. It was wonderful and only made him all the more nervous for her.

A few minutes later, George looked like he would cry when she told him she wasn't staying, but then again he always looked like that. Henderson was happy about Haley's decision—he hoped her star power would come in handy in sticky situations. Roland wasn't ecstatic and groused in a manner that wasn't like him.

"I'm just tired I guess," he said. "An old man needs his sleep, or so that's what I hear." He didn't seem all that sleepy to Phil, but the ex-Inquisitor was too busy haggling with Joseph to pay all that much attention.

Phil demanded the return of their uniforms and pistols. He received the uniforms, minus underwear, and only one of the pistols with just three rounds of ammunition. Joseph thought he was being generous.

"I didn't even have to let you live," he said. This was his defense for basically stealing. Despite the bad bargain forced on them, Roland voluntarily gave up his work boots to a man who wore a pair of ancient loafers that were held together by filaments only. Roland claimed if he needed anything more the Lord would provide.

Henderson sneered at the idea of charity and propped his feet up, happy to be back in his government issued shoes. Feeling slightly guilty over his most prized possession, Phil kept his Chinese made shoes out of sight as they sat down to a late lunch.

Perhaps because the word stealing had been mentioned in their previous bargaining, Joseph gave back all of the food that Colonel Heinrich had packed for the trip, but then the governor held up a tiny round cylinder.

"George says you're in need of a twenty amp fuse." Most of the food was bargained away in the next few seconds. The Dwellers needed food more than they needed a few fuses and a van that they claimed was basically worthless and would only attract the army to them.

It wasn't quite as worthless as they said.

When the four of them got to the van, tired and hungry hours later, they found it stripped of everything that didn't actually involve driving. The interior was a shambles—there wasn't a touch of cloth left to the upholstery, so they sat on rusting springs. Parts of the engine and its attendant wiring had been removed so that the heater, windshield wipers, interior lighting, and odometer didn't work. But the worst was the tire situation. Not only had the spare been stolen, but also each tire was missing three of their five lug nuts.

"It should be fine," Roland said with insincere cheer, when Haley started to pull at her own hair.

"Just keep to the center of the road, especially near any drop offs. And...and whatever you do, go slowly."

Phil did just that, putting along at a dreadful pace. The odometer, if it had been working, wouldn't have clicked over fifteen miles an hour during the whole trip. For him that wasn't the most annoying aspect of the drive; it was the lack of mirrors. He was so used to having them that not having them made him antsy, and despite having the mountain road to himself, he continually wagged his head about checking his many blind spots.

For the most part, during the slow ride, Henderson and Haley slept, but for all his supposed sleepiness, Roland stayed awake as Phil drove.

"I kind of wished that I had stayed with the Dwellers," the old man said after a long sigh. "They had so much to learn."

Phil wasn't feeling as generous and said sarcastically, "I know what you mean. They left the handle on my door. Who taught them how to field strip a car?"

Roland smiled. "No, not that. I'm talking about religion."

"Yeah, I guess," Phil agreed. Having only been converted that day, he knew next to nothing about the subject, yet the Dwellers seemed to have even less insight. "I heard them mention hell a lot. Is that normal?"

"Yes. Many people fixate on consequences rather than benefits. As an example, a mother might tell her child to eat her vegetables or she'll get sick, as opposed to eat them to stay healthy."

"It seems like the same difference to me," Phil replied.

"What happens if the child doesn't eat her vegetables one day and doesn't get sick? Since that's very likely, what's reinforced is that the mother's position as an infallible authority figure is weakened and the child begins to think the whole 'vegetables are good for you' concept is a myth. You see?"

Phil nodded in a bobbled disjointed fashion. "Kind of. I think. So what you're saying is if someone sins and nothing bad happens, the next sin becomes easier?"

"Yes. Hell gets put off and off. For the living, death seems remote. Even under our own circumstances, I don't feel particularly nervous. And for a person in a normal situation, death can feel like a life time away."

The talk of death seemed to depress them both and they fell into a silence that was only punctuated by random moments of excitement. Roland loved the mountain views and would exclaim happily at things Phil found ordinary: birds, squirrels, symmetric pine trees, valley scenes.

"I miss so much about the world," Roland said. "Sixty years is a long time without the sun. And the stars! When it gets dark, please pull over and let me see the constellations."

"I can do that."

The sun went down a little while later and Roland cried. He would not say why, but Phil guessed: the old man's time was running down and he knew it. There wouldn't be too many more sunsets for him and that was maybe true for all of them. The thought added to his depression and so Phil went to stand with Haley. They shivered together. Her hand was cold and he gave her the black coat of his uniform. She thanked him with a kiss, which banished any remaining cold in his body.

Despite the draining battery, Phil let them park on the deserted hilltop until the stars came out. He sort of wished he hadn't, because Roland didn't get much better. He sat on a tree stump, just off the road and stared with his head cranked back until Venus hid herself among the stars and Orion curved into view.

"The battery is at thirty percent and it's getting cold!" Henderson shouted. He had refused to get out of the car and sat in it griping at the delay.

Phil went to the old man and touched his shoulder. "We have to go, Roland."

He turned to Phil and said, "Night is the natural order of things. It is greater than the day. That's how it is. In the universe there is always more dark than light. But not for us. God gave us light even at night."

"He did, but we have to go."

After this, the ride was gloomy. Phil tried to engage Roland but he was terse. "I need to pray," he answered a few times in response to Phil's attempts.

Phil brought out what he hoped was a sure fire subject to change the old man's mood. "What about Jesus?"

"What about Jesus, what?" Roland cranked.

This made Henderson snort. Phil ignored him and asked, "I meant, why did he come down. You said he was the son of God and that he died for our sins. I just don't seem to understand. Isn't it God who is the one who forgives?"

Fug had begun to build up on the window where Roland leaned with his elbow posted up. He wiped it away with the back of his hand and continued to look out at the approaching lights of the Capital.

"If I could slap you, it might be easier for you to understand."

"Why would you want to slap me?" Phil asked. "Are you saying I'm stupid or something?"

Roland sighed more fug onto the window. "No, I'm not saying you're stupid. I'm saying mankind can be very, very stupid."

"Especially priests who never shut up," Henderson said.

Everyone ignored him, something they had been practicing for the better part of the ride...at least the parts in which he was awake.

"The bible may seem like a big complicated book," Roland went on, warming to the conversation. "However, the truth is that it's very simple. The problem comes when people start interpreting it more than they should. This is especially true of the Old Testament. Most people view it in one of three ways.

The hard liner will tell you that every single word in the bible is fact and that each line came from God's mouth to man's ears. At the other end of the spectrum are the people who dismiss the stories as simply legend or myth.

"In between lays the great majority of the people who believe that most of the old testament contains seeds of truth but over time the seeds were layered upon with supposition and exaggeration so that the exact truth is hard to know. These people, and I am one of them, believe that the exact truth is less important than what each story is designed to teach us. You see we believe that many of the stories are allegorical; that is: stories that have a meaning or a moral to them. The reason I am affixed to this third group is that God created man as a thinking, reasoning creature.

"People in the first group tend toward the robotic. For them the bible lines up as a list of do's and don'ts. If God said: wear a cheese hat, they'd wear a cheese hat without question. If God said Keep holy the Sabbath, they'd be at church every Sunday with their cheese hats on or be riddled with guilt if they were to miss a week. In their mind committing any sin, be it murder or a white lie, is equal in evil.

"People in the second group who want to believe the bible is a bunch of myths tend toward the chaotic, though they frequently are also atheists. We live in their world now. And we've discovered the concept they championed to replace God: the concept of the 'greater good', is evil right to its core.

"People who fall in the final category look for meaning. There are many stories to the bible: Noah and the Ark, David slaying Goliath, Jonah and the whale, Daniel in the lion's den, and in each these we find wisdom if we search for it."

"And what does all this have to do with Jesus?" Phil asked. Ahead he saw an elevated portion of road and breathed a sigh of relief. It was the main highway back to the Capital that he'd been hoping to come upon for the better part of the last half-hour. The van was down to a twenty percent charge and getting lost would've meant a long walk.

"I'm getting there," Roland said. "Now for the third group there is a question as to which of the Old Testament bible stories is of the greatest importance. If you had to take one and give it to the world, which would you take? Most would choose the story of Moses bringing the Ten Commandments to the people."

Roland paused significantly as if he expected Phil to gainsay him. "And they would be wrong?" Phil asked.

"What do you think?"

Phil grimaced and said, "You know I don't know much about the bible. I know only what you told me." Roland had given a brief overview of it the night before during their long vigil. Of the Old Testament, he had learned about the creation, Adam and Eve, Abraham, Jacob and Joseph, Moses and especially Job. Phil guessed Roland held a special place in his heart for the trials that Job endured in keeping faith in the lord.

"Pick one," Roland said.

"I really don't know. Moses...or the creation?"

"That's two and you're wrong with both," Roland said with a smile. "But don't feel bad, like I said, most people would go with the story of Moses."

"Well it should be Moses," Phil insisted. "He brought the Ten Commandments down from that mountain and where would we be without them?"

"Having a lot more fun," Henderson said groggily from the back seat. "Can you two shut up? I'm trying to sleep."

"No," Roland told him. He then said to Phil, "Answer your own question and you know the reason why the story of Moses isn't foremost. Where would we be without the Ten Commandments? Would it be chaos in the streets? No, it wouldn't. The reason being is that even in Moses' day the Ten Commandments weren't that much of a revelation. Thou shalt not kill? Were people allowed to commit murder before Moses' time?"

"No. I doubt it," Phil said with a shrug. "So why isn't it the story of the creation then? You'd think that was important."

"It is important, however like the Ten Commandments it's intuitive. We know instinctively that lying and adultery is wrong, just as we know this earth, this universe is a miracle creation of God's. Atheists deny this and they do so angrily. It's because they are fighting what their soul knows is true."

"You're not going to tell me the most important story is Job!" Phil said. "The man was tortured for his whole life simply to satisfy a bet between God and the Devil."

"It was a story about keeping faith in the lord, but still not the most important story in the Old Testament."

Phil squinted at the dark road, thinking. "Was it Abraham? Jacob? Joseph?" Roland shook his head at each guess. Phil had to laugh at what remained. "Adam and Eve? Of all the stories you told me, that was the most simplistic and childish one."

"Yes," agreed Roland. "Yet just because something is childish or simplistic doesn't make it wrong." The old man spread his arms in the van and gazed out the window. "The Lord gave us this paradise. He said: it's all yours—enjoy yourself, just don't sin, please. Do you see how simple that is? God gave us life and a few simple rules and said have fun. And that's what we should have done."

He sighed and dropped his hands. "God made it simple and for some reason we made it hard and complicated. People did that, not God. Rules in the bible began to pile on rules. Statutes about food preparation, alter construction, and accidental ox goring! These were man's laws, not Gods. God wanted it simple like you said, and maybe even childish."

"I guess I see how that would be important, but...but what about slapping me and the reason for

Jesus?" Phil asked to get back to the original question.

"God sent his only begotten son because he knew the hearts of men. He had tried the easy approach in the beginning. He then tried again with Moses, giving him Ten Commandments, saying, focus on these. But people wouldn't. So he sent his son down with the simplest message of all: love. Love God and your fellow man, and everything will be alright."

"Right, I get that, but you said Jesus was predestined to die on the cross. Why would God do such a thing?"

"Because God knew that humans needed a slap in the face. He gave us this wonderful being; a man who performed miracle after miracle, knowing that he'd be arrested and killed for breaking the stupidest laws. Man's laws, not God's. The Lord did this because he knew that without the slap in the face—without him up on that cross, Jesus' teachings would be forgotten. He knew that the miracles would be doubted. He knew that people were weak—were afraid of committing unless someone went first, unless someone else had skin in the game.

"So the Lord sent his son and Jesus went first to show us the way, and his message lived on: live your life in peace and love. Do not fear death for you will rise to be with the Lord, just like Jesus."

"And you don't fear death?" Haley asked Roland.

Surprised that she was paying attention, Roland turned to her with a smile. "No, child, I don't fear death in the least. I am averse to pain; it's not something I like to experience, but actual death? What is there to be afraid of?"

"I know what I'm afraid of," Henderson said, pointing to the highway in front of them. A Homeland Security roadblock was set up just at the range of their headlights. With the missing lug nuts on the van, it was too late to try to yank it around and make a run for it. They were caught.

Chapter 37

Into the Fire

"I need my coat," Phil said to Haley. "Quick, hand it over."

Phil drove and struggled into his coat, while Roland held the wheel steady. In the back seat Henderson adjusted his tie and checked the load of the pistol; he'd been given the pistol since Phil couldn't stand to have it on his person anymore. Not to mention, no one believed he would have the nerve to fire it.

"I don't want to hear one word about God. You hear me? Not one word," Henderson threatened. "And you, Phil try to remember that you are an Inquisitor. Act like it."

The roadblock consisted of four HS vehicles, a couple of blinking lights, and a few rows of spike strips that would leave their tires in ribbons if they tried to run the checkpoint. As the rest of the patrolmen sat in their cars trying to stay warm, a single uniformed man stood outside with his hand raised.

"Stop the car, turn off your lights and shut off the engine," he ordered.

Phil could only do two of these. He left the engine humming and popped the hood. "I can't turn it off. I got a bad fuse." He turned to Henderson, "Show him."

The under-inquisitor hurried out and spoke low. He pointed to the ducted tape fuse box and then went into a story about having to stop for their news gal, Haley Baker, who needed to use the bathroom out in the woods. When they got back, they found people stripping the van and now it was barely operable.

"Haley Baker?" the patrolman asked.

"Yes indeed," Henderson said. "Come here I'll introduce you."

"We don't have time for that crap!" Phil growled. "We're late for a, uh meeting with the commissioner." He felt like a bad actor in a bad play; reciting unrehearsed lines. It worked somewhat on the patrolman, who had to tread carefully around an Inquisitor.

"I still need to see your papers, and some ID," the patrolman said coming to shine a light in Phil's face. He held it only briefly before turning it on Roland and Haley. The latter cast a demur hand over her eyes and the light switched off.

"Sorry about that Ms. Baker. I love your work, by the way. You do a great job; everyone thinks so."

She gave a smile and held out her ID card. He stared at it a long time before returning it. Henderson was next and then Phil, both IDs getting perfunctory glances only. Roland didn't have ID and there came a tense moment as the patrolman looked at him quizzically. It was the mass of wavy, white hair on the man's head that had him gawking.

"I'm a prisoner," Roland explained. "That's why my hair is the way it is and it's why I don't have ID."

"Prisoner?" the patrolman asked, glancing down at the travel docs he had secured from Phil. "These say that you are a mechanic...and where are the other two? It says here that there's supposed to be a George Tuney and a Colonel Heinrich traveling with you. This colonel even signed it."

The four looked one to another in growing panic and then Haley touched the patrolman's arm and said, "George became ill, and...and the colonel changed his mind about coming back to the Capital. Had some business he said. And Ro...the prisoner used to be a mechanic. The form does say occupation, and prisoner is hardly an occupation."

"I guess," the patrolman answered. He shown the light on each of them again and held it longest on Phil and his death's head key lapel pin. "I should run this by my superior. Wait here." He left with their IDs and travel docs.

"What's going to happen?" Roland asked as the patrolman walked back to the other vehicles.

"I don't know," Phil said. "I was pulled over with incorrect papers once as an under-inquisitor. It was a headache but they let me go; only that was a matter of a typo on the date. This...I don't know. Traveling with an undocumented prisoner is bad, but without George and Heinrich here this looks really fishy."

"We're screwed," Henderson said.

"We should pray," Roland advised. "And what's more we should think on the concept that the ends do not justify the means."

"I don't know what you mean by that," Haley told him. "But we need something more than prayers and weird advice. Tell me, Phil, what would you have done three days ago? I mean as an Inquisitor if this had happened and you had never met Roland? How would you be acting right now?"

"I'd be angry," Phil replied at once. "Annoyed that some peon was getting in my way, making me sit out here and freeze."

"Then be that," Haley said. "Go over there and get mean. And play up the cold part. I'll come join you and you give me your coat. We can work on their sympathy."

The idea of lying didn't sit well with him and worse was the idea of becoming an Inquisitor again, even if only for a few minutes. But he didn't feel he had much of a choice.

"Alright," he agreed.

It felt as though Phil rode in the body of a stranger as he exited the car. He could feel the muscles of his face slide into an accustomed sneer. His chest tightened, his muscles bunched; tension and violence rippled across his shoulders. His left hand curled into a fist and his right went to his tie and touched the fabric—only inches from where his empty holster sat beneath his left arm.

This was him as an Inquisitor. A man who cared for the lives of others only if they enhanced his and only so long as they continued to do so. It made him want to gag. How had he lived like this for so many years? How had he been so willing to kill or maim or torture without the least qualm? How had been so inhuman?

He went to the lead patrol car and stood staring at it until the door came open and a balding man stepped out. Phil said nothing. He really couldn't. A part of him rebelled against what he had been and his insides were so torqued that he could only muster a glare.

"I'm just checking your papers," the man said.

Phil had to say something. He took a deep breath and buried his newfound conscience. He would be Godless for the next few minutes.

"Well, you can stop," bristled the Inquisitor. "You have three choices: you can put a call into People's Farm 332 and ask for Colonel Heinrich. Only that won't work seeing as of yesterday the phone lines were all down. Two: you can call the commissioner of Justice Ari Loman and explain to him that a paperwork error is causing him to delay his dinner plans. Only you may not live too long if you do."

"What's number three?" Haley asked coming up, doing her best to shiver in the cold evening. "Whatever it is I hope it's quick, I'm freezing. Hi, I'm Haley Baker."

Her presence was difficult to gel with his clashing personalities, except that both the new and the old Phil were head over heels for her. Phil slipped off his coat and slung it over her slim shoulders. She seemed almost childlike and angelic and he had to refrain from kissing her. It took a moment to get back into the character of Inquisitor.

"Number three," he said after another long steadying breath, "is the good sergeant here chalks this up to a case of bad paperwork and nothing more. Those are his choices...or he comes with us and stands a charge of interfering with an Inquisitor in pursuit of justice."

The man tried to stand his ground. His lips pursed and his eyebrows crinkled in determination, but then Haley gave him a smile and a shrug. "You don't see what I see when the cameras are off," she said. "He does his best work then; you'll confess to anything. I'd go with number three if I were you." She walked back to the van.

"It's bad paperwork," the sergeant said and handed the stack of papers back to Phil.

"Did it work?" Haley asked as he climbed into the van. He nodded and she squealed, "Yes! You were great, just like the old Phil Tarsus." She took a relaxed breath and said, "I think we have a chance. We can do this."

The sergeant and the patrolman peeled back the spike strips and waved them through. Phil drove past and then took a peek back at Haley. She had a wild look to her that couldn't be hidden beneath a warm smile.

"We can do what, exactly?" he asked.

"You know, get through this," she answered still enthused. "I've got a feeling we can."

Roland eyed her with a curdled look and then turned away with a 'Humph' sound, but said nothing more. He only stewed in silence until the lights of the Capital were very close and then even Henderson had enough.

"Let's have the lecture you old coot," the under-inquisitor said. "We can all tell that you are dying to explode in self-righteous bull."

If he wasn't going to explode before he looked seconds away from it now. He even hissed between his teeth as though he were venting gas. "Perhaps the one thing the communists have taught us is that the ends *do not* justify the means!"

Phil felt the need to apologize but wasn't sure what for. "What does that even mean?"

Next to him, Roland looked to deflate from his explosive state. He slumped in his unpadded seat and said, "It means that no matter what outcome you hope to achieve, even a noble one, it will be undone or warped without noble actions. Any deceit, any subterfuge, any sabotage that you use to gain your goal will ultimately tarnish it and turn it evil. For you Phil this notion leads to a very fundamental question: are you going to put your faith in lies or are you going to put your faith in God."

"God," Phil said immediately. "But it's not like I lied back there."

The choices he had given the sergeant were all true. The phones were down at the camp. Loman would probably kill the sergeant along with everyone else, and Phil could've brought the man in on any charge he felt like.

"You were completely truthful?" Roland asked, peering in at Phil with sharp eyes. Phil nodded, which sent a bushy eyebrow up. "You know who I saw taking to that sergeant? I saw an Inquisitor. Is that who you are?"

"No."

"But we may need him as an Inquisitor," Henderson said. "Stop filling his head with crap. It's more than just his life at stake here."

"Then Phil has a difficult choice," Roland said. "And you'd be wrong if you thought I don't care about your life, Nick or yours, Haley. The difference is that Phil has chosen to learn while you...two...wait. Where are we? What is that river?"

Phil first glanced at Roland, concerned at the panicky note in his voice and then down at the black water. "That's the Potomac."

"The Potomac? No, it can't be! And this is highway 66?" Phil nodded and was about to speak when Roland almost screamed, "Then where is Arlington? You can see it from here. It should be right there...right where those buildings are. What are those?"

"Dom-boxes," Phil answered. "They're just dom-boxes. Relax."

"Dom-boxes," Roland whispered, his face up against the window. "But where is the cemetery? You should be able to see it from here and...and...oh my Lord! Where is the Washington Monument? And the

Reflecting Pool? They should be right there!" He banged on the glass with his index finger, pointing across the water. "Lord help me where is it all? Why can I only see these stupid ugly buildings? What the hell are they?"

"Dom-boxes," Phil answered again. "Apartment buildings."

Roland melted against the glass, his wrinkles going flat and sagging. "The White House is gone too...you tore all that down and put up apartment buildings? That's insane."

Chapter 38

Bullet Exchange

"Where is my country?" Roland whispered as he stared out the window at the passing buildings. They were all grey concrete; each identical to the next. "Where is my city?" For the previous fifteen minutes, he had been inconsolable and was now just able to talk.

Phil had heard rumors that there had been monuments erected to this or that capitalist scattered about the city at one time or another, but he had never seen one. For him the city had always looked like this.

"I take it there was some stuff here," he said to Roland. "Some statues or something?"

This caused the man to begin cackling. It only lasted a few seconds before he went to weeping again. Henderson rolled his eyes and said, "Let's forget him; he's clearly cracked. So what do we do? Go straight to the Justice building? It's only half past seven. Loman is almost surely still there. We can go pop him easily. I've been thinking we can make it look like a suicide."

"Hold on," Phil said. Though the traffic was so light he could have stopped in the middle of the street without a worry, he pulled over. "I don't know if that's really a good idea."

What Roland had said before his breakdown about making a choice had set within Phil like quick-drying cement. He wouldn't kill; he wouldn't even lie. This gave him a sense of well being, but also a sense of being somewhat purposeless. What was he even doing there in the Capital? What sort of atonement could he manage as a fugitive? He gave a peek Roland's way but the man hadn't recovered from his shock enough to give him guidance.

Haley shook her head and said, "Phil's right. That's the wrong play. The smart thing to do is find out what Loman is so scared about. That way we can blackmail him. We can finally be connected. Think about it." She raised an eyebrow provocatively.

"I have thought about it," Henderson shot back, ignoring the eyebrow. "I'd love to be connected but Loman won't be so easily blackmailed. We'd have to find a hiding spot for the file...and we'd have to make copies and then...I don't know what. I just know that it won't matter what we do. He's not like the other commissioners; he's the Commissioner of *Justice*. He will find out all of our secrets and then, *poof*, we'll all disappear. But, if Loman were to die, we'd be in the clear."

"No, you'd be in the clear," Haley said. "I would be screwed. My boss knows I went out to that prison. What is she going to say when I come back without my cameraman and the news van? There'll be questions I can't answer, not without someone higher up on my side. So that means blackmail is our only play."

"You get to decide?" Henderson asked. "Is that it?"

Haley became cool and suspicious. "We should vote on it. And I'm sure I can count on Phil to be on my side."

Phil was a non-entity in this conversation. Neither way, murder or blackmail was moral in his mind. He had found God. His eyes were open and they weren't going to be closed again. He was just about to say this when Henderson pulled the gun from his holster and held it up for them to see.

"This isn't a democracy, Haley. What we have here is a dictatorship. What I say goes and I say we kill Loman. After which we dump his body in the Potomac and then head over to your office to get that file."

"What then?" Haley asked. She didn't seem frightened by the presence of the gun so much as she appeared just plain tired.

"We play it by ear."

Haley rallied, "Not good enough. Play it by ear means that you'll kill us. That is not going to happen at least not easily. You have three bullets and yes, there are three of us, but you'll need one for Loman. You're one short."

"Wrong," Henderson said. "I don't need a gun to kill you, Haley. And I think the old man will just about have a heart attack if he sees one more dom-box. And Phil? He's gone soft; it won't take much."

Phil shook himself as if waking from a deep sleep. "I'm not as soft as you think. I'll defend myself and others. I can defend the innocent and the weak."

"What about Loman?" Henderson asked. "He's neither. Will you defend him?"

"I...I don't know," Phil said. "Roland?"

The old man was grey and lethargic. His head rested against the glass and he didn't turn it when he spoke to Phil, "I don't know my destiny...I feel like Moses. He was denied the Promised Land just like me. I...I won't live to see it either. They built over it. It's here beneath all this...this horrible uniformity. America is here but all this has to be wiped away."

"What about me?" Phil asked. "I came all this way and now I don't know what to do."

"Follow your conscience. Follow your heart," Roland replied. "You can never go wrong with that."

"Oh, what a load of crap!" Henderson exclaimed. "We're going to the Justice building and that's final. And Haley, I meant it when I said we'd play it by ear. I don't know what's going to happen with Loman. And I don't know what's going to happen after. I'd much rather kill your boss than you."

"That's sweet," Haley said. "You really know how to sweep a girl off her feet."

"Ha-ha," Henderson laughed sarcastically. "We're still in this together. Loman is our enemy. We should concentrate on him and soon."

"If we're in this together, give me one of the bullets in your gun," Haley said. He gave her a look as though he thought her insane and she explained, "I know you could kill us without the gun, but it would be loud and messy. We would fight back. We would run. It wouldn't end well, not for any of us. However, if you were to give me a bullet, maybe I'd trust that we were really in this together."

This time Henderson smiled sincerely. "A bullet; *your* bullet you might say, interesting. And what do I get in return? Trust goes both ways."

She peered out of the window, thinking. She came up with nothing more than a shrug. "I have an idea," Phil said, putting the car in gear and heading to the Justice Building. "In return for the bullet, Haley will stay with Roland in the van and keep it running."

"While you and I go in after Loman?" Henderson said, considering. "That's not bad. I was wondering how I was going to keep the van without killing all of you. Here, you can have your bullet." He jacked the slide back and handed one over.

It took only minutes for Phil to drive to the Justice Building and during that time his mind was a whirl of confusion. He had been led to the Capital by what he had felt to be a prophet, only Roland turned out not to be one. He was an old man, one filled with faith and love for the Lord, but still only a man. He had no magic powers; no divine insight.

And neither did Phil.

All he had was the directive to follow his heart. His heart said to leave, which made no sense since not too long before his heart had been certain that coming to the Capital had been the absolute right thing to do. Now he couldn't understand why. The

Capital with its dull sameness had never seemed so bleak. The people hurrying against the cold had never seemed so wretched. The city seemed more dead than alive.

A woman tripped over a curb and turned her ankle badly; no one glanced her way to see if she was ok.

An old black man, with bowed and spindly legs, and a face made sharp by near starvation, limped along coughing up blood. He would be dead soon—old age and communism didn't mix well—and no one cared. They only cared to get out of his way.

A young man stood against a building in a line with many other young men. He was pale and thin lipped. He was going to war. A war that was never ending. A war that was used as justification for so many atrocities. A war designed to hold the population in a constant state of terror from external enemies.

The young man would go to war and kill because he had no choice. The old man would die because he had no choice. The woman would go on, broken ankle or not, because she had no choice. The State owned them.

The State didn't own Phil Tarsus. It once had but not now. His eyes were open. He had known the misery the State produced before this, yet he had never thought there could be another way.

What if the other way is death? the voice in his mind asked. Death was still a choice, and a noble choice if the alternative was a life of endless sin and pain.

Phil pulled the van over and yelled to the injured woman, "Are you alright? We could give you a lift."

"What the hell are you doing?" Henderson said, hissing the words through gritted teeth.

"He's helping the less fortunate," Roland answered, sitting up. "Something we should all do."

The help was declined. The woman took one look at the black Inquisitor uniform that Phil wore and practically began to cry. She stood immobilized in place and no amount of explaining or placating had the least affect on her.

Eventually Phil had to drive away, which left Henderson weak from laughter. "You are such a moron!" he said when he could speak. "Do you think that you'll be able to save these people? You think they can find God?"

"That's my hope," Phil answered. "I think that's why I've been called back to the Capital. But..."

"You bet your ass, there's a but," Henderson said, turning suddenly angry. "First off, there is no God. And even if there were, those people out there would never listen to you. Look at them. They're not even people. They are simply a glomping of cells that have been trained to walk and talk. They have no ambition, no drive. They eat when the State tells them. They sleep when the State tells them. They even procreate when the State tells them. They are robots only."

Phil opened his mouth to deny this, however the truth of it was a little too obvious.

Henderson nodded in malevolent glee. "That's right. It's too late, isn't it? Those people out there are the very definition of hopeless. The State owns them. If they have a soul, the State owns that too. What did you think would happen when you got here? Did you think that you'd walk around preaching and making converts of every other person? The State would never allow it and even if it did you would fail."

"Maybe...but I should try," Phil said uncertainly. "I should try, right?"

Roland looked deep in thought and said nothing. Henderson scoffed, "Go right ahead and try. First you should ask yourself what would happen."

"Homeland would arrest me," Phil said, thinking aloud. "It wouldn't take more than an hour. In another hour I'd be transferred to the Justice Building. There they'd torture me and in a day or two they'd stone me to death for treason. I wouldn't be able to save anyone."

"Exactly," Henderson said. "You wouldn't save a single person. And you know what's worse? You wouldn't be able to save anyone even if the State allowed you to preach. What would you say to those people out there, what exact words would you use to counteract everything they've been taught; everything their parents have been taught?"

Phil's first response was to look to Roland—the old man kept his eyes away and again said nothing. "I'm not sure," he answered eventually.

"You're not sure because there isn't anything you could say. Look at yourself, Phil. It took the threat of death; it took a prison burning down on top of you; it took the fact that you've become an un-person in order for you to have your 'sudden' conversion. Words alone wouldn't have changed you."

This was true and undeniable. "You're right, Henderson. So what do I do? Roland, please say something."

"I've told you everything you need to know," Roland answered. "Sometimes people need a slap in the face. You needed a building to burn down on top of you. The question is, what does America need in order to unchain its soul?"

Phil began to sputter in more uncertainty, but Roland held up a hand. "I don't think that's for you to worry about. You should follow your heart. That is my advice."

"Then I'm going to the Justice building," Phil said. A block away, it loomed above the other buildings. It was grand and shining, while they were squat and ugly. It dominated them, just like it dominated this part of the city. "I need to confront Loman."

Chapter 39

The Commissioner

With Roland and Haley neatly tucked around the corner in the van, Phil and Henderson approached the building at a fast walk. Phil breathed easy, his heart was a steady beat, he knew an inner calm. Surprisingly Henderson looked just as confident.

"We can do this," he said, moving with firm determination. "I can feel it in my bones."

A sardonic laugh escaped Phil. "Be careful. You sound like Roland. Maybe God is speaking through you."

"If God wants Loman dead then we're on the same side on this," Henderson replied, fishing out his ID. "Let's cut the chatter." The guard station stood thirty feet away; it was their first test. Had they been declared dead? Were they on the Most Wanted list? Or had they been sent to their deaths in Polk and nobody even knew or cared that they had been trapped in a fire?

It turned out to be choice C. The guards looked on them as they did the other twelve Inquisitors operating out of the building, meaning they sweated and shook long enough to wave the two on. "The elevator is in the green, sir," one of the guards said.

Henderson beamed. "Excellent."

"You may not have to kill him," Phil said, hitting the button for the top floor. "Think about it. You only have two bullets. What if his secretary is still here?"

"Strangulation is pretty quiet."

"I'm saying we should talk to him," Phil insisted.

"For what reason? He's as guilty as they come. Even a God-lover like you has to see it. And he's tried to kill us. The old man said you could kill in self-defense, remember?"

Phil did, yet the idea of killing a man, even an evil man like Loman, in cold blood didn't sit well. It felt too much like murder or assassination. He wished Roland was there to tell him what to do. *Follow your heart.* Yep, that's what he would say. So Phil did just that.

He punched Henderson square in the jaw.

"Sorry. I really am," he said to the unconscious man as he lowered him to the floor of the elevator. Phil then hit the seven button. The seventh floor was where the offices of the middle managers were kept. It was deserted, as Phil knew it would be. He dragged Henderson to a cubicle and, taking a phone cord, tied his hands and feet.

There was a pause as Phil contemplated taking the gun from Henderson. He didn't. Just having it was a temptation that he didn't know if he could resist in the moment. Foregoing the elevator, he went to the stairs and started up two at a time, but stopped after only a few. There was someone unseen ahead of him, moving slowly.

Phil couldn't wait. Henderson wouldn't be out for long and the cords that bound him had been hurriedly tied. He would get loose. After the briefest of hesitations, Phil moved up the stairs as if he had every right to and came upon one of the dark workers that cleaned the building.

A sigh of relief slipped out before Phil even thought to hold it back, but it seemed to make no difference. The man's eyes went wide at the sight of an Inquisitor so close and he stepped aside to let Phil pass, only he did so awkwardly. He was trying to hold both a mop and water filled bucket with his left hand. Some of it sloshed out. Leaping over the plastic edge in a moment of suicidal revenge, the water splashed onto Phil's pants and expensive Chinese made shoes.

"Careful there," Phil said with a little laugh.

He made to keep going but the moment held him in place and he only took a single step. Something was wrong.

Yes, you would normally be so furious over spilt water on your shoes that you would break his other arm, the voice in his mind spoke.

His other arm? Phil gave the man a closer look. Despite that the black man shivered in uncontrolled fright, Phil knew him. It was the same man he had stepped over a few days before...the man who had fallen down these same steps and had broken his wrist...the man he hadn't given a second thought to except in regards to how his blood would adversely affect the shine on his shoes.

Just then it felt as though something broke in Phil's chest. How had he been that person? "I'm sorry," Phil said. "About before when you fell."

The man shook his head, looking at Phil as though his apology was so foreign as to be spoken in a different language.

"You fell a couple days back and I didn't do anything to help," Phil tried to explain. "I'm sorry, it was mean of me. Here let me take that bucket. I'll carry it for you."

The man's eyes went wider in disbelief as Phil took the bucket and mop from his hands. "What floor are you going to?" Phil asked and even as he did a sudden dread hit him. What if he was going to the tenth? Would Henderson try to kill this man as well?

"Nine," the man said in a little voice. It was a lie. Phil could sense a lie from miles away. The man was going to ten and it would be very dangerous if he did.

"Ok, you can go to nine," Phil said. "Nine is good. You should definitely clean on nine."

He didn't wait for anything more from the man. Taking the bucket and mop he started up as quick as he could, without making it look like he was hurrying. Time felt to be running down, yet he didn't want to look suspicious even to a janitor.

"Here you go," Phil said at the landing to the ninth floor. He opened the door to a dark hall and set the bucket in. "Try to be more careful. You don't want to trip and break your neck...it's just an expression," he added as the man froze at what he construed to be a threat.

Phil didn't have time for more of an explanation. "Just an expression," he said again and nudged the man into the hall. The second the door shut, Phil launched himself up the final flights of stairs.

He found the tenth floor lobby deserted. Ms. Adleman's desk was dark and had a cold feel to it. Beyond her desk was a length of hall from which seldom-used conference rooms sprung on either side. They were empty and dark. Practically the entire floor, all of which was dedicated to one man, was empty and dark. The only real glow came from the office at the end of the hall. It was Ari Loman's.

In all his time as an Inquisitor, Phil had never been in that office and had never wanted to. It had an evil reputation. Frequently people went in and corpses came out. Its occupant had a worse reputation. Ari Loman was said to personify evil. Even the Inquisitors that worked for him shunned his presence and if ever they were summoned to his offices, they would go pale and shaking. Few ever returned.

Phil hurried to see him; he didn't even pause at the door to knock—what would be the point? Instead, he strode in, fearing that he was out of time.

"Commissioner...Loman?" Phil asked, feeling a touch of bewilderment. The room was sumptuously furnished with polished wood; the floors gleamed with buffered marble; the glass windows were spotless and sported a wonderful view of the city. The Commissioner's desk was huge and practically screamed power.

What was so bewildering to Phil was the man who sat behind that great desk. He was little and appeared to be slipping out of middle age without grace. He was pudging in the tummy and his comb-overed, thin hair was flopping off the side of his head ridiculously. He had a mean face that belonged more on a toddler in the middle of a tantrum than on a man.

"Commissioner Loman?" Phil asked again when the man did nothing but sit there staring at him.

Now Loman moved. He reached into his desk, and Phil took a breath and steeled himself for what was coming, he expected to be shot out of hand. Only Loman simply brought out a lighter and lit a cigarette with shaking hands.

"She sent you already?" Loman asked after a huge drag on the fag that turned it half to ash.

"No," Phil said, shaking his head. "No one sent me. I'm Phil Tarsus."

Loman took another drag, and shot twin jets of smoke from his nostrils. "Oh, yeah?"

"I'm Phillip Tarsus," Phil repeated. Loman didn't seem to recognize him or his name.

"You said that," Loman commented. "Now what do you want, Tarsus? I'm busy." In front of him was an ashtray filled to overflowing and a deck of cards laid out in a game of solitaire.

"I worked the Crown case...you know, Stephen Crown?" Phil's bewilderment grew. Loman clearly didn't recognize any of these names. "He was a gay from Stadler Academy? No? What about Roland Gentry?"

"No. Who are these people? What do they have to do with me? And you, what do you have to do with me?"

"You sent me to Polk," Phil reminded him.

Loman stuck out his chin and squinted up at Phil, he then shrugged. "I'm sure I had a good reason...and that was?"

How could Loman not know him? Or Crown, or any of it? He hadn't batted an eye at the mention of Polk. The only explanation that Phil could come up with was that he hadn't been sent to his death at all. It had been a series of freak coincidences that found him in that prison.

That meant he wasn't being hunted. That meant no one was after him.

A laugh slipped out. It was giddy and manic. He turned from Loman and stared at a gilded writing table that sat opposite the desk and smiled. Everything he had gone through—all the fear and worry—had been for nothing. He was in the clear! His life was back!

Just like that, the specter of death that had haunted him for so many days vanished. The laugh came again, louder this time. He was himself again, Phil Tarsus, Inquisitor.

He hadn't really done anything wrong that would keep him from reclaiming that title. There was no law against escaping from a fire. And it was Henderson who had killed Heinrich. That was his deal not Phil's. All Phil had to worry about was Roland, and he could explain that away as being enthusiastic for the truth.

He could say that he had only saved the old man so that the people could have their revenge.

Or better yet, he could just kill Roland. No one would know and no one would care. Down the Potomac he would go just like so many others and who would ever care?

Follow your heart.

The voice! Phil's smile vanished in an instant. The voice would never stop.

What about God? What about Heaven? the voice demanded.

Phil fought back: What about living *my* life like everyone else? What about living like a person and not like a hunted animal in a cave?

What about atonement? What about saving souls?

What about my misery? God doesn't seem to care about that! What about my happiness?

What happiness?

With Loman watching and doing nothing but puffing on his cigarette, Phil went to the writing table and slumped against it. He had never been happy. His life before had been a run of misery, punctuated by times of slightly less misery, and the few time he thought that he'd been happy were just a mirage. If he had been asked what the happiest day of his life was he would have claimed it was the day he became a full Inquisitor. Except that he had spent that day plotting revenge against everyone who had ever slighted him. That's not being happy.

Sleeping with Haley curled up to his chest, that was being happy. The strange, "old" feeling within him died away forever in that second.

Movement in the corner of his eye had Phil turning just in time to see Henderson step into the room with his gun drawn.

"What is this?" Loman said, his hands coming up to light his next cigarette. "I do my duties as agreed!"

"He doesn't know," Phil said, smiling. "He doesn't know who we are or..."

Henderson fired the pistol. Loman's death was odd and beguiling. Phil couldn't take his eyes from it. The little man clutched his chest with one shaking hand and took another drag from his cigarette with the other. He began to choke on the smoke, but it seemed the tobacco was all he had to live for and he died trying to get the cigarette back to his lips.

"He didn't know us," Phil said. "You didn't have to kill him."

"Please," Henderson scoffed. "You believe that guy? How many times do I have to tell you, people will say anything with a gun pointed at them?"

"Do you see a gun?" Phil held out his arms.

"I guess not, but that doesn't mean..." Henderson left off, thinking.

"Trust me, Henderson, he didn't know me. He didn't know you. He didn't know Crown or Roland or anything about Polk. This has been a mistake."

Henderson's thinking wasn't rational. "Or maybe he just forgot our names. To him we're nobodies. To him we're peons. You see? Maybe he just..."

"Forgot?" Phil supplied the word. "And he forgot that he burned down a prison? No one forgets something like that. I'm sorry, but he just didn't know anything about us or Polk."

"Then who's after us?" Henderson demanded fiercely, grabbing Phil's jacket with his free hand.

"Maybe no one. Maybe it was really just an accident."

Henderson didn't seem to comprehend this. He stared at the body of Loman flopped onto his desk. The corpse still held the cigarette in his fingers, a thin trail of smoke drifting up silently. If Loman had anything left of his rotten soul, Phil figured it wouldn't be much different looking than the tiny wisp.

Henderson shook his head at the corpse. "You're wrong. Somebody's after us, and if it wasn't him then it had to be someone else. In fact, he was probably working for someone else. Someone bigger. If you ask me I think I did us a favor." The under-inquisitor was trying to convince himself.

Phil blew out wearily through puffed cheeks and said, "No one is bigger."

"Well something's going on!" Henderson cried. "No one gets sent to a prison on the day it burns up by accident. No way that happens. Wait, I got it! You know what we need? We need that file. We need that damned file! Come on!"

With his gun still out and his eyes wide and unblinking, Henderson raced out of the room. He ran to the elevator and began jabbing the button frantically. "Come on...come on!"

"Look, Nick. We should..."

The gun flashed in Phil's face and he found himself nose to barrel with it. The smell of spent powder was pungent in his nostrils. "Don't start with me," Henderson hissed. "That bastard deserved it."

"I'm just saying you need to calm down. You're going to attract attention to yourself."

He didn't calm. "That's easy for you to say. You didn't just kill the damned Commissioner of Justice! Or that damned colonel. That was a mistake. It was you. You were egging me on. You practically made me kill him."

Henderson was near to hysterics and Phil decided not to argue, especially with the gun pressed into his cheek. "That's in the past, Nick. You need to calm down and put the gun away."

"I can't. It's all I have," Henderson admitted, cradling the gun now, as if Phil was a parent threatening to take away a favorite toy. "I'm not like you, Phil. I can't pretend there's something more. For me there's just this."

The way Henderson was acting gave Phil pause. There was doubt in the under-inquisitor where before there had only been the surety of righteous zeal. There were questions in his eyes where before there had only been rigid thinking. "I'm not pretending, Nick. There is more to life."

Henderson flared into anger again. "There's more? What is it? Fairies? Magic?" The anger was greater than it needed to be. Phil knew that type of anger. He had used it himself to cover his uncertainty.

"Yes," Phil said without hesitating for a breath. *Yes*, he thought to himself. When he'd been a citizen, he had only what was allowed by law. Now, as a person—a real person, there was not just more, there was everything. He felt the gift of life like it was meant to be lived.

"There is magic," Phil assured. "Life is magic."

"No," Henderson said grimly. "Magic? You are cracked. You're so far gone that nothing can help you, except maybe death. I should do it. I should pull this trigger and put you out of your misery. You were once a man to emulate and now you are this. I didn't think it was possible."

Henderson brought the gun back up but Phil only smiled past it. "Nick, with God, anything is possible. Open your heart and you'll find magic. Don't laugh. I have something you don't. I'm happy. Actually happy. And I have hope. I have hope for the future. And I have love."

Phil expected another round of mocking to come from Henderson but instead the man drew back in confusion. "Even if you're right," Henderson said. "It's too late for me."

Phil grabbed his shoulders and said, "That's what I thought. You saw me, blubbering and afraid. But then it felt like a light switch. Just like that. Just that quick. You either believe or you don't, and the moment I allowed myself to believe I felt it." Phil snapped his fingers to show how quick it was and that was when the door to the stair came open with a bang.

With the lobby dark and the stairs lit the man who stood there was only a black shadow with unknowable features. In his hand was the cylinder of what seemed to be a gun.

Henderson didn't have the reflexes Phil did; he was a hair slower, which meant all the difference in the world. Phil would've been able react faster, turn quicker, and would've been able to bring the gun up in a blink. He would've had a fraction of a second more time to evaluate the situation; to recognize that the dark figure was only just a man and what he initially took for a gun was only the handle of a mop.

Henderson, however was only fast enough to turn and fire, before Phil could fully grab his arm.

Chapter 40

Henderson's Doubts

The dark worker, with his bucket and mop clutched in his one good hand, staggered back. His mouth came open in a silent scream, showing off his teeth; they were a sharp white in contrast to his skin. His eyes went wide in surprise and pain...and then he toppled backwards. Too late, Henderson put out a hand to him—too late for the man and too late for Henderson.

He turned to Phil and said in desperate explanation, "I didn't...it was an accident."

Phil pushed past him, slid on mop water at the top of the stairs and stumbled down to where the janitor lay. The man was very dead; his heart had been shot through.

Henderson stood at the top of the stairs like a man on a tiny island. "It was an accident. Like Loman...I mean Heinrich. It was just a," he paused and his face screwed up tight. "Wait. Why should I care? He was just a..."

Phil cut across him angrily, "He was a man. Just like you and me."

"No, he was a waste of a bullet. That was all. And now this thing is useless," he said of his gun. He looked at it, while his face contorted. He tried to form it into its accustomed sneer, but only half succeeded. "It's as useless as you are. Here."

Henderson tossed the gun to Phil and then wiped his hand on the black of his coat. He then started down the stairs in a hurry, not looking at the man he'd killed.

"Wait," Phil said and grabbed his arm. "We should pray. I think. Roland did when you...after Heinrich died."

"Do what you want," Henderson said in a ghostly whisper.

Phil stood over the body for a moment staring down. What was he supposed to say? He wasn't a priest, in fact, he had never even cracked a bible. Still he felt the need to say something. If Roland was there, he would have for certain. If he could kneel and pray over the body of what was basically a slave master then he definitely would find words for this simple man.

Feeling odd, Phil knelt and then stammered, "Lord...please...um...I want you to look after the, uh, soul of this man." He wanted to use the man's name in the prayer, yet he couldn't remember it. Phil had seen him three or four times a week for the last seven years and in all that time, he hadn't ever given him more than a passing thought or a harsh order to move his ass.

"Do you know his name?" he asked Henderson.

"No and I don't want to," Henderson said. "Come on." He left, rushing down the stairs as if he were being chased.

"Damn," Phil whispered. He stood and had just enough time to say, "God bless you," as a final prayer before he heard an erratic thumping from a few flights below. This was followed by a low moan.

Phil turned from one dead man and raced down the stairs in time to see another—or rather one who would be very soon. Henderson lay sprawled in an unnatural heap of blood and water. He had slipped in the spill that Phil had caused earlier and now there was a jagged, white bone coming up out of his neck. It was his collarbone and along one side of it, blood pulsed in an eerie shower onto Henderson's face. He blinked at it blearily.

"I can't move," Henderson said in a throaty voice. "What happened?"

In a second, Phil was at his side, uselessly trying to hold the blood back. "You fell." He could think of nothing else to say.

"Oh," Henderson said. "I didn't mean it about the janitor. It was an accident. Was he really dead?" There was a pleading note to his voice that had never been there before.

Very badly, Phil wanted to lie, but he couldn't. "Yes, I'm sorry."

"And I'm going to die." It wasn't a question. They both knew he wouldn't live. There was just too much blood. It ran down the stairs like a small river.

Phil watched it flow from step to step and then he slumped, defeated. He thought he had come back to the Capital for atonement; he thought he had come to make amends, but he had done nothing more than preside over the deaths of three men.

"Help me," Henderson whispered.

The blood shooting up from the wound had little force now and Henderson's eyes were nearly closed. "I can't. There's nothing I can do..." Phil paused. There was one thing he could do. "Nick, don't reject God, please."

"It's...too late. I killed that man." His voice was barely audible.

Suddenly energized Phil leaned over Henderson's face and yelled, "No! It's never too late. Beg forgiveness. You can do that."

"I...wanted to be...nice," Henderson said.

Phil nodded hoping Henderson would continue but he didn't. He only grew weaker. "Yes, you were nice. It's why I picked you. But now I need you to say you're sorry, Nick! Say you're sorry for killing those men, please. God will forgive."

"You wouldn't...let me...be good." The man's eyes went blank and he died.

"Nick! Look at me. Look at me," Phil pleaded. Henderson couldn't. "Oh man! God, please forgive him. It wasn't his fault, it was mine. I did it. I killed those men. It was me. I taught him how to be a..." He choked suddenly on the air in his lungs and gagged on the truth of Henderson's last words.

Every under-inquisitor learned from his Inquisitor. Phil had been taught to hate and to hurt without remorse and he had passed that on to Henderson. "His sins are my sins, Lord. Please forgive me. Henderson...Nick, I need you to forgive me too. I'm sorry. I made you like this."

The grey of the stairwell spun and Phil felt a sudden desperate need for air. A minute later he left the building, however the steps from Henderson's body to the street went unnumbered and unaccounted for. He was just suddenly there in the biting cold, feeling the tears on his face burn.

A white-faced Haley asked: "Where's Henderson?"

Phil pointed up at the magnificent skyscraper—a building he hated. "Dead. So is Loman and this...other fellow. I don't know his name." Roland had his blue eyes sharp on Phil. "I didn't kill them. I followed my heart and it led me...nowhere. It was a waste to come here. Loman didn't have a clue who we were, or what had happened at Polk. He wasn't what I expected."

Haley's chin dropped. "Then you weren't the target. I was. They were after me all along. It's the only explanation."

Had Phil heard this the day before he would've been elated that no one was after him, now he was only tired. "Why. What do you know?"

"I don't know what I know," Haley replied with a weak shrug. "But the answer is in that file. We have to get it back."

"Or we don't," Phil said. Perhaps because of the violence of the last few minutes, a surety of death hung about him. It was a gloom darker than the night. "I failed Henderson. I didn't just let him die, I made him into a killer. I say we leave. I say we get in the van and just get out of here. We could make it pretty far tonight."

"I'm not like you," Haley said, triggering a shock of déjà vu within Phil. "I can't live like a hunted animal."

"And you can live like a caged one?" Phil cried. Desperate to leave, he turned to Roland. "What do I do? I came here for atonement and all I've gotten is more death. I don't want to go on like this. I failed Henderson. I'm afraid I'll fail both of you."

Roland put out a warm hand and said, "Follow your heart."

A sad cry mixed with a laugh escaped Phil's throat. "My heart? I don't know my own heart. My heart..." he hesitated as he caught the look of fear on Haley's face. Despite the emotions twisting his soul, there were some things in his heart that were very clear. "My heart says I can't leave Haley. I can't leave her unprotected."

"Then you'll come with me to get the file?" Haley asked with relief.

On this his heart was clear. "Yes," Phil replied. "Though I don't know why you want it. Not anymore. I see this city and I see these pitiful people. They walk around waiting to die. Now I see that was me! I never truly lived...I only staved off death. My purpose to life was simply to put the end off for another day. But I never really lived. I wonder why anyone would want this life, especially not after seeing what there is outside of it."

"I didn't see much that was better out there," Haley said. "A farm where people starved to death or a city that surrounded itself with bones? I know the Capital isn't great, but for me there is still a chance here. A chance to be happy or maybe a chance to be someone."

Phil climbed into the van. "If you had seen Loman you'd have known there's no chance for happiness here. Even if you are someone."

He started the van on course for the entertainment district, the one part of the city that seemed alive. It was here that the State ran its approved movies and it's politically driven live theater. The buildings were clean and newly painted. They were well lit and the streets more crowded—but only with pedestrians and filled to capacity buses.

The secondary streets of the entertainment district were another story. They were dark and seedy; the buildings showing their age worse than the rest of the city.

"Right through that gate," Haley pointed. Phil could barely see what she was talking about until a security guard shown his flashlight. "Hey, Jerry," Haley said, waving. "It's me Haley. These two are with me."

Jerry let them through to an underground garage where they were checked by another guard whom

Haley also knew. Their outfits, dark blue jumpsuits emblazoned with the two masks: comedy and tragedy —the symbol of the Board of Entertainment—made Phil take a closer look.

"These guys aren't Homeland. Who are they?" He had never been beyond the glittering facade of the main strip before.

Haley handed over her ID card to yet another guard who peered at it briefly and then scowled in Roland's direction. Haley didn't see the look and said, "We have our own security force here. There are lots of crazy stalker types and Marilyn doesn't trust Homeland."

"Marilyn?" Phil asked.

"Thanks Bill," Haley said, taking back her card and showing them into a lobby. She went to the elevators and hit the up button. "Marilyn Jennings is the Commissioner of the Board of Entertainment. We all call her Marilyn; she is so nice."

"She lets you talk to her?" Phil asked, amazed. They stepped into the elevator and he added, "Tonight was the first time I ever talked to Loman. Not that I ever wanted to."

They exited onto the fourth floor and despite that the entire level seemed deserted, Haley warned them with a quick finger to her lips to keep quiet. Her office was clean and warm—no little junky space heater for her.

"What should we be looking for?" Haley asked, thumbing through the copied Crown file. She had pulled it from behind a full-length mirror, but only after she cast a look at herself and made a sour face at what she saw.

"It's got to be one of his students," Phil replied. "Is there anyone named Jennings?"

Haley's eyes flared. "Marilyn wouldn't hurt a fly...and no, there isn't a Jennings on the list. Nor any of the big names, like I said."

"What about your boss?" Roland asked Phil. "You mentioned someone other than Loman."

"Conner?" Phil replied. "He doesn't have near the power to do any of this. He's a paper-pusher; he's worried about budgets and rationing."

"I checked already," Haley said, holding up the paper. "There's no Conner. I'm just going to read down the list. Tell me if anything rings a bell...Atkins, Adleman, Clark, Davenport, Grant, Ingram, Kent..."

Haley choked off her words as a woman walked in, followed by three burly guards. "See, no Jennings," the woman said with a beaming smile. She was older but still beautiful. Her angles were fresh; her creases sharp but at the same time her curves, from the gentle waves of her golden hair to the swell of her hips were as soft as nature could make them. She had a glow about her and a presence that filled the room.

"Marilyn," Haley breathed. "I didn't know you were here."

The Commissioner of the Board of Entertainment laughed easily, like a woman without care or worry. "Oh, Haley, it's you who is the surprise. I never thought I'd see you alive."

"You know about the fire?" Roland asked.

Marilyn turned to the old man and paused before answering. "My what a specimen," she said approaching him. "Look at that hair...beautiful! And those eyes...so much wisdom. I could do so much with you if I were so inclined. And if you weren't a prisoner. Yes, I know about Polk. We got some great shots of it burning away as well, but I didn't know you were going, Haley and when I found out. I wasn't happy."

"Nor was I," Haley said. "But I had no choice."

"May I ask how you knew about the fire?" Roland questioned. "It seems to have gone overlooked by everyone else."

"It was overlooked because it was just a prison," Marilyn said, waving her hand, dismissing the death of thousands. "We didn't even cover it as a news story. The shots we took were to hold for future use; stock footage is the term. And as for how I knew? It's my business to know. Knowledge is power."

"True power derives from God's love," Roland said.

This brought a happy laugh from Marilyn. "Yes, I love it! This is the stuff writers can't even dream of. How's this: to escape an inferno three unlikely people band together: a prisoner spouting biblical lines, a beautiful reporter and an Inquisitor in love. Don't deny it Tarsus; I can see it in your eyes. This should be good. Oh, I can't wait to hear your story. But first, Charles be a dear and relieve the Inquisitor of his gun."

Chapter 41

Language is Leverage

The guards were quick, thorough, and rough. They searched Phil, taking his gun from him and holding him with his arms cranked behind his back. With far more gentleness, they took the Crown file from Haley, and then searched Roland as if they didn't know what would happen to someone so old if they did more than look at him odd. After this, the group was escorted to Marilyn's sumptuous office where they were seated around a long conference table.

"The gun was empty, Commissioner," one of the guards said holding it out to her. "It's been very recently fired."

"Ooh, the plot thickens," she said, sniffing the barrel and smiling mischievously. She plunked the useless gun on the table and then pointed to the guards. "You three leave us and you, Haley, tell me everything that's happened."

Without hesitation, Haley launched into the full and true story of what had transpired to all of them from the moment they first heard of Stephen Crown. She went on right up to the point they returned to the Capital and then she turned to Phil to describe what occurred with Loman and Henderson in the Justice building.

When he hesitated, Marilyn drummed her fingers on the table for a moment before saying, "Look, Tarsus, I may not have Inquisitors working for me, but I'll find out the truth, even if it kills you. Now spill. Did you find out who was after you?"

For some reason Phil didn't want to let on that, the Commissioner of Justice had been killed. "No. Loman didn't know a thing about any of this. We're going on the theory that Haley was the target."

Marilyn turned away and stared at a piece of art that hung from her wall. It was of a field of flowers, which Phil had barely given a second look. "Yes. Maybe," Marilyn mused aloud. She then brightened her smile and said to Phil. "Never trust Loman. He walks around in a daze, but he's a snake. He's the one commissioner who stumps me. But that's neither here nor there. The probable truth about all of this is that I am the intended target."

Roland found this funny. Laughing he said, "My goodness, your ego is amazing."

"Yes," agreed Marilyn. "But that doesn't make what I said any less true. You see the balance of power is always in flux. Each board represents a fiefdom and its commissioner is a veritable king within it, yet there is overlapping and it's at these margins that power is gained or lost. Take the case of Ellen Mathews."

Marilyn went to her desk and typed a command into her computer. This dimmed the lights slightly and the face of Ellen Mathews, sprung up on one of the large monitors that sat around the room. The commissioner sighed and shook her head. "Look how beautiful she was. Look at that jaw line; so regal and commanding. What a waste. She was spoon-fed false information by the Board of Productions in order to cover up their incompetence."

"And how does this affect you?" Roland asked.

"She was my lead reporter!" Marilyn snapped. "Now she's a traitor, and you better believe this casts a shadow on all of us in Entertainment. My power derives from the belief that the news we report is complete, incorruptible fact. When people start to doubt, it can take years to bring them back around. And now someone is going after one of my up and comers."

"Me?" Haley gushed happily. Phil and Roland shared a look that said: *How could she be happy that someone was after her?* A second later, she answered the unasked question. "I don't believe it. Marilyn Jennings thinks I'm an up and comer."

"You were," Marilyn conceded. "Now you're a fugitive."

"But I didn't do anything. You said yourself that someone is only using me to get to you. I'm innocent."

"Sorry, Hun," Marilyn said patting Haley's arm. "You're a liability. Even if we find out who set you up, I can't use you anymore. There'll be questions and likely investigations. All of which creates more doubt in the minds of viewers."

"Then what are you going to do with me?" Haley asked in a small voice.

"I don't know," Marilyn said, thinking. "It might be best if I disappeared you."

"Disappear me?" Haley gasped.

"I'll make it quick, which compared to the alternative is the best you could ask for. You've been on the Justice beat long enough to know what is waiting for you if I don't. Now don't pout and let's see that file. Maybe the fag knew something of interest."

Obediently Haley pushed the file across to Marilyn and as she flipped through it they sat in silence—except for Roland. He was curious and asked, "So the different Boards undermine and attack each other? How does a government run itself like that?"

"Somehow we do," Marilyn said absently as her eyes went back and forth on the page.

Roland shrugged at this and then went to the picture of the field of flowers. He ran his fingertips gently over its surface; the sensation of which made him smile. Marilyn cleared her throat in warning and he pulled his hands away quick, like a child caught in the act.

Phil wished he could smile as well. His sense of impending doom was still upon him and the words of this commissioner had only increased the feeling. He tried to fight it by putting on a show of bravado. "Haley seems to think that you run a powerful board, Commissioner. I don't see it. Other than a few guards that look more like bar-bouncers than anything else, you don't have much here."

"This file is useless," Marilyn groused, tossing it onto the table next to the gun. "And for your information, Inquisitor, Entertainment is by far the strongest board. We tell people what to think and feel. We define right and wrong. We define fact."

"That's not possible," Roland said. "A fact is unchangeable. You just think you're changing them but you're not. All you are doing is deluding yourself."

Marilyn leaned back in her chair and said, "The result is the same. If we want you to think food shortages are the result of neocons—it's what you'll think. If we want you to think the world is getting hotter, you'll sweat on a spring day. You see language is leverage, and whoever controls the language controls the country."

Roland snorted in disgust. "It's a lesson you picked up from the old liberal media, I see. Back in my day, they changed the meaning of words with impunity. Taxes changed to become fees. Income became wealth. Wealth became greed and of course, greed became the greatest evil imaginable. The definition of any word was subject to change so long as it furthered the liberal's needs. Illegal immigrants became undocumented workers and then that changed again to undocumented Americans. Mother and father became interchangeable and eventually were switched out for 'parental figure' so that over time the word family became so warped as to be unrecognizable. Even simple things you wouldn't think mattered were transformed: pets became animal companions, Christmas break became winter break and drug users became self-medicators."

The commissioner raised an eyebrow but didn't argue. Haley did however. She was pale and shook with anger or fear. "Maybe you're wrong, Roland. Not everything is a conspiracy. Who would care what a person called a dog or cat?"

"I wish I were wrong," the old man sighed. "As Marilyn said, words were used to shape thinking. The word pet was changed in order to make the idea of animal rights palatable."

"What right does an animal have?" Haley asked in a mocking tone, glancing toward Marilyn as she did, hoping for some support.

"None. But giving them rights wasn't really the point at all. It was just another wedge to destroy the dominant culture. The liberals took up the cause of animal rights because they wanted to appear as if they cared, not because it made any sense. They thought it was all right for a wolf to tear the belly out of a sheep and eat it alive, but they thought it was the height of cruelty for a rancher to kill the same wolf in a second with a bullet. And they would rather see a thousand deer starve to death rather than allow hunters to cull them in a humane manner."

"You're exaggerating," Haley said. "You just want to make the liberals, and by extension everyone here at the Board, look stupid."

"Not at all. The liberals called hunting cruel and barbaric; and no one wanted to be thought of as cruel. They positioned the argument so that if you weren't for animal rights, you must be in favor of animal suffering. Ask Marilyn."

They turned her way and she shrugged. "No one likes to see animals suffer," she said, in effect agreeing. Haley dropped her eyes to her hands which were squeezing themselves in a show of anxiety.

Phil glared across the table at the commissioner and asked, "But you'd see an actual person, your own employee, someone devoted to you, suffer?"

"It is the way it is," Marilyn said. "I got to my position not through compassion, but through strength. It's survival of the fittest here at the top and if that means I have to make it look like Homeland Security murdered one of my top reporters then that is what I'll do."

"You think it was them?" Phil asked.

"I don't know," Marilyn said. "Loman and I both lost mid-level players with the blame pointing toward Horace Fielder over at the Board of Corrections. However his position is so weak it would be suicide for him to take on the major players like this."

"If you ask me, it was the Army behind the prison fire," Phil said. "It was a professional job and I don't think those morons at Homeland could've pull it off."

Marilyn shook her head. "Of course it was the Army. I'm not questioning who burnt it down. It's been slated to go for months." Roland and Phil shared a look of incredulity over how cold-hearted she was about it. She saw the look and rolled her eyes. "It was a question of budgeting; maintaining prisons are expensive. The deaths of those prisoners served a purpose...just like your deaths will serve a purpose. A greater purpose."

"By that you mean *your* greater purpose?" Phil asked.

She smiled wickedly. "In my mind there is no greater purpose."

"But I was loyal," Haley said without strength.

"Yes, you were great, Hun." Marilyn tried to pat Haley's hand again but the younger woman pulled back. The commissioner gave her a sour look and turned back to Phil. "We know who started the fire, the question is how you and Haley...Haley what are you doing?" Haley had stood and picked up the gun. She was now digging through her pockets.

Marilyn looked ill at ease. "Sit down before I call the guards."

"Am I supposed to be scared?" Haley switched the gun to her left hand and searched her front right pocket.

"You should be," Marilyn said. "Those boys will show you what loyalty is all about. They'll break your legs if I so much as snap my fingers."

"But you're going to kill me anyways. You just said...ah, here it is." She held up a bullet and before Marilyn's eyes could go wide, Haley slid it into the chamber and sent the bolt home with solid thunk.

Chapter 42

Haley and Her God

"I'll call the guards," Marilyn said. "They'll be here in a blink."

Haley scoffed at this. "You'll be dead in a blink. So go right ahead."

Marilyn gritted her teeth into a warped smile, but said nothing. Phil sighed and asked, "Is this going to help us at all? First we kill the Commissioner of Justice and now we hold the Commissioner of Entertainment hostage?"

"Loman is dead?" Marilyn said in shock. She blinked a moment and then an idea struck her. "Haley we could use that. We can turn this to our advantage. We could say...the old man did it." She pointed at Roland for emphasis, jabbing her finger in the air toward him. "We could say...we could say that he broke out of prison and went after Loman out of revenge...and that you tracked him down and killed him when he was on his way to get me."

The gun in Haley's hand drooped as she considered. Phil crossed his arms over his chest and asked, "What about me? What crazy story are you going to cook up about me?"

"That's up to Haley. We could say that the insane prisoner managed to overpower you. Or we could say that the two of you worked as a team. People will like that."

"Does Roland have to die?" Haley asked in a little voice.

Roland laughed at this. "Haley, please. She's lying to you. There's too much downside for her to concoct a story that can be disproven so easily if you were brought before an Inquisitor."

"Are you lying?" Haley asked.

Marilyn had regained her composure and now her personality was a force. "No Haley. Please don't listen to an old zealot. What does he know? Does he know that it was I who picked you out of obscurity? Remember that day? Remember what I said?"

"You said I was going to be a star."

"That's right. And you still can be. Right now, your opportunity is even greater. We can go whichever way you want on this... a deranged zealot breaks out of prison, kills the Inquisitor sent to bring him to justice and he has you at knife point..."

"No," Haley said shaking her head. "Roland's too nice. He wouldn't do that."

"Then how about this?" Marilyn offered, her eyes shifting back and forth. "The prisoner saves you from the fire...and...and the two of you are hunted by an Inquisitor. You find out that Roland was innocent all along..."

"No. That's not the truth."

"Since when do you care about the truth?" Marilyn demanded in angry desperation. "I've seen your reporting. Hell, I even saw the Crown execution. That man hadn't done a thing wrong yet you were there smiling your way right through his death. The point is, truth is malleable. We change it to suit our needs and right now the unvarnished truth will get you killed, Haley."

Haley looked to Roland who gave her a fatherly smile. "You know what truth is, and you know what the value of it is. Just like you know how much to value a lie."

"Not at all?"

"Exactly."

Haley's mouth came open and her eyes went back and forth from the old man to the commissioner. Finally, they came to rest in the middle, on Phil. "What do I do?"

"Follow your heart; that's what Roland says."

The gun came up from where it had sat in her lap and came to rest pointing at Marilyn who made a sound of frustration. She then turned angry. "Is that your decision?" she demanded. "That's fine by me. Because you'll pay. I was trying to be nice before but now I don't think so. You're going to wish you had died in that fire."

Haley looked green, but Roland hopped up in a jolly mood. "Look at this old computer," he said going to Marilyn's desk and giving the mouse a shake.

"It's state of the art," grumbled Marilyn.

Roland chuckled. "Computers were my business. This was state of the art before I was born. Whoa. Well look at her." He swung the monitor around so that they could see that the backdrop to the password screen was a pretty blonde girl in a white dress. "Is that...?"

"It's Marilyn Monroe. I was named after her. And stop messing with the keyboard. You'll never guess my password and I'm not telling." Ignoring her, Roland turned the monitor back and kept up his typing.

"So what do we do now?" Haley asked. Phil shrugged and she grew angry. "Weren't you the one with some sort of idea about coming back to the Capital?"

Phil ran a hand through his hair and tried his best to avoid the smug look on Marilyn's face. "I came back here because I thought I was meant to. Like destiny. Roland had me convinced...no, I had myself convinced that I was going to change things somehow."

"Change does not come easy," Roland said, still squinting at the screen.

"Yeah," agreed Phil. "I just don't think I'm the one to do it. We can only hope that they'll destroy each other. Roland! That's it. Maybe we can use Loman's death to start a war among the Boards."

"Not going to happen," Roland answered without looking up. "Marilyn will tell you."

"He's right; it won't happen," she said. "Whoever takes over at Justice will be happy that someone did him a favor in knocking off Loman. And a war between the Boards won't ever happen, because we keep ourselves in check."

"Yourselves in check? How would you stop the military," Phil asked. "You'd think the Commissioner of the Army could take over anytime he wanted to."

"That was always the worry from day one," Marilyn replied. "Yes the army has brute power but it's offset by two things. The military is technically split into three distinct Boards: army, air force, navy. They hate each other with a passion and squabble all the time. Also, we keep them busy. It's why we're always at war. It doesn't matter what sort, or against who. Big war, small war, medium war; the whole idea is to keep them busy and to keep them somewhere else."

"That's your check?" Phil asked, skeptically. He had seen the army in action and didn't think that the air force and navy combined could do much but slow it down.

"I also have the power to hold them in check," she replied haughtily. "Though how is a secret I won't reveal; just be satisfied that I'm telling the truth."

"What about you?" Haley asked. "Who holds Entertainment in check?"

"Good question, Haley. I'm not all-powerful. The Board of Justice checks me. If I started a power grab, they could come in and arrest half my staff in a blink. And before you ask, Homeland Security with its quasi-army of police thugs checks Justice. No one can get too big or two strong."

"But you were worried someone was after your power," Haley said.

"Only at the margins. I should have said no one can get too big too quick," Marilyn answered. She then changed the subject. "Tell me, Haley, did you find God like these two? Are you a zealot? Don't be embarrassed and don't be worried about getting in trouble. After all it can't get too much worse for you."

Now Roland lifted his eyes over the monitor. Haley took one look at him and went pink. "I don't know. It sounds nice and all: love and happiness, but what good has it done us? We're still in big trouble. No magic spirit has come to save us."

"It depends on how you define the word save," Roland said.

"I think any way you look at it you aren't saved." Marilyn stood. "Well...I'm not going to sit here all evening. I have a nine o'clock meeting of the Board of Commissioners."

"Wait," Haley said as Marilyn started to leave. "I have a gun."

"Yes you do, but you also came with only one bullet, which was very stupid. So you have to come to a quick decision: shoot me and then die in about five seconds or put the gun on the table and live for a little longer."

"What should I do?" Haley asked Roland. The old man hit a key and stood.

"You won't be able to look to me for much longer. Decide for yourself or ask Phil for his advice, though he will likely only say follow your heart."

"My heart says Marilyn doesn't deserve to live a second longer," Phil said and felt a churning in his stomach. "That doesn't seem Christian, does it?"

"Remember, Phil. Thou shall not kill is actually an injunction against murder. Render unto Caesar that which is Caesar's. What I mean by that is the body of a man is his and his fellows to protect or harbor or slay. It's his soul that belongs to the lord."

Phil laughed. "Do you ever just answer a question plainly?"

Roland smiled in his grandfatherly way and said, "Sometimes it's moral to take a life, especially when that life is such a danger to all of humanity. Is she that threat?"

"Not alone she isn't," Phil said. "She is self-serving and small, and her death will be meaningless. Another will take her place just as another will take Loman's place."

"I think you've got it," Roland said.

"Got what?" Haley asked desperately. "What do I do?"

"If you kill, kill for a reason," Phil said. "Do you have a reason to kill her?"

"She betrayed me," Haley hissed angrily. "And she already said she'll kill all of us." She raised the gun and it rattled in her hands. Marilyn leaned back away from it as if that would do her some good. "I can't," Haley said a second later, putting the gun on the table.

Marilyn squinted at it. "I wonder what I would have done if I were you. Probably the same.

Breathing may not be everything but sometimes it's all we have. Guards! Get in here."

The three burly guards came in and eyed the group. They sensed something had gone wrong and they were nervous. The commissioner picked up the gun and swiveled it toward the newcomers making their eyes grow large. Her eyes in contrast narrowed to the slits of a viper.

"Freddy, you overlooked something when searching the prisoners. I should give..."

"Ms Jennings," Roland said with a warning note in his voice. The two locked eyes for a moment and then her lip curled.

"Fine," she said with a sour smile and tossed the gun down. "There's a new Commissioner of Justice," she said to her guards. "I want these three gift wrapped for him with my compliments."

"Wait!" Haley cried. "No, not the Inquisitors. They...they're your enemies. You'll only make them stronger. Remember, you said that."

"At the margins, my dear," Marilyn said, touching Haley's hair. "Only at the margins. And there is this, an early peace offering with a new Commissioner can pay great dividends in the future. It's all a give and take; keep that in mind. Besides this may give you a day or two longer to find that God of yours. I wish you luck."

After their close call with the furious commissioner, the guards were in no mood to go easy on them and each was searched once more in a rough manner so that even Haley had her face smashed into the wall as she was groped. Phil barked at them, but only received blows in return.

"It's ok, Phil," Haley said through tears. "Don't worry about me."

This was a useless suggestion. His heart burst at her treatment and he couldn't help himself and he begged them not to hurt her. They ignored his pleading and tied her hands as cruelly as they did his own and tossed them into the back of another van.

"Not the seventh level," Haley moaned through her tears. "Freddy! It's me, Haley. You know me. I was nice to you..."

Freddy went to punch her in the face and Phil threw himself over her and received the blow and many more besides. But he wouldn't move from atop her no matter what they tried and after a while, they left him alone and drove to the Justice building.

How badly he wished the ride would take hours or days, but this van was in perfect order and in minutes, they stopped.

"Haley keep quiet," Phil warned. "Don't say a word. Don't beg."

"Yes," Roland agreed. "It won't do any good. These guards do indeed know you and so it makes it a thousand times harder to do what they've been ordered to do. It'll come out in their fists...but..." Here he lowered his voice to a whisper. "If you get alone with one of them that's when you beg. You hear me."

The van door opened and they were pulled out one after another. The building loomed above them cold and inhuman, like a totem of evil. Haley could barely stand her fear was so great and Phil found his breath wouldn't leave his throat like it should. It seemed to catch there so he thought he would choke on air. Compared to what awaited him inside it would be a godsend if it did.

There were very few instances of a fallen Inquisitor being brought back to the seventh level alive, but those instances were legendary for their unabashed cruelty. Gone was the inner calm he had felt earlier in the evening and now it was replaced by a dread that vibrated along his every nerve.

"Courage, my friends," Roland said. "Trust in the Lord."

"I can't!" Haley wailed. "Freddy please. Don't do..."

Freddy was a mountain of a man, thick and wide, his hand was the size of a dinner plate. He clamped it over her mouth, crushing her lips to her teeth. "Say my name again and I'll smash your teeth down your throat." As he said this, he shot a nervous glance at the building. Beneath his hand, Haley nodded and he released her. She dropped her head and her tears lipped onto the pavement at her feet.

Then they were bustled into the building and there were the security guards that Phil passed with his nose in the air on a daily basis. They eyed him— some in surprise—some with nasty smiles.

"Delivery for the new Commissioner of Justice from the Commissioner of Entertainment, Ms Marilyn Jennings," Freddy announced. "I'm ordered to accompany them."

He was such a presence that the guards allowed it and in seconds they were all in a single cramped elevator riding to the tenth floor. What would they find? Phil wondered. Had Loman's body been discovered? Was there really a new Commissioner already? Phil hoped to God that it was Darryl Conner and not Russ Steiner the Secretary of the Inquisitors. Russ was the devil.

Phil had to squeeze his eyes shut against the thought of Russ and his gleaming tools and the screams he caused to vibrate the building hour after hour.

"Here we are," one of the security guards said when they got to the tenth floor. Unlike earlier the floor was well lit, all save Ms. Adleman's desk, which was still dark and empty. "At the end of the hall."

They were at the door at in a blink and now Haley drooped in Freddy's arms; she was only a blob of flesh and tears and overwhelming fear. The guard knocked and Ms. Adleman stepped from the office wearing a look of shock at what she saw in front of her. She said nothing.

"A delivery for the new Commissioner of Justice from the Commissioner of Entertainment, Ms Marilyn Jennings," Freddy announced a second time. "I'm ordered to accompany them in to see him."

Ms. Adleman glared. It was a thing to see Freddy wilt before it. "You will wait downstairs in the lobby for any message the new commissioner may wish to send back," she said in a tone that froze the air around them. "Or these men will shoot you. Whatever authority you think you've been granted by the Commissioner of Entertainment was invalidated the moment you set foot in this building. Good night."

Freddy took the smart road and turned on his heel. The building security guards left at a look from Ms. Adleman and were only too happy to.

"Tarsus, you bastard," she said next through gritted teeth, glaring with all the ferocity she could muster. This caused the strangest reaction—he smiled. She had been Loman's secretary and it was highly unlikely that the next commissioner would keep such a hag around. He was suddenly unafraid, at least unafraid of her.

"That's Mr. Tarsus to you," he said, feeling that eerie calm. He hoped it would last.

She laughed so hard at this that the folds of fat in her sagging face crumpled in on themselves, turning her usual hideous face into that of a pale goblin. And then she stared at Phil as if trying to figure out what could bring him to say such a thing.

She then smiled with villainy beneath and said, "In you go. Time to meet your destiny."

Chapter 43

A New Justice

The calm disappeared when Phil stepped through the door. Russ Steiner sat relaxing in the very chair Loman had died in less than an hour before. The ash from Loman's last cigarette still sat in a little heap on the desk next to Steiner's elbow.

"Well, what is this?" Steiner asked. "Tarsus? Haley Baker? What the hell is going on?" This he asked of Ms. Adleman.

"I'm not exactly sure," she replied. It was a lie, Phil could tell. She knew something or perhaps everything. "They were delivered by Jennings' people."

"What a night," Steiner commented as if it had been arduous for him. Outwardly, he seemed quite content. "Let's hear it, Tarsus. You have a little run in with Loman and then maybe a disagreement with your under-inquisitor?"

"My hands are clean," Phil replied without elaborating.

"They are not," Ms. Adleman said. Phil's hands were tied behind his back and she had a good view. "There's blood all over them. Henderson's I'm betting."

How did she know that name? As far as Phil knew, they had never spoken a single time. He gave her a look but she only stared with gathering wrinkles around her eyes.

Steiner got up and turned Phil around. "Look at that." He went to spin Haley around as well and knocked her into the wall as she stumbled.

Phil slammed his shoulder into Steiner, sending him back. "She's clean," Phil growled. "Leave her out of this."

"Wow. You are amazing," Steiner said, genially. He then kicked Phil in the stomach, sending him to his knees and gasping for air. "Listen carefully Tarsus: you don't give me orders. At the moment, you are a murder suspect three times over. And since one of those killed was the Commissioner of Justice, you are also suspected of treason. You know what that means?"

It meant that Steiner would have him down in the seventh level where he would eventually confess to anything that Steiner wanted him to confess to. Steiner was the best; everyone knew it.

"I understand," Phil said.

Steiner beamed. "Excellent. Now what in the name of Pete is this?" he asked looking at Roland. "It's an antique human." This he laughed loudly over; no one else joined in. "Are you going to protect him also?"

"I don't want to see him hurt," Phil replied. This made Steiner laugh some more. Before this Phil had never seen Steiner so much as crack a smile, and he liked it better that way. Steiner's laugh was creepy.

"I knew you were going soft," Steiner said. "Didn't I, Ms. Adleman? Two weeks ago I told her you were going soft, soft, soft. And now look at you, Tarsus. Acting all chivalrous and pathetic. You know who's to blame? Conner. If he wasn't already dead, I'd have him on charges of treason also."

"Conner's dead? How...when?" Phil asked.

Steiner laughed again—it was a cold noise. It was what a corpse would sound like if it laughed. "Like you don't know, Tarsus. Henderson, Conner, Loman all dead? Are you telling me you don't see a connection here? What's the piece missing out of this puzzle?"

"Me?" Phil guessed.

"You."

There was something else missing from the puzzle. Something glaring. Yet what it was he didn't know.

"Take a look at this," Steiner said pulling out a photograph. "Maybe it'll jog your memory." It was a picture of Conner slumped over his desk. There were two little holes in his forehead and a mass of gore slung out the back. Steiner made to pull the picture back but something caught Phil's eye.

"Hold on," he said. "Let me get a better look." Steiner hesitated and then decided to humor Phil. "This wasn't a professionally done," Phil murmured. "Look at the first shot. It's high up on the forehead. That shot almost missed."

An expression of puzzlement crossed Steiner's face and he took a closer look at the picture. "How do you know which shot was the first...I see. And the second shot had a different angle; he was lying on the desk. You can tell by the splatter."

The piece of the puzzle clicked into place. The way things were set up the chain of command went: Henderson, Tarsus, Conner, *Adleman,* and then Loman. Everything went through the commissioner's secretary. Phil glanced her way and they locked eyes. She had killed Conner. But why?

Perhaps she couldn't stand the idea as Conner as her boss, or maybe she thought he had murdered Loman and she had been exacting revenge. She was notoriously protective of Loman, so much so that Phil thought they were romantically involved. The thought was repellant and nearly drove a fact from Phil's head. Nearly.

"May I see the picture one more time?" Phil asked.

Looking suddenly uneasy, Steiner acquiesced and turned the picture toward Phil. He was looking to see if he could catch a glimpse of Conner's desk clock, but it was turned to the side and he couldn't tell the time exactly. However, it didn't matter. Unlike Phil's, Conner's office had windows and there was a definite low glow competing with the overhead light. The picture had been taken just at sundown, when Phil was still ten miles outside the city and Loman was still alive.

"What are you looking at?" Steiner asked.

At the moment, he wasn't looking at the picture at all. Movement to his right had him turning and had he been armed and untied he would've been able to stop Ms. Adleman. She was slow and very deliberate. The gun seemed to take ages to show itself from beneath the shawl she wore against the cold.

Though slow, she didn't hesitate and pulled the trigger with a deafening crack. Steiner looked surprised as the first bullet entered his chest, and afraid as the second one did. He crumpled and died, while Phil and the others backed away from Ms. Adleman.

"Tarsus, you pain in the ass," she said. "This is all your fault."

"I actually don't know what's going on," Phil admitted. Despite having a gun trained on him, he felt the inner calm coming back. Steiner was dead; the world was a better place. "I know you killed Conner earlier this evening, only I don't know why. Did Loman order it?"

Ms. Adleman smiled in her unfortunate manner and said, "You're an idiot. Loman couldn't order a sandwich without me."

Flummoxed, Phil glanced over to Haley and Roland but they were as stunned and puzzled as he. "You killed Conner without Loman's permission?" Phil asked. "Why? If he found out you'd be...wait. Loman didn't send me to Polk. He didn't have a clue about that. It was you. Now I get it. You sent me to Polk to die."

"Yes."

"And you had Crown's building burned to the ground," Phil accused. She nodded and he went on, "And you rushed the execution...and your last name is Adleman! Was it a granddaughter?"

"Yes," she said looking slightly impressed. "My granddaughter, the only thing in this world that matters to me was in Crown's class. He was a good teacher."

"You had him killed!" Roland said. "How could you say that?"

She shrugged. Phil was beginning to understand. "Ms. Adleman was afraid someone would use the fact that a gay had taught her granddaughter against her. But how did you get her into Stadler Academy in the first place. You're just a secretary." She raised her eyebrow at this and now Phil understood completely. "You aren't just a secretary, aren't you?"

"I am the real Commissioner of Justice and have been for thirteen years. Loman was just a figurehead."

"Is that how it is with all the boards?" Phil asked. "There's someone behind the scenes pulling strings like a puppet master?"

Ms. Adleman seemed to like the image as puppet master. "No. As you said I was just a secretary under Commissioner Roberts, but then he began to grow senile. Day to day decisions had to be made and gradually I came to make them. I just spoke in his name and forged his signature. When he died, I handpicked his replacement. Loman was a burned out under-commissioner with skeletons in his closet. His entire job was to sit in this office and keep up appearances."

"Did Conner find out?" Roland asked. "Is that why you killed him?"

"Yes," Ms. Adleman replied. "Crown was arrested before I was aware and Conner took one look at Mary's name and knew that something was wrong. He started digging around and found out that I basically run the entire operation. You got to hand it to him, Conner had balls. He wanted Loman's position and tried to blackmail me."

"So why did you go after us?" Haley asked. "We didn't do anything wrong. We didn't know."

"To be on the safe side," Ms. Adleman said, waving her hand as if shooing a fly. "A woman in my position can't be too careful. If Conner could figure it out, I knew that Tarsus would as well. So I sent you to Polk. It had been scheduled to be reduced anyway and what with a prisoner suddenly confessing to a crime of treason." Here she raised her eyebrows at Roland. "I figured I'd be able to clean up a lot of loose ends before I took out Conner."

There came an awkward silence among them as each silently asked the same question: what was to come next. Haley couldn't remain silent for long. Her fear drove her to ask. "So what are you going to do with us?"

The gun still sat in Ms. Adleman's hand and she gave it a long look before answering: "I think that I'm going to have make a bargain with Mr. Tarsus. I need a new figurehead and you fit the bill well enough: you know my secret and I have leverage over you. It's all I need."

"Even if I wanted the job, I don't think that it'll work," Phil said. "I'm just an Inquisitor. Who would take me seriously? Aren't there under-commissioners in line for the position? And won't there be questions? I mean everyone in my chain of command has been murdered."

She laughed. "Around here, murder is a resume enhancer! People will be too afraid to question you, and we'll use that fear to keep them in line." Ms. Adleman took a deep breath and glanced down at Steiner's body. "I was so worried when Steiner found out about the bodies. He isn't the kind of man who plays second fiddle when..."

"I don't want the job," Phil said interrupting. With the choice between swinging the whip and feeling it, Phil couldn't bring himself to swing it anymore.

Ms. Adleman's dark eyes flashed and then she took a few faltering attempts at laughter. "You don't want the job? This isn't an interview. You take the position or I cut out all your tongues and send you down to the seventh level for interrogation."

"I can't do it," Phil said.

"Please!" Haley cried. "For me; do it for me. She won't make you kill anyone. You won't have to do that anymore."

Well..." Ms. Adleman made a face. "That's not entirely true. Marilyn Jennings knows too much. I'm going to need some evidence implicating her in the death of Commissioner Loman; just to hold over her head as a threat to keep quiet. I think a few confessions—two or three will do it. We'll start with old man; I don't like the look of him."

"I said I won't do it," Phil repeated.

"You'll do it," Ms. Adleman said confidently. "I saw how you looked at Ms. Baker. I probably won't have to crush more than two or three of her toes before you cave in."

Phil dropped his head, unable to look Ms. Adleman in the eyes. She was right. He'd do anything to keep Haley safe. But what did that mean for Roland? Would Phil be able to torture the old man to death to keep Haley safe?

As usual, Roland seemed to know Phil's mind. He said in a clear voice, "Take the offer, Inquisitor."

"Don't call me that," Phil said. "It's an embarrassment."

Roland nodded in understanding. "Take the offer, Phil. Thou shalt not regret it."

Chapter 44

A Temptation Too Great?

Thou shalt not regret it?

Why had Roland used such an odd choice of words? The only other times he had used the words thou and shalt was when he had gone down the list of the Ten Commandments. Did that have meaning here? Was the old man suggesting that God would want him to take the position of commissioner?

Didn't Roland understand the inherent evil that the position would require of a person? Roland looked at him steadily with just the tiniest head nod.

"All right, I'll do it," Phil said. "But, I need to know that Haley will be safe from harm. And...and if I'm going to interrogate Roland it's going to be a fake. Haley could help out with the editing. We can make it look real."

Ms. Adleman raised an eyebrow at what she took as a sign of a man going soft. "Fine. But if it's not convincing I'll have to take over." She then gave Haley a glance and added, "I have a place outside of town that I can keep her safe. You can even visit on the weekends. It's very cozy. Now I have stipulations of my own. You will do everything I tell you to, without hesitation or backtalk. For every infraction of this very simple rule, I'll have Ms. Baker beaten and you will be forced to watch. My guards on the farm are mine. They will not listen to you and will kill Ms. Baker at the drop of a hat."

"I understand," Phil said.

"I hope you do," Ms. Adleman said. "Because I won't tolerate the least nonsense. Turn around."

Phil had the ropes cut that bound his hands; Haley and Roland did not. Ms. Adleman went to Loman's desk and took from the drawer a three-inch long rectangular box that had wires trailing from it.

"You're going to begin your tenure as Commissioner of Justice tonight. Sorry for the short notice, but there's a meeting of the Board of Commissioners in less than an hour and it would be very dangerous not for you to attend. Here." She held out the box. "This goes on your belt. It's a transmitter and this tie clip has a camera right there. I'll be able to hear and see everything you do."

"Everything?" Phil asked clipping the box to his belt. "Even when I go to the bathroom?"

She glared. "No. It has a battery life of little over an hour. Turn it on when you get to the building. But don't think I won't know what's going on between now and then. I'll have one of my men babysitting you at all times. Now this goes in your ear. I'll be telling you everything you need to say. You got it?"

"Yeah. I'm your puppet."

"Good. Stay here in this office. Don't even think of leaving until the car comes to pick you up. I've got a thousand things to do and no time to do them in. Let's go," she said to Roland and Haley.

They left the room and even before the door had shut, Ms. Adleman was shouting orders down the hall. "Greg! Take this old geezer to the seventh level. Ernie, I want every guard who was at the front door pulled and liquidated. No questions. Tim, tell that big moron from Entertainment that..."

The door shut leaving Phil alone with the body of Russ Steiner. "I'm the Commissioner of Justice," Phil said. He went to the desk and slumped into the seat, feeling weak. "How on earth did that happen?"

He sat there for a good five minutes, staring at nothing before he noticed Steiner's head hung canted toward him and his eyes stared vacantly in Phil's direction. It made him queasy. He got up and nudged Steiner's head with his shoe and then laughed at himself for being such a wimp.

"I can't even touch a corpse. I..." Phil stopped as he realized that no one had said anything on behalf of Steiner, a man Phil had secretly referred to as 'the prince of evil.' What could he say? Steiner made Loman look like a saint.

Wearily Phil knelt and said, "Lord...help him...I guess. Though he doesn't deserve it. I mean, I don't know what I mean. I'm the one that needs help not him. Oh boy...I mean, bless him, please, but bless me too. Haley needs me and Roland..." he trailed off from his blathering and gazed down at the body, unable to find the words for any sort of proper prayer.

A long sigh escaped him and he was just about to heave himself up when he caught sight of something beneath Steiner's black Jacket. It was the leather of his holster. Ms. Adleman had completely overlooked its presence.

With growing excitement, Phil fumbled the service pistol from the dead man's holster and checked the load. All accounted for.

"Now what?" he asked Steiner.

He had one pistol with fifteen rounds to take on a building with maybe thirty guards roaming the halls. And then there were all the service personnel, the secretaries, the under-inquisitors, and Inquisitors. It was getting late, however there would still be some running around.

That was a lot to go against, yet worse than all that was the fact that he didn't have any sort of plan. All he had was the vague idea to free Roland and track down Ms. Adleman and Haley before it was too late. Only he didn't know how to start and worse, a part of him wanted to give up on the whole idea.

It seemed so dangerous and for what? A new chance to be hunted down and killed? Why would he want that when he was sitting at the pinnacle of one of the strongest boards in the government? If he had Ms. Adleman killed, he'd be one of the three most powerful people in the country.

He could be warm for once...and full; he had no doubt that commissioners ate like kings. And his house would be grand! There were rumors that mansions still existed hidden in the forests north of the city. Great sprawling properties with fountains and pools and manicured lawns. What a life! People would fear him—women would throw themselves at him, and men would kill for him.

It would take almost nothing to have that all for himself. "I would just have to give up my soul," Phil whispered. With his hands still stained with Henderson's blood and his wrists raw from the ropes that had bound him, it didn't seem like such a bad price, not just then. He was tired after days of stress and fear, and his new belief in God was a weak little thing. Something that could be easily forgotten in the gluttony of a feast and the arms of a fine woman.

Haley's face swam into his mind. *They'll kill her. They'll kill her slowly*, his inner voice spoke. It was true, and it would be Phil's fault. Now Roland's stern visage came to him. *They'll kill him too*. Yes, and again it would be Phil's fault. How many more would die because of him...because he did nothing?

"What am I supposed to do? I'm just one man!"
You fight.
"But I might die."
No, you will die. Everyone dies.

"Right. Everyone dies," Phil said to himself. He didn't even know what fighting entailed. Was he supposed to fight the entire country by himself? The answer didn't come to him from his inner voice, but a face did: Roland's once again. He would know the answer.

Casting aside the images of the pools, and the giant four-poster beds, and the tables filled with food and wine, Phil went to the door. He would fight, even if it meant he wouldn't make it past the door to his new office.

Tucking the pistol into his own holster, Phil was just about to peek out when he hesitated. "A commissioner doesn't peek," he told himself. With that in mind, he strode out of his office with purpose and nearly blanched at the sight of a security guard standing right there.

"Uh, Sir?" the man said timidly. He put his hands out, palms up in the universal gesture of stop. "Commissioner? Ms. Adleman told me not to let you wander around. It's for your own good."

"What do you know about my good?" Phil asked, trying to sound haughty though his insides were like water. "Probably nothing I bet."

"I'm just following orders, Sir. I'm supposed to keep you in your office and call Ms. Adleman if you don't stay there."

Perhaps out of habit Phil fingered his tie; his hand inches from the butt of his pistol. This always calmed him. It relaxed him enough for him to step closer to guard. This wasn't one of the men who had accompanied them up from the lobby. He knew this man...it was the kiss-up who usually worked the front lobby. The guard was lucky he hadn't been there earlier.

The guards who had been there were all soon to be murdered for the crime of being in the wrong place at the wrong time. They had seen the new

Commissioner come in under arrest and Ms. Adleman wasn't taking any chances that a rumor would start.

"I'm not staying in my office," Phil said. "So make your call. Just know that if you do I'll be aware of who you really work for."

"Who's that?"

"Ms. Adleman," Phil explained. "I plan on firing her and every one of her cronies at the first opportunity. Is that going to be you?" The guard shook his head rapidly. Phil clapped him on the shoulder and said, "Good. Come with me. I've got to consolidate my power before things get out of hand. So keep your gun ready."

The man was a nervous wreck being so close to the Commissioner of Justice. "My gun? Why do I need my gun ready? What's going on?"

"There have been five deaths in the building tonight," Phil answered. "There may be a coup d'état in the works and so..."He paused at the blank look on the guard's face."There may be an overthrow in the works. Do you understand?"

"Yeah, I got that."

"Good, so do exactly as I say without hesitation. Even if I ask you to pull your gun on another guard. We're going to detain as many people as we can and then sort out loyalties later. We'll start at the bottom."

They raced down the stairs taking three at a time and very soon they found themselves at the seventh Level. Phil knew it intimately. It was laid out in a capitol T. Offices to the right of the stairs; interrogation rooms and the execution room to the left; and down the long corridor in the center, holding cells by the hundreds.

There was a guardroom just inside that long hall and in it, two men sat playing cards. There should've been a third.

"Where's the new prisoner?" Phil demanded as he strode in, his hand touching the new clip on his tie.

The guards here were less inclined to fear the Inquisitors since they worked with them on a day-to-day basis. These two didn't even stand up. "Grady is checking him in. Room forty-eight at the end of the hall."

Phil turned to the guard he had brought from the tenth floor and glanced at his nametag. "Wait here, Noonan," he said and then tipped him a small nod. Noonan swallowed loudly and nodded back, his hand landing and re-landing on the butt of his gun like a moth kissing a lamp.

Phil hoped Noonan wouldn't shoot himself by accident and hurried down the corridor passing one sad prisoner after another until he came to cell forty-eight, which was about mid-way down. Roland was on the ground being stomped by the guard named Grady—this was standard operating procedure for people imprisoned for treason.

"Hey there, Inquisitor," Grady said with an easy smile. The man enjoyed his work, something the old Phil Tarsus had always appreciated.

Phil pointed to Roland and said, "Turn him over."

When Grady bent to his task, Phil pulled his gun and bashed him in the back of the head. Grady slumped over Roland who struggled to free himself from the weight of the man. Phil didn't help. Time was against him.

"Cuff him and stay here unless you here gunfire and then come running," Phil ordered and then turned on his heel heading back to the guardroom. His heart beat in his chest like hammer against his ribs. If any more guards came by or if a stray Inquisitor decided to check on a prisoner things would turn bloody and quick.

The two guards were still playing cards and unsuccessfully trying to engage Noonan in conversation. Phil entered with his gun still in his hand; he leveled it at the now wide-eyed guards and said, "We have reason to suspect that one of you two is involved in a plot against the new commissioner."

The two looked at each other and then immediately pointed at his opposite. "That's what I thought," Phil said. "I just need to check your pockets. Hands up and face the wall." Since neither was actually involved in any plot, they obeyed readily.

"There's a new commissioner?" one of them asked. Phil grunted out a yes as he relieved them of their guns and handcuffs. "What are you doing?" the same guard asked.

Phil had cuffed the two men together. He didn't answer, but turned to Noonan. "If anyone comes in, hold them at gun point and don't let them leave." Noonan nodded and held his gun in jittery hands.

Seconds later Phil had the two guards down in the cell with Roland. They started to babble out questions and declarations of innocence; Phil hushed them with a glare and then locked them in.

"I need my proper clothes," Roland said as they made their way to the guardroom.

"I'll get you something better," Phil assured him. "How would you like to be an Inquisitor?"

Chapter 45

The Clash

Noonan pointed his gun Roland's way and demanded, "What is this? He's a prisoner. He should be in a cell."

"He's a wrongfully accused prisoner," Phil explained. "We're going to figure this all out, Noonan. But first I need one second." He pulled Roland aside and said, "Check that office right there for a uniform and then figure out how the hell we're going to find Haley, and hurry."

When Roland scampered away, Phil gave Noonan a grim smile. "Let's clear this floor. You and me." He had a burning need for atonement and nothing seemed to satisfy that, like locking away Inquisitors.

This turned out to be an easier chore than he had expected. There were only eleven men in the various offices, and Inquisitors, by the very nature, were solitary, it was nothing to go from room to room and take them into custody. Another fact that helped them was that Inquisitors tended towards anger rather than exuberant outbursts; every one of them went quietly to the cells muttering threats under their breath.

When they were half done Roland appeared with his hair slicked back, wearing the black uniform of an Inquisitor. As tall as he was he fit into a spare uniform of Henderson's though it hung loosely on his thin frame.

"I feel horrible," Roland complained. "Like I should be asking forgiveness for just putting this on."

"Ask forgiveness later," Phil said opening a door to an office belonging to a man that he had worked with for years. He pointed the gun he had taken from Steiner and said, "Zane, you're under arrest. Sorry, it's just a formality, but you have to come with me."

They were done with ten minutes left before the car was supposed to come get Phil. "What do we do now?" he asked, Roland.

"I found Haley," the old man replied. "Or rather I found the apartment building in which Ms. Adleman lives. It sits catty-corner to the Board of Commissions building. An Interesting fact—there are no other tenants in that building. She has it all to herself."

Phil stared in amazement and asked, "How did you find that out so quickly?" A large part of him expected God to be the answer, but Roland pointed to the computer in Phil's office.

"Despite that the modem on that piece of junk is archaic even by my standards...I mean how can you not have ethernet? When I was a kid ethernet was old news. They had protocols that could run..."

"Roland!"

"Sorry. The easy answer is that I hacked into Ms Jennings computer when we were in her office. I thought it unlikely that she had been named after a movie star from over a hundred years ago. I figured it far more probable that she named herself after Marilyn Monroe and from there I just typed in various permutations of Norma Jean Baker, Marilyn Monroe's real name and there it was. She wasn't kidding about information being her forte', she had information on everybody and everything."

"Including Adleman's address."

Roland laughed. "Including the door code for the rear entrance." Phil was moving to the stairs in a flash, but Roland held him back. "We're not done here."

"We don't have time!" Phil insisted, throwing off Roland's restraining arm.

"You're wrong. We have ten minutes. Remember, you can't even leave the building without an escort of handpicked men." Phil moaned, but Roland steadied him. "Here's the plan. You leave with whoever comes for you. Act submissive and then once you get around the corner put a gun to his head. I'll be there."

"And then what?"

"We change places," Roland answered. "One of us has to continue onto the meeting otherwise Adleman will know we've cooked up a plan."

"But you don't look anything like me!" Phil bellowed. "It'll never work."

"The camera's going to be on my chest, pointing out, not up. She won't know. She'll think it's you and thus she'll have her guard down. It's the only way you're going to get into her building."

Phil nodded at the logic of the plan, taking it in. He then said in a whisper, "I might have to kill someone." In order to save Haley, he would kill if he had to, whether or not Roland said it was all right.

"You might have to kill a lot of people," Roland replied, laying a hand on his shoulder. "In a world filled with sin, hatred, and evil, war is inevitable. We are at war. And now we have to figure out what to do with the prisoners of war." He pointed down the hallway where the majority of cells held people who had done nothing, yet were condemned to death.

"I know what to do," Phil said. He grabbed the keys and searched out one prisoner in particular: Ellen Mathews.

"Ellen?" She didn't look like herself. Every inch of her visible skin had been abused in some manner or another: there were burns, lacerations, punctures; the list went on. "Ellen Mathews can you hear me?"

She cowered in his presence and he had to repeat himself before she said, "Yes, Sir."

"My name is Phil Tarsus. I'm a friend of Haley Baker's and I'm here to free you."

"Haley?" she said in wonder, coming from her crouch in the corner of the cell. "You're freeing me? She said you were nice. She said...but...but it doesn't matter. I can't leave. *He* will know and *he* will hurt me."

"Russ Steiner is dead. He can't hurt you anymore," Phil said. "Come on. Let me show you." He took her hand and drew her forth and then walked her down the hall to where the Inquisitors sat glaring from their new cells.

"What's going on?" she asked. There was so much fear still in her voice that Phil began to doubt that she would be able to help in anyway.

"We're escaping, tonight. Here's..."

"Yes!" she cried, raising her hands in the air, tears running from her eyes. "We're escaping!" she screamed and the prison went wild. Phil had to drag her down to where Roland and Noonan stood so they could hear each other.

"They can't escape. It's against the law," Noonan said.

Phil made a sad face. "I've got bad news, Noonan. You are now an accessory to treason. If you don't escape with us, they'll stone you to death."

While Noonan turned white, Phil outlined his simple plan. There wasn't much to it and it only took a minute. Ellen was to release every prisoner, and arm those with military backgrounds with the fourteen pistols they had confiscated. They were to then wait fifteen minutes and make a charge at the four guards at the front lobby, while another group was to head to the garage and take as many vehicles as they could. They were to make a break for the mountains around Williamston.

A simple plan for them. Phil's plan for escape was a little more complicated and after running over it, he and Noonan chanced the elevators and rode back up to the tenth floor. They hurried to his new office.

Standing in the doorway Noonan asked, "Am I really a criminal? You know I didn't do anything."

"Does that ever matter around here?" Phil asked. The guard's face drooped, answering Phil's question. "You'll do well where we're going. They need men who aren't afraid to do the right thing."

Noonan actually blushed at this. A moment later, the elevator dinged and he shut the door.

Phil had barely enough time to scurry to the seat behind the desk and glance once at the body of Steiner before the door opened again and a burly guard stuck his head in. He looked about the room and then asked, "Are you the new Commissioner of Justice?"

It was like an accusation in Phil's ears. It was as if the guard had asked him if he was the country's top murderer. He restrained the surge of anger within him and said, "There's no one else here but me and that guy." He pointed at Steiner.

The guard went to the phone, punched a few buttons and said, "He's here, ma'am. We're leaving now."

There were two guards with him. One, a blonde giant of a man, who stood by the elevator and the shorter thicker one who had made the phone call. Of Noonan there was no sign. He'd been dismissed, which worked out great. The second part of his plan was to rush downstairs and escort Roland out of the building.

So far, things were going to plan—with the one exception: there were two guards with Phil and probably a third as a driver. Three against one were dreadful odds even with Phil being dead fast. He had to bet these fellows were trained killers and in that line of work, nothing succeeded like speed of hand.

Still, he had the element of surprise on his side...or so he thought. The elevator doors opened onto the lobby and there was Roland with his hands above his head and a few feet away, a very nervous looking Noonan had his hand inching toward his pistol.

Confronting them were four guards, each with weapons drawn and aimed at Roland, but at the sound of the elevator the guards swung their pieces toward Phil and the men that Ms. Adleman had sent.

Surprise had been lost...and a second later judgment went out the window as well. There might have been a chance that, as the new Commissioner of Justice, Phil could have explained away the presence of an ancient looking Inquisitor as a visitor from Boston, however, inexplicably Noonan pulled his gun and fired.

In a span of seconds, an unknown number of bullets blazed back and forth across the room, tearing the air with the shrieking of their passing. Roland displayed his age, slowly going to the floor like a rusting robot, while Noonan went down in a heap still firing, but mostly hitting nothing but the expensive windows on the far side of the room.

Even caught so unaware Phil's gun appeared in his hand like magic and he fired with the intent to kill. Roland—his mentor, his spiritual guide, his friend—

was in danger and he gave no thought whatsoever to the consequences to his soul or body. Nothing mattered to him but protecting the man he had come to love as a father, and with anguish in his heart over the thought of Roland feeling the least pain, he fired.

And he missed. The men with Phil were trained bodyguards; just as he went to fire, one of them pulled Phil back behind him, spoiling his aim. The guards in the lobby turned from one attack to another and returned fire at the elevator. They held a significant advantage over the bodyguards, who were both huge targets confined to a small space.

Bullets came whizzing in, hitting flesh and bone; metal and wood. Both of Phil's guards were hit in the first exchange, yet with their size and the vagaries of bullet trajectories it was no wonder that one, the giant blonde, stayed upright, though he dropped his gun to clutch the wall. With the cold heart of the Inquisitor he once was, Phil took the man by the back and held him in place with one hand while he fired with the other.

His human shield lived long enough for Phil to kill two of the guards in the lobby and then the blonde went over and Phil had to press himself against the wall of the elevator to keep from being hit.

Now there came a lull that Phil couldn't allow to last. Time was against him. He had precious few minutes to get Roland to that meeting before Ms. Adleman began to suspect a problem. In a blur of black cloth and pistol fire, he leaned partially into the doorway and fire off two quick rounds at the guards.

One was a clean headshot, the other a through and through gut shot, which he counted as a miss, seeing as the man was still alive and still firing.

And there were others firing. More guards, maybe three or four, had come running at the sound of the fight and now bullets from all angles pinned Phil to the corner of the elevator. He couldn't move without getting hit, yet he had no other options. If he stayed and cowered, a ricochet would eventually get him and both Haley and Roland would die because of his lack of courage.

The gunfire was loud, a tremendous din that vibrated the walls and it took all of Phil's lung strength to hear his own battle cry as he leapt from his hiding spot with his gun and soul at the ready. He was prepared to die, yet strangely, he didn't as he thought he would. The clash had transformed in the last few seconds; it had grown amazingly. The freed prisoners hadn't waited the fifteen minutes as they had been told to do and now they were swarming everywhere.

And the numbers of security guard too had grown. It was mayhem. It was battle. And there stuck in the middle of it was an old man.

Chapter 46

Roland Gentry, Inquisitor

The rational brain quails in response to the imbalance of battle. In the soldier's mind, every action seems to equate to an increase in the chance of death or pain, while only the non-action of immobility offers a fleeting safety.

The mind is not meant for warfare, whereas the unthinking heart reacts with purpose. The heart guides the soldier. It gives him strength. It allows him to charge through a hail of bullets to come to the aid of a fallen comrade.

Phil sprinted across the lobby, grabbed the collar of Roland's coat and commenced to drag the man toward the lobby doors. Around him, the air snapped and cracked with the passage of blazing hot lead and behind him on the gleaming marble lay a trail of blood.

The blood was no matter. The sudden galvanizing pain in his side was no matter. Only gaining the door mattered. Only escaping mattered. Only saving his friend mattered.

The window of the door came apart just as he reached it and showered him with glass. Blinded, Phil threw himself into it and then the winter air had him.

It was sharp and burned his lungs, and at the same time it froze the moisture on his exposed skin and brought the congealing damp on his shirt to the forefront of his mind. He had been hit.

Yet he was still moving. Phil ignored the battle behind him and the spreading pain and drug his friend down the stairs to where a black sedan waited making a noise that Phil hadn't heard in a long time; not since his army days. The sound was the steady thrum of an actual engine. This thing wasn't a windup toy. It had the healthy, throaty grrr of a big block V-8.

These weren't made anymore. A car with a combustion engine hadn't been made in decades. Only trucks and tanks for the army had these now. Phil had just a second to amaze over this fact before the driver of the car opened his door. The man was smaller than the two bodyguards and he held his gun pointed up and not out.

"Commissioner Tarsus?" he asked.

"No," Phil replied. He wasn't Commissioner Tarsus, nor was he Phil Tarsus, Inquisitor. He was only Phil Tarsus, Enemy of the State. The driver's eyes went wide at the denial. Too late he brought the barrel down with a jerk and Phil shot him; running a tunnel through the top of his head.

"I'm sorry," Phil said and meant it. The act—the way he had killed so easily and with so little thought —was very much something his old self would've done. More than the bullet wound, this pained his insides.

"Don't be sorry," Roland said from the curb. "Pray for his misguided soul, but don't be sorry. And don't accept the guilt of those who die in battle. God has given you life. It is not for others to take away or hold in bondage. You are guiltless in fighting a war for freedom."

"I don't feel guiltless...far from it," Phil said. "Come on. Get up."

"I don't think I can without help," Roland said and pulled back his coat. His white shirt was a mural of blood running across his abdomen.

"No!" Phil cried, and despite his own pain, he knelt over Roland, while his fingers searched out the wound. "A gut shot."

Roland looked down at himself, grimacing. "Fitting isn't it? I've had a long, slow, painful life and now I can look forward to a death that matches it. I guess I can say I one-upped Job on the misery scale. He at least got his donkeys back in the end. What do I have?"

"You have me," Phil told him. "You have me as your friend."

"I do...and that's worth at least two donkeys," Roland said with a sudden smile. "And I've got something to look forward to."

"Heaven?"

"I was thinking of an earthly pleasure. If you can get me there in time, I'll have the gratification of seeing the Board of Commissioners destroyed. Come on...get me in this car."

There was no time to be gingerly about moving the man. Phil heaved him up, both of them grunting in pain as he did, and pushed him into the back of the car. He then pulled the transmitter from his belt and gave it, along with the earpiece and tie clip, to Roland.

"How on earth are you going to destroy the Board," Phil asked as he hurried around to the driver's side. When he got in he added, "The prisoners we freed aren't going there. I told them to head up to Williamston."

"Can't explain...just...right now," Roland gasped out. He was struggling the little box onto his belt. He had to twist his torso to do so and the pain was obvious on his face. "Just get me there...hurry."

Phil glanced down at the controls to the car—to the Chevy—the word was imprinted on the steering wheel. "Hurrying won't be a problem," he commented. He gunned the engine and the Chevy leapt forward like an animal un-caged. It fishtailed to the right and Phil had to fight the wheels back to the center of the road. He grinned as he did.

"No wonder they outlawed this," Phil said. The car represented the ultimate in freedom—it was fun.

And it made short work of the trip. The streets and dull buildings flashed by in a blur. So fast was the car that he had to slow down and wait a block away from the Commissioner's building until the dashboard clock said the time was one minute to nine. His gut told him that being too early would be as bad as being too late. While they sat there letting the engine

442

rumble pleasantly, Phil took stock of his wound. It was hardly more than a scratch; a three inch gash that cut through his inter-costal muscles and nicked a rib.

"Maybe you should be glad for your bullet wound," Phil said, looking in the rear view mirror. Though his own wound wasn't incapacitating it was painful nonetheless and he had trouble turning. "If you're going to try to destroy the Board, they'll kill you."

Roland agreed, "You're right. Which makes this good bye. Have you learned everything I taught you?"

"No," Phil laughed. "I'm sure there's a God...after that I don't feel like I know anything."

"Good," Roland said. "A man who can admit ignorance is a far greater man than a man who thinks he knows everything. Help me out."

Phil was far more gentle easing Roland from the car and when they were standing on the sidewalk feet from where heavily armed men stood prepared to open the door for them, he whispered, "What am I going to do?"

Roland shook off his pain long enough to smile and say, "Save the girl."

"I meant after that."

"Save the country."

"I meant what am I going to do without you?" Phil said. "You're the one with the brains and the faith. You're the one who always knows what the right thing to do is."

This brought a touch of red to the old man's cheeks. "The right thing to do is to pass that mantle on to you. Follow your heart. That's the best I got...now announce me."

"Announce you?" Phil asked. Roland tilted his head toward the guards at the door and Phil understood. They would be waiting on the new Commissioner of Justice. Phil cleared his throat and spoke with authority: "Make way for the Commissioner of Justice, Roland Gentry."

Clutching his stomach as an eighteenth century emperor might, Roland appeared regal as he slowly made his way to the door. Phil couldn't watch for more than a second. He had a girl to save.

The Chevy spun its tires as he roared away and only too late did he realize that he had never got the code to the back door to Ms. Adleman's building, which was coming up fast. But then he saw it didn't matter. A small box sitting on the dash began blinking, and there up ahead a large door began to roll up on the side of a non-descript dom-box.

He would be able to drive right in. Perhaps right into trouble. Phil slowed the car and transferred his pistol to his left hand where he could fire out the window if he had to. However, he was in luck. There was only a single guard in the garage and the Chevy's headlights blinded him.

"Cut the lights, damn it!" the man said. Phil didn't; he turned off the engine but left the light purposely on as he slipped out. "Roger, stop being an ass. If you don't..." The man stopped as he saw Phil holding his gun pointed right at him. "You're not Roger."

"No, I'm not," Phil said. "Tell me where the girl is or you die."

In his bloody Inquisitor uniform, and with his face a controlled fury, Phil seemed more monster than man. The guard went fish-belly white and stammered, "She's with Ms. Adleman in the third floor lounge, I think."

Lounge? The word had very little meaning to Phil who lived in a ten by ten dom-box like everyone else. "Take me there," he ordered.

"Yes sir." The man moved crab-like toward the door, unable to take his eyes from the barrel of Phil's gun. He moved with such fear that Phil grew angry and grabbed him and propelled him on. They went through a doorway and down a hall, coming to a set of elevators.

"It's the fastest way," the guard said. There was a lie in his voice. Yes, the elevators were fast but were they monitored? Phil guessed they were.

"We'll take the stairs," Phil said. "Go! Now!" The man felt the urgency and saw the white knuckles of Phil's gun hand and began to take the stairs as fast as he could. He was practically running from Phil, but the ex-Inquisitor was in too good of shape and stayed right behind.

"Through there," the guard said of the door.

"You're coming too," Phil said as he frisked the guard from behind, coming up with a pistol and two magazines.

"She'll kill me," the man said desperately.

Phil shrugged. "Maybe not. She's lost her power. But I definitely will if you don't listen to me, now go." Phil kept his left hand on the back of the man's collar and guided him through the door to the third floor. The "lounge" wasn't anything like he expected. The interior of dom-boxes were as grey and lifeless as the exteriors, but this was something else.

The center of the third and fourth floors of the building had been hollowed out to form a huge room. It was practically an auditorium in its dimensions, though not in feel. It was more like a garden. Plants of all sizes from small shrubs to towering trees gave the room a hidden feel, and as they walked to the rear of the room they discovered cozy nooks that sported soft couches or tables with chairs. These were all empty.

There were people in the room, however they were all further on, hidden from view. The people laughed and joked and this stewed Phil's anger all the more and he pushed the guard along until he came to the last bit of foliage. Peering through, he saw that the end of the room opened up into a larger sitting area. Though the area could accommodate fifty or sixty people only eleven were there. Four were clearly servants, one was Ms. Adleman, and the other five were doughy, indolent looking people, lazing on couches. Phil guessed these last were relatives of hers.

Haley was nowhere in sight.

None of the eleven even noticed them; their eyes were fixated on a large monitor that showed an unsteady picture: it was a shot coming from Roland's tie camera. He was being led into the inner chamber of the Board of Commissions.

Phil was just about to announce himself and demand that Haley be brought forth when Marilyn Jennings spoke in a loud voice.

"What is this?"

The gun nearly went off in his hand and his eyes shot to the monitor. The angle of the video was odd and the feed grainy but it was definitely the Commissioner of Entertainment looking angry enough to claw Roland's eyes out.

"We were told that the new Commissioner of Justice would be a surprise, but this is too much!" Marilyn frothed.

"It is what it is," Roland said in a low voice. To Phil, the voice was obviously not his, yet no one in the lounge so much as blinked at it.

Ms. Adleman was the one exception, she grimaced. "Wrong!" she said into a microphone that sat on a table in front of her. "Tell them that you hold a monopoly of power at Justice and that rivals are even now being put down." After a moment of hesitation Roland complied, still in a voice he held unnaturally deep.

"You're not going to get away with this," Marilyn stated and then turned away. With her not taking up the entire screen, Phil had a better look at the setting that Roland found himself in. He stood in a large room; a proper auditorium though not one of tremendous size. On a dais sat a long table with six chairs and Roland eased his way toward it.

"Hurry up," Ms. Adleman growled into the microphone.

"All in good time," Roland replied with a slight cough. As he got close, the camera swiveled to take in the people in the chairs. Five were jowled white men who scowled at Roland or raised a questioning eyebrow. They were commissioners of the most powerful boards: Army, Air force, Navy, Homeland security. Marilyn was the lone female among them, representing Entertainment. The last chair was empty. It belonged to the Commissioner of Justice.

Roland sat in the chair, the wheezing in his chest obvious to Phil, but apparently to no one else.

"Don't say anything just yet," Ms. Adleman said into the microphone. "It's normally Crawford from Army that usually..."

"As you can see," Marilyn Jennings' voice cut across Ms. Adleman. "The rumors have proven true. Commissioner Loman has been murdered and..."

Ms. Adleman hissed into the microphone, "No. Stop her. Stand and tell them he had a heart attack!"

"Excuse me," Roland said and grunted his way to his feet. He was slow to do so and Marilyn went right on talking.

"...by the very man who is claiming his seat among us."

"You are wrong," Roland said. "I did not kill Loman."

"He had a heart attack," Ms. Adleman prompted.

"The truth is that I wasn't even there when he died," Roland stated. "Though I don't see how that matters to you, or to anyone in this room."

Ms. Adleman grabbed the microphone with a shaking hand. "Say what I tell you to! Tell them...tell them that the inner workings at Justice are none of their concern." She then covered the microphone and said to a man who stood nearby," We're going to need the girl after all. Get her."

Roland said his line and Ms. Adleman continued feeding him his script. Dutifully he asked Marilyn, "Ms Commissioner, did anyone delve into how you came to head Entertainment? The same question could be asked of you General Crawford, did anyone ask how your predecessor, General Murray ended up in a building that just happened to get bombed by our own men?"

There was a murmuring from the lesser commissioners in the room and then Marilyn spoke again: "This is different. This man was a prisoner! Look at him. He escaped from Polk when it burned down, and now he wants to be one of us? He can't be trusted."

The view from Roland's tie camera didn't show Marilyn, but it did give a great shot of a middle-aged man in the second row, who stood and announced importantly, "As Commissioner of the Board of Corrections, I can assure you that no one escaped from Polk. We took precautions against that."

"Then how do you explain him?" Marilyn asked.

"Maybe he came from one of the outlying regions," the man said. "There are all sorts of long haired criminals running around up in the hills. And that would be Homeland's issue and not mine; have him explain."

"Long haired?" Ms. Adleman said in confusion. She looked around the room briefly as if searching for a familiar face but when she didn't see it she turned back to the monitor. "You need to change the subject, Tarsus. Tell Marilyn that you'll look into the matter of Polk and hint that investigations are under way. Even better: tell her we have Haley Baker in custody and that she's revealing some very interesting information."

Roland did as requested, except he referred to Haley as Ms. Baker. This caused Ms. Adleman's eyes to go to squints.

"Is this you, Tarsus?" she asked into the microphone. Phil felt his insides go cold—Roland wouldn't lie. The best he could do is not answer the question, which would not be enough to fool an old fox like Ms. Adleman. If she figured things out without Haley present, then threats to the girl Phil loved would be used against him. And it would work.

Marilyn Jennings' voice put off discovery for a few more seconds: "Is that some sort of threat? Try to have me arrested. See what happens!"

Roland cleared his throat; a prompt for Ms. Adleman to give a line for him to repeat, but she wasn't put off the scent. "If that's you Tarsus, let me see your hands. Put them up the camera."

Chapter 47

The True Justice

Roland put his gnarled hands up and Ms. Adleman growled into the microphone, "Where's Tarsus?"

"Adleman," Phil said in a carrying voice. He didn't yell or shout. It wasn't really necessary. She looked over, angry at first that someone would have the temerity to address her in such a way, but then her face displayed frank surprise.

"Who is that?" she asked, pointing at the monitor.

"That's Roland Gentry," Phil told her. "The old man who was with me."

Ms. Adleman eyes flicked about as she took in the unforeseen shift the evening had taken. "And what do you think you're going..."

Her words were interrupted by Marilyn Jennings. "No? You don't want to test me?"

Ms. Adleman turned back to the microphone and started, "Tell her that she..."

"Tell her whatever you want," Phil hollered.

Rolland chuckled and said quietly, "I will. And you do what you need to do."

"You aren't going to do anything, Tarsus," Ms. Adleman said. "Someone get Ms. Baker into the punishment room. I think we may be able to convince Mr. Tarsus that his little game is over."

One of the servants hurried to obey, but before he had taken three steps, Haley Baker came in from a side door being held by one of the guards. Phil trained his gun on the man who stopped with his mouth open.

"Get her out of..." Ms. Adleman started to say but then Roland spoke and she seemed to lose all interest in Phil and Haley.

"Ms Jennings, there will be no formal investigation against you," Roland said. He finally turned toward her and now her face, red and indignant, could be seen. "I'm afraid the people will pass judgment on you without one."

"The people?" Marilyn asked. "Why are you talking about the people? The people are sheep. They believe everything that comes out of my mouth."

"That's what I'm counting on," Roland replied.

Phil hadn't budged. He still crouched over the kneeling guard he had dragged up from the garage, but he couldn't stay in his present position forever. The man with Haley hadn't drawn his gun, so Phil swiveled his back to Ms. Adleman. "Give me the girl and I won't kill you."

Absolutely unafraid of the gun pointed straight at her, she waved her hand to hush Phil and said, "Just a second."

On the screen, Marilyn's face took on a hint of suspicion. "Why would you count on that? Whatever you think you got cooked up won't work. Polls indicate that almost a hundred percent of the people believe everything I say is the truth. I control the truth."

"Not anymore," Roland said with a little cough. "I do."

"Do you hear him?" Marilyn asked the room of commissioners. "He's trying to grab power. I told you he can't be trusted."

"That's too bad. I want your trust," Roland answered back. "I want you to believe me when I say that your time is over." Roland had a way about him —when he spoke, he exuded truth, so instead of doubting him Marilyn grew afraid.

"What do you mean?" she asked.

A fraction of a second later Ms. Adleman nearly repeated her. "What does he mean?" she asked Phil.

"Exactly what he says," Phil answered. "The man never lies. Never."

"But what..." Ms. Adleman started, however the amplified voice of Marilyn Jennings cut across her.

"Whatever you think you're doing has gone too far. We need the guards in here. You are under arrest old man. You hear me?"

Someone off camera said, "Guards aren't allowed in chambers."

"And it wouldn't matter anyway," Roland said. He then gave a low groan and clutched his abdomen. Softer, he said, "I've initiated Operation Black Monday. Norma Jean can tell you there's no turning back."

"Norma Jean..." Marilyn breathed. Looking weak, she lowered herself into her chair.

Stunned, Ms. Adleman turned from the screen and said, "Shoot me now, Tarsus. We're done."

Phil had no clue what the operation entailed and he wasn't the only one. People off camera began demanding answers. Marilyn shook herself and then jumped up. "Maybe he's lying. There's no way he could have done this. I need a phone! A simple call will tell me..."

"The lines aren't working!" someone cried.

Roland nodded. "Cutting off telephone and radio communication is step one of the operation. I have to say that it's a genius plan."

"What the hell is this operation? We have a right to know," the Commissioner of the Navy demanded and the room broke into a frenzy of shouting.

Phil was equally as curious, but his main concern was Haley's safety. "Damn it, Ms. Adleman, give me the girl or I will shoot."

Ms. Adleman sat thinking and biting her nails. She looked over for only a second and said, "Shut up with that."

She was so apathetic to the danger Phil posed that he had to give up on even threatening her. Instead, he threatened the man who held Haley. He had yet to draw his gun, which was why he was still alive.

"Do you care about dying?" Phil asked. The man nodded and released Haley who stepped away, timidly coming to Phil's side. Once there she hid behind him and was practically invisible in the foliage.

"We should go," she said, pulling at Phil's coat.

It wasn't a good idea. If they tried to make a break for it, Ms. Adleman could have her guards all over them with only a word. Of course, staying put wasn't a good idea either but it kept them safe for the moment.

"Not yet," Phil said, as Roland began asking for quiet. The old man's strength was fading. It came out in his voice, which was a low gravely sound, interspersed with a soft, wet cough.

"May I?" Roland asked when the volume of the room dropped to a murmur and it became clear that Marilyn Jennings wasn't going to answer. "Operation Black Monday is the Commissioner of Entertainment's method of holding the other, stronger, Boards in check...to keep them from grabbing power all for themselves."

"They would never do it," someone shouted.

"Why not?" Roland asked. "History is replete with strong men attempting takeovers. In this case, the threat was mainly to counter the Army, due to its brute strength and Homeland Security because of its police powers. Black Monday counters them by threatening the stability of the entire government. It's a MAD scenario—Mutually Assured Destruction."

"There's no way. Entertainment is too weak," a commissioner in the first row called out. "They have no real power."

Roland coughed again and shot a fine spray of blood onto his hand. "If entertainment is so weak, why do they have a permanent seat on the security council? The truth is Entertainment, with its ability to alter the news and warp people's perceptions is the sustaining force behind this, the most corrupt government on the planet. The Board of Entertainment holds the people in line with displays of pseudo patriotism, and with its subtle suggestions of fear coupled with the demonstration of outright terror. The people live their lives as abject slaves in vile misery, yet always Entertainment offers them the tiniest scrap of hope to keep them motivated. The hope they peddle is that things will get better...someday."

"Who gives a crap about hope?" The Commissioner of the Navy barked. "And you haven't answered my question. What the hell is Black Monday?"

"It's simply the truth," Roland replied. The power of truth seemed an unlikely source of fear to the gathered commissioners who began to whisper skeptically among themselves. A few even laughed.

Not so the Commissioner of the Army. He stood, seething in a rage. "Did he really do it, Marilyn?"

She nodded vaguely. "Norma Jean was my pass code. But how did he know?"

"Damn it!" the general thundered and then began to storm away. "I've got to head this off."

"You can't," Marilyn said. "You saw the specs. Once Black Monday is set in motion it plays out, no matter what. Any minute now the broadcasts are going to start. It's going to be chaos."

"By my estimation," Roland said. "You have about fifteen seconds." There was a great twenty-foot monitor on the wall to his left and all eyes went to it.

Next to Phil, Haley seemed stunned. "Truth? That's all he has? That's crazy. The truth is not magical. It won't bring down the government. It won't save us."

"The truth of God saved me," Phil said. "There's no telling what it will do..."

Just then, the screen flashed red and the word: ALERT! began to blink on it. Both rooms went silent as they waited on what Operation Black Monday would mean.

Marilyn Jennings' pre-recorded face appeared. She was composed yet saddened. "My fellow Americans, I come before you to announce a historic moment for us all. The government has fallen. Note that I did not say *your* government. The Board of Commissioners was not composed of normal Americans like you and me. No, it was comprised of men and women who lived like princes and acted like dictators. They cared nothing for your lives. They cared nothing for your feelings. They cared for nothing but themselves."

Though Marilyn kept speaking, the image of her face left the screen and what replaced it was a film litany of horror. "Every commissioner was a culprit: here is the Commissioner of the Army, General Crawford ordering a human wave attack against the Mexicans on the Texas front. Those are unarmed

American soldiers that he forced to charge against machine guns."

The film was almost nauseating to watch. Men came apart under the direct fire, with blood and body parts going in every direction. Haley turned away.

"This is the bombing of Corpus Christi, ordered by Commissioner Mendel of the Air Force. In order to deny the enemy use of the city he commanded that it be leveled. Over forty thousand American civilians were killed by our own planes..."

"Turn this off!" screamed General Crawford. The Marilyn Jennings in the auditorium only shook her head as her likeness on the monitor went on to describe horrors perpetrated by the other branches of the government. Some were obvious, such as the everyday villainy that occurred at the Justice building. While others were less so, such as the corruption in the Board of Electrical Production that allowed children to freeze to death every winter, or the complete ineptness in the Board of Agriculture that led to the deaths by starvation of half of the state Oklahoma.

"Because of the incompetence of the Commissioner of Agriculture and the criminal nepotism of staffing the Board with useless family and friends, you can see here entire fields of corn left to rot on their stalks. And here fields of..."

Roland had been turned toward the monitor, but he jumped as gunfire exploded in the auditorium and the calm but sad visage of Marilyn Jennings on the TV went to grey static. General Crawford waived his smoking gun now in the direction of the real Marilyn Jennings.

"This is your fault!" he roared. "Your paranoia caused this."

"We both know it wasn't paranoia," Marilyn replied with venom. "You had plans to take over. I saw the timetable. I saw the logistics..."

General Crawford shot Marilyn three times and she disappeared from the view of Roland's tie camera in a mist of red. The general, looking crazed, turned to the old man. "You son of a bitch," he swore, bringing his gun to bear.

"God loves you..." Roland began but then the general's gun flashed and roared. The old man wheezed with a wet and phlegmy sound and then coughed blood onto the camera. "May...he have...mercy..."

The gun flashed again.

Phil felt the pain of those bullets as if they had torn into his own chest. His breath came ragged in a throat that choked and he clutched himself with his free hand trying to soothe a deep ache. It felt that a part of him died the moment Roland did. Just like that, his confidence left him. And so too did his strength. In the span of two pulls of a trigger, Phil Tarsus was reduced to a weak nothing who wanted to crawl into a corner and cry.

Behind him, Haley let her body slip down against a wall. She began to sob, and she wasn't the only one. The room broke into a chaos of cries and tears. Then came a minute where everyone turned to the person next to them and began blabbering questions without receiving any answers.

Ms. Adleman sat through it, stewing in anger and fear until one of her pale guests found the courage to tug on her sleeve and ask: "What does this mean for us?" He was a young man but already looked old. His hair was thin and greasy and his face looked incapable of forming any expression beyond haughty.

"It means this is done," she answered through dry lips. "This life...this life I've built for us is over."

"But what does this mean for *us*?" the man asked again.

"I just said what it meant, damn it!" Ms. Adleman shrieked. "Black Monday will tear this country apart. Are you satisfied with what you've done, Tarsus? You and that old man have just plunged this country into civil war. It's inevitable. Every poll; every computer scenario predicts it with absolute certainty."

For a second Phil was so lost within his grief that it took him a second to respond to the sound of his own name. "Am I satisfied?" he asked, seeing again in his mind the gun firing into Roland's body. "No. I'm not satisfied at all. But...but I am hopeful."

"Hopeful?" Ms. Adleman couldn't believe what she was hearing. "You are hopeful that very soon Americans will be killing Americans?"

"No. I'm hopeful that soon Americans will be fighting for their freedom."

"Kill him!" Ms. Adleman cried pointing at Phil. "Someone kill him!" The servants were unarmed and only stared, while the guests looked from to another,

460

each hoping someone else would step up. None did. Ms. Adleman switched her accusing finger to the guard who had brought Haley in. "Do it," she said in a voice gilt with frost.

At the death of his friend, Phil's hands had gone numb. He had stepped back from the hostage he had brought up from the garage and now he just stood there with the gun at his side. Phil didn't think he could lift it again even in self-defense.

The guard saw the change in Phil—the near exhaustion of his mind and body—and placed his hand on the butt of his pistol. Yet he did not draw it. Something within the guard had also changed in the last few minutes.

He shook his head. "I won't. You said yourself that this is done. It'll start with me." The man nodded at Phil and then turned and walked away.

"Come back and kill him!" bellowed Ms. Adleman. He wouldn't and the man's steadily fading footfalls seemed to only increase her anger. "Get back here now! Right now!"

When the man's footsteps were gone completely, Phil felt the air in the room change. The queen had been defied in her own realm and there hadn't been consequences. Phil shook his head at Ms. Adleman and the spirit of Roland seemed to speak through his lips, "The problem with using terror to hold power is that when you are no longer terrifying you no longer have power. Let's go, Haley," Phil said putting his hand to her.

Chapter 48

Epilogue: A New America

Haley had only the beginnings of a gossamer faith in the Lord yet her faith in Phil Tarsus was a deep reservoir. In her eyes, he had assumed the mantle of Roland Gentry, a man of seemingly endless wisdom. This wisdom gelled with Phil's own natural courage and toughness formed, at least for her, a perfect man.

She needed this sort of man like she had never before. Her life had been thrown into such a whirlwind that she could put her trust in nothing else but him. The words of the actual Roland Gentry came back to haunt her: *You're a disgrace to your gender*.

Now she smirked when she thought of how angry she had been when he had said it. She smirked because his words had been the essence of truth, and she had been child-like in the face of them. She *was* a disgrace. All her life she had excelled at beauty and little more. Haley still had her beauty—a few ragged days would not change that fact—but now she knew there were so many things that were more important.

Freedom was one. How funny that concept was. A few days before she would've laughed off the very notion as a trick of the neocons. Now it opened the world to her. She could do anything and be anything she wanted.

Love was another concept that had blossomed into her consciousness. Before, love was the means to an end. It was a tool to be used; a chisel to pry or a weapon to hurt. Now, her eyes had been opened: love was not the means, but the end—the thing worth striving for.

A sudden golden light struck the side of the car and she glanced over at Phil. The new light framed him and she felt a heat inside her. He loved her. She knew this as fact. He had come for her. He had risked his life, while she had played the damsel. She felt somewhat ashamed of this and wished there was some way she could be there for him as he had for her.

"So what are you going to do?" she asked Phil as the sun rose on the valley that held what once was the cozy little town of Williamston.

Hours earlier, they had left Ms. Adleman's third floor lounge and had walked in no real hurry down to a parking garage. They met a few people along the way and every one of them had scurried out of their path. Those who saw Phil Tarsus saw a man with red-rimmed eyes and a wild air about him; he appeared a second away from committing mass-murder. Haley knew better; Phil had never been further from killing in his life than in those terrible minutes after Roland had been shot.

Thinking over her question, Phil slowed the Chevy, taking a turn off the two-lane mountain road, following the tracks of a number of vehicles that had recently come this same way. "I'd like to be a farmer," he answered.

This surprised her. "You won't help with the revolution? They'll need men like you."

"I thought you meant afterwards," Phil said with a little laugh. He had laughed frequently on the trip from the Capital and she had joined him every time. Though Roland's death was still so near, the weight of their enslavement had been lifted from their souls and it was all either of them could do not giggle at every passing tree.

He turned somber for a moment and said, "I'll help, but not in a way you'd expect. The thought of killing has me...I don't know if I can be involved in that anymore."

Haley crinkled her nose. "Are you talking about helping out spiritually? Because if so, I don't know how well that'll be received. You remember how Governor Joseph reacted to what he called God-talk. He wasn't the only one; most of the Dwellers didn't believe in God."

Another laugh escaped him. "You know what Roland would say to that, right?"

She had to smile and not just because she did indeed know what the old man would've said, but also because she knew suddenly her purpose. She knew how she could be there for Phil.

"Roland would have said: Then all the more reason to bring God to them," Haley answered. "But it may not be that easy, not by yourself. They'll resist change."

Phil hesitated and then asked, "Would you help me?"

"Yes," she said easily, touching his arm. There could be no other answer.

The End.

Timeline of A Perfect State

2023— Defense of Marriage Act declared unconstitutional

2024— Mid-term elections. "Do-nothing" Republicans blamed for stalled budget process and fading economy. This, coupled with sudden, mysterious cash donations given to Libertarian candidates mean GOP losses in both houses. President continues to legislate through Executive order

2024— Top Marginal Tax rate increased to 44% to cover revenue shortfall.

2025—President offers blanket pardon to all illegal aliens. "No human is illegal!"

2025— Full implementation of the Patient Protection and Affordable Care-2 act.

2025— Republicans take a last stand on lower taxes and decreased spending—and are portrayed as the party of the rich—Libertarian candidates continue to run flush with money from unknown sources, splitting every important race. Democrats win White House. Gain majorities in both houses.

2025— Cost of Patient Protection and Affordable Care-2 act greater than expected. Top Marginal Tax rate increased to 49%. Healthy Americans Law— among other things the law prohibits use of Transfats and restricts the amount of sugar in canned beverages and cereal.

2025— Tancredo V Colorado- Supreme court rules marijuana use legal. Writing for the 6-3 majority, newly appointed Justice Mader states: "It's natural and as healthy as drinking water."

2026— Family Aid Act increases assistance for single mothers. Percent of all births to unmarried women reaches 40.8%

2026— Fairness Doctrine enacted. Its equal time clause destroys profits and Talk radio as a medium lasts only another six years and is replaced by "Government Programming"

2027— With a 5-4 liberal majority in the Supreme Court, the Hunter's Protection Act is pronounced constitutional. Hand Guns and semi-automatic weapons are made illegal

2027— Border Patrol budget slowly and quietly reduced. Dream Act II: all immigrants without prior convictions are given a fast track to citizenship. Democratic voter rolls explode.

2027— Cost of Patient Protection and Affordable Care-2 greater than expected; to cover budget shortfalls, top marginal tax rates are increased to 58% Corporate tax increased to 41%

2029— Republicans, again depicted as the party of the 'rich and the rednecks' pick a presidential candidate seen as "Liberal-lite" He caves on every conservative issue. Democrats easily win White House and both houses of congress. They are not seriously challenged for 24 years.

2029— Citizen Protection Act limits the number of bullets a person can purchase per year to one hundred. Weapons tax: $.05 per bullet and $100 per firearm.

2029— With a solid 7-2 majority in the Supreme Court the Religious Protection act is declared constitutional. Bans all reference to all religions on state and federal land. In God We Trust is removed from currency. Nativity scenes, Christmas trees and any reference to the Ten Commandments are stricken from all public land.

2030— Death Penalty abolished.

2030— Protection of Motherhood Act: provides federal funds for all abortions.

2031— Internet Fairness and Truth Doctrine passed. Taxes all internet entities and adds a layer of "Protective" regulation.

2031— Cost of Patient Protection and Affordable Care-2 greater than expected—the first Wealth Tax is introduced. 2% of accumulated wealth is to be paid annually.

2031— Family Assistance Act—increase aid to single mothers. Percent of all births to unmarried women: 46.4

2031— Wealth tax increased to 3%

2031— John Roberts-last conservative member on Supreme Court dies. All laws are now rubber stamped by highest court.

2032— Weapons Tax increased to $.50 per bullet and $250.00 per firearm

2032— Good Citizenship Act makes it illegal to shelter or remove wealth from the USA for the purpose of avoiding tax.

2032— Balanced Budget Act: Wealth Tax increased to 5%. Top marginal income tax increased to 81%. Corporate tax increased to 48%. Ends all deductions for Charitable giving. Salvation Army, Catholic charities, and Red Cross cease to exist within a few years.

2032— Unemployment chronically above 11%—Job Protection Act makes it illegal to fire employees as long as company is deemed profitable by the IRS

2033— Weapons tax increased $1.00 per bullet $375 per fire arm—sales of weapons plummets.

2033— Child Protection Act II Increases aid to single mothers. Percent of all births to unmarried women: 51.9%

2035— Patient Protection and Affordable Care-2 is more expensive than expected: Pharmacy outlays per person capped at $1,000 a year. "Experimental" drugs are no longer covered. This includes nearly all new drugs on the market.

2036— Inflation hits 11% Unemployment 13%

2037— School Uniformity Act. Spending and curriculum must be equal in every school district effectively ending local control of schools. Department of Education takes over.

2037— Defense Parity Act states that Military Defense spending must be equal or less than the spending of the next highest spending nation

2037— Child and Mothers Protection Act: Increased aid to single mothers. Percent of all births to unmarried women: 54.9%

2037— Patient Protection and Affordable Care-2 is more expensive than expected: Executive order 24639 institutes the five year rule—a patient must have a 50% percent chance of living five years to qualify for any major surgery. Hip surgeries and transplants become rare. DNR(Do Not Resuscitate) orders are placed on all individuals under the "five year rule." Life expectancy in US drops to 70.1 years by 2035 To help cover costs, taxes are increased on cigarettes, alcohol and a catch-all term: junk food.

2037— Fairness in Budgeting Law: Wealth Tax increased to 6%— Top marginal rate- 92%— Corporate tax 60%— Weapons Tax to $5.00 a bullet and $500 per firearm.

2038— Supreme Court decision Adison V Smith & Wesson. Weapon makers can now be held liable for any death or injury attributed to gun use. Last of Gun makers goes bankrupt later in the year.

2041— Patient Protection and Affordable Care-2 is more expensive than expected: Below the age of forty yearly check-ups and mammograms no longer covered. Five Year Rule is changed to the seven year rule—Life expectancy in US drops to 69.1 years by 2043.

2041—Child and Mothers Protection Act II Increased aid to single mothers. Percent of all births to unmarried women: 59.9%

2041— Last stand of the Republicans. The shrinking base tries to rally around staunch conservative David Chandler—in the media he is portrayed as a pro-greed, anti-health, anti-mother, religious zealot, a strict constitutionalist in a time of a fluid constitution. He loses in an election that is rife with fraud, voter intimidation by government officials and an estimated 2.2 million illegally cast ballots, the Supreme Court does not take up the case, "For the good of the country."

2042— inflation hits 14% Unemployment 16.3%

2042-2046—Of the 106 Conservatives left in congress all are subject to continuous ethics violation charges and most are eventually removed from office.

2045— Child and Mothers Protection Act III Increases aid to single mothers. Percent of all births to unmarried women: 65.9%

2046— Victory: Ideal Governance Act—Decrees that only Political parties that espouse the ideals of America will be able to run candidates for public office. Conservatism, long pilloried as the last bastion of greed and racism is effectively outlawed.

2048— Inflation hits 18% Unemployment 17.6%

2048— The People's Workers Party (PWP) started under Ayers and Stadler as a Socialist alternative to the Democrats.

2048— 2nd Amendment declared unconstitutional.

2046-2078— Series of domestic terror attacks against local, state, and federal officials. Though right wing groups are blamed, some believe that most of these were undertaken by PWP operatives.

2057— End of the Democrats. After 40 years of miserable economic output the PWP lays the blame at the feet of the Democrats. The Party resurrects "Hope and Change" and sweeps the Democrats out of office. Begin one party rule.

2057— Profit(referred to repeatedly as theft or price gouging) declared illegal.

2058— Inflation hits 22%. First Revaluation of the American Dollar. Unemployment 18.6%

2058— Government takeover of the following industries: oil, gas, and coal production, pharmaceutical, automobile production, telecommunications, banking.

2058— Trial of Albert Fishman televised. He is accused of sabotaging automobile production. His trial(The first of a long series of "Show-trials") is a masterpiece of theatrical production that keeps the country hanging on for weeks.

2059— Fishman found guilty of treason. The death penalty is revived specifically for cases of treason.

2059—Percent of all births to unmarried women: 73.9%

2059— First Child Allegiance school opens, ending the practice of foster care and adoptions. These children are now wards of the state and are raised in Allegiance camps until the age of eighteen.

2059-2067— The State arranges for headline grabbing trials to cover for increasingly bad economic news. The trials are similar to soap operas in their complexity and drama.

2065 Census shows a strong decline in population brought on by alarmingly negative population growth coupled with mass emigration out of the country(particularly by Hispanics)

2066— Patriot Project #4 begun. Building of the north and south border walls. By '65 America's borders are ringed by cement, concertina wire, and machine guns.

2069— With the trials starting to wear thin the State looks for a new scapegoat: the "New" rich… specifically Homosexuals. The show-trials of '64 –'69 are exclusively of Homosexuals and from these it is "discovered" that large portions of the Homosexual population are in league with Neo-cons to over-throw the government. Hefty rewards bring forth a constant stream of new suspects—though tens of thousands rot in jails, few if any are guilty of anything.

2075— Census shows steady population decline and continued negative population growth. Percent of all births to unmarried women: 81.9% Population Integrity Law passes outlawing homosexual acts. To combat the lack of productivity in single mothers caring for children, Allegiance camps become mandatory for all children beyond the age of eight. Within twenty years this drops to the age of three as a minimum, though many mothers give up their children within the first year.

2073-76— Homosexuals, en masse attempt to flee America. Those who can't, go into hiding.

2076— Second Revaluation of American Currency. Restructuring of Social Security payouts—retirement age pushed to 75. End of Welfare—the State introduces "Work-fare" creating a virtual slave class out of the growing number of poor.

2076— End of Affirmative Action beginning of the "Color Blind" society. Attempted race riots are put down by the Army, using maximum force. Minority leaders are arrested on charges of treason.

2077— Official Government takeover of the entertainment industry. It is replaced with the Board of Entertainment. News is now officially filtered. People are fed a steady diet of 'good news'—while food rations decrease.

2078— Arrest of Teamster Boss Harvey Emanuel— first of the Union show trials. Within the year union leaders arrested en masse and are blamed for the poor economy.

2078—The State creates the Board of Rationing.

2079—Marijuana declared illegal

2079— Private ownership of business declared illegal

2082— Freedom of Speech(Including freedom of the Press) is curtailed, determined to be of "less importance" than the protection of the State and the Party.

2083—Fourth and fifth Amendments declared unconstitutional.

2085—Census shows steady population decline and continued negative population growth. New Population Laws are passed—cash rewards are given per child.

2086— Religion is declared illegal. Worship of God is considered subversive.

2087— The Greater Constitution of America ratified —this mainly dictates the rights of the State and the obligations of the citizenry.

2095— Census shows steady population decline and continued negative population growth. Abortion is declared illegal. Child compulsion Law sets a minimum of two live births per female before the age of thirty-three—last of the paleo-feminist leaders arrested. Neo-feminist espouse motherhood as the highest purpose a woman can attain.

2122—Present day

*It could never happen here?

1933— Hitler assumes power in Germany

1941— First Nazi death camp begins operations.

Author's note:

A Perfect America was inspired by two things: the 2012 election and the Bible.

The reelection of Barak Obama was a bit of a shock to many conservatives. It seemed that a perfect storm had aligned against the president--terrible economic news, bad job reports four years running, skyrocketing debt, and poor performance in foreign policy--made it seem like the republican nominee would be a shoe-in. After all Mitt Romney was handsome, smart, successful, and best of all he didn't do anything idiotic. Yet he still lost badly.

It made me wonder: if Romney couldn't win in this situation when could another Republican ever win and what would happen if they never won again? I took the thought and ran with it. Though with history as a primer it didn't take much imagination. We don't have to look past the Bolshevik revolution to see that a culture could be utterly destroyed and replaced with something almost exactly like what is described in A Perfect America. Scary indeed.

But a setting is only part of a novel. The bible showed me the way for the actual story. Paul Tarsus is clearly Saul of Tarsus who most of us remember as the Apostle Paul. Before his conversion, the Apostle Paul was infamous in his day for his persecution of the early Christians and was witness to the stoning of Saint Stephen one of the first Christian Martyrs. Then on the road to Damascus he was blinded by a vision of Jesus. He was blind for three days and from then on became the most devout follower of Christ.

Merge the two halves of the story and A Perfect America is born.

For those of you who enjoyed the novel may I suggest The Sacrificial Daughter as a follow up? Once again politics and religion collide but this time the setting is small town America in the grips of its own economic depression. The only thing that could make the townspeople's lives any worse is the serial killer that walks among them.

Finally, on a self-serving note, the review is the most practical and inexpensive form of advertisement an independent author has available in order to get his work known. If you could put a kind review on

Amazon and your Facebook page, I would greatly appreciate it.

    Yours,
    Peter Meredith

Fictional works by Peter Meredith:

A Perfect America
Infinite Reality: Daggerland Online Novel 1
Infinite Assassins: Daggerland Online Novel 2
Generation Z
Generation Z: The Queen of the Dead
Generation Z: The Queen of War
The Sacrificial Daughter
The Apocalypse Crusade War of the Undead: Day One
The Apocalypse Crusade War of the Undead: Day Two
The Apocalypse Crusade War of the Undead Day Three
The Apocalypse Crusade War of the Undead Day Four
The Horror of the Shade: Trilogy of the Void 1
An Illusion of Hell: Trilogy of the Void 2
Hell Blade: Trilogy of the Void 3
The Punished
Sprite
The Blood Lure The Hidden Land Novel 1
The King's Trap The Hidden Land Novel 2
To Ensnare a Queen The Hidden Land Novel 3
The Apocalypse: The Undead World Novel 1
The Apocalypse Survivors: The Undead World Novel 2
The Apocalypse Outcasts: The Undead World Novel 3
The Apocalypse Fugitives: The Undead World Novel 4

www.ingramcontent.com/pod-product-compliance
Lightning Source LLC
Chambersburg PA
CBHW052031260626
47163CB00005B/20